The WAY FROM HERE

JANE TURNER

ORION

First published in Great Britain in 2022 by Orion Fiction,
an imprint of The Orion Publishing Group Ltd,
Carmelite House, 50 Victoria Embankment
London EC4Y 0DZ

An Hachette UK company

1 3 5 7 9 10 8 6 4 2

A CIP catalogue record for this book
is available from the British Library.

ISBN (Mass Market Paperback) 978 1 3987 0589 0
ISBN (eBook) 978 1 3987 0590 6

Typeset by Input Data Services Ltd, Somerset

Printed and bound in Great Britain by Clays Ltd, Elcograf S.p.A.

www.orionbooks.co.uk

For Vesta women everywhere.

Part One

September 2011

The Finish: *The end of the drive phase of the stroke when the blade is extracted from the water by tapping down. In coaching it is often thought helpful to consider it as the start of the recovery phase, rather than the end of the drive phase.*

I

KATE

'Pontefract?' The blue sign flashed past.

'I'm not supposed to be here! How did that happen?' Kate glanced at the satnav perched on the dashboard. The screen was black. The cable hung free, guiltily.

Oh fuck! she said to herself, as a mounting sense of dread tightened its grip on her chest. *Fuck, fuck, fuck! Breathe, Kate, you can do this.* Ella was plugged in to her headphones, oblivious to the impending crisis. Kate tapped her gently on the thigh to attract her attention.

'What?' asked Ella irritably, as she dragged the speakers away from her ears.

'I must have taken a wrong turn. We're in Pontefract and we're not supposed to be. Can you look at the map for me?'

'Mum! We'll be late!' wailed Ella. 'I'll miss registration and everyone will have made friends and I'll have to spend the next three years on my own!' If Kate didn't love her daughter quite so much, right at that moment she could have found her a bit of a brat. But she did love her, and

Ella was entitled to be stressed about starting university. Allowances needed to be made.

'It's in the pocket behind my seat – the map.'

Ella was tapping away at her phone. 'Oh, Mumsie, you're so last century. No one uses maps any more.' That stung. She was quite sure if Tim had been driving he'd have insisted Ella map-read the whole way, old-school. Perhaps she should have done the same. But then Ella would have puffed and sighed and that really wasn't what she wanted today of all days. Even if Ella had been map-reading they might still have missed the turn after so many hours on a straight road. No doubt Kate had been lost in thought at the crucial moment, relying on her dodgy technology to prompt her when the turn was imminent.

That was the problem with a long journey: too much time to think. Ella had expressed surprise at how far it was to Durham, a fact that had clearly escaped her when she was filling in her UCAS forms. In fact, it had been news to Ella that you could go that far north and still be in England. So much for her A* in GCSE Geography. If she'd intended to put distance between herself and her mother, she'd certainly succeeded.

'No harm done. We'll still be there in bags of time.' She squeezed her daughter's arm and smiled encouragingly at her.

'My app says we should be there at 16.52.'

'There you are – you'll be fine.' And Kate plugged in the satnav again giving the connector an extra shove for good measure.

Planning the trip, Kate had imagined a memorable experience she and her daughter would look back on fondly in years to come. It wasn't quite working out that way and Ella wasn't helping. She hadn't removed her headphones since they left Bath, so frankly might as well have not been in the car.

It seemed ridiculous to admit that Ella's leaving had come as a shock as she'd had eighteen years to get used to the idea. In fairness, there had been considerable uncertainty over whether Ella would have done well enough to go to university that year. Once she had her results there'd been a week or so of celebration and then the rest of the time had been filled with all the preparations needed for the next stage of her life: printers and vaccinations, kettles and dental appointments.

Kate did know, deep down, that Ella could still go to university with a residual amount of stubborn plaque and would survive the experience. However, oral hygiene was one of the few things she could still control in Ella's life. She remembered the summer before Poppy, Ella's older sister, had started senior school. Kate had experienced a recurring nightmare that it was the first day of term and she hadn't finished sewing name tapes on her daughter's uniform. It had finally dawned on Kate that her anxiety wasn't actually about the name tapes. This time there was no gym kit to be named, but Kate could still contrive to make a long list of tasks without which she was sure her daughter could not possibly thrive.

Their most important appointment had been their lunch yesterday at Ella's favourite restaurant. The beginning and end of every term at school had been marked by Chicken Katsu and Ella did not want to stop the tradition now. Kate had been so pleased her daughter didn't feel she'd grown out of the habit. While knowing she had to let her daughter go, Kate still wanted to hang on to some keepsakes of her childhood. This meal would always be one of them.

Driving at 50mph on the M1, past endless orange cones, listening to Ella humming along to some unknown melody, Kate could finally stop worrying about her lists and confront what was happening: her younger child was leaving for university. From now on she would be completely alone all week and at weekends it would just be her and Tim. And it would be like that until Christmas. She noticed she was chewing absentmindedly at the side of her finger. The nail was already gnawed down to the quick. Frustrated with herself, she placed her hand firmly back on the steering wheel and heaved a sigh. Ella reached across with a perfectly manicured hand and patted her mother's leg:

'It's fine, Mum. I'm going to be just fine. You really don't have to worry about me.'

'I know, darling. Don't mind me. I just wish there weren't so many bollards.'

Kate looked at her daughter, singing along to the silent music.

> We are young
> Let's live our lives,
> Strong and free . . .

She looked happy. She was so obviously ready for university, excited about meeting new people and exploring the world beyond the bubble she'd grown up in. She was also enthusiastic about her subject, which always helped. No doubt she would find a way to negotiate all the challenges that lay ahead.

It was funny how everyone seemed to think Kate should be worried about how Ella would cope. Tim was concerned. He kept asking Kate if she thought Ella would be OK, seeking reassurance which Kate gladly provided. No, she was not worried about Ella. This was so obviously the right thing for her. Ella was going to be just fine.

She'd miss her. Of course she would. Out of choice she'd probably have spent her entire life hugging her children and breathing in the smell of them. But little by little, from that first day she'd left Poppy at the nursery to go back to work, she'd learnt to accept and adjust to the physical separation.

Kate remembered the raw, visceral pain she experienced as she made herself walk away from the cheery nanny holding her baby, her breasts leaking into the freshly laundered bra so carefully selected for her return to the workplace. It was her first lesson as a mother in letting go. She knew it had to be done. It was Poppy's first lesson in learning to trust the world and to feel secure in it without her mother's comforting presence.

Step by step over the years Kate had ever so gradually given her girls the opportunity to extend their orbit further and further away from her. Always they came back to her, the centre of their universe, for encouragement and reassurance. But as they grew, they needed to check in less often. Poppy had already been at university for two years, and in term time she generally only called once a week. But when she was upset or in trouble, or when she had some good news to share, it was Kate she reached out to.

The bond was not broken. It was as strong as ever, even if it was invisible much of the time. Kate had done her job well, she knew that. Poppy was thriving and Ella would do the same. If a mother's goal was to eventually make herself obsolete, she was right on track. If one day her children had to manage without her, she knew they would not just survive but would flourish.

No, Kate's anxiety had nothing to do with Ella. It didn't seem to have occurred to anyone, least of all Tim, that what she was actually worried about was herself. She was well aware the endless tasks concerning Ella's departure were a sort of displacement activity. She felt she was standing at the edge of a yawning chasm, a great belching, black void of nothingness that was drawing her towards it. What was to become of her? What had become of her?

Kate had been so busy making a place in the world for her daughters, she'd somehow forgotten along the way to take care of herself. The life she'd ended up with was not the life she'd planned. Everything was a compromise. She'd been so full of optimism and ambition all those years ago on her own first day at university. She'd been the first pupil from her comprehensive to storm Cambridge's ivy-clad courts, and she'd believed the glittering prizes were hers for the taking. She was going to be a human rights lawyer: respected, fulfilled, making a difference. And yet here she was with her niche, mummy-track job, processing endless identical claims for clients. It was one unfulfilling Groundhog Day after another.

The worst part was she felt it was almost impossible to voice her frustration. Uninspiring it might be, but it was still a decently paid, flexible job that had allowed her to work three days a week and to be the parent on call for the girls 24/7. She was well aware many of her friends envied her. It just wasn't the life she'd imagined for herself.

Then there was her marriage. Kate sighed again as she took stock. Tim was a good man, a good father and a good provider. Her mother considered it a good marriage. But then Kate was not willing to burden her or anyone else with descriptions of her loneliness. It had seemed a sensible enough decision after the girls were born for Tim to stay in London during the week for his job while Kate made their home in Bath. She hadn't foreseen how the arrangement would set them on separate paths, which would eventually lead to a massive gulf between them.

You make one simple decision and eventually, one day, you find yourself in bloody Pontefract when you were supposed to be going to Durham.

So many times over the years Kate had made this mental checklist. She knew she should be grateful for what she had. Yet somehow she couldn't help feeling there was supposed to be more. To an outsider she was the girl who had everything: the house, the job, the husband, the kids.

It's all just so . . . disappointing.

Still, it was a glorious day for a long drive. After a slightly underwhelming summer, just as the days were shortening and the nights turning cold, the sky had turned a brilliant and positively un-English blue. For days now they had been bathed in sunshine, the strength of which had taken everyone by surprise.

Kate mused about the way people obsessed about summer. They spent so much time planning for it and talking about it. Then, when it finally arrived, it was so often disappointing. But just as they thought it was all over and were packing away the barely used paraphernalia of fine weather, they discovered the best was yet to come.

They finally pulled into Ella's college in the late afternoon. As they walked up to the main building, hand in hand, Kate felt Ella's palm clammy in hers. Her normally self-assured daughter was working hard to hold it together. Kate was also feeling intimidated. Once upon a time she'd been so sure of herself and so full of courage. At Cambridge she'd dived head first into an exotic world with a language all of its own, full of 'bedders' and 'butteries'. She remembered striding in to drinks parties full of strangers, apparently the only girl present not wearing a pearl necklace. She'd never seen anyone in pearls before who wasn't someone's mother. It made her laugh. She'd been fearless in those days.

She wondered what had become of that girl and how she'd turned into such an anxious, apologetic old woman. It was as if, as her children grew, she herself had been diminished. As they sucked the milk from her breast, somehow the life force had drained away from her. As Poppy and Ella developed into beautiful, poised young women, so Kate had been reduced to this lesser version of herself.

Conscious of her daughter's nervousness, she started talking a little too fast, telling Ella how lovely the college and grounds were, in fact how lovely everything was. She said 'hello' to everyone they passed, possibly a little too enthusiastically. It was as if she were back at Ella's first day at infant school. Then she had told herself:

'So long as she doesn't wet her pants, everything will be OK.' It didn't feel too far from the mark this time. It didn't occur to her that, ironically, despite all the pelvic floor exercises, she was actually the one most at risk of this humiliation.

As they carried on up the path Kate was conscious of the heads turning back to check out her daughter as they passed. Ella was tall like her mother, with the same long, rangy legs. Her streaky blonde hair was long and straight, the way Kate's had been in her youth. She'd finally cut it short the third time she caught nits when Poppy was in nursery.

Ella was the spit of her mother in old photographs, with the same sharp cheekbones and generous mouth. From her barely concealed smile Kate could tell she was enjoying the attention. She remembered from her youth what it felt like to be the focus of men's gaze, how powerful it had made her feel. Their attention had drifted away so gradually, she only realised it had gone when she first found them staring past her at one of her daughters.

Two more male students walked past, and one was so distracted by staring at Ella he tripped over a paving stone and had to be hauled back to his feet by his friend. Kate noticed Ella standing fractionally taller, her shoulders pushed back ever so slightly. Then there was the unmistakeable hair toss. Kate smiled to herself. But even as she did so she felt herself drooping, momentarily defeated. Ella glanced at her mother and then stopped and embraced her in a hug:

'Don't worry, Mum. I'm going to be fine!'

Kate laughed and freed herself from her daughter's hold and rummaged in her bag for a tissue. She blew her nose and said, 'I know you are, darling. Ignore me, I'm just being silly.' Today was about Ella. The black pit, drawing her in, would have to wait.

Having collected the key to Ella's room, they hauled the endless bags and boxes up three flights of stairs. Once everything had been moved Kate decided it was time to christen the kettle and make some tea. Somehow the milk was still stacked in the fridge at home, along with the fruit juice and smoothies they'd selected so carefully from the supermarket. How had she forgotten them? She could kick herself. She'd wanted everything to be perfect and she couldn't even remember the sodding milk.

At least they'd remembered the brownies and wine. Kate remembered enough about her own Fresher's Week to know that social anxiety was eased by cake and alcohol, and she had packed a copious supply of both. Ella was despatched to knock on her neighbours' doors and scavenge for milk. While she waited for the kettle to boil, Kate stood looking out at the view from the large sash windows.

There was no doubt it was an enchanting spot. The college lawns swept down from the accommodation block, past mature chestnut trees, until they reached a red brick boathouse ornamented with white timber gingerbread and topped by a flagpole. Massive doors at one end opened onto an expanse of concrete and a series of narrow terraces led down to a wooden dock. The River Wear swept past the pontoon and off into the distance, magnificent and stately.

As she stood admiring the light playing seductively on the surface of the water, a women's eight rowed past, doing slow firm. Kate caught her breath. It was something she hadn't witnessed for nearly thirty years. It was a sight so familiar and so dear, it came as a shock to see it again. She almost found herself trying to identify her old crew from their distant outline – was that Hatty at bow? Or Paula at Seven? These young women could have been the students she'd rowed with all those years ago. The image was timeless.

Suddenly Kate found herself choking up with emotion. She was overwhelmed by a yearning to return, to be the one embarking on a new chapter of her life. She wanted to be the one going to Freshers' Fair and signing up for new experiences, forging new friendships and exploring new terrain. She wanted to feel again that excitement, that enthusiasm, that passion. The sudden longing was almost unbearable.

Later, having said her goodbyes and kissed her daughter for the last time, Kate made her way back to the car. Fortunately Ella had assumed Kate's tears were for her. There were occasionally advantages to the adolescent's egocentric view of life.

The light was fading. She sat with both hands on the steering wheel, but made no attempt to start the engine.

She was quite alone. Somewhere in the city a budget hotel was expecting her, but the thought gave her no comfort. She would be on her own in the efficient but soulless room, just as she would be when she arrived home tomorrow. Now there was no avoiding it: the abyss was right in front of her. It was impossible to see a way forward, to find a reason to continue. Everything looked so bleak.

Her phone burst into life with a perky tune. Tim.

'Hiya. All well?' she asked, putting on a pretence of cheeriness.

'I can't find the mango chutney. Are we out of it?'

'There's a jar in the fridge. Top shelf. You'll have to move things around to see it.'

'You got there OK? Traffic not too bad?'

'Yes, fine.' Kate decided not to mention Pontefract. 'I just said goodbye to Ella. I'm off to look for the hotel.'

'How was she? Settling in OK? No tears, I hope?'

'Not from her. No she's absolutely fine. It's really lovely here.'

'I wish I could have taken her. I feel I'm missing out. I simply couldn't afford to take tomorrow off, not with this client meeting. God knows whether I can sort things out with them.'

'Oh, I'm sure you will. You always do. You're good at your job, sweetheart. And clients love you.'

'Well, yes. We'll see. Top shelf you say? Better go. See you Friday. Have a good week,' and he rang off.

And how are you doing, Kate? she asked herself. She had thought she couldn't feel more alone than she had five minutes earlier, but somehow the call from Tim had made it a whole lot worse.

She sat for a long time, staring through the windscreen. The river shimmered in the last rays of the setting sun but

Kate looked straight past it into – nothing. She wished tears would come again as a good cry might help, but she was beyond that. Finally she roused herself, blew her nose and gave herself a stern talking-to.

You're just going to have to get a grip. Find something else to do. Something to fill your life.

She thought of the women in her book club who'd taken up a variety of hobbies in recent years. One woman had explained how 'golf really helped take my mind off the menopause'. Another friend had been obsessed first by sailing, then gardening, then had finally found Jesus. The memory made her smile, but none of those would do.

She didn't just want something to fill the time. She wanted something she was passionate about. Most of all, she wanted to recapture the person she used to be. Suddenly, with a fierce clarity, Kate realised that if she were to escape the dark chasm, she had to make it happen.

And just then the women's eight came back into view, rowing back to where they'd come from.

***Backstops**: The 'ready' position. The rower sits with a straight back, leaning backwards slightly. Legs are flat and straight. The blade is held flat on the water with the handle against the body. This is the position the rower adopts immediately before commencing rowing.*

2

KATE

> From: Womenscaptain@albionrowingclub.org
>
> Good to hear from you, Kate. We're always on the lookout for experienced rowers. Our senior women's eight are going out at 8.00 a.m. this Saturday, if you'd like to try out.

'Are you sure this is a good idea?' Tim's shaved head was buried in the fridge as he foraged for fuel for his cycle ride. He emerged clutching a couple of pork pies and a Scotch egg. He was tall and skinny and his stretchy cycle gear somehow exaggerated his resemblance to a pipe cleaner. 'I mean – should you be doing this?'

Should I be doing this? Kate was already doubting herself. Getting ready had been a nightmare. Make-up? No make-up? She didn't want them to think she was some sort of gym bunny who worked out in thick war paint. *Oh God – what am I doing?* This was possibly the hundredth time she'd asked herself this question.

And what on earth to wear? If only her girls were at home. They'd know exactly what to do. She really missed them at times like this. At Cambridge she'd worn a motley collection of rugby shirts nicked from boyfriends and baggy tracksuit bottoms. They'd festered in a large pile in a corner of her room like a gently steaming compost heap. She hadn't been as hot on laundry in those days.

Back then it wasn't done to try too hard with what you wore. Admittedly, when only 10 per cent of students were female, it was the men that did the chasing. It was all so different now. Young women seemed to try hard all of the time. It was as if they had to be Instagram ready at every waking moment, their hair freshly straightened and their eyeliner perfectly applied. Vigorous physical activity was clearly incompatible with this level of grooming. Kate had not been surprised when she'd read somewhere how few of her daughters' generation took part in sport. Disappointed, yes, but not surprised.

'Plain black Lycra. Not the Lululemon.' Kate could almost hear her daughter's voice. That was one problem solved.

It was fortunate she'd allowed plenty of time, as the way in to the club was not obvious. *Don't they want people to join?* The entrance was through a gate at the end of a lane overgrown with nettles. A placard hung on the rusted metal bars announced 'Albion Rowing Club' beneath a faded crest. The river remained hidden.

She headed over to what looked like an agricultural outbuilding clad in corrugated iron. Surrounded by fields, it was eerily quiet. There were half a dozen boats on trestles in front and a number of people milling about. No one paid her any attention.

As she reached the building she hesitated. She looked for an eight but couldn't see one amongst the boats outside. Stepping into the gloomy boatshed she could just make out a group of women at the far end. The rough concrete floor was thick with dust and clods of mud.

'Excuse me, I'm looking for the Senior Women – or the Women's Captain?' asked Kate. The women stopped talking and stared at her. Kate cringed under their scrutiny.

'She's down by the river – she'll be here in a minute,' said one, and they resumed their conversation without missing a beat. Kate tried to make herself invisible. They were having a debrief on the night before and dissecting what one of the group may or may not have done with one of the men's first eight. It was like listening to Poppy and Ella with their mates – in fact, all the women were young enough to be Kate's daughters. They had long swishy ponytails and were dressed almost identically. Kate was wearing the wrong leggings and the wrong fleece. It was all a terrible mistake. She didn't belong here.

Finally a wiry looking woman in her early thirties appeared.

'Oh. You're not what I was expecting.'

Kate had debated whether to say how old she was in her email to the club, but had settled on, *I stroked my college first eight at Cambridge but haven't rowed for a while.*

'Sorry, I'm the Women's Captain. I see you've met the rest of the crew. Everyone – this is Kate. Kate rowed at Cambridge and is here to see if we're good enough for her.' This was said without a trace of irony. 'Is Beth here yet?'

A woman with auburn hair replied, 'This is Beth we're talking about – she's only five minutes late at the moment. Give it another quarter of an hour.' This produced a chorus of cackles from the group. Kate made a mental note to give that particular rower a wide berth.

'Well, let's get the boat out,' said the captain. 'Hopefully our cox will be here by the time we're ready. Hands on!'

Everyone strode off to the next bay in the boathouse and ranged themselves along the length of a yellow eight resting upside down on wooden supports. Kate dithered, unsure where to go. 'What number did I say you were rowing at?' asked the captain.

'Four.'

'OK, so you're in there,' and she pointed to a slight gap in the line-up between two equally tall and slender young women with matching manes of blonde hair. The one in front had an impressive collection of metalware clipped down the length of her ear. The one behind sported carefully applied eyeliner that ended in extravagant flicks. Kate moved into place.

'Ready to lift – stroke side going under!' barked the captain. The crew lifted the boat a couple of inches off the rack in unison and gently started moving it out.

'That's you – stroke side! You need to go under!' This was directed at Kate by Three with the eyeliner. Every alternate person had ducked under to the far side of the boat and she was the only one missing. She quickly moved to fill the gap.

'To shoulders – go! Mind the riggers on the way out!' At the captain's command the crew raised the boat onto their shoulders and carefully made their way out of the shed towards the waiting trestles. Having not seen an eight being moved in years, Kate marvelled that they could move a piece of equipment the length of a bus and manoeuvre it in such a tight space.

'To heads – go!' shouted the captain, and before her brain could register the command, the boat was swept out of Kate's grasp and above her head.

'And down on to the trestles – go!' Again, before Kate could react, the boat was being manoeuvred down to one side and gently laid on the green canvas slings.

'OK, everyone adjust your feet as quick as you can. Beth's here so we're going in five minutes.'

Kate was completely befuddled. The commands were like echoes from the past, but they no longer produced a response in her muscle memory. She recalled being part of a well-drilled crew, moving together with perfect synchronicity. It was the only way women could move heavy boats. Men could do it with brute force. But for women, lifting an old boat, its carbon fibre honeycomb full of water and filler, the task was at the limit of their strength. Unless they did it together. Kate felt like the incompetent squaddie on parade, her foot clicking to attention after the rest of the platoon. If her plan had been to go unnoticed, she was failing miserably.

For the umpteenth time that morning, Kate felt in need of a pee. She knew it was nerves, but she was also far from confident in her pelvic floor since having the girls. She turned to Three and asked her where the toilet was.

'Toilet? In your dreams,' laughed Three. 'Try the bushes at the back of the boatshed. I tell you what – you go and I'll sort your feet out. You look about the same height as me.' Grateful for the kindness, Kate jogged off in the direction Three was pointing. The ground was thick with nettles and she lowered her naked bottom cautiously, hovering in an uncomfortable position to stay clear of the stingers. This really summed up her morning so far: awkward, undignified and slightly risky. When she arrived back, everyone was standing ready.

'Better?' asked Three.

'Much. I shouldn't have had that last cup of tea before I came out.'

'Me, I can't even think straight with a full bladder, let alone row.'

Just then an older woman appeared, wearing a life jacket and carrying a cox box. This must be Beth, the coxswain.

'Don't forget – when we separate you go to the right!' hissed Three.

'Whole crew!' shouted the cox.

'Hands on!

To heads –

Go!'

At the cox's command, the crew swung the boat to their heads and separated to their respective sides, the boat resting on their shoulders as if they were pallbearers. They walked it down the steps to the river.

'Thanks for the heads-up back there. It's all a bit of a blur,' Kate said quietly as Three handed her an oar with a number four painted on the side.

'Here – let me,' and Three secured her blade in the rowlock. 'Don't worry, you're doing fine. Just make sure you're holding on to that rigger when I get in. If we end up capsizing you will be my newest ex-friend.'

'Stroke side holding,

Bow side getting in,

Go!' shouted the cox. Kate watched the other stroke-side rowers pushing the ends of the riggers down onto the pontoon, and did the same. Crouched on the dock, Kate watched Three slip off her wellies, push her seat back on the slide, then gracefully step onto the black rectangle painted on the board under the seat. Having sat down she secured her oar in the rowlock. With her blade flat on the water and the boat no longer in danger of tipping over, Three secured her feet into the shoes attached to the footplate.

I remember this! I can do this!

Once all of bow side had their oars in place the cox called, ***Two getting in!*** Then once Two was in her seat,

'Four getting in!' This was the moment of truth. Kate took off her trainers and pushed her seat back the way Three had done. She put her left foot on to the black mark. She went to step across with her right foot and wobbled.

Shit! Shit!

She bent down and steadied herself. Both feet in place, she went to lower herself onto the seat. This was easier said than done. She clung on to the rigger and then landed heavily. She wriggled into the correct position and then, holding on to her oar, strapped her feet in. The wooden handle of the blade was rough to the touch. Her hands remembered the coarse texture, the weight and balance of the blade.

'Well done,' whispered Three. 'That's the hardest part over with.' Kate was not entirely convinced, but was grateful for the encouragement. Close to the water now, Kate breathed in the familiar river smell, part rotting vegetation and part diesel oil. The gentle lapping of the water against the side of the boat sounded like the voice of an old friend. Her gaze fell on the trim buttocks of Five in front of her. Kate groaned inwardly at the thought of Three having to spend the whole outing studying her own expansive bottom.

'Testing! Testing!' came the cox's voice through a speaker by Kate's feet. That was something new. At Cambridge they'd made do with coxes with penetrating voices.

'Can you hear me in the bows?'

Three tapped Kate on the shoulder. 'Don't forget – when the cox says "Bow Four", that's us. Got it?'

'Got it.'

'Number off when ready!' said the cox.

'Bow!'

'Two!'

'Three!' The cogs in Kate's brain couldn't move fast enough to process what was happening.

'Four!' hissed Three.

'Four!' shouted Kate

'Five!'

'Six!'

'Seven!'

'Stroke!'

'Pushing off!' called the cox, and the rowers closest to the bank pushed the eight clear into the river.

The cox commanded stern four to row light pressure, and the four women in front of Kate started rowing. She had to move her hands forward and bring her knees up to avoid the oar in front becoming tangled with hers. She was glad of this chance to observe and remind herself how they warmed up, building up the stroke, piece by piece.

They began sitting bolt upright, legs flat and using just their arms. Next they started hingeing from the hips, legs still straight. Gradually they brought in the legs. With each new command the rowers brought up their knees slightly higher and slid their bottoms closer to their feet. With each addition to the stroke, the arc circumscribed by the oar increased. Finally they were at maximum compression and taking full-length strokes. Kate felt the familiar lurch of the boat with every stroke. It was like cantering on a horse – a backwards and forwards movement that you had to ride out. With every surge she felt her heart lift.

'Next stroke –

Easy there!'

And with this, the four women stopped rowing. Kate knew what was coming next: her turn. *Dear God, can I remember what to do?*

'Stern Four –

Sit the boat!
Bow Four –
Backstops,
Light pressure,
Go!'

With that Kate pushed her arms away, rocked over, moved up the slide and placed her blade in the water. She was rowing. It felt as natural as breathing.

'Bow – make sure you're in time with Four,' the cox called. ***'She's setting a nice rhythm. Make sure you're following.'*** Kate almost purred. She could do this. She was exhilarated by the movement and the water. But more thrilling still was being reminded of her own ability. Of who she was.

Once Bow Four had warmed up, cox called for Stern Four to join in. Now they were rowing as an eight. Even though they were using minimal effort the boat was zipping along. The river slipped away behind the cox with narrowboats and pleasure cruisers moored at its sides. Kate was conscious she had no idea what the river ahead looked like. It was a curious sensation to be travelling along an unknown river, backwards: to be able to see so clearly where you had come from but to have no clue where you were going.

They rowed on with the cox making calls to focus on different aspects of technique. Kate struggled to understand some of the instructions. As they progressed down a straight, a number of single and double sculling boats passed on the other side, making their way back upstream. There were no boats moored here. Overgrown willow trees jostled for space on the banks, their branches trailing in the water, narrowing the river.

When they finally halted, just short of a weir, Kate was all in. She could barely breathe and her arms and legs felt like jelly. They paused for a few minutes to drink water.

As Kate concentrated on bringing down her heart rate and steadying her breathing, she studied the view down the river, back towards the Albion boathouse.

The land to the left rose sharply to an escarpment. A couple of imposing Georgian houses sat smugly on the plain above the ridge, looking south over the river. To her right, there was nothing to see but open countryside. As Kate brought the focus of her gaze back to the river, she noticed with a start the menacing outline of a grey heron, poised motionless on an overhanging branch. In stark contrast to the bucolic scene beyond, the limbs of the trees lining the river were draped with shrouds of blackened plastic. Remnants of last winter's floods, they were a reminder of the river's changeable nature.

Once everyone had drunk and talked their fill, they spun the boat and rowed back, working on technique. Kate was concentrating so hard she was surprised when they arrived back at the landing stage. Getting out was much easier than getting in, but as she went to straighten up, her back crunched and a pain shot through her buttock. She was already stiff. This was going to hurt.

They lifted the boat out of the water. Grimy with oily filth and duckweed, it bore a distinct tidemark. As they raised it above their heads, the foul-smelling water ran down Kate's arms. They carried the eight back up to the boathouse. Bow Four collected the blades and put them away while Stern Four washed the boat. Kate couldn't remember washing a boat in her university days.

The oars were stored vertically in the boathouse, resting in the rack by their collars. Bow was making a fuss because Two hadn't put the blades away in number order. Two was arguing it didn't matter as they got jumbled up when you took them out anyway. Once Two walked off, Bow took them out and rearranged them. Kate thought to herself that Bow probably had very tidy kitchen cupboards.

With the boat safely away, the crew huddled together to discuss how the outing had gone and what they'd like to work on next time. No one said anything to Kate. She was so overwhelmed by the experience, it was difficult to untangle her emotions. She couldn't honestly say she'd enjoyed the morning as she'd felt uncomfortable and out of place for so much of it. But there had undoubtedly been moments of exhilaration. No – moments of joy. She was hugely relieved to have survived and not made a complete fool of herself. But it was even harder than she remembered, both technically and physically. She'd have to work hard to regain the form she once had, if it was even possible.

As the meeting broke up, Three caught Kate's eye and whispered:

'Well done, Cambridge – you're in!' Before Kate could say anything, Three was walking away from the boatshed, her arms looped round the waists of two of the other young women. It reminded Kate of the camaraderie of her old college crew. They'd learnt to row together, won and lost races, bickered and made up. They'd been more like sisters than friends. It was hard to imagine she would ever feel that with this crew.

Just as Kate was about to make a move, Beth the cox came over. She was about Kate's age and similar height. She was probably more slight, although it was difficult to tell under the multiple layers of clothing, waterproofs and life preserver. Her hair was a tangle but was dark brown and chin length. A hairdresser may once have intended it to sit in a layered bob. She had an endearing grin and the white lines that fanned out from her eyes suggested a habit of smiling. Her mouth hardly moved as she spoke with the clipped tones that identified her as from a different world to Kate's, an impression at odds with her stained orange over-trousers that had seen better days.

'You must be Kate. I didn't get a chance to have a word before we went out. Um, you're not . . .'

'What you were expecting? No, I gathered that.' Beth laughed, and for the first time that day Kate started to relax.

'How was that for you?' asked Beth. 'You did brilliantly, you know.'

'Really? I absolutely loved it. It was so kind of everyone to let me have a go.'

'Nonsense! They were lucky to have you. I think it's amazing you wanted to do it.' Beth's eyes crinkled into a warm and slightly mischievous smile as she said this.

'What – at my age?'

'I meant after such a long lay-off.'

'To be honest – I hadn't realised how unfit I was. I don't think I'll be able to walk tomorrow. I'm stiffening up already.'

'How are your hands?'

Kate lifted up her palms for inspection, livid with several large, raw blisters.

'Ouch. Do make sure you give those a good clean before you tape them up. Don't want you going down with Weil's Disease.'

Kate was touched by her thoughtfulness.

'Was there anything in particular you found difficult?'

'This is going to sound ridiculous, but it wasn't the rowing itself. The hardest bit was carrying the boat. And then getting in to it. I don't remember it being so difficult when I was twenty.' Beth knotted her brows together as if she were considering this information.

'Look, I don't know if you're interested, but as it happens,

I'm a physio. I could show you some exercises to help with that. And some stretches. If you'd like.'

'Oh my God – would you? You have no idea – that would just be amazing.' Kate was struck by how much this small gesture of kindness meant.

'No problem. Give me your address and I'll drop by tomorrow, before you seize up.' Beth smiled and waved as Kate limped away from the river towards her car. She felt battered and bloodied – but triumphant. She had lived to fight another day. And she would. She would fight another day. She was not going to stop fighting.

***The Drive Phase**: after the blade is placed in the water the rower applies pressure to the oar, levering the boat forward.*

3

KATE

Kate reached over to put an arm round Tim and found instead a cold empty space with the duvet peeled back. He must have sneaked out for his Sunday morning bike ride without waking her. She wanted him there. So much. She'd woken up to an empty house every morning during the week and now she ached for him. She hadn't realised how much she'd been looking forward to seeing him, and how disappointed she was not to have him around.

They were so used to their weekend routine, with Tim heading off early to conquer his next hill climb. It hadn't occurred to her she'd feel differently after a week alone without the girls for company. Still, it was early days. No doubt she'd get used to it in time.

When she finally surfaced she found she could barely move. Either her muscles refused to respond, or if they did the pain was unbearable. She was trapped, pinned down by her goose-feather duvet. *This is what it must be like when you're old and have a fall. You spend all night lying on the kitchen floor, unable to move until someone finds you lying soaked in your own urine.*

Determined to escape she worked her feet to the side of

the bed, and then slid out until her bottom was on the floor. She crawled to the bathroom, turned on the bath taps and reached for the painkillers. After a maximum dose of anti-inflammatories, a scalding-hot bath plus several cups of tea, Kate began to feel human again. She was absolutely fine so long as she kept moving. If she sat down for any length of time her legs and back locked into place.

Kate was relieved Tim hadn't been there to see the state she was in. No doubt he'd have told her once again she was mad to be doing this to herself at her age, even as he headed out of the house in fluorescent Lycra, cycle helmet and cleats. Self-awareness was a gift not granted to everyone.

As Kate walked along the landing to the airing cupboard, she passed the door to Ella's bedroom. She paused and then opened the door to reassure herself the room was clean and tidy, even though no one had been in there since last time she checked. She sat on the bed. It felt quieter than the rest of the house. Emptier. She wasn't used to being able to see the carpet in here. She ran her hands across the damson velvet counterpane. It was soft and comforting against her ragged palms. Kate lowered herself gingerly onto the bed and laid her head on the pillow. She buried her face in the icy cotton and breathed in the smell of her child. She lay there, lost in memories of her baby, remembering the soft skin at the back of her neck that always smelt just like this.

Eventually she roused herself. She taped up her blisters and busied herself clearing up the kitchen and making an apple pie for later. Plus some totally unnecessary cherry tray bakes. Preparing meals and baking cakes was how Kate expressed herself, and she wanted Beth to know how grateful she was for her kindness.

Beth was as good as her word, and dropped round after her morning outing. Her cheeks were pink and as Kate hugged her, she could smell the outdoors clinging to her hair. She put the espresso pot on the hob to brew, and while they waited for the coffee, Beth took her through a series of stretches. They all hurt. No – they were all total agony. But with Beth's encouragement Kate breathed deeply through the pain. Once they'd finished, her poor aching body did feel a great deal easier.

'I'm sorry. It must hurt like buggery. You'll need to keep doing these every two or three hours for the next few days. That will help with the stiffness. And keep taking the anti-inflammatories.'

'You know, it's feeling better already.'

'Grand. There are a couple of other things I want to show you.' Beth took her through some exercises to help build up her upper-body strength, using a couple of old milk cartons filled with water as weights. That was to avoid injury when moving the boat. She was extremely particular about how Kate was holding herself, and making sure she was breathing at the appropriate point in the movement. Kate felt safe in Beth's care. It was a good feeling.

'Sorry for being fussy, but it's really important you do this correctly, right from the start. By the time we've built up to a heavy weight, you need to make sure you have a good technique.' She then showed her how to practise standing up from a deep squat. Doing this would help build up the core and leg muscles Kate needed to get in and out of the boat.

She could go through this routine every morning in the kitchen while she waited for her porridge to cook. By now the air was filling with the enticing aroma of coffee. Kate put four slices of the freshly baked cherry cake on a plate and they both sat at the battered pine table.

'This is a treat.' said Beth. 'I don't ever bake,'

'I'm so in the habit of baking every week for my family, I keep forgetting the only person who's going to eat my cakes now is me.'

'What about your husband?'

'He doesn't do carbs.' Kate pondered the irony of the situation as they sat in companionable silence, sipping at their coffee.

'Tell me something – do you row? Or do you just cox?'

'Gosh, yes, I used to, for years. I was mad about it.'

'So why did you stop?'

'Oh, I don't know . . . my last crew broke up when one of them – Lesley – had an injury. I carried on sculling for a bit but people started asking me to cox. I sat in for other crews but I got sick of never being picked to race. I pretty much only cox these days although I keep saying I'm going to start sculling again.'

'Do you miss it?' asked Kate.

'I miss being part of a crew, but – you know – it is how it is.' Kate wondered if Beth was always this accepting. As they drank their coffee, she glanced down at Beth's left hand, bare of rings.

'Do you mind me asking – do you have a partner? '

'No, I don't mind you asking,' she replied smiling warmly, clearly appreciating Kate's tact. 'And no, I don't have a partner. Somehow it just never quite happened.' She paused. 'There was someone. Once. I really thought he was "the one". But it seems it wasn't meant to be.' She hesitated. 'And I guess it's not going to happen now.' There was an awkward silence. Kate began to wish she hadn't asked the question. Beth drank her coffee looking lost in contemplation. She picked at her cake and extracted a whole cherry. She chased it around the plate with her finger. She had the easy charm and expensive vowels of people who'd been to public school. Kate wondered to herself how different their childhoods must have been.

'Do you realise,' said Beth, 'you've got everything I was supposed to have: the lovely home, the husband, the children? That's what was planned for me.' This came out in a bit of a rush, like a confession.

'My parents didn't believe in educating girls – they thought it would be an "obstacle to a good marriage". At school we spent more time with our ponies than our books. It was great fun but we all left complete noodles. It was a total fluke I scraped the grades to train as a physio.'

'Lucky for me you did. You're really good at it.'

Beth didn't seem to notice the compliment. She seemed preoccupied with her train of thought.

'When you're young you have this idea of how your life will look one day, even if that idea is someone else's. Then, somehow, you wake up in your late forties and it isn't anything like that. You sort of wonder – how did I get here? This isn't what was supposed to happen.'

'I know exactly what you mean – life not turning out the way you expect.' Kate paused, unsure whether to continue. She lowered her voice slightly, as if she might be overheard in the empty house. 'You do know things aren't necessarily as rosy as they look on the outside, don't you?' She got up to put on a second pot of coffee and offered Beth another slice of cake. 'I look at you and I envy you: living your life on your own terms, doing a job you enjoy and pursuing your passions. It's a long time since I did that.' Kate lifted her head as she finished saying this and glanced cautiously at Beth. She looked intrigued.

'Well, it's about time you started again. Next weekend?'

'Try and stop me.'

*

It was late by the time Tim limped in from his cycle ride. Kate had already made a start on peeling the potatoes for supper. She put down her knife and staggered up to the front door. She was so pleased to have him back. He was bent over the village newsletter lying on the hall table, clad in red and black Lycra.

'How was it? I'm glad you're back in one piece.' There was no reply. Then Kate saw the telltale wire dangling from Tim's cycling helmet. She tapped him on the shoulder and he turned round with a start and removed his earpiece.

'I didn't see you there. What time's supper?'

'Another hour or so. How was your ride?'

'Annoyingly, I got a puncture early on but I managed to fix it – a couple of them waited for me.'

'That was kind of them.'

'Wasn't it? Do you know, I'm so used to spending my time at work with everyone out for themselves, it almost comes as a shock when someone's nice to me like that.'

Kate felt quite touched by this admission.

'Someone apart from me,' she added.

'Well, obviously. You're my wife. It's your job to be nice to me.' There was a silence that neither of them seemed to want to fill.

'Well, I'll go and get a bath, seeing as there's time.'

As Kate turned to go, she'd stiffened up and was limping.

'You OK? Have you hurt yourself?' Tim sounded concerned.

'I'm fine. Just a bit stiff.'

'Are you sure this rowing is a good idea? You're going to do yourself an injury if you're not careful.' With these words of encouragement floating in the air, Tim hobbled his way upstairs. Kate sighed and returned to her vegetables, wondering whose job it was to be nice to her.

Bow: *The rower closest to the front or bow. In coxless boats, often the person who keeps an eye on the water behind them to avoid accidents.*

4

KATE

By the following Friday, as she ploughed through the stack of files in front of her at work, Kate felt almost back to normal and her blisters were nearly healed. It was only when she attempted to get up to fetch another document that she found her entire body had been welded into place.

Kate's office had no window, being in the centre of the building, but instead the wall to the corridor was made of glass. While this let in no natural light, it did help to relieve the potential for claustrophobia. The feeling of working in a goldfish bowl was harder to escape. As colleagues passed by, they smiled at her or gave her a wave. While she appreciated the gesture, it was a distraction she could have done without.

It was not an attractive office. More to the point, it was not a desirable office. The lack of an external window, the absence of furniture beyond Kate's desk and chair, all semaphored Kate's lowly status within the firm. This was at least part of the reason quite so many colleagues waved at Kate as they passed. She was not a threat so it cost them nothing to be pleasant.

Kate had rationalised the situation many times over: she

was only in the office Wednesday to Friday, so it made no sense to occupy a better room. She used one of the meeting rooms when she saw clients, so really it made no odds. Except it did. It rankled. In a quiet, low-grade sort of way, like a small paper cut suffered on a daily basis. Over time the accumulation of barely perceptible slights built up, like the constant irritant in her clients' lungs that eventually turned into cancer.

A partner at the firm had represented one of the earliest claimants suffering from an industrial disease called mesothelioma and a flood of other victims had followed. On the strength of this they'd created a highly specialised part-time job that was perfect for a woman returning from maternity leave. For a long time Kate had been so grateful for any work that would fit in with her family, she'd been happy to accept whatever terms and conditions were offered. It was good for Kate – and even better for the firm who could pay her less than a man would want. And of course, in the beginning when it was all new, it was fascinating. But gradually, as the years went by, the interest had vanished.

She'd lost count of the number of clients she'd represented, who for all intents and purposes, were identical. The challenge had faded as her experience grew, and she was left exposed to the shortcomings of the arrangement. She occasionally wondered whether her dissatisfaction with her job was as much about her status as the work itself.

The legal profession had become so specialised since she first trained. Almost everyone now worked in the narrowest of fields, seemingly doing the same case or transaction over and over again. That complaint was not unusual. But her contemporaries who hadn't been side-tracked by child-bearing seemed to be less dissatisfied. She debated whether she'd have found industrial negligence more fulfilling if it paid five times as much and had earned her a partnership.

It wasn't even as if she derived any personal satisfaction from the job. She could kid herself she was doing something worthwhile, getting compensation for the men and their families. But she couldn't stop them dying. And they all did in the end. She'd learned that the hard way. Mesothelioma was a dreadful disease. Caused by exposure to asbestos, it rotted the lungs, and by the time they'd received a diagnosis they deteriorated rapidly.

She'd made a point of getting to know her earliest clients, hoping to make the legal process less daunting. But their deaths had hit her hard and she learned to distance herself. But if she wasn't personally involved, there wasn't the same satisfaction in winning. Even so, Kate knew she should count herself lucky. But she still occasionally wondered to herself whether a window was really too much to expect.

She'd arrived early that morning to deal with a backlog of cases running up against court deadlines and after several hours of devilling at the pile she needed a break. She grabbed her coat and walked to a nearby café. The coffee was decent enough, but the reason for Kate choosing this particular establishment was their almond croissants, surely the most luxurious treat known to man.

Kate had spent her entire adult life considering her calorie intake. That was not to say that she was particularly controlled in what she ate, simply that nothing passed her lips without Kate having an internal debate as to how many calories it might contain and whether the enjoyment would justify its consumption. Almond croissants almost fell into a category of their own. They contained about a gazillion calories, but the pleasure was transcendental. First the crisp outer layer with shards of buttery almonds, then within, the sweet, unctuous cache of almond paste.

Her mouth was salivating at the thought of the treat to come as she joined the back of the queue. It was busy. As she waited, she mulled over the work she'd accomplished that morning and mentally triaged the pile remaining. Service was slow. After a few minutes she'd advanced one place, but several more people had joined the queue behind her.

'Wotcha, Kate. Mind if I join you?' It was Rick from the office, one of the trainees who'd recently qualified.

'Sure. You needed some fresh air too?'

'Oh, I can't drink the coffee in the office. Filthy stuff. I come here every day about this time.' Kate was surprised Rick could afford an expensive coffee habit at this stage in his career. Not to mention disappearing from the office every morning. When she was doing her training she barely went out for lunch, so desperate had she been to impress the partners with her diligence.

'Who's next?' One of the baristas had suddenly come free and was scanning the queue. Before Kate could speak Rick had leapt in.

'I'll have a flat white and an almond croissant.'

'Coming up,' said the barista. Kate was speechless. She thought Rick incredibly rude for barging in ahead, but she didn't want to make a scene. So she stood next to him fuming, while she waited to be served.

'See you then,' said Rick, as he grabbed his spoils and headed back to the office.

'What can I get you?'

'I'll have an Americano with hot milk and an almond croissant,' said Kate, forcing herself to calm down. Rick's rudeness had spoilt her break and she didn't want it wrecked any further.

'Sorry – we just sold the last almond croissant. Can I get you something else?' Kate was silent. She clenched her fists.

Her nails dug into her palms. She wanted to scream. She wanted to punch something. Hard. Instead she swallowed down her anger, composed herself and said, 'No, thank you. I'll just have the coffee.'

As she walked back to the office she felt as if her head would explode.

Don't be ridiculous, Kate. It was just a bloody croissant. He's done you a favour saving you from all those calories. Now calm down and enjoy your coffee.

But she couldn't calm down. Her anger seemed to be completely out of proportion to the loss of a sugary treat. She already knew Rick was an obnoxious twerp, so why should one more piece of oafish behaviour annoy her so much? As she walked, she imagined herself explaining the incident to Beth, and the problem became clear. She wasn't angry with Rick. She was furious with herself for not saying anything, for letting it happen.

She'd spent her whole life just accepting it when people treated her as less than she deserved. She'd been brought up to believe that ability and hard work would be rewarded. If she wasn't getting what she wanted, she was told, she just needed to try harder. To lean in. She was privileged to have been allowed into a man's world. She was expected to fit in and not make waves. Not be difficult.

She recalled the daily litany of trivial slights. The clients who assumed she was a secretary, no matter how severe a suit she wore, how serious and unflattering a hairstyle she adopted. She'd always been the person in the meeting expected to pour the coffee or fetch a photocopy. Back when she'd started, men had licence to make sexist jokes freely and you had to pretend to find it amusing, no matter how humiliated you felt. You had to laugh off the casual sexual harassment as well.

There was so much she'd endured without even realising. They had a name for it now: micro-agressions. Day by day, year by year, biting her lip and letting the insults go unchecked had taken its toll on Kate. Of course it was much better now. But behind the politically correct behaviour it was still there, the automatic assumption of superiority. It had shown itself the week before when one of the partners had talked over her in a meeting and then repeated exactly what she'd already said. The way she was paid two-thirds of what a man would be given. The way they'd allocated her an office without a window. And of course, she now had the double-whammy of being not just female but middle-aged to boot.

Back then, she could have made herself unpopular by objecting to pouring the coffee in client meetings, might have kicked off about somehow always being given the worst training seat and the least prestigious assignments. But the trouble was, apart from the fact women just didn't complain in those days, she didn't actually know why it was happening. Surrounded by men who assured her it was the luck of the draw, she was gaslighted into believing she was just, well, really unlucky.

Then, as time went by and she didn't make the progress she was expecting, she believed them when they patiently explained this was due to some inherent character flaw that she needed to remedy. It had been bewildering. She saw so many men she considered mediocre overtaking her. Each tiny incident was too insignificant to challenge without appearing ridiculous, but she internalised the message that she deserved to be treated this way, that she had no choice. So when a dickhead like Rick behaved as if she didn't count and he had a God-given right to be served before her, he was touching an incredibly raw nerve.

By the end of the day Kate had regained her equilibrium and was pleased with the amount she'd achieved. Crisis had been averted and her work was now well under control. As she started to pack up, she turned her thoughts to supper. It was Friday and Tim would be home after working in London all week. That was something to look forward to.

When they first made the move to Bath, they'd thought he'd be able to spend a couple of nights at home during the week. But it soon proved impossibly tiring to make the long journey back, and they accepted the enforced separation. On a Friday he tried to be home in time to eat supper together and they normally had a takeaway that Kate picked up on the way back from work.

Without thinking too hard about why she felt the need to make a change, Kate decided to cook tonight. As well as making an effort with supper, she thought she would shower and change. Rather than pulling on something comfy with an elasticated waist, she put on a pair of skinny black trousers and a black silk tunic she never got round to wearing. It was too fashion-forward for the office and too smart for home, so it sulked in the back of her wardrobe.

With the table laid and both Kate and the house looking their casual but elegant best, she sat with a gin and tonic, listening to the radio. A text came in from Tim: a trespasser on the line at Swindon so his train would be late in. Kate poured herself another gin and tonic and found a packet of crisps at the back of the cupboard. She was hungry, and she munched her way through the whole packet as she listened to a panel of politicians explaining to the good folk of Barnet why they were mistaken about nearly everything. When Tim finally made it home it was nearly 9.00 p.m. and the gin had gone to Kate's head.

'You cooked? Did I miss something? Is it our anniversary?'

Kate assumed this was an attempt at a joke but it made her feel silly to have made so much effort. Tim seemed awkward for a man in his own home, as if unsure of what was expected of him. His shoulders were hunched and his eyes wary. It always took them a while to decompress after the working week, to make the transition to being a couple again. Kate reminded herself to give it time, to let Tim unwind. She didn't want an argument, although what with the gin and the waiting she could easily have started one.

'I just thought how much I'd missed you during the week. I wanted to do something nice for you.' Kate forced her brightest smile. She so wanted to reconnect with Tim, to rediscover the man she married. The one who could make her laugh until she wept. The one whose kindness made her feel safe and utterly contented.

She remembered Friday nights when they first moved here. She would hear the front door go and Tim would rush through the house to find her without taking his coat off. He didn't even greet the kids first in those days. Ignoring their squeals he made straight for Kate. He would gather her up in his arms and embrace her with an ardour that told her what she needed to know: he had spent all week missing her and wanting her.

That's what she needed now. For Tim to take her in his arms, to kiss her and ask if she were OK. Ask her if she missed their daughters. Ask her if she was coping with the emptiness.

'What a pity the train was so late. I bet this lamb would have been delicious an hour ago.' Despite the state of the meal, Tim enthusiastically heaped the meat and vegetables onto his plate and started shovelling it into his mouth.

'Slow down a bit – you'll give yourself indigestion.'

'I'm so hungry. Plus I've got some work I need to get

sorted out as soon as I've finished. I'd have done it on the train but the Wi-Fi was on the blink.'

Now Kate really was disappointed.

'I thought we might play Scrabble after supper.'

'Scrabble?'

'Yes – you know – the board game. I found it in the old toy cupboard.'

'But you don't like Scrabble.'

'Don't I? I was remembering the fun we used to have playing with Danny and Charlotte. Before we got married. I just thought it might be nice to play a game, spend some time together rather than you with your laptop and me watching telly.'

Tim looked at Kate as if he hadn't seen her before. His face softened.

'Scrabble eh? Well, I'm sorry, but I've got work to do, and then I need an early night. I'm up early tomorrow – we're cycling to Wells, apparently.'

'Wells? Not to worry. Another time perhaps . . .' And as Tim disappeared to his study, Kate scraped the half-eaten meal from her plate into the bin with slightly more force than strictly necessary.

Squaring: *To turn the oar so that the spoon is at 90 degrees to the water. This action should be done early during the recovery to ensure good preparation for the catch.*

5
KATE

The next morning Kate arrived early at the rowing club for the session and looked around for her crew. Five of the women from her boat were huddled together, heads practically touching. There was no sign of Three or Beth, so she took off her jacket and clambered onto one of the line of rowing machines to warm up. The seat felt warm and the handle was slippery as she grabbed it.

She felt self-conscious working out on her own, but decided to focus on rowing for a whole ten minutes. By then, hopefully, the others would have arrived. As she concentrated on her technique and the points she'd learned the previous week, she became aware that her crewmates were now watching her.

'Setting a good example, Cambridge, I see,' called out Three as she strode down the boathouse towards them. 'Presumably you lot have already warmed up?' With that Three flung her things down on the floor and sat down heavily on the machine next to Kate. 'So glad to see we didn't frighten you off last week.'

'You'll have to try harder than that. I'm a sucker for punishment.'

The pair of them rowed in unison for a few more minutes until the Women's Captain appeared in the doorway and shouted:

'Hands on!'

This week Kate had more of a sense of what she was about and she could understand the instructions if she listened hard. They were in the same seats as the week before and Kate was grateful to have Three sitting behind her. Despite being a clone of the other crew members and very much part of their group, she was open and welcoming.

The outing went well. Kate was gradually feeling more at ease, although she could not in all honesty claim the exercises Beth had shown her were helping yet. Still, it felt reassuring to know the cox was on her side. With Three behind her, Kate was almost starting to feel comfortable in the boat. It was also getting easier to focus on her technique rather than worrying about what was coming next.

After the outing the rest of the crew made arrangements to go out for breakfast, although no one included Kate in the conversation. Chloe, the number Six, was the Queen Bee of the group. She was as tall as Kate but elegantly slender with long ginger hair swept up into a pert ponytail. On the back of her neck was an inked symbol of infinity with a row of small birds. It reminded Kate how relieved she was her own girls hadn't got themselves a tattoo. Yet. The tattoo notwithstanding, Kate smarted at being excluded and was relieved when Beth sidled over and whispered in her ear.

'You got five minutes to give me a hand? Then back to yours for coffee?'

Kate silently gave thanks that she lived so close to the rowing club.

'Don't forget ergs on Tuesday evening,' bellowed the captain. 'We're doing a 5k test.' This produced a groan from the crew and grimaces all round.

'What's a 5k test?' asked Kate.

'You'll soon find out,' said Beth.

In fact Kate couldn't do much to help Beth except keep her company as she expertly checked the cox boxes over.

'Novice coxes will insist on leaving them unplugged,' she muttered, 'Or worse still, shoving the charger in and damaging the connection. It's maddening if they're not available to use just because people can't be bothered to look after them.'

As she worked, Kate asked her about some of the exercises they'd done during the outing to make sure she understood them properly. Rowing technique had changed so much since her university days, and it was really useful for Kate to be absolutely clear what she was trying to achieve.

Once the cox boxes were organised, Beth moved on to the buoyancy aides to store them neatly so they could dry. This was more within Kate's area of expertise, creating order out of the detritus left by young people with more important matters on their minds than hanging things up. Now Beth was the one standing with her arms crossed watching Kate work.

'Tell me, Kate, what are you hoping to get out of rowing – assuming you're planning on carrying on?'

Kate paused in what she was doing and thought hard about Beth's question.

'I don't know. I suppose I want to get back to rowing as well as I can. And I want to race – although I don't even know what races Albion does.' With this she bent down to retrieve an orange life jacket that had become wedged under a box in the corner.

'Well, the next big race the women's squad are training for is the Women's Head of the River on the Tideway—' She broke off as if unsure whether to continue. 'Look, Kate, I feel I should warn you . . .' She stopped, then went on, 'The way teams are picked in a club, well, at Albion at any rate. It's all done by the captain. And the thing is, they do look at erg scores and how good your technique is and everything. But at the end of the day, everyone likes to row with their mates . . .' Kate wasn't really sure what this meant, or why Beth was saying it.

'Well, I'll just have to get so good they can't say no to me.' Kate said defiantly.

'That's the spirit,' said Beth who sounded less confident. 'And you know, training on an erg will really help with your technique. You should try to get to the squad training session.'

'Really? I've never trained on an erg. We didn't have access to them in my day. I suppose it can't be any worse than a water session. Can it?'

Kate arrived early on Tuesday evening but there were already a few of the women's squad milling around.

'Nice to see you, Kate,' said the captain. 'I suggest you crack on and do your test now before the rest of the squad arrives.' She explained the task was to row 5,000 metres which would take about half an hour. They would set up the distance on the monitor and it would count down to zero as Kate rowed.

She needed to keep an eye on the number of strokes she was taking per minute: this was displayed in large digits on the screen. For this drill she had to maintain a steady rating of twenty-four strokes per minute.

She also needed to focus on her 'split'. This metric

calculated how long it would take to row 500 metres at the current level of output and was a measure of how much power was being applied.

'The main thing is to keep your split fairly constant,' said the captain. 'I'd have thought at the moment you want to be aiming for two minutes thirty to two minutes forty seconds. Don't worry about today's score. You're just setting a benchmark. What I'm looking for is your progress over the coming months.'

What on earth am I doing here? Kate felt sick with apprehension. At least on the water no one could see her. Here in the boathouse under the fluorescent lights there was nowhere to hide.

'Do your warm-up, then I'll set up your monitor for you.' With that the captain moved on to chivvy a group of young women chatting in the corner.

Kate strapped her feet in. To the side and in front were floor-to-ceiling mirrors. She gazed ahead at the reflection of a slightly puffy middle-aged woman and put one hand up to smooth her hair. There were more grey than blonde highlights these days.

Summoning all her courage, Kate sat tall, engaged her core muscles and pulled her shoulders back. At the end of the warm-up drill she was glowing. She let go of the handle and peeled off her sweatshirt. As she attempted to rearrange her hair, the captain appeared at her side and tapped away at the buttons on the monitor.

'OK, Kate. You're good to go. Just remember – keep it steady for the first k.

'Come forward!
Attention!
Go!'

Kate pushed back with her legs on the first stroke and

watched the wildly fluctuating numbers. It took her a while to adjust her cadence to fit the rating. *4,000 metres to go.* Having finally found her rhythm, Kate turned her attention to the split. It was somewhere up around three minutes. *Hang on – the captain said it should be two minutes thirty!* Experimenting, Kate worked out if she concentrated on driving off her toes, she could bring the split down without increasing the rating. On a good stroke she could manage two minutes twenty. On a bad one she was back up around three minutes.

3,000 metres to go. She gradually homed in on two minutes forty as an achievable target for the split and focussed on keeping each stroke as close to this as possible. *2,500 metres to go.* Kate saw the distance left and panicked. It was too far. *Count it out, Kate. Just focus on the next twenty.* She concentrated hard on the next stroke, making it as good as she could, as close to the rating and split as possible. Then the next stroke. Then the next.

2,000 metres to go. She couldn't do this. She really couldn't. Should she just stop? Make her excuses and leave? If she did, she'd never be able to come back. She had to finish. She had to. Moisture was running down her back. Her hands, greasy with sweat were slipping on the handle. She was on the point of giving up.

'Sit tall, Kate! You can do this!' From afar, above the thumping of dance music and her own misery, Kate heard the captain's voice. Somehow this simple exhortation brought Kate back from the brink and reminded her of who she really was. She was a woman of courage who did not give up.

She checked her posture and immediately her split fell. She found her resolve returning. She could do this. She was going to do this.

'Come on, Cambridge! Keep it going!'

'You can do it!'

'Dig deep, Cambridge!' The many voices calling out helped her rise above the screaming coming from every part of her body, the pain telling her to stop. *1,000 metres to go.*

'Last k – that's just like rowing down the straight. Anyone can row down the straight!' Kate didn't know who shouted that but she held on to it like a mantra. She felt completely destroyed, and yet still she kept going.

By the last 200 metres, it seemed like the whole squad were cheering her on. As she pulled herself over the line, there was nothing left. She was spent.

The women around her cheered as Kate let go of the handle and fell back, gasping for air. She released her feet from their straps and sucked in great drafts of oxygen. Just as her breathing started to relax, she felt an unmistakeable churning as her diaphragm went in to spasm. Unable to stand, she leant across from her seat and retched violently. She opened her eyes to confront the appalling mess on the floor – and was astonished to find that the plump girl at Bow, had caught her vomit neatly in a bucket.

'Here – have some tissues,' she whispered.

Gratefully Kate wiped her mouth and fumbled around for her water bottle. The rest of the squad had already moved on and were busy with their own training. So she staggered to the changing room and, staring into the mirror, she assessed the damage: her hair was everywhere and her face an unattractive mix of deep puce and white. Her vest was soaked in sweat and clinging to the rolls of fat. She ran a comb through her hair and put her sweatshirt back on. *What an old fool.*

Of course she was relieved she'd finished, but her time

had simply confirmed what she already knew: she was incredibly unfit. She looked a complete mess, and as for throwing up . . . Kate shook her head as if to erase the memory. They were right. All of them. Tim included. She was too old for this. She couldn't do it. She picked up her rucksack and headed out through the boathouse, head down.

'Good effort, Kate – see you Saturday,' the captain called after her. Really? She still wanted her after that performance? She thought back to what the captain had said, about tonight being a baseline to measure her progress. Then it dawned on her: the captain thought she could improve.

For goodness sake, Kate. Of course you can improve. It might take longer than when you were in your twenties, but there's no reason you can't get fit again. When she got to her car, Kate scrabbled around in her bag for her mobile phone.

'Beth – I need to work on my erg performance. How would you feel about training with me?'

They arranged to meet that Friday, but when Kate arrived at the boatshed the grey metal door was locked and the place was deserted. There was no sign of Beth. So Kate stood and waited. She was starting to get cold, so she walked down the slope towards the river and stood at the top of the wooden staging. There were wide steps the width of the dock leading down to the water. The wood was treacherous with lichen and slicks of water.

She checked her watch. Twenty minutes. She climbed back up to the boatshed and found it as empty as before. She phoned Beth's mobile but there was no reply. Just as she was on the point of giving up she saw Beth emerge through the gate.

'Sorry to keep you,' said Beth as she hurried up the path.

'No matter. I was just worried something had happened.' They let themselves into the gloomy boatshed and the strip lights blinked into life. Neither of them said anything. It was as if Beth's late arrival had set a distance between them.

Kate took off her jacket and looked around. Thick cobwebs hung from the rafters, and a deep layer of dust covered everything. There was a sticky orange stain on the floor by her feet. Everywhere were discarded wrappers, blackened banana skins and mugs with a skin of green mould. It reminded her of Poppy's student house. She was still amazed how her daughter could have grown up in a clean, orderly household and yet be perfectly content living in squalor.

'I got hold of a copy of the club's land-training programme from Stanley, the head coach,' said Beth. 'I suggest we do a "pyramid".' This involved changes in ratings every two minutes. 'The main thing is, we need to try to keep our splits consistent throughout. OK?'

'Let's give it a go,' said Kate. She felt far from sure but with Beth there it felt less intimidating. She wanted to improve and this had to be a better option than training with the whole squad.

While Beth fiddled with her training schedule and the monitors, Kate fished around in her sports bag and produced a portable speaker. Beth looked up.

'What's that?' she asked.

'I thought we could do with music so I put together a playlist.'

Beth's face erupted in smiles. 'I feel like when I was fourteen and a boy sent me a mix tape.'

'Don't get too excited. I asked my youngest for some suggestions so you may not like everything.'

'Anything to take my mind off the pain.'

They climbed on machines next to each other and began their warm-up to Motown, the music they'd sung along to in front of bedroom mirrors with a hairbrush for a mic.

It was easier training next to Beth than on her own. Kate could achieve the correct rating simply by making sure her body mirrored Beth's. They began the pyramid and Kate realised her split time was varying wildly. She sneaked a look at Beth's monitor and was shocked to see her split was a rock-solid two minutes twenty seconds. She resolved to concentrate harder and brought her own under control.

Motown segued into eighties disco with memories of flicky hair-dos and knickerbockers. By the third change of rating Kate was dripping wet. Her face was red and sweat was coursing down her back. But her breathing was steady and it felt sustainable.

By halfway, Kate was only too aware that if Beth hadn't been there she would simply have stopped. But she was there. And Kate kept going, matching her stroke for stroke. She drove herself on, giving herself up to the music.

Two-tone was the sound of youth club discos, then punk took Kate back to student parties. By the start of the final protocol, they were done in. Empty. As Beth called the last change in rating, an unfamiliar song came from the speaker:

I used to always be alone
Said I didn't need anyone
I could do it all myself
Then my crew adopted me . . .

They both glared at their monitors, straining every sinew to maintain their splits. As they counted down the final strokes of the drill and willed themselves to the finish line, the chorus erupted from the speaker:

We are young
Let's live our lives,
Strong and free . . .

As they finished and the clock on the monitor counted down to zero, Kate let her handle go with a thwack, released her feet and slumped forward.

'Well done us,' said Beth, once she'd recovered sufficiently to speak. 'That was great. I haven't done a workout like that in ages.' They both sat quietly, enjoying the afterglow of their exercise, draining their water bottles. Finally they got up and went through their stretches, then Kate unzipped a cooler bag.

'What's that? Champagne to celebrate keeping going for a whole thirty minutes?'

'Milk!' said Kate triumphantly, holding it aloft. 'I read you're supposed to have protein straight after hard exercise.'

'Wow. That's brilliant. You're absolutely right. The lads all have those ghastly protein shakes, but honestly, milk is just as good.'

Kate filled a plastic beaker and Beth knocked it back. She let out a small burp, a white moustache decorating her upper lip.

'It's lovely to have someone looking after me, for a change,' said Beth.

'My pleasure,' said Kate.

'Of course, as well as the protein, the milk's good for calcium. I hate to say it, but at our age, we need to start thinking about our bone density. Before it's too late.'

'Well, that's a cheery thought,' said Kate as she drained

her cup and smiled back at Beth with a white moustache of her own.

They turned out the lights, locked up the boathouse and headed back to their cars thoroughly contented. Feeling encouraged by their camaraderie, Kate asked, 'You know I asked you the other day whether you had a partner? I was wondering whether you're seeing anyone? You know – dating?'

'Dating?' Beth's hesitation made Kate regret asking the question.

'I'm not sure if you'd call it dating.' Silence. Kate sensed there was more, but she felt she was crossing a line. Given they were just getting to know each other she didn't want to spoil things. She had an idea her friendship with Beth could be important and she didn't want to jeopardise it talking about men.

'Same time on Tuesday?' asked Beth.

'Sure thing – it was 5.30 p.m., wasn't it?'

They continued working their way through Stanley's training programme over the next few weeks. They saw each other on the river at weekends and shared a coffee together afterwards when they could. But their Tuesday and Friday evening sessions gradually took on an important place in their lives. Now when Kate woke up to an empty house on a Monday morning, she comforted herself with the thought she'd be seeing Beth the next day, and their Friday workout was the perfect way to unwind before Tim arrived home.

She was beginning to get used to being alone during the week. She was sleeping better and was no longer troubled by the silence when she woke up. She'd started appreciating the luxury of not having to cook a meal every night, or feeling the need to stay in. She'd begun going for a swim after work and was now a regular at the local cinema. There were definite advantages to having the house to herself. Plus she no longer went to the fridge to find a swarm of locusts had cleaned it out. If she bought a pot of yogurt, it would still be there when she came to eat it. It was a small thing, but Kate thought it important to appreciate the positive aspects of this new phase of life.

She was feeling so much better than when Ella had first left, but she was conscious it was still work in progress. She still had days when it all felt utterly hopeless, but they happened less often. Even amidst her rejuvenated schedule, Kate was aware her sessions with Beth held a special significance. Apart from the real pleasure of spending time with her friend, there was a purpose to them. When it came to her rowing, Kate was on a mission: she was determined she was going to match Chloe and her mates on the erg, however long it took.

Part Two

February 2012

***Washout**: When the blade is extracted before the end of the stroke which results in a loss of power and drive. Washing-out may be caused by finishing too low, or by a loss of suspension.*

6

BETH

February 2012

The light was still the thin grey of early morning when Beth walked out of the Radisson Hotel. She was wearing gym clothes under her down jacket and had a rucksack over one shoulder and a yoga mat tucked under the other arm. A close observer might have noticed that her mat, while dusty, appeared never to have been removed from its leather strap. Someone paying attention might also have noticed that, curiously, Beth had exited the hotel's lift, not the door to the gym. They might also have remarked that Beth exited the hotel lift every Tuesday morning at the same time, wearing her gym kit and carrying her unused yoga mat. But Beth had come to realise that no one did pay attention. She'd been doing the same thing every Tuesday for years.

Beth didn't really think about her weekly ritual any more. She'd been doing it for so long it was now just part of her routine. In the first few weeks of meeting up with Mark she'd realised it wouldn't be long before someone she knew saw her weekly walk of shame and started asking too many questions. It was Mark who suggested the sports kit, saying people would assume she had membership of the hotel's facilities and used the gym before work. The yoga mat had been a stroke of genius.

As predicted, she'd been quizzed about her movements more than a few times over the years, but the enquirer always lost interest once she launched into a run-down of the cardio equipment available at the Radisson gym. Mark was clever at things like that, the tiny details most people don't even notice but which eat away at the brain until a pattern emerges. He should have been a spy. He was wasted in Human Resources.

As she hurried away from the hotel, Beth felt the familiar emptiness that always accompanied her on that walk. She'd never known loneliness like those early mornings. Once she was at work and getting on with her day she'd gradually shake it off. She'd be fine for the rest of the week. Really. Then Monday would come round again and she'd be reminded what it felt like to be the centre of someone else's world. Mark would hold her in his arms and make her feel wanted. Then dawn would come and another small part of her spirit would be crushed.

Despite the inevitable cycle of joy followed by loss, Beth had never looked for more than this, whether it had been on offer or not. She knew the limitations of the arrangement. In fact, Beth had never quite admitted to herself, but deep down she knew that, even if Mark were free, she wouldn't be interested in a normal relationship with him. She didn't think for a second her friends would like him, and her mother certainly wouldn't approve. Wouldn't have approved.

She couldn't quite remember how it started. It was five years ago – or was it six? She'd met him a couple of times when she was going through a bad time. Somehow she'd just drifted into the arrangement. A big part of the appeal was that, as she only met Mark in secret, she didn't have to worry about what her mother thought of him. Even after her mother's death a couple of years ago, this still seemed an important consideration.

Nor did she discuss it with any of her friends. She didn't suppose for a second they'd understand and she had no interest in trying to justify herself. She'd learnt to compartmentalise her life and subterfuge had become a habit. So when Kate had asked her about her love life, she'd ducked the question the way she always did and studiously avoided wondering how Kate would have reacted.

If Beth were honest, there had been a time when she'd first realised this wasn't a fling that she'd debated the rights and wrongs of continuing. But she was feeling particularly badly used by life at that point. She'd decided that if the universe had not seen fit to provide her with a suitable partner, then she was entitled to take care of herself as best she could. Beth could see now her moral compass might have been on the blink for a while. But as time had gone on the arrangement had seemed so mundane it was difficult to get worked up about it. She was not the one doing the cheating, after all, and she was realistic enough to recognise that if it were not her, Mark would almost certainly be meeting someone else. He never talked about his wife and Beth never thought about her.

It was only a fifteen-minute walk back to her house. Her route took her past a building site with a new advertising hoarding. It featured a grinning male athlete and the Olympic rings. Everything just then was about the coming games. Back home in the shower her mind drifted to the athlete's larger-than-life six-pack. She wondered to herself what was being advertised and realised she had no idea. She glanced at the clock. 8.30 a.m. She'd need to hurry. She was never late for work.

However, Beth was nearly always late for rowing. It was Saturday morning. The pips came on the radio as she reached the roundabout near the club. *How did that happen?* Rowing had to be a punctual affair or you could spend half your life waiting for crew members to show up. Beth knew she was never one of the first to arrive, but she convinced herself no one noticed the odd occasion she was a few minutes late.

For some reason, it didn't seem to matter what time she set the alarm. In fact, it sometimes felt like the earlier she got up, the later she arrived. She'd be so relaxed she'd put on some laundry or do the crossword and completely lose track of time. Still, one of the advantages of coxing was you were doing the rowers a favour so they were ill-advised to criticise. Coxing was often cold and always uncomfortable. There was no exercise involved for the cox, so unless they had a romantic interest in a crew member, it was essentially quite tedious with only the occasional moment of drama.

'Nice of you to join us, Beth!' called the captain. She had the happy knack of remaining friendly while making it clear that Beth's tardiness had been noted.

'Sorry. Won't be a second – I'll just grab my things.' As she ran into the boathouse, she caught Kate's eye and they exchanged conspiratorial grins. Beth dumped her rucksack and pulled on her waterproofs. She was already wearing a down jacket and wellies with extra socks. A woolly hat and ski gloves would complete the outfit. She headed out, grabbed a buoyancy aid and cox box, and signed out the boat. She joined the crew just as their coach was starting the briefing.

'Ah – Beth. Nice of you to join us,' said Mike.

'We've done that bit,' said the Women's Captain.

'Sorry,' mumbled Beth.

Mike was the Senior Coach and Club Captain. He was exceptionally tall and skinny – the perfect rower's build. Although he was only in his mid-fifties, his hair was quite white which he carried off thanks to a tanned complexion. Without his grizzled hair you would have taken him for a much younger man: he was fit and lean with not a spare ounce on his muscular frame. He would have looked younger still if he'd ever smiled.

'Right, ladies. We have one month until WEHORR.'

Mike went on to explain all about the race, even though most of them had rowed in it before. According to Mike, its full name was the 'Women's Eights Head of the River Race'. It was a processional time trial and the largest women's race in the world. It took place in March on the River Thames in London.

'We rowers refer to it as "the Tideway". This is probably because it's tidal.' Beth looked round at the rest of the crew to see whether anyone else was offended by Mike's patronising explanations, but they were all gazing at him in rapt attention. It occurred to Beth that Mike must love having this crowd of women hanging on his every word. He went on to say the race was from Putney to Mortlake, the same as the Boat Race they'd all seen on telly.

'The men's Boat Race. The women's race isn't televised.' Everyone turned to stare at Kate. *What are you doing, Kate?*

'And the women's race is held at Henley.'

More silence. Then Five said: 'I never knew there was a women's Boat Race.' At this everyone started saying what a shame it was they'd never seen it on telly growing up and why hadn't it ever been on *Blue Peter*?

'Thank you, ladies. Thank you, Kate for that contribution. As I was saying, the course is seven kilometres although it doesn't feel that far because we race on the outgoing tide, so the river does quite a lot of the work for you. It'll still feel like a heck of a long way. But you've worked hard all winter. You're all rowing well and you've done your training on the ergs. You know you can do the distance.'

Beth turned to check on the crew and counted how many were there. Controlling a crew of eight could be like herding cats.

'Where's Bow?'

'She's just gone for a pee,' said Three.

'Typical!' said Chloe. Beth and Kate exchanged amused glances. It was a standing joke between them that Chloe could not pass up the opportunity to make a bitchy comment. As they waited for Bow's return, Beth watched Kate laughing and joking with the rest of Bow Four. Kate had earned their respect through perseverance and hard work. Most of the crew had come to recognise Kate's quiet kindness and decency.

How she'd changed from that first Saturday morning back in the autumn: her technique was crisper, she was significantly fitter and stronger than five months ago, and her flexibility had improved enormously. Her erg score at the latest 5k test placed her well amongst the rest of the WEHORR crew.

Beth was so pleased she'd been there at the beginning to help Kate with her stretches and weight training. That, plus their erg training through the winter, had made such a difference. And it wasn't just Kate who'd got fit: Beth was now in better shape than she had been for years. It was an added bonus they'd become firm friends.

To be fair, Kate had thrown herself into the challenge:

within a couple of weeks of returning to rowing she'd signed up for sessions on both Saturdays and Sundays. A month later she'd offered to do a double session on a Saturday for another crew who were one short. Unfortunately, as Beth had feared, Kate had not been picked for the WEHORR race crew despite her erg scores. However she'd acted as a sub pretty much every outing. Some of the crew were so flaky.

For Beth the biggest change in Kate was her confidence. She was still fairly quiet in the main squad, especially when Chloe was around. But she held herself tall and looked everyone in the eye. All the same, she'd surprised Beth by daring to speak out like that during Mike's monologue.

Down on the dock, Beth stood with one foot inside Stroke's rigger to stop the boat drifting off. Once they were all in, she told them to number off from Bow. As soon as the captain called 'Stroke', Beth put one foot in the boat and lowered herself into the narrow seat. She attached the cox box to the boat's wiring, arranged the microphone's headband around her head, and switched it on.

'Testing. Testing. Can you hear me?'

'All good,' came a voice from the far end of the boat.

Beth turned around to check the river was clear, had a good look upstream as well, and then gave the command to push off.

As they made their way across the river, she pushed the toggle in her right hand forward to adjust the rudder and the boat gradually altered course to head for the far bank. Once she was halfway across the river, she pushed her left hand toggle forward to bring the boat around, parallel with the bank.

Steering an eight was tricky. The boat was nearly twice the length and width of a double-decker bus. The rudder was kept as small as possible to avoid slowing the boat, but this limited the cox's ability to steer. As Beth altered its position, it moved the stern sideways, pivoting around the position of the bow, which remained fixed. Once the boat was pointing in the new direction, it would travel forward on that new trajectory.

What Beth couldn't do was steer around an obstacle as if she were driving a car. Changing course took time, during which the boat would travel a considerable distance. Beth had to anticipate well ahead and make continuous small adjustments. On top of all this she couldn't actually see the end of the boat as she had eight rowers in front of her. In part, steering was achieved by the crew pulling harder on one side when instructed, but this relied upon the rowers doing as they were asked.

When Beth was growing up in the 1970s it was normal to hear comedians on family television shows making jokes about how women were terrible drivers and couldn't park. The world had evolved but some attitudes lingered on: there were still those who thought when it came to big or fast vehicles, driving was a man's job. Steering an eight was extremely testing, with narrow margins and serious consequences to mistakes. However, any doubts the men might have about the ability of women were set aside as crews needed their cox to be as close to the minimum weight of 55 kg as possible. That made it a pink job. Most of the time.

As they progressed down the river, Beth took the crew through the warm-up. The day was fine with only a light breeze. The Avon was at its normal height with a steady stream but the forecast had said there would be bad weather moving in, and although in theory it was not due to arrive until the afternoon, she needed to keep an eye out for the conditions deteriorating.

Once they were rowing as an eight, Beth took them through a couple of exercises to address the balance. Every time the boat lurched down to one side she felt a twinge in her back as the muscles absorbed the shock. Why did so many of them take so long to start concentrating? It was painful and frustrating. They reached one of the few places on the river where it was safe to park an eight without obstructing other boats and Beth gave the instructions to bring them in tight to the bank. Mike pulled alongside in the launch.

'Right – I want you to do the rest of the outing as one piece and remember: we're focussing on rowing together as a crew rather than eight individuals. You're not following the person in front – you're all following Stroke. When her blade goes in, your blade goes in. When her blade comes out, your blade comes out. Stroke has lovely fast catches, but at the moment the only person going in with her is Kate at Four. The rest of you need to sharpen up your ideas.'

The crew were shaken by the criticism, but Beth set them off and settled them into their piece. She made regular calls to remind them about their catches, interspersed with the routine reminders to sit tall, hold their legs down on the recovery and engage their core muscles.

Mike was quite right about the catches: Kate was completely synchronised with Stroke and had the same deft, light movement at the start of the sequence. The rest of the crew seemed to be performing a Mexican wave. As the session progressed, Beth could see definite signs of improvement with almost all of the crew now in time except for Bow and Six. With the timing improved, the balance had miraculously sorted itself out, and without increasing the pressure or the rating, the boat speeds were starting to come up. Would they be able to maintain this if they wound it up? They turned the last corner and in front of them lay the final 600 metres to the club's dock.

'OK, chaps – we're on the home straight so we're going to wind it up.

With Stroke!

Wind!'

On this command Stroke gradually started to increase the pressure. As the power applied to each stroke increased, the rhythm gradually speeded up until they were flat out at race pace.

'Last twenty strokes!' Beth yelled, in spite of the cox box.

'Keep it together!

Keep it strong!'

The boat was flying and with every stroke Beth's back was rammed again the hull of the boat. This was why she coxed. It was exhilarating.

'Last ten!

Give it everything you've got!

Leave it all on the river!

Go!

Ten!

Nine!

Eight!

Seven!

Six!

Five!

Four!

Three!

Two!

One!

Wind it down.'

At this command the rhythm slowed and the synchronisation fell apart.

'Keep it together!
Right to the end of the outing!
Mike is still watching.'

The technique immediately became more taut and focussed. Beth slid the eight alongside the dock with practised ease.

When the boat had been put away, they huddled together in the boathouse, their backs to the cold wind coming from the open shutters. Mike joined them for a debrief.

'How do you think that went?'

No one said anything so Beth volunteered, 'Well it got better. I was doing loads of calls about catches and timing and there was a good response. By the last 1,000 metres I felt we were together and the boat speeds were coming up.'

'Anyone else?' asked Mike.

'I could really feel the difference when everyone was taking the catch with me,' said the captain. 'It was like rowing in concrete for the first part of the outing, but it was much lighter once everyone was backing me up.'

'It definitely improved as the outing went on', agreed Mike, 'but you should get it right from the off. If you're good enough to row WEHORR, you shouldn't need telling. The only person backing up Stroke right from the start was Four. Well done, Kate. Most of you got there with reminding. However, Bow and Chloe at Six were consistently late. Bow – I know it's hard from that far back to keep time with Stroke. That's why Bow is the hardest seat to row in. You almost have to aim to beat her in. Anticipate her stroke. Six – you have no excuse. You're in direct contact with Stroke. Why weren't you in time? Why were your catches so sloppy?' This drew a synchronised intake of breath from the crew and Chloe looked as if she was about to explode.

'Sort it out, Six. I expect a serious improvement next outing.' As Mike left, it felt as if the air had been sucked out of the shed.

'Right now, ladies,' said the captain, ignoring the atmosphere. 'You'll be thrilled to hear Chloe has organised special WEHORR T-shirts for you all. Do you want to hand them out, Chloe?' Chloe pulled herself together and collected a box from under a bench.

'I guessed at the sizes, so if they don't fit you'll have to swap amongst yourselves as I'm not going to sort it out. Come and get them as I call your name.

'Stroke – Medium.' The captain walked over and took the plastic bag in Chloe's hand.

'Seven – Medium.'

'Six – that's me, obviously. Extra Small.

'Five – Small.' Here Chloe paused with her list and fiddled with something inside the box.

'Four's not here but I've given it to her already.

'Three – Small.'

'Two – Medium.'

'Bow – Extra Large.'

Bow kept her head down and peered out through her fringe as she went to collect her parcel. There was a small rosy circle on each of her cheeks like badly applied blusher. The women were busy taking the shirts out of their plastic bags and admiring them. Three asked, 'What about Kate? Don't you have one for her?'

'Kate's not in the racing crew so she doesn't get a T-shirt,' Chloe spat out.

'That seems a little harsh as she's sat in on pretty much every outing,' said Three.

'Well, perhaps you'd like to organise the shirts next time,' snapped Chloe, and she turned on her heel. As

Chloe disappeared, the rest of the crew tried on their shirts. Several of the crew had to be reassured that, no, it didn't make them look fat, and yes, that shade of green worked with their colouring. In the midst of them, Beth saw Kate standing quiet, eyes glittery.

'You OK, buddy?' Beth whispered.

'Not really,' said Kate, and she walked out of the boat-shed towards the river. By the time Beth had dumped her equipment and caught up with her, she was sitting on the deserted dock, staring at the calm, still river flowing past. Tiny swirling eddies hinted at the treacherous currents below.

'I'm so sorry that happened,' said Beth as she reached the dock and sat down beside Kate. 'You know what a bitch Chloe is. You rowed brilliantly today. You should be really proud of the progress you've made. Don't let a stupid cow like Chloe ruin that for you.'

'Yes, but it's not just Chloe, is it?' Kate had stood up now and was pacing up and down the dock. All around were still, empty fields and the silent river. 'It's not about the bloody T-shirts. It's about the race. Why can't I be in the crew? Do you realise – I'm the only one in the squad who hasn't missed an outing? You know how hard we've been training on the ergs. My 5k score is better than at least half of them, and Mike himself said I was rowing as well as Stroke. What more do I have to do? I've been kidding myself they'd ever want me in their crew. It's like – no matter how fast I make the boat move they'd be embarrassed to be seen racing with someone who could be their mum. They'd rather have someone with a cool tattoo and hair extensions, even if she couldn't row for toffee.'

Kate's voice had grown to a crescendo. Once she'd finished, quiet descended on the river. A couple of swans beat their wings languidly as they made to take off. Beth didn't know what to say.

'Sorry,' mumbled Kate as she sat down again. 'I don't normally throw tantrums – I usually leave that to my kids.'

They sat side by side, gazing into the calming waters rolling past.

'You asked me once why I didn't row any more, and well – this is why. I reached a point where I'd been passed over one time too many. By then they were all so much younger than me, and I wasn't part of their gang. I didn't want to go out drinking cocktails or clubbing with them. I just wanted to row. But when it came to racing they wanted to be with their mates. So somehow, I just never seemed to make the cut. Eventually I just couldn't put myself through that any more. You know, we train too hard to do it without the promise of a race down the line.'

'Hang on – you've been training with me the last few months and you weren't even in the squad.'

'True, but I had you as my motivation. I wanted you to get fitter, so I knew I had to do it with you. I've always found it too hard on my own so I figured you'd find it easier with a training buddy.'

'Oh, I have. There's no way I'd still be rowing without you. You've been such a pal.'

'Well, Pal – you haven't asked me why I didn't get a T-shirt,' said Beth.

'What do you mean? I assumed it was just for the rowers?'

'Nope – it's normally for the whole crew including the cox. It's because I'm not coxing the race. I just heard they asked Dan because "he has more experience on the Tideway".' As Beth said this she was aware there was a slight edge to her voice.

'Fuuuck!' said Kate, her jaw nearly touching the wooden

planks beneath her feet. 'What have I got to complain about? You've been out there, every outing in all weathers, putting up with Mike's bad temper, Chloe's passive aggressive bullying, not to mention everyone's whingeing.' Beth realised she was starting to tear up, but her friend must have seen this and pulled her in for a hug.

'Fuuuck,' breathed Kate, and they held each other tight.

Overlap: *The amount by which the scull handles overlap when the athlete holds them horizontally at right angles to the boat.*

7
KATE

A peal of church bells exploded through the oppressive darkness of the bedroom. Kate was lying on her back, staring at the ceiling. She'd been awake for hours, eyes fixed on a small stain left years ago by water damage. There was nothing she had to do and nowhere she had to be. She was alone in the house.

'Bloody bells,' she grumbled to herself. She was regularly irritated by the noise, but kept it to herself, knowing it didn't reflect well on her. After all, she had chosen to buy a house next to the church. 'I wouldn't mind if they knew how to ring them properly. It's such a din.' The discordant clashing continued, and she rolled over to switch on the radio. She was met by a jaunty folk tune. 'Bloody *Archers*,' she groaned and smashed her hand down on the radio to silence it.

She resumed her position lying on her back and, as she stared into the gloom, a small tear escaped and ran down the side of her face. After a few minutes her neck felt quite damp. Resentfully she hauled herself out of bed, went to the bathroom and grabbed a handful of tissues. She blew her nose, wiped her face and leant on the washstand, peering at the mirror. She looked into the sad eyes, heavy with dark shadows.

'What are you going to do?' Kate had no idea. But being a middle-aged English woman, in the absence of a more constructive answer her default response was, 'make a cup of tea'. So she heaved on her shabby dressing gown, and made her way down to the kitchen. It was a shambles, with dirty plates and mugs stacked haphazardly on every surface. Pans and dishes were piled in the sink, swilling in cold rancid water. Kate ignored the mess and switched on the kettle.

She'd only just settled herself, elbows dumped on the kitchen table and both hands hugging the hot mug, when the front door bell rang.

'Damn, damn, damn,' she muttered to herself as she walked to the hall to answer it. She glanced in the mirror as she passed and shuddered. 'I'll say I'm going down with a cold.' In her near-catatonic state it didn't occur to her to wonder who might be calling on a Sunday morning. It was Beth. She was still bundled up in her coxing gear with water dripping off her jacket and down her water-proof trousers.

'Are you OK? You look terrible.' Kate couldn't answer. She felt unable to speak. Unable to move. She felt herself swaying slightly, and put out a hand to steady herself.

'Can I come in?' said Beth. Kate still had no words, but she stood back to open the door wide. Her friend stood dripping on the mat and peeled off her wet layers.

'It's absolutely filthy out there. You picked the right Sunday to give it a miss,' Beth said, as she tried to disentangle one of the trouser legs to allow it to dry. She hung the sodden garments on the radiator by the front door and then put an arm around Kate's shoulder to steer her towards the kitchen. 'I could do with a cup of the Best Coffee in the World. And a bun, if you've got one going,' and she gently lowered Kate into a chair and started rifling through cupboards looking for the coffee. When the espresso pot was finally on the stove, she sat down opposite Kate and bent her head towards her, her eyes soft and concerned. 'I was worried when you weren't there this morning.'

Kate was still unable to speak.

'They said they'd asked you to sit in for Chloe. She's away on some hen do.' Kate tried to formulate a response, but abandoned the task due to its sheer impossibility. 'They had to get in a new girl from the development squad. She was so hopeless, I can't tell you.' Beth was examining Kate's face, presumably hoping for a reaction. Kate felt as if she were listening to her friend through a thick pane of glass.

'Everyone missed you,' Beth said quietly. And at this a tear escaped from Kate's brimming eyes and coursed down her face. Beth reached over and took her hand. 'What is it, Kate? What's wrong?'

Kate breathed in heavily and fumbled in the pockets of her dressing gown for a tissue. She mopped her face. She tried to think what to say, how to answer her friend. Then a whistle signalled the coffee was ready. The moment was broken, so Beth got up and found the mugs and the cake tin. Once it was organised, she tried again.

'I was concerned when you cancelled our erg sessions last week. I nearly came round then.' Both women sipped at their coffee. Beth continued to study Kate's expression. Kate averted her eyes to avoid the scrutiny. Finally Beth seemed to find her courage and asked cautiously,

'Are you still upset about the whole T-shirt thing?'

'No,' said Kate almost with a laugh through the tears and mucus, 'I'm not still upset about the T-shirt thing.'

'So what is it?' asked Beth almost wheedling, sounding faintly desperate. 'Kate, why did you cancel our erg sessions last week? Why didn't you row this morning?'

'I cancelled last week . . .' Kate hesitated, as if she didn't know herself what the reason was. 'I'm sorry, I know it wasn't fair on you. But on Tuesday I just didn't want to do it. Then Friday came and I still didn't want to do it. Then I got the email about sitting in today and I realised – I don't ever want to row again.' With this Kate dissolved into gulping sobs and Beth got up to put her arms round her.

'Oh, Kate. I'm so sorry. I could murder that bloody Chloe.'

'Oh, it's fine.' As she said this Kate sat up and shrugged off Beth's embrace. 'It's not Chloe's fault. I mean – yes, she was a bitch, but no, I'm not upset about her.'

'Oh Kate, you can't give up now. You've put so much into it. You've come so far. We've come so far. You're bound to be upset thinking it might be over.'

'Of course it's over! I failed and that's all there is to it. I tried my hardest but it just wasn't enough.'

Beth looked thrown by the force of her response and continued studying Kate, her head cocked to one side.

'I tell you what – if Tim's not around, how about we go to the pub for lunch? My treat?' Kate started opening her mouth to object, but Beth had clearly decided this was what they were going to do. It was what they needed to do.

'So you go and jump in the shower and I'll clear up the kitchen while you get ready. Go on, Kate. I'm not taking no for an answer.'

Kate opened her mouth again but no words came out. She sighed and shuffled her way to the bedroom as instructed.

She switched on the shower and while she waited for the water to run warm, she sat on the edge of the bed. She didn't know what she was going to say to Beth. She was absolutely clear she was never going to row with Chloe and her mates again. She was sick of trying to ingratiate herself in their clique. It was the same at work. The same everywhere. She just wasn't good enough.

She just couldn't keep training knowing she'd never be picked to race. It was as simple as that. She'd failed, just like she'd failed in her career. In her marriage. In pretty much everything except having her daughters. And now they were gone. All that was left was failure. A fat tear broke free and slid down her cheek.

What was she to do? She felt terrible and she was only too well aware when she last felt this bad. She couldn't have told you the exact day it began. It had sort of crept up on her over – well – years. Nor could she have told you when it ended, as there wasn't just one day when the sun started shining again, when she'd felt like singing. It was more like someone gradually adjusting the TV from black-and-white to fully saturated colour. It was imperceptible, but ever so slowly the pleasure and joy began to return to her world. Once she was on the right medication.

Although she couldn't identify the beginning and the end, there was no mistaking the endless months of sleepless nights, of waking up to blackness, of stumbling through the day lost as if in fog. Her lost year. She would never forget that dark place and she did not want to go back there.

Steam was snaking out of the bathroom door, so Kate climbed in the shower. She held up her face to the spray of warm water and surrendered herself to its cleansing power, in the hope it would wash away her misery. She stayed there a good long time.

Once dressed, she looked sternly at herself in the mirror. 'You know what's happening, Kate. Be honest for once.

You're slipping into depression and it's been coming for a while. You need to do something.' It was one thing to recognise the problem, but it was quite another to know how to address it. The way Kate was feeling she could barely manage to put one foot in front of another.

As she waded downstairs, Beth was waiting for her in the hall. She got up and looked anxiously at Kate.

'Feeling any better?'

'A bit. Thanks, Beth.'

'I don't know if this will help, but I've had an idea. How about I teach you how to scull? Then you can keep rowing but you don't have to deal with Chloe and her mates?'

'Sculling? Ooh, I don't know . . .'

'Promise me you'll at least give it a go?' There was something in Beth's face that suggested she somehow knew what was going on and just how important it was to keep Kate rowing. Important that Kate got regular fresh air and exercise. Important that Kate spent time with her friend on the water. Important that Kate did something that gave her joy.

What Kate wanted to tell Beth was that her very life was on the line. But she couldn't possibly tell her friend that. She couldn't tell her about the blackest time of her life. The months when it had felt like the only way out of the darkness was to end it all. How every morning she woke before it was light. How she'd lain in bed for hours wrestling with the illness, desperately trying to find the willpower to make it through one more day. How each morning she'd postponed the end, forcing herself to crawl through another horrendous twenty-four hours. How she promised herself release if she would only do that. Then playing the same terrible game the next day, again and again. Tricking herself into keeping going. Just one more day. For the sake of her children. Just one more day. No.

She had never told anyone and she couldn't possibly burden Beth with that now.

And yet Beth was here. She'd come round because she was worried about her, even though she was soaked through. Christ, she'd even cleared up the kitchen for her. She wanted to help. Hard as it was, Kate knew she needed to let Beth in. She needed to let Beth help her.

By the time Beth dropped her back later that afternoon, Kate was feeling a whole lot better. Simply getting washed and dressed had helped, but a change of scenery and a meal cooked by someone else had really lifted her spirits. Most of all being with Beth made her feel so much better about everything. It was hard to wallow in self-pity when she was with someone who so evidently liked and respected her. If Beth believed in her then she couldn't give up. Not yet. Even if she had absolutely no desire to learn how to bloody scull.

***Catch a crab**: When the oar becomes caught in the water at the moment of extraction and the blade handle strikes the athlete. Often causes unintentional release of the blade and significant slowing of boat speed. A severe crab can even eject a rower.*

8

BETH

A few days later, Beth drove over to Marlborough for a school reunion. The Talbot was surprisingly busy for a Wednesday lunchtime in early March. Although as Beth didn't normally go out for lunch on a weekday, let alone in Marlborough, she didn't have any experience by which to gauge it.

Most of the patrons were middle-aged. The men were dressed in the sort of tweed jackets you bought in Jermyn Street rather than as an afterthought at Mole Valley Farmers along with the cattle nuts and baling twine. A number of them were accompanied by surprisingly young women with a less firm grip on the Wiltshire dress code. The older women had clearly received the memo: polo-neck sweater with sheepskin or quilted gilet, set off by a silk scarf. Everyone was wearing sensible footwear. Of course: it was match day at the local public school and the inn was full of parents who'd driven down from London to watch.

As Beth wove her way between the tables, she saw Bunny waving madly from a room at the back. Good old

Bunny. She'd been head girl in their final year, and half a lifetime later still took her responsibilities seriously. Every six months there was a lunch for their year in Wiltshire, and then one in London. Both involved a day off work for Beth, but it was one of those things you just did, like a family obligation. In fact, since her mother had died, these women were the closest thing Beth had to family. They'd known each other since the age of eleven and were more like sisters than friends. Their lives might have little in common now with Beth's but there was a loyalty and affection so profound it didn't need to be mentioned.

Beth slid into the remaining seat and her friends broke off their conversations to greet her warmly. There was so much to discuss and time was short. First there was a complete rundown on the current status of their children: where had they gone to school; how had the exams gone; what plans they had for their gap year; which uni they were at. Beth was struck how earnestly they were comparing the admissions policies of Russell Group universities, when not one of them had been to university themselves.

Finally they moved on to the interesting bit: the scandal. Whose daughter had got pregnant; whose son had been expelled for drugs; whose pony had broken its leg at Pony Club camp; whose husband's shooting syndicate had to disband after being targeted by animal rights protesters.

As the women chattered away, Beth looked around the table with a warm, benevolent feeling. Most of them were wearing more or less the same outfit, which had barely changed since their heyday in the 1980s. Bright cashmere featured heavily, accessorised by chunky faux pearls, Hermès scarves or jaunty cotton shirts with the collar turned up. The more fashion-forward amongst them wore ponchos in tasteful shades of beige, usually embellished with fur.

Nearly all of them were blonde with expensive honeyed highlights.

They looked ludicrous, of course, and Beth could imagine some of the choicer vocabulary her colleagues might use to describe them. Yes, there was no doubt they were all privileged, Beth included. But that didn't mean they were bad people. Knowing them as she did, Beth just saw them as people, like anyone else. They had their faults and their foibles, but they were largely decent, well-intentioned women trying hard in their own way to leave the world a better place than they'd found it. Not that this would have stopped her colleagues feeling the urge to mock them.

Beth had dressed appropriately for the occasion. She had felt like a spy putting on a disguise. She'd dug out an oatmeal sweater her mother had given her not long before she died and one of her mother's many scarves that hadn't made it to the charity shop. She was also wearing a pair of her mother's earrings: Mabé pearls in a heavy setting of twisted gold. She wouldn't have dreamt of wearing them to work, and she didn't have the sort of social life that called for them. So they languished in a box in her knicker drawer.

Despite the odd sense of putting on a foreign uniform to infiltrate behind enemy lines, Beth did not feel out of place: she knew these women and she was one of them. She belonged to this world. However she also belonged to the world at the hospital and on the river and in her street. She was only too well aware how her friends and colleagues would have reacted to this gathering. Beth knew how to dress like these women and she spoke the same language. She could still pass for one of them. Just like she could blend in to her everyday life.

No, she did not feel out of place. But she did feel what she'd always felt, from that very first day at school through to the dances and parties they attended later: like the runt of the litter. They'd all fulfilled their destiny, had married well and had children. They'd all had the life Beth's mother had intended for her. She was the only one who'd failed.

Perhaps it would have been different if she'd listened to her mother when she left school and had followed the same path as her friends: secretarial college followed by a job in the City. Or cookery school followed by cooking directors' lunches in the City. Or a sinecure at one of the grand auction houses or art galleries. They all did the same sort of thing back then, smart jobs that paid a pittance but brought them into the orbit of the 'right sort of men', jobs that signalled they were the 'right' sort of girl. Instead, she'd dug her heels in and insisted on training to be a physio. Looking round the table at her blonde friends, Beth realised none of them would have found their husbands at physio college as the 'right sort of men' didn't become physios.

The conversation flowed between the whole table, peppered by jokes made funny by experiences shared thirty years before. Beth hardly tasted her game pie, so keen was she to keep up with the chat. She suddenly realised she was letting it go cold, and so for a moment concentrated on her meal. It was surprisingly delicious.

'And how's your job going? Still at Weston Park Hospital?' This was Caroline, sitting to her left.

'My job? Oh it's fine, thanks. Same old, same old.'

'And what else have you been getting up to? Still rowing? I expect you'll be looking forward to the Olympics.' Beth was surprised and slightly embarrassed Caroline remembered so much about her. She couldn't even remember how many children Caroline had, let alone what stage they were at. She had a vague idea she'd mentioned training as a counsellor last time they met.

'As a matter a fact I am. Still rowing, that is. We had a new member join recently who's my age and a fantastic rower. I've just promised I'll teach her how to scull.'

'That's generous of you.'

'Well, yes and no. It will do me good to get back in a scull again. And I need to do something . . .' Beth paused, unsure whether to continue, but she felt a need to confide in someone. 'To be absolutely honest, Caro I'm worried about her. She's had a bit of a hard time at the club since she joined and I think – no, I'm worried . . . I have a suspicion she's more fragile than she seems on the surface. I'm worried it's making her ill.'

'Hmmm. There are a lot of people like that about,' agreed Caroline. 'If you look round this table, we all seem to be so on top of things. But I suspect half of us have been on anti-depressants at one stage or another. By the time you get to our age most people have been through some sort of rubbish.'

'I just want to help. It sounds so lame, but teaching her to scull was all I could think of.'

'Well, it sounds like a great idea to me. Regular exercise does wonders for mental health. I should imagine being out on the river with you is exactly what she needs. I wish you luck with it.' Beth gave her the warmest smile she could muster. She didn't remember eleven-year-old Caro being this wise.

'By the way – I was sorry to hear you lost your mother. It must be a while ago but I don't think I've spoken to you since it happened. I know how much she meant to you. She was . . .' Caroline seemed to be choosing her words carefully. 'She was obviously a big influence in your life.'

Beth hesitated before replying, checking her emotions were sufficiently under control.

'That's so kind of you. Yes, she did leave a large void.' Beth ate another forkful of her pie. Caroline seemed to be waiting for her to say more.

'Funnily enough, I was just thinking about her. How all of you have the lives she wanted me to have. How she should have had one of you as her daughter.'

'Oh Beth, that's a terrible thing to say. And utterly ridiculous. You do know you're the one we all look up to?'

'Caro, I know you're trying to be kind but even I wouldn't fall for that.'

'But it's true. Haven't you heard them talking about their daughters? They all want them to have lives more like yours than their own. Sure, they might still want them to get married at some point, but most of all they want them to have an education and careers, to have some meaning to their lives beyond the next gymkhana or shoot dinner. They want them to have choices rather than having the decisions made for them.'

'Is that what happened to us? Did we have the decisions made for us?' asked Beth.

'Well, I certainly don't think we were encouraged to think for ourselves. Our parents thought they knew best and it would have taken a great deal of courage to rebel against that. I don't think you realise how extraordinary it was that you went to college to train.'

'Well, maybe. But I still know my mother died disappointed in me.' Beth realised she sounded bitter and slightly tearful.

'Well – shame on her!'

Beth gasped at this.

'I'm sorry Beth, but it needs to be said. I'll be incredibly proud if my daughter turns out like you. I would think it a job well done. If your mother was disappointed – and I'm not saying she was – but if she was, then it says more about her than it does about you.'

Beth took her old comrade's hand and squeezed it. 'Bless you, Caro. Bless you.'

As she drove home late that afternoon, Beth pondered on their conversation. It was the first time she'd heard anyone criticise her mother. She'd so obviously been right about everything. Her friends had always been terribly respectful when they came to stay. But then girls from St Mary's, Pusey were always polite, now she came to think about it. In fact, Bunny ran a business selling scatter cushions with that embroidered on the front. A Pusey girl would never have said a word against her hostess.

Come to think of it, they were all still jolly polite. Old habits die hard. But growing older must have given some of them new perspective. She could imagine Caroline reflecting on her own upbringing when considering what she wanted for her own children. She'd always been a thoughtful girl.

In a way she and her old school friends were all dinosaurs, the last generation to be brought up solely to marry well. It was like the remaining handful of elderly women in China with bound feet. They were a reminder of a world that no longer existed.

'Shit! I'm not a failure,' shouted Beth as she thumped the steering wheel. 'I was just ahead of my time!'

Her little house felt cosy and welcoming after her noisy lunch. She loved having it just the way she wanted it, without having to consider anyone else's tastes or obsessions. She was lucky to live there.

Beth didn't have anything else to do for the rest of the day. Even though she hadn't had a drink, she felt soporific after such a big meal in the middle of the day. Of course the chat was exhausting as well. Having to be alert and react to everything over several hours really took it out of you. She'd have a quiet evening and an early night. She might even have a bath, take the time to enjoy the designer bath oil someone gave her that she never got around to using.

Beth filled the kettle to make tea and, as she waited for it to boil, her eyes fell on the photograph on the dresser. Her mother's hair was arranged in a chignon, her shoulders were bare and she wore a pearl choker. She was leaning in to the camera with an unnerving steeliness to her gaze. She'd have been so annoyed to see how tarnished Beth had let the frame become. It was filthy. Beth looked into her reproachful eyes and remembered what Caro had said. And without a second thought, Beth grabbed the picture and slung it in a drawer. With that simple act she felt lighter and more optimistic than she had for a long time.

As she drank her tea, Beth was totally at peace. She felt blessed to have such old friends still in her life after all these years. There was something about people who knew you when you were really young, not least the sense that if they'd stuck with you this long you were never going to lose them. They were lovely women, even if completely ridiculous.

Despite her huge lunch Beth felt the need of something sweet to go with her tea. It was too wet on its own. She rootled around in the cupboard and found a packet of chocolate biscuits Kate had brought over a while ago. Kate. What on earth would she have made of her school friends? Beth knew her well enough by now to know she'd have a number of astute observations, but she'd have kept most of them to herself. She was also pretty sure Kate would have recognised how kind the women were. Especially how kind they were to Beth. Mind you, if Beth were to comment on how they dressed or their obsession with Pony Club, she knew they'd both have roared with laughter. Kate was a good friend and they saw life the same way, despite their different paths.

As she sipped her tea and thought about her friend, her thoughts turned to Mark, and she allowed herself for the first time to wonder what Kate would say about her affair. Of course, after all the time they'd spent together, Beth knew exactly what Kate would think. She wouldn't be judgemental, but she would tell Beth she deserved better. She wouldn't tell her there were 'plenty more fish in the sea' or use other such unhelpful phrases. Kate was better than that. But she would point out how damaging the affair was to Beth's self-esteem.

It was funny how clearly Beth could see it now she had someone in her life she knew loved and respected her and wanted the best for her. And after a wonderful day with old school friends who also made her feel cared for, she felt strong enough to take the affair out of its compartment and hold it up to the light for scrutiny. And that was it. That was all it took.

In the clear light of day Beth could not ignore the shabbiness of her arrangement with Mark. However much she enjoyed her time with him, it did not compensate for the loneliness it made her feel the rest of the time. Without really acknowledging it she had come to believe this was all that life had to offer. Every time she walked away from the hotel the self-loathing reinforced the sense this was all she deserved.

But she did deserve better. Kate would tell her that in an instant, and Caro and Bunny and all the others believed the same. She was so much more than that. Her life was so full.

She did not need to keep harming herself in this way. She knew Kate would describe the set-up as destructive. And she'd be right.

She sent the text to Mark and went upstairs to run her bath, humming to herself as she went.

***Front stops**: The position at which the rower sits forward with arms straight and out, legs fully compressed, ready to take the catch.*

9
KATE

It was May and the river was bountiful with vibrant new growth. The new leaves of the gnarled crack willows appeared almost fluorescent in the sunlight. Families of mallards and moorhens went about their business, cajoling stray ducklings into line. Motionless herons punctuated the length of the river. Every so often a flash of azure rewarded quiet observation – a kingfisher. Kate always felt as if she'd spotted a unicorn, and even after all these months the sight never failed to thrill her.

She and Beth had been sculling regularly now for several months and the outings with the WEHORR crew were a distant memory. Together with their land-training sessions, barely a couple of days went by without them seeing each other. Every time they met, Beth would peer at her intently and ask, 'So how are you? Really?'

It always made Kate laugh. They never actually said the words out loud, but it was clear they both knew what she was asking. It was a huge comfort for Kate to know someone was looking out for her and would be there to catch her if she started falling.

'Hiya. How was your day, dear?' called Kate as Beth arrived looking harassed.

'Oh, the usual NHS stress and psycho-drama. How was yours?'

'Sadly, no stress and no drama. Nothing but utter tedium.'

'That doesn't sound good,' said Beth as she rummaged in her sports bag. 'Oh bother, I forgot my sports bra. I'll have to row in this one.'

'Ouch,' said Kate. 'You could just leave it off, it's not like anyone's going to see us.'

'So what's wrong with work?' asked Beth.

'Oh, nothing really. Don't mind me, I'm just a bit fed up. I was so lucky to have a job that fitted in with the girls when they were growing up, but now, to be honest, it's just – well – boring.'

'Why don't you look for something different then, now they've left home? I mean, if you could do absolutely anything, what would it be?' This last question was slightly muffled as Beth bent over trying to pull her trainer on without undoing it. She finally accepted it was hopeless and put the shoe on her lap to unpick the knotted laces.

'I always wanted to do Human Rights law, but there's not much call for that round here.' Kate did a sort of fake laugh as she said this as if it was actually funny. 'Poppy called earlier.' She wondered whether Beth would notice she was changing the subject. 'She's got her finals in a couple of weeks. She's so stressed.'

Beth finally had both trainers on and laces tied.

'Right, I'm ready – let's do this!'

Like many people who first learned to row at university, Kate had never been in a scull before Beth started teaching her. Although essentially the same technique, rowing in a sculling boat presented significant new challenges. Most obviously, you have a blade in each hand and coordinating the two was tricky. Many times Kate ended up with her hands jammed together and scraping the skin off the top of her right hand, or jamming her thumbnail between both handles.

They'd started in a double, which meant Beth could steer and manage the balance while Kate got to grips with the stroke. Once she'd mastered that and could sustain it over a whole outing, Beth persuaded her to move into a single. Kate had really needed persuading. Single sculling was difficult, and capsizing was a normal part of it. Bad weather, collisions with other boats, collisions with the bank, collisions with debris in the river, loss of concentration – there was no end to the hazards that could lead to a ducking. Kate was a strong swimmer, but still the thought of ending up in the river terrified her.

Yet Beth was insistent. Reluctant as she was, Kate felt she owed it to her friend to try. She'd succeeded in mastering many physical challenges over the last year that at the time she'd thought beyond her. She knew she needed to start trusting her body again.

The biggest problem was the lack of stability. With far less weight in the boat than in a four, it felt like balancing on a tightrope. Beth taught her to keep both hands at the same height on the way forward to front stops, and on the way back in to backstops. Once they overlapped, they had to be in contact with no gap in between. For weeks Kate either crashed her hands together, or kept her left hand too high, sending the boat lurching over to one side. Gradually it improved and her hands eventually found an invisible track at the right height. The hardest part was at front stops. Kate had tried to explain it to Tim.

'Imagine you're rocked over with your core muscles

engaged. You're in a squat position with your knees up against your chest, your arms are wide open and you have to make sure your hands are at the same height. Oh – and you're doing this balanced on a knife edge. Going backwards.'

What Kate didn't mention to Tim, probably because his eyes were glazing over at that point, was that as well as performing this trick repeatedly, the most important thing was to be relaxed, because if you didn't relax you would capsize. You had to relax, even though in the beginning you were either banging your hands together or the boat was lurching to one side. Or you became impaled in an overhanging bush. Kate knew she was making progress when they could get through an entire outing without a near-death experience. Gradually she started to release the tension. Kate was a quick student, and her experience of sweep rowing meant much of it came naturally. However, embedding it into her muscle memory took time.

She persevered and gradually the balance and steering fell into place. It was a virtuous circle, of course: the better her technique, the straighter she rowed and therefore the easier it was to steer.

Ideally Kate was only supposed to look over her shoulder to see where she was going every few strokes – even at light pressure a single scull would travel quite a distance in that time. If the boat were travelling straight, then all would be well until the next time she took a look. However, the smallest differential of pressure between her two hands would result in the boat being pulled round a couple of degrees. After a couple of strokes she was either on the wrong side of the river – potentially with a university eight bearing down on her – or wedged in a bush. The temptation was to look every stroke, but that didn't work either, as she would then struggle to take proper, even strokes, which just made the whole problem worse.

Whether it was becoming a mother or simply getting older, Kate had a greater sense of self-preservation than in her youth. Rowing backwards at speed did not yet feel like a natural occupation. However, she trusted Beth to keep watch and warn her of impending disaster and she gradually let go of her fear.

That afternoon the conditions were perfect and Kate was feeling surprisingly in control. It almost took her by surprise, but there was a smoothness and fluidity to her rowing that had been lacking before. As they worked their way down the river, the boat soared. They paused at the top of the straight and then set off to row it as one piece. As her boat picked up speed, Kate found herself gradually increasing the pressure with her legs and allowing the rating to come up. It felt as though she were flying. As she slowed down at the bottom of the river, she was euphoric. When Beth caught up with her she was sitting with her handles under her arms, hugging her knees, laughing and crying at the same time. How incredible did she feel?

'Did you see that? Did you see that? I did it! I can't believe I did it!'

Beth seemed as thrilled as Kate was.

'Oh my goodness – you so did. That was epic. You've cracked it.' They stayed a long while in the shade of a budding horse-chestnut, relishing the moment. Never had the river, the surrounding fields and distant hills looked more beautiful. Kate couldn't remember when she'd last felt this good about herself and about life. Energy coursed through her veins and she fizzed with optimism.

'Right at this moment, I feel I could do absolutely anything,' said Kate. 'I feel incredible.'

'I feel pretty great just watching you.' Beth was grinning like mad, slumped in her seat with her head thrown back and her eyes closed. 'It's powerful stuff you know, Kate – doing something that frightens you and conquering it.'

Back at the dock they carried the boats back up to the boathouse and found the shutters open and one of the men's squad mowing the grass. He waved at them. Beth filled her in about him as they walked back to the river to collect the blades. His name was Jack and he'd rowed in the same four for years. They were a few years younger than Kate and Beth.

'Most of them are overweight and they're all immune to coaching,' whispered Beth.

As they walked back up to the boathouse, Jack turned off the mower and walked over to say hello. Kate had seen him before and warmed to the permanent smile that stretched from one side of his face to the other. He seemed congenitally cheerful.

'You two are getting out a lot. You planning to race?'

'Not sure about that,' said Beth. 'It's great getting out together and enjoying the river, but I'm not sure either of us want the pressure of racing in a scull.'

'I can see that. You always see them capsizing at regattas. Makes you realise there is something worse than your four always coming last. At least we've never had to swim home.' Jack was clearly tickled by this cheery thought.

'You're so lucky to have a crew your age – even if you don't, ahem, always win. We'd love that, you know, to row in a four or an eight with women our own age.'

'So why don't you go out and find a masters crew of your own?'

'What – from other clubs?'

'Well, you could do that. But just think how many

women your age used to row here. Most of them still live in the area. Why don't you see if any of them want to give it another go?'

'Jack – you're a genius. Why on earth didn't I think of that?' said Beth.

'It's a gift, Beth. It's a gift,' and he grinned to himself as he returned to his mower.

Walking back to the car, they discussed Jack's suggestion. Feeling inspired after their outing, Kate was gripped by the idea.

'Can you imagine – a crew with women our own age? How much fun we'd have? Right now, if I could have one wish, that's what I'd ask for.'

'Gosh, it would be incredible, wouldn't it?' They carried on to their cars in silence, deep in thought. When they reached Beth's VW, she turned and said to Kate, 'I've had an idea. You ever played skittles?'

Saxboard: *The sides of the boat above the water line made to strengthen the boat where the riggers attach.*

10

KATE

'I've been meaning to ask – are you planning to go and see any of the Olympics?' Kate was hunting around in the cupboard for her second shoe as Beth asked this. Despite Beth being over half an hour late to collect her, Kate still wasn't ready.

'I really must tidy this cupboard out. It's a disgrace. Honestly, half of the stuff is the girls.' They've just dumped it here and forgotten about it.' Kate emerged holding a black boot and sat down on a chair to put it on. 'Olympics? I'm not sure I'm that bothered about watching sport. I'd rather do it myself. Tim talked about putting in for tickets but he never got round to it. Anyway, they say the traffic's going to be gridlocked in London. How about you?'

'I'm looking forward to watching the rowing. It's not often you get to see it on telly.'

There was quite a crowd at the Little Tidsworth village hall. The skittles night always enjoyed a good turnout and Kate followed Beth to the bar, threading her way in between the statuesque club members. Having bought their drinks they leant against the bar and surveyed the hall. The members were clustered together in crews, so each group was of the same gender and a similar age. They also seemed to share their own dress code and mannerisms.

Close to the bar stood a group of large, jovial men. A number were carrying considerably more weight than was ideal and all of them were holding a pint of beer in one hand, with the thumb of the other looped in the waistband of their trousers or hooked in their trouser pocket. Their legs were set wide apart, jaws jutting and shoulders braced in an exaggerated display of masculinity.

At the far end of the hall, Chloe was perched on an outsize wooden chair with her acolytes from the Senior Women's crew buzzing around her. She seemed to be exercised about something. After a minute or two, Bow picked up a full glass of wine from the table in front of Chloe and walked over to the bar. She deposited the drink on the counter next to Beth with a heavy sigh.

'You OK?' asked Beth.

'Not really. Apparently, I messed up Chloe's order and got her chardonnay rather than sauvignon.'

'Crikey, that is serious. Talk about First World Problems.' Bow smiled at Beth's attempt at a joke. When the bartender came over she ordered a glass of sauvignon.

'Sorry, love, it's house red or house white.'

'Thanks – I'll leave it,' said Bow. She picked up the drink that had already been rejected once and grimaced at Kate and Beth. She looked as if she'd have preferred to stay and chat rather than returning to her own crew.

'Who makes a fuss about grape varieties – we're in a village hall for pity's sake?' Kate whispered to Beth.

'Clearly Chloe does. She probably thinks it makes her look sophisticated,' Beth whispered back.

'I could tell you what it does make her look, but it's not a very nice word.'

The pair watched mesmerised, even though they could not hear what was being said. Bow's explanation did not seem to have impressed, and she slunk to the back of the group. Everyone stared at the offending glass of wine languishing untouched in front of Chloe. As they watched the pantomime Kate felt relieved she was no longer trying to be part of their squad. She'd loved the rowing but she wanted a crew she could feel part of, made up of women like her.

Someone called for quiet and read out the names of the first two teams to play. Beth was amongst them and Kate followed her into the skittle alley. It was a lean-to, cheaply constructed at the back of the village hall. The cold walls were shiny with condensation.

The players hurled their balls in the general direction of a cluster of wooden pins set up in front of the far wall. They skidded along the wooden floor. Many of them missed altogether, then a hooked shot would ricochet off the wall and wipe out the target. While an element of skill and accuracy no doubt helped, the slightly random nature of the results made it an ideal game for all comers.

Once the player had despatched his final throw, a couple of young lads leapt up to rearrange the pins. The balls were fed into an oversized drainpipe lashed against the wall, and gently rolled back to the next player at the far end. It was a Heath Robinson arrangement but served its purpose well. There was no doubt that a game of skittles and a pint of cider was a taste of authentic Somerset.

Beth was the last to play and missed completely with her first two balls. With her final throw she changed technique and attacked the target with more gusto than finesse. The ball bounced heavily a couple of times as it progressed down the alley, as if destined to demolish a dam. The third time it came down to earth it landed squarely in the centre of the pins and sent them flying, to rapturous cheers from Beth's team. The two boys dived for cover.

'Come on,' said Beth, 'let's talk to Molly. She's married to Stanley, our Head Coach. I bet she'll have some ideas.'

The two friends weaved in and out of the crowd until they reached a group of men their own age sitting in the corner together with Stanley, his wife and Jack. Stanley was no athlete. He was amongst the shortest of the men in the room and nearly spherical. He had short grizzled hair and a weather-beaten complexion. He sipped his pint of stout as if he had a grudge against it.

'Evening,' said Beth. 'Have you met Kate? She's a new member.'

The group all made polite noises and Jack gave them his sunniest smile. Then they carried on their discussion about the pros and cons of replacing the club's lawnmower. Apart from Jack, the other men were around fiftyish, tall and wiry. It struck Kate they were the fittest men in the hall, even if they were the oldest.

She turned to Molly who was perched on a bar stool to her left. She was a miniature version of Stanley: barely five foot but with a round body like a dumpling, with skinny limbs protruding from her oversized and hairy jumper. Her short hair was pure white and her pale eyes pierced like lasers.

'I'm Kate. You must be Molly.'

'Pleased to meet you, Kate. How are you getting on? Are the Senior Women playing nicely with you?' Kate was thrown by the question.

'Everyone at the club's been really friendly.' Kate was always keen to avoid giving offence. 'Do you row, Molly?' Kate suspected she knew the answer but wanted to move the conversation along.

'I used to,' said Molly, which surprised Kate. 'I've mainly coxed of late.' This surprised Kate even further.

'I don't think I've seen you on the river,'

'No, you won't have. My damned knee – I finally had it replaced last year but I haven't managed to get back into a boat since then.'

'How is it? The new knee, I mean?'

'The knee's fine. The trouble is just everything else packed up while I was out of action.'

Kate told Molly about their idea of a masters women's squad, and asked if she'd be interested. Molly scrutinised Kate as if she were weighing up how seriously to take her. Then deliberately Molly said, 'I won't row, but I will cox you.' It took a moment to absorb what she'd just said. 'Give me a call when you've got a crew.'

Kate turned to Beth to share the news with her, but she'd been drawn into the lawnmower debate. When the topic was finally exhausted, Beth launched an opening gambit about their project. She explained what they had in mind, and asked if the men knew anyone who might be interested. They came up with a number of suggestions and made encouraging noises.

'How about Mike's Lesley?' said one of them.

'What, Mike the Club Captain?' asked Kate.

'Yeah. She used to be quite the star of the Senior Women's crew. I tell you what, why don't you give my wife a call? You remember her? She's still in touch with some of them. Of course she's far too busy to row herself between work and the kids.'

'Don't you have work and kids?' asked Jack, and the man glared back at him.

'Thanks,' said Beth. 'We'll take you up on that.'

'If you manage to get an eight together you should try to do the Vesta Head,' he replied.

'What's that?' asked Kate.

'It's a masters head race on the Tideway. You get hundreds of veteran eights from all over the world. You've never seen so many old farts rowing in one place.'

'Plus a few women's crews,' added Jack. 'It happens in March. That should give you something to aim for. My crew talk about it every year but somehow we never quite get around to it.'

'Well, maybe we'll all get to Vesta next year.'

***Come forward!**: Instruction used by the cox or athlete to bring the crew to the front stops position ready to row.*

11

KATE

There was a warm fug in the kitchen and a faint smell of onions. Kate and Beth had been out sculling earlier and their Lycra was still damp. Kate had cooled down a while ago and so was enjoying the fetid atmosphere which was a comfort to sore muscles. They were reviewing the potential candidates for their masters squad and the results of their many calls and emails. The phone rang and as Kate stood up to answer it, a pain shot through her buttocks. It was Ella.

'Hi, darling. How nice to hear from you on a Sunday morning. You having a nice weekend?'

'The best, Mumsie. We had this massive night last night. We went to Newcastle, clubbing. And you'll never guess what – Rob's asked me to go to his College Ball with him.'

'How lovely.'

'Thing is, I haven't really got anything to wear to it.'

'Right . . .'

'But I've seen this dress online. I'll send you a link.'

'Righty ho. Look, sweetheart, I've got someone here. Can you call again later? We can have a proper chat then.'

Kate hung up the phone and limped back to her seat.

'Why do I get the impression my girls only call when they want something?'

'Well, at least they call,' said Beth.

'True.'

There were endless lists and pieces of paper scattered over the long table – most of them had been tipped out of Beth's Bag for Life that served as her briefcase. Kate had been tempted to make a comment, but she realised her friend was self-conscious about her filing system and resisted the urge. She had her laptop open and her black-rimmed glasses planted halfway down her nose. She was in her element, surrounded by paper, bringing order to chaos.

'Your husband around?' asked Beth. 'I was wondering whether he minded me being here on a Sunday morning.'

'Oh, you're quite safe. He goes out cycling with a bunch of his mates on a Sunday. He's rarely back before late afternoon – and then he normally wants to go straight to bed for a nap.'

'Gosh, is this what domestic bliss looks like?'

They continued with their sorting and organising. Then Beth announced she needed a pee as the coffee had gone straight through her. As she waited for Beth to return, Kate gazed at the screen saver on her laptop: a photo of her with Tim and the girls on a sponsored walk. They surely looked the picture of domestic bliss. It wasn't how Kate would describe it, but it was a marriage, the result of decisions taken long ago with the best of intentions.

It had seemed rational enough at the time, and they knew other families who lived the same way. After all, few jobs in Bath commanded a salary high enough to afford a house in the city. They seemed to cope, and they kept hoping an opportunity might come up for Tim to work closer to home. But it never happened. Gradually over the years their lives had diverged and they just became used to it.

At the weekend when the girls were young they'd go swimming as a family, or on bike rides. The joy and laughter they packed in to two days sustained them through the rest of the week. And it wasn't as if the rest was so awful. Everyone was busy getting on with their lives and they really had a wonderful time when they were all together. But it began to change as the girls grew older. The girls had their activities and someone had to drive them around to all the sports and music lessons and birthday parties. As Tim had been away all week, Kate normally ran the taxi service.

He worked long hours in London all week and he needed time to unwind. She had two weekdays to herself at home, and even with all the domestic admin she could normally find time for a swim or a coffee morning. She'd have liked to join him in his weekend sport: before cycling it had been golf. They'd occasionally played together before they got married and it would have been wonderful to go round the course together at the weekend, but it was hardly practical with two children. Even after the chauffeuring was finished there was homework and music practice to be supervised and meals to be cooked.

As Beth was still not back, Kate took the opportunity to put another pot of coffee on. She banged out the used grounds into the composting bin and washed the holder under the tap. Peeling back the seal on a fresh tin of coffee was one of those quiet pleasures that made life worth living. She breathed in the heady aroma then scooped out the soft rich grains. Kate loved the ritual of making real coffee.

She looked back at her screen saver. At the time, every decision had seemed perfectly reasonable. But she could see now that right from the beginning their lives had started to run along different parallel tracks. Perhaps if one of them had begun an affair or lost their job, they might have been forced to confront what was happening. But no, it all ran smoothly. Their daughters were growing up and Tim's career was progressing solidly. However, with every passing week the connection between them died just a little more.

For the longest time, Kate didn't even realise what was happening. Everyone had challenges bringing up a family: sorting out childcare, making ends meet, negotiating extended families. Moaning about the various difficulties along with the nits and forgotten PE kit was part of the glue that held together friendships with other mothers. Then every so often you met someone who had real problems, like the woman who'd just received a devastating diagnosis for her child. That brought Kate up short. Seriously, how could she possibly complain about anything in her own life?

Still, every morning when she woke, the first thing she thought about was the hard lump of sadness that seemed to have lodged itself in her breast. But she brushed the feeling aside and got on with her day. Then, in the quiet of the night, when the girls were fast asleep and she sat nursing a glass of wine and listened to the ancient house groaning, it felt as if the malignant knot would burst out of her chest and she ached to be with another adult.

She assumed it was the physical lack of adult company that was the problem. But Kate could have been in a roomful of people and would still have felt lonely. So even when Tim was home at weekends, with the distance that had grown between them, the feeling didn't go away. Kate was just distracted from it. Given that she didn't understand what was wrong, it wasn't surprising they'd never talked about it. So Kate just kept herself busy and avoided the problem. Until she'd been confronted by her empty nest.

She wondered whether Tim ever regretted the decisions they'd made. She might carp on about being relegated to the slow lane, but he might feel he'd missed out on time with his children. It was easy to focus on the negative aspects of her job, but the flip side was she'd been there at the beginning and end of every school day. She'd sweated blood with them learning spellings and tables. She'd read every word in their reading scheme. Twice. She'd watched the girls' friendships develop. She'd counselled them on how to react to some minor betrayal or misunderstanding, conscious she was teaching them skills to manage relationships when they were grown up. She'd been intimately involved in their lives. She'd helped shape them.

She wondered whether Tim ever thought he'd missed out on that. The girls loved him dearly, of course they did. But it was a more distant relationship. There were references and jokes he didn't get and so many memories he didn't share. Did he regret that now? Was his professional success and personal fulfilment a price worth paying? Kate wondered if Ella's leaving had prompted him to reflect. He'd said that thing, on the phone, the day she took Ella up to Durham. He'd said he wished he could have been there. Perhaps he'd meant it. Now it was too late. The girls were gone and there were no second chances. At least Kate had a second chance at life. This was her time and she was determined to make the most of it.

She heard Beth in the corridor walking back to the kitchen.

'Do you know you're out of loo paper?'

'Sorry – you should've shouted. The housekeeping in this establishment is very shoddy.'

Beth sat down in her seat and surveyed the piles of paper and plastic bags around her.

'Right,' said Kate, peering over the top of her glasses at Beth, 'let's do this.'

They beavered away, pulling all the scraps of paper and remembered gobbets of information into one orderly database. Before long the chaos on the table had been organised into one neat pile held together by a bulldog clip, and Kate had printed off two copies of the list. Beth looked at her friend visibly impressed.

'You're good at this. You available next January to help with my tax return?'

Kate laughed. 'What do you mean, next January? Haven't you done it yet? It's June already!'

It was depressing. Despite the endless calls and emails, not one of the women they'd contacted had been convinced. Beth had even met up with a handful of them. Still she couldn't persuade them. Kate broke off to pour the coffee and set out a plate of greyish squares.

'What are you delighting us with this week?' asked Beth, peering at the plate.

'Dutch apple cake. I haven't tried it before. It's got apples in. And cinnamon.' Beth looked dubious, but cautiously took a small bite.

'You know – they taste better than they look.'

'Cheeky,' said Kate, and the two friends worked their way stoically through a large square each.

'Do you remember the first time you came round here for coffee? When you came to rescue me with your stretches after my first outing?'

'As it happens, I do,' said Beth. 'We had cherry tray bakes as I recall.'

Kate snorted with pleasure. She was always pleased when Beth appreciated her baking.

'I remember you saying something about a boyfriend

who might have been "the one". I was wondering what happened.' Beth put her coffee mug on the table and looked down at her hands.

'What can I tell you? He was absolutely lovely.' As she said this, Beth looked quite wistful. 'We met when we were training together. He was a physio as well. He wasn't particularly exciting or good-looking, but he made me laugh. Actually, the truth is, I found him incredibly attractive. He wasn't conventionally handsome, but he worked out which was unusual in those days.' Beth leant forward and whispered confidentially, 'I'm a bit of a sucker for a ripped abdomen.' Kate contemplated this admission and had to acknowledge she probably felt the same way. Beth resumed her story. 'He was the kindest man I've ever known. I genuinely don't think I've ever met anyone as kind.'

'Except for your sculling buddy,' said Kate.

'Well, clearly except for you.' She continued, 'We were friends from the moment we met, and it gradually turned into love. Yes, I can honestly say I was in love with him, and I know he was in love with me.' Beth was quite emphatic as she said this last part.

'How wonderful,' said Kate. 'It's a great gift to have such certainty.'

'Well, it's easy to see now after all this time.'

'So what happened?' Kate radiated concern for her friend.

'At the end of the year I went home to Dorset for the holidays and he came to stay. It was a disaster. An utter disaster.'

'How? In what way?'

Beth blew out hard as if attempting to suppress mounting emotions.

'I don't know why, but when we were at college, I hadn't realised how . . . different he was. To my family, I mean.'

'Different? In what way was he different?' Kate was gazing at her friend as if to decipher the mystery from the contortions of her expression.

'This is going to sound absolutely terrible, so please don't judge me.'

'Of course I'm not going to judge you,' said Kate, now genuinely alarmed. 'You're my friend, nothing you could say would make me think any less of you.'

Beth gave her a weak smile. 'Well, at college we were a really mixed bag. I think that was part of the reason Mummy hadn't been terribly keen on the idea. But you know me. I get on with anyone.'

'And everyone,' said Kate. Beth gave her another half-hearted smile.

'There were so many things I hadn't really noticed. Well – of course I'd *noticed* – I just hadn't thought about them, not until he came to Dorset.'

'What sort of things?' asked Kate, braced for a terrible revelation.

'Well, it all really came to a head at dinner. I know this sounds dreadful, and it is dreadful, but it was his table manners. I could see my mother watching him and I knew exactly what she was thinking. You know how it is, when you've spent your whole life with someone nagging you at every mealtime: "Hold your knife properly, eat with your mouth closed." I just knew that was what she was saying to herself.'

'Oh my God, do I hold my knife properly?' asked Kate mockingly, possibly out of a moment's insecurity. Beth looked irritated.

'Kate, I do know it doesn't matter how you hold your knife. The problem was my mother thought it did. I know what mattered was that he was kind and decent and treated me well. Unfortunately, all my mother cared about was whether he was from a family like ours.'

Kate sensed that this was a painful subject for her friend, and that she was being less than her normal sympathetic self.

'So what happened?'

'I just couldn't bear to hear what Mummy had to say about him, so I avoided the whole issue and ended it.'

'You ended it?' asked Kate, incredulous. She looked at her friend, misery etched on her face.

'It's hard to believe now I could have done something so cowardly. Or so stupid. I just didn't want the confrontation.'

'What happened when you went back the next term?'

'It was dreadful. I couldn't bear to see him looking so hurt. He was such a nice man . . .'

They sat in silence and then finally Kate spoke.

'You know – we all make mistakes, especially when we're young. God knows, I've made my fair share.'

'Have you really, Kate? I thought you were practically perfect.' Kate gave Beth a playful punch on her arm. 'It sounds so terrible now to say my mother was judging someone based on their table manners. I mean – it was the 1980s not the 1900s. But that was my world and it was all I knew at that age. I thought it was normal. It was only as an adult, when I got to know people who hadn't been brought up like me, that I finally realised how rigid and judgemental my mother was. How wrong it all was.'

Beth paused, staring at the wall. Kate stayed quiet, allowing her friend to unburden herself.

'You know, I regret allowing myself to be so brainwashed by my mother. I look back and wonder why on earth I never stood up to her. I should have told her she was wrong about so many things. But what can I say? I loved her and wanted her approval. And I do think in her own way she was trying to do what she thought was best for me. However misguided that was. I just didn't want to have to choose between a man and my family. I know that makes me sound pathetic and weak, but there we are.'

Kate contemplated what her friend had said, straining to consider it properly and to respond fairly. Shaking her head slowly she said, 'I don't think it's the worst crime in the world to want your parents' approval. It doesn't make you a bad person.' There was silence and she added, 'Your mother sounds quite a handful, though.'

'Oh, she was. She died a couple of years ago but the shadow she cast still looms large.' Beth sighed.

'Well if it helps, buddy, you have my total approval. And we need to see about getting you out of that shadow.'

They reapplied themselves to their task and were deep in concentration when the kitchen door opened and in came Tim. He was dressed in black Lycra cycling shorts with padded codpiece and a pillar-box red top plastered with obscure Italian brand names. He limped slightly, his legs a little bowed and he click-clacked across the stone kitchen floor.

'Any coffee going?'

'Oh hi, sweetheart,' said Kate leaping to her feet to put another pot of coffee on. 'You're back early. Nothing wrong, I hope?'

'My knee's giving me gyp so I decided to cut it short,' he said as he peered into the fridge before extracting a cold sausage.

'How was the cycle until then? It was dry at least.'

'Oh it was fine. It's all a bit frustrating.'

'Darling – this is Beth . . .' Tim removed his head from the fridge and took a hard look at Beth.

'Hi, Beth. Don't think we've met before.'

'I'm sorry – I'm probably in the way.'

'Oh, don't mind me. I've a lot of work to do anyway. I'll be in the office,' and he hobbled out of the kitchen.

'I'll put a coffee on . . .' Kate's voice trailed off as he tapped his way down the corridor. 'Sorry about that,' she muttered, slightly flustered and suddenly less sure of herself. 'That was Tim.'

'I should go. Leave you two in peace.'

'No, don't,' said Kate, possibly a little too quickly. 'We're going to finish this. It won't take long. And it's important.'

'Is it, though? It's only rowing.'

Beth had probably only been making a flippant remark, but for Kate it was as if she had lit the blue touchpaper, and she exploded with a mixture of pent-up frustration and righteous indignation.

'But it isn't though, is it? It isn't just rowing. It makes me so angry. All of the women I've managed to speak to about our squad, when I ask them why they stopped rowing it's always the same answer. And do you know what? I'm pretty sure if I called up the women from my year at Law School and asked what happened to their careers, the things they used to do, the people they used to be, I'd get the same answer: children, elderly parents, husbands, no husbands, being overlooked, passed over, being considered too old, no longer relevant . . .' Just then the coffee pot on the Aga shot out a blast of steam at high pressure.

Beth looked at her and cleared her throat.

'I'm sorry, Kate. I didn't mean to trivialise it. You're right, this is important. Really important. I do that – when I think I can't do something I make a joke of it. I'm sorry.'

'And you apologise too much.'

'I know – sorry about that too.' The two friends smiled at each other, relieved to have defused the situation.

'Right, let's look at it.' And with an uncharacteristic amount of grip, Beth summarised the position: by asking around they'd identified twenty-one women aged between forty and fifty-five who used to row at a high level and were still living in the area. While none of them had actually said 'no', they hadn't quite persuaded any of them to say 'yes'. 'We have to find a way to make the decision easier.'

They kicked the problem around for a while, and came to the conclusion they needed a one-off taster session. It was too big a decision to 'go back to rowing' with an open-ended commitment. It would be easier to persuade them to give it a go for just one Sunday afternoon. All they'd be agreeing to would be a fun paddle. And tea and cake afterwards. No one ever said no to cake.

Although Kate was trying to feign enthusiasm, in truth she had no confidence this approach would be any more successful than their previous efforts. But it was one last roll of the dice and she felt she had to go along with it. If this didn't work they could abandon the project and Kate could start looking for something else to fill her life. Maybe pottery was more interesting than it looked. After much deliberation they plumped on a date four weeks later in the middle of August.

'Gosh, – it's not long until the Olympics start,' said Kate, looking through her diary.

'Actually, that reminds me – a few of the members are planning to watch the women's coxless pair final in the Waterman. Believe it or not the GB pair learned to row at Albion and by all accounts they have a pretty good chance of making it through to the final. If you're not working you should come.'

As she closed the front door on her friend, Kate decided to draft the invitation to the taster day in August while she had the momentum, and went to the office.

'How's the knee, darling. Did you take something for it?'

'Yeah – it's murder. Who was that?'

'That was Beth, my sculling partner, I told you about her.'

'More like your witchcraft partner the way you two were cackling away. What's for supper?'

'I haven't got that far yet. I normally go out to the supermarket on Sunday afternoons, before you get back from your cycling. Anything in particular you want?'

'Can you get ginger beer while you're there. And pork pies.' Throughout this conversation Tim hadn't taken his eyes off the screen of his computer. Kate hesitated, wanting something from him but unsure how to ask for it.

'Tim . . .' He turned his head slowly to look at her, as if it took an immense effort of will to detach his eyes from the screen.

'What's up?'

She didn't know what to say. She wanted to tell him, 'I miss you. I want to be close to you and I don't know how.' Somehow she just couldn't say that. The distance between them felt unbridgeable.

'Hmm?' Tim waited for an answer and looked as if he wanted to say something as well. But instead he turned back to his screen and started typing again, and the moment passed.

Abandoning the taster day invitation she retreated upstairs to their bedroom, and sat on the side of the bed, gazing out of the window. The garden was at its glorious best, exploding with colour and unchecked growth. The clouds parted to allow glorious sunshine to spill over the lawn. It was a day for a barbecue.

She imagined families squabbling good-naturedly over burnt sausages and bowls of potato salad. She thought back fondly to when the kids were small. They'd have been playing in the garden on a day like this. She had a memory of Tim playing French cricket and the girls shrieking with laughter when he smacked the ball for six and broke a window upstairs. Kate had been in the kitchen getting lunch and watching through a window. Suddenly the memory became coloured by her current frame of mind: she recalled how at that precise moment in their family's history, Kate had been apart from the others, observing rather than participating.

She realised with a jolt she was starting to wallow. She forced herself to remember the next part: after she heard the window shatter she'd rushed outside. Tim was standing in the middle of the lawn with his hands on his head, cursing himself as if he'd done something truly terrible. Kate had peeled his hands away from his head and put them around her waist and kissed him and held him. Poppy and Ella had danced around them squealing and laughing, relieved the crisis was not really a crisis after all and rejoicing in the obvious affection between their parents.

Kate wondered if she should go back down to the study now and peel Tim's hands away from the keyboard and put them round her waist and kiss him. But when she tried to picture it, the Tim of her imagination kept his eyes clamped to the screen and she somehow ended up awkwardly kissing the top of his smooth head. It was hopeless. She sighed and roused herself. She had work to do.

The following was posted in the award-winning rowing blog – 'A Girl in a Boat', Wednesday 1 August 2012

We seem to have been waiting for this moment all year, and now it's finally here – the first rowing final of the 2012 Olympics. I expect like me you saw the opening ceremony on Saturday. I have a confession to make. I'm afraid I can't stand those Soviet-style displays of thousands of synchronised dancers they normally have. They're not really British, are they? Plus the budget for our version was titchy.

As Saturday's opening ceremony loomed, I think it finally dawned on all of us we were the ones hosting the wretched thing. Not only were we about to do something utterly uncool, but we were going to be really rubbish at it as well. The temperature rose, the air crackled. How bad could it be? The pundits started making our excuses early:

'You have to understand, this isn't our sort of thing at all. We're only doing it because it's expected. As a nation we prefer our entertainment a little more . . . idiosyncratic.'

Boy, did they give us idiosyncratic. It was completely bonkers and totally British. I mean – smoking chimney stacks, steeple-jacks and dancing beds! They didn't have beds in Beijing! The sheer imagination captivated the world. Did you see the Queen and James Bond skydiving into the opening ceremony? Of course you did. How could you have missed them? It was brave. It was genius. We were hooked. Everyone was ready to see our athletes showered with gold medals.

But then the hot and steamy weather that held for the opening ceremony finally broke and storm clouds gathered. So much has been expected and when athlete after athlete tipped for gold failed to deliver, we've suffered each blow like a National Disappointment. By last night I'm pretty sure I detected panic in the voices of the commentators. After all the hype, everyone is asking: who's going to win the first British gold medal?

So much attention had been focussed on the handful of athletes selected for the media campaign, a number of world-class competitors have gone under the radar. It seems it's only just occurred to the fourth estate that the first British gold medals are probably about to be won by two women no one outside of rowing has ever heard of.

I wish all our rowers the very best of luck. Bring it on!

The catch: *The moment at which the spoon of the blade is immersed in the water and propulsive force applied. Immersion and force application should be indistinguishable actions.*

12

KATE

When Kate arrived at the Waterman's, half a dozen Albion members in green baseball caps clustered self-consciously by the door, blocking the way. Mike was holding court.

'So my phone goes last night, and when I answer, some bird says: "Is that the captain of Albion Rowing Club? This is ITV. We'd like to come down to your club tomorrow morning and film you all rowing, to show where Kirsty Jelbert and Karen Manning learnt to row."

'"Well," I say, "that would be absolutely fine, except no one rows on a Wednesday morning – everyone's normally at work."

'"Well how about we come and film you in your clubhouse and interview you about them?" she says.

'"Another nice idea," I say, "but we don't have a clubhouse." Anyway, I told her we'd all be here to watch the final of the women's coxless pairs on telly. I mentioned there'd be bacon sandwiches.' The members clustered around Mike hung on his every word, amazed by what was happening.

'So where did the rest of them come from?' asked one

of the men. At this Kate peered over the shoulders of the members blocking her way and was astonished to see the pub filled with TV cameras.

'Well, after that my phone just kept buzzing. Word must have spread, because I'd lost track of them by the time I switched the damned thing off so I could get some sleep.'

It was quite bewildering. Kate squeezed past them and made her way to the bar to order a coffee. A couple of bar staff stood at the far end, chatting. Neither of them took any notice of her. After a few minutes trying to catch the eye of one of them, Kate was beginning to wonder if she was actually invisible. She finally called out and waved. The taller one gave a sigh and slouched towards her. They'd run out of bacon sandwiches.

As she waited for her coffee, Kate surveyed the room. There were half a dozen TV cameras being set up by an assortment of scruffy men in dirty jeans, T-shirts and facial hair. Each of them was accompanied by a couple of crew, busying themselves with cables and clipboards. The cameras were focussed on a long table at which were seated half a dozen Albion members wearing various items of clothing in Albion green. They were facing the large TV hung on the wall. Jack was there and he signalled for her to come over. Kate recognised a couple of the others from the skittles night. Just then Beth arrived.

'Your daughters with you?' asked Beth. The girls were both home briefly for the few weeks of the holidays for which they did not have a better invitation. Not that Kate had seen that much of them even when they had been at home. They seemed to be either out or asleep. Beth had heard so much about them but had never managed to meet them.

'They were both still asleep when I left. They were out

last night and I've no idea what time they got back. Heard from anyone about the taster day?'

'Afraid not,' said Beth. 'But there's still time.' She sounded as if she didn't believe this any more than Kate did, but they comforted each other with positive noises. It had been such a wonderful idea but they'd known all along, deep down, it was unlikely to work. After all, if it were that straightforward the club would have a women's masters squad already. It was disappointing, but Kate was determined not to let it drag her down.

They joined the other members at the long table. Jack found a couple of free chairs and dragged them over for them. Despite the depressing conclusion of their failed project, both women felt positively chirpy in his company. Nonetheless, it really felt terribly odd, sipping at their cappuccinos with half a dozen TV cameras pointing at them. A young woman with a clipboard came over to Beth and Kate.

'Hi. I'm Jax with Sky News. Would one of you be willing to do an interview with me after the race? It'll only take five minutes of your time.'

'Sure,' said the man sitting next to Kate, leaning across her to shake the young woman's hand. 'Anything I can do to help. I'm David. I'm on the committee at Albion, you know.'

'Great,' said Jax. 'See you after the race.' Kate had not met David before but she'd come across his type many times: good-looking but not terribly competent, with a tremendous sense of entitlement, elbowing in front of anyone he did not perceive as useful. Fortunately Kate had no desire to be interviewed on television, so she was only mildly irritated by his rudeness.

'Tosser,' Beth mouthed at Kate.

There was a palpable air of tension in the pub. Voices were low and conversations stilted. No one knew how to behave. It was all slightly unreal. The minutes ticked by and finally the race was about to start. All eyes were on the TV screen. The British pair were in lane three as the fastest qualifiers. Kate counted up the lanes on the screen to identify their boat. An official lay prone on the pontoon, his arms stretched down to the water holding the tip of their stern. The two rowers slumped, nervous. They stretched and flexed in their seats. Anxious. Focussed. Ready.

The umpire called out the nationalities taking part, lane by lane:

'In lane three, representing Great Britain . . .' The rest of the announcement was drowned out in the most extraordinary roar from 30,000 spectators banked along the finish. It was the first stirring of a beast of monstrous proportions. Both athletes looked as if they were about to vomit. Manning fiddled with the straps on her vest; Jelbert stared hard at the water. Kate gripped the seat of her chair and sat forward as if it would somehow afford her a clearer view.

'Attention!' And the Olympians took their start positions. Then an electronic noise like the horn of a tram sounded the start of the race. With their blades buried in the water, the rowers drove with their legs and heaved their boats into motion. By 250m Jelbert and Manning were half a length ahead. At this point the BBC commentator mentioned the girls had learned to row at Albion Rowing Club and the Waterman erupted in its own version of the Dorney roar.

As they reached the 500m mark, the announcement over the PA system at Dorney Lake that the British pair were two lengths ahead provoked the beast. A wall of sound met the rowers. Communication between them would be impossible. Had they gone out too fast? Could they sustain the power to the end? Kate found the tension unbearable.

By the halfway mark the Brits had a lead of three and a half seconds. They looked commanding. Was it too good to be true? Kate was still not ready to believe they were going to win. There was so much that could still go wrong. Could they do it? They looked so strong. Kate could feel the emotion welling up in her throat, watching these two goddesses.

The noise was incredible. It sounded as if every British spectator at Dorney was willing them on as each stroke took them a few metres closer to that gold medal. The towpath was a blur of bicycles.

As the British pair approached the 1,500m mark, to Kate's eye they appeared unbeatable, remorseless in their pace. As she watched the screen and saw those two powerful, beautiful women conquering the world, tears started coursing down her cheeks. All around her Albion members were screaming and shouting, waving their arms and jumping with hysterical anticipation.

The commentator had finally worked out the British pair were going to win this race and the enormity of it slowly dawned on him. This was going to be the first British gold medal of the home games, won in spectacular and convincing style.

'Their names are going to be up in lights! Their names are going to be on the front page of every newspaper in the country!' While he was saying this, Kate could imagine him kicking his research assistant to find something, anything he could say about the two women.

But despite their commanding performance, it would take only a momentary lapse of concentration for it all to go terribly wrong. In the last 250m their boat speed dropped as the Australians and New Zealanders sprinted for the line, their lead shrinking with every stroke. Could they hold on? Could they make it to the finish line?

Every man, woman and child in the stands were screaming louder than they had ever screamed before: this was for Britain! The pair had judged it perfectly and they crossed the finish line with one metre of clear water remaining between them and the Australian crew. As they did so, the Waterman erupted with a roar. Kate fell into Beth's arms and the two of them cried their hearts out.

On the television, the GB pair finally stopped in front of the battery of sound coming from the stands, Manning collapsed backwards onto Jelbert's legs and Jelbert slumped over her partner, wracked by sobs. They had done it. They had rowed their race. They had met their destiny head on. They had won Olympic gold.

In the pub everyone jumped up and down, hugging whoever was next to them and screaming and shouting. The six TV cameras were lapping it up. Part of the crowd were now doing a conga round the pub. Beth had let go of Kate to get up and hug the other members and take part in the collective rejoicing. In the midst of all the noise and confusion, only Kate sat quiet and still at the long table, oblivious to the chaos around her, staring at the television screen. Tears trickled down her cheeks. She was simply overwhelmed by what she'd just witnessed. She felt such unbridled joy and pride as if Kirsty and Karen were her own daughters. She did not want to let go of this moment.

The din finally settled down and the conga line had danced its way into the beer garden. Beth and Kate were just discussing whether a cup of tea was needed or something stronger, when one of the TV producers came over to them.

'Would you have a couple of minute to share your thoughts on the race?' the producer asked, looking at Kate.

'Me? Are you sure you want to know what I think? I expect I can find Dave from the committee for you.'

'I definitely want to know what you think.' As she said this Kate realised one of the cameras was trained on her, its red light glowing. She didn't know how long it had been filming her.

The producer had Kate stand next to the fencing in the beer garden with the river in the background. The conga line could be heard at the far end of the lawn, crashing into some tables laden with glasses. Despite this, there was a stillness around them, with the restful sound of the river and a robin singing in the willow trees.

'I'm talking to Kate, a member of Albion Rowing Club, who first learnt to row at university. Kate, how did you feel watching the race?'

'It was obviously very exciting,' said Kate, not sure if she should look at the producer or into the camera, and alternating between the two. 'We had a good idea the girls were going to win as they've been performing so well all season. But in rowing there's so much that can go wrong. You haven't won a race until you cross the finish line.'

'You seemed to be quite emotional watching the race,' said the producer.

'It was incredibly emotional for me. I was lucky enough to start rowing at university but back then I'd never seen women rowing on television. Not many people realised women could row. I never thought that in my lifetime I would see images like that on national TV, British women rowing and beating the world. I feel so proud of Kirsty and Karen and what they've achieved. And I hope their example will encourage lots of other girls and women to take up rowing. It's a fabulous sport.'

'What is it about the sport that you love so much?' asked the producer.

'Well . . . firstly, it's a very technical sport. There's a real joy in getting it right. You know, doing it properly. It's obviously physically demanding and lots of people will appreciate the pleasure of an intensive workout. A huge attraction, though, is being on the water. There's something quite zen about it. I mean – wouldn't you rather work out here than in a gym?' Kate swept her hand across the distant view of the river disappearing around the bend. 'But the thing that really keeps you going is the crew. It's the ultimate team sport and you develop a bond that you rarely experience in normal life. I'm sure Kirsty and Karen will be like sisters for the rest of their lives.'

'Well, you've certainly sold it to me,' said the producer. 'This is Melanie Abbott for the BBC at Albion Rowing Club.' When the camera stopped filming, Melanie consulted with the cameraman about the other pieces they needed.

'If you do use it, where and when will it be?' asked Kate, assuming it would take some tracking down on the red button in the early hours of the morning.

'The main coverage of the games starts at 7.00 p.m. I'm sure Kirsty and Karen will be the lead story. It'll probably get picked up on the news bulletins as well. Thanks again,' said Melanie, and she and the cameraman moved on, leaving Kate slightly shell-shocked.

The women's coxless pair was indeed the main story of that evening's Olympic coverage. Much was made of the fact that Kirsty Jelbert had not been in a boat until 2008 when she'd joined the Olympic development scheme and been taught to row at Albion Rowing Club. Kate was fascinated by the skilful way the film shot at the Waterman had been edited to create a lively narrative. The film of the Albion members reacting to the race was television gold. She was less comfortable with a lingering shot of her own tear-streaked face just before the pub broke out in uproar as the pair crossed the line.

As it turned out, the producers loved her interview and it made repeated bulletins as well as the main evening programme showing the day's highlights. Kate was all over the media. The clip was picked up by other networks and tweeted and shared on Facebook, and generally went viral in a low-key, short-lived sort of way.

Kate found the whole thing excruciating, and was contorted with embarrassment as she watched the evening coverage with her daughters. She was so wrapped up in her own shame, she was in no position to judge the impact the piece had made. Halfway through the segment she fled to the kitchen. Loading the dishwasher was therapeutic and helped restore some order to her thoughts. She'd nearly finished clearing up when her daughters burst into the room.

'Mumsie! That was amazing!'

'Way to go, Mum!'

The two girls scooped up their mother in one big hug and the three of them laughed and embraced and bounced up and down, until Kate almost believed it had been amazing too.

Capsize: *When a boat turns over in the water due to poor technique or a collision. Not uncommon in sculling boats.*

13

KATE

The next morning Tim called first thing from his office in London to ask Kate to collect his bike from the repair shop.

'What time are you back Friday?' asked Kate.

'Not sure. I'll let you know. So what are you up to today? Giving a match debrief on the boxing? Or is it the weight-lifting?' This could have been meant as a joke, but Kate thought she could detect the faintest hint of a sneer.

'Actually, I'm taking the car in for its MOT then working from home' said Kate. As she hung up the phone, she realised it had stung, and she remembered the shot of her tear-stained face. Oh the shame! The embarrassment! Why on earth had she agreed to be interviewed? Just then her phone beeped with a text from Beth.

Too early for a coffee?

Come right over, you're just what I need texted Kate right back. Her daughters wouldn't be up for hours. She put the coffee on the stove and checked her emails. Her inbox was full of messages about the broadcast: random journalists wanting to interview her; friends congratulating her. What on earth were they thinking? She'd just made an utter fool of herself. She was still shaking her head and going through the whole ghastly experience for the umpteenth time when Beth turned up.

As she opened the door Kate said, 'Whatever you do, please don't say anything about yesterday. I'm just trying to forget the whole thing ever happened.'

'What on earth are you talking about?' Beth seemed terribly excited. 'You were incredible, Kate. You really expressed how we all felt, about the race and about rowing and everything.'

'That's kind of you to say, but I don't think that's true.'

'Really? Well, I can prove it! Look at that,' and she brandished her smartphone in front of Kate's nose.

'What am I looking at? I haven't got my glasses on.'

'That, my friend, is an inbox stuffed full of rowers wanting to go on our taster day. They all replied after they saw the race. Every single one of them. They all want to do it. You only went and jolly well did it!' With this they both threw their arms around each other and jumped up and down together like a pair of teenagers who'd scored tickets for a One Direction concert.

It was unbelievable. They'd more or less given up on the idea as a lost cause. They'd put so much work in to it and got absolutely nowhere. And yet here, as if by a wave of a magic wand, they had a potential squad signing up for their first outing.

After much hugging and shrieking, they repaired to the kitchen for a celebratory coffee. They had work to do and a taster day to organise. Once they'd talked excitedly through what was required, they decided to give Stanley a call on speakerphone. They didn't necessarily need him to coach the session, but it would be reassuring to have someone in the launch as backup.

'Not that backup will be required,' Beth had added hastily. 'But it's no bad thing to have someone from the committee involved from the start.'

According to Beth, Stanley was a decent enough man but he did not suffer fools gladly. In fact Stanley tended not to suffer fools at all. There were those who suspected Stanley might be on the autistic spectrum, given his complete oblivion to the sensitivities of others. There were others who said he was simply normal for Yorkshire, the county of his birth. Whatever the reason, Stanley required careful handling and Beth was at pains to make sure she was on top of her brief before she made the call.

'Hi, Stanley. It's Beth. Sorry to bother you. I'm on speakerphone with Kate. How are you?'

'Wasn't the race marvellous? Bloody marvellous. Now, what can I do for you, Beth?'

She explained about the taster session and the plans already in place. Stanley was clearly shocked.

'I did talk to you about it, Stanley – a couple of weeks ago. You didn't seem to think it would be a problem.'

'Well, to be honest I didn't take it that seriously. I didn't think anyone would be interested.' Kate exchanged a conspiratorial look with Beth. They really had defied the odds getting this far.

'You do know Molly's said she'd cox us?'

'What – my Molly?' This really seemed to throw him, so when Beth asked if he'd be prepared to coach them, Stanley mumbled something about 'consulting the committee'. Kate threw Beth a concerned look. Given her profession she was a stickler for doing things by the book, but this sounded like yet another obstacle being put in their way. Undeterred, Beth explained to Stanley what they wanted him to do.

'Our main objective is to remind the women why they used to love rowing so they want to come back. You know – all those things Kate said yesterday on the telly.'

'Yeees – that thing. By the way, have you seen the Club Facebook page this morning? Molly just showed it to me,' said Stanley.

'No – should I?' asked Beth.

Stanley said that they both might want to take a look. 'Right. Got to go. Speak at the weekend?' and he hung up.

Kate fetched her laptop and while she bustled about heating up milk and arranging chocolate tray bakes on a plate, Beth tapped in the address of the website. She seemed to be having a certain amount of difficulty in remembering her username and password and there was much muttering and cursing under her breath. She finally found the right combination and scanned down the page. Suddenly she stopped reading and closed the laptop.

'Christ, what's happened? You look as white as a sheet.' Beth hesitated, then opened the laptop, scrolled down again and pushed it over towards Kate. The club's page was plastered with photographs of the golden girls: rowing, collapsed in the boat after the finish, on the podium with their medals. The main photograph on the club's page had been changed already to a spectacular shot of the two women smiling, heads close together, holding up their medals. Someone had posted a clip of the TV coverage of the race, and there were the usual comments:

Ben Duncan: Fanbloodytastic! What a race!

Marcus Hawkes: Congratulations to Kirsty and Karen. Albion members win Olympic gold. Amazing.

Kayley Nokes: I can't believe she learnt to row in the same boat I learnt in! Why can't I make it move that fast?

Simon Cooper: Go Albion! Whoop whoop!

And so it went on. Until there was a post that took a darker turn. Someone had taken the footage of Kate being interviewed and made a meme out of a gesture. In context, in the film, there was nothing odd about it. Kate was shrugging and blinked. If you watched the whole clip you would not even notice; that's how normal people behave. The meme was not in context. It was the same brief movement repeated like a hideous tic. It made Kate look demented. Above it were a flurry of comments.

Blue skies: How embarrassing we couldn't find someone more appropriate to speak for the club. At our finest hour, what a shame we give the world the impression our club is full of emotional, menopausal women. #whoneedsthem

Joe Connell: As we're trying to recruit men under twenty-five for our men's first eight we should be showing off the many hotties we have in the club #Albionhotties

Mark Fry: Did anyone give her permission to speak on behalf of the club?

Emma Miles: Someone should put in a complaint about her.

Chris Whetherly: Why hasn't the committee got a grip on this? We should have a vote of no confidence.

Emma Miles: Vote! Vote! Vote!

Ben Duncan: I thought she spoke very well. Surely it's good to show that we're inclusive as a club? Let people know that we're not just about Olympians.

Chris Whetherly: Of course we're inclusive otherwise why would we have a fat boy like you as a member? #Albionfatboy

All colour drained from Kate's face. She read on, frantic. Suddenly the screen blurred and black spots danced in front of her eyes. She felt giddy, detached. Her head was light as if all the blood had left it. Then a pair of hands was steadying her and guiding her to a chair. Her head was gently pushed between her knees, and it all went black.

Puddles: *Disturbances made by an oar blade pulled through the water. The farther the puddles are pushed past the stern of the boat before each catch, the more 'run' the boat is getting.*

14
BETH

Beth hung up her buoyancy aid on a rust nail and plugged in her cox box to recharge. It was such a joy at this time of year not to have to put on bundles of clothing and waterproofs to cox. It could still be chilly on the water as you were immobile for so long, but one extra layer was sufficient. Plus sunscreen and sunglasses, of course. She did occasionally think that on a day like today people would pay good money to be rowed down the river.

It was glorious weather. She toyed with the idea of taking a single out. It was perfect for sculling. It was unbearable that Kate felt so terrible about the whole Facebook thing that she couldn't be persuaded to come down to the club. She'd love being out on the water today, to see how the breeze ruffled the leaves on the willows and left trails of pollen on the water.

It was just so unfair. How could they pick on her friend like that? She knew all Kate wanted to do was crawl under a stone and never come out again. It had only been a few days since it happened but she knew there was no way Kate would go down to Albion again on a Saturday or Sunday morning when the main squads were there. Too many of them had said too many hurtful things.

Beth had tried to point out it was just a handful of people, and that most of the club thought they were talking rubbish. Kate, not unreasonably, asked why all these sensible members had not come to her defence, if that was the case? The answer seemed to be that they 'didn't want to get involved' and they thought it would just 'blow over'. Stanley had said as much. It obviously hadn't occurred to him that Kate might benefit from some specific kindness after what had happened.

At least Kate had her kids home for the holidays. Beth had offered to take her out for a walk or a bike ride but Kate insisted she had plans with the girls and would be fine. The only thing Beth could think of now to help was to do everything she could to make the taster day happen. If they couldn't achieve their dream of a veteran women's squad, she couldn't see Kate would be coming back to rowing. Ever. Christ, Kate had even been talking about pottery classes when she called yesterday.

'Hi Stanley. Mike.' The two men were huddled close together by the opening to the boathouse, deep in conversation. They both looked up with guilty expressions on their faces.

'You had a chance to think about our taster day?'

Stanley and Mike exchanged a meaningful look.

'Yes, about that. I haven't managed to call an emergency committee meeting yet . . .'

'You've lost me,' said Beth, completely confused. 'Why do you need a committee meeting?'

'Well, there's a lot to think about. There's the insurance, for one, plus we'll have to do a full risk assessment,' said Mike.

'That's fine,' said Beth. 'I can sort that all out.'

'We'll still need to get the committee to approve it. It needs careful consideration,' said Mike.

'You do realise they're all former Albion members? They were all in the senior crew at one time. It's not like they're novices or anything. We know what we're doing.' Beth was conscious her voice was rising in pitch. She was starting to panic. Her natural inclination was to back off at this point, but she couldn't let them stop this.

'Yes, but that was a long time ago,' said Mike wearily. 'Like I say. We'll have to see what the rest of the committee have to say.'

'You do know Lesley has signed up?' said Beth, conscious this was not her usual style.

'Lesley? What, my Lesley?' asked Mike. Now he was confused.

'Yes, your Lesley.'

The two men left and Beth stood watching them disappear down the path. She'd never realised before how hateful the club could be. There again, she'd never tried to do anything for herself before. She'd just gone along with everyone else's schemes and done her bit to help.

'Penny for them.' Beth turned and saw Jack on his knees next to the lawnmower. Had he been there the whole time?

'I'm afraid you don't want to know what I'm thinking right at the moment. It isn't terribly charitable.'

Jack clambered slowly to his feet, dusting down the front of his voluminous khaki shorts. He was smiling, as ever, but he looked serious as well.

'I'm so sorry about what happened. You know – the Facebook thing. Someone told me about it this morning. I hope your friend's not letting it get to her.' His face was the picture of concern.

'Thanks, Jack. I'm afraid she's terribly distressed. Between you and me the Senior Women had already given her a bit of a rough ride. Now with this, if I can't make our taster day happen I don't think I'll ever be able to persuade her to come down to the river again.'

Jack blew out hard, pushed back his baseball cap and scratched the back of his smooth head.

'That's awful. I'm so sorry.'

Beth gave Jack a weak smile. 'The stupid thing is, I thought the hard part was getting the veteran women to sign up. It didn't occur to me the committee might not agree to it.'

'Well, why wouldn't they? We regularly have crews of old boys borrowing a boat to go out for a reunion. I've never heard the committee expressing the slightest concern about them. This is a new one on me, Beth. Looking on the bright side, once they've had a chance to get their heads round it I'm sure they'll see there really is nothing to object to.'

Beth was not convinced, but she appreciated Jack's support.

'Would you like me to have a word?'

'Ooh, I don't know. It might look like you're interfering. It could just make things worse.'

'True, but then I can point out to them something you can't.'

'What's that?'

'That they're only being difficult because you're women. And they're not allowed to do that.'

'Wow! Is that what the problem is?' asked Beth, genuinely shocked. 'I thought it was just because we're old.'

'Double whammy, innit?' said Jack, grinning his broadest grin.

*

Beth never found out if Jack had intervened, but a week later she received an email from Mike giving grudging permission. He itemised a number of requirements that had never been asked for before in the long history of Albion Rowing Club, but Beth was not going to argue. She knocked off the risk assessment and sent it back by return, along with the list of participants and their completed temporary membership forms. She didn't tell Kate about any of this and simply kept reassuring her that everything was set.

Beth was worried sick about her. Kate had been saying she wasn't going to the taster day. In fact, she'd made up her mind to give up the whole notion of rowing. But Beth had called round unannounced one evening, and enjoyed a glass of rosé in the garden with Kate and Poppy and Ella. They were lovely girls. The younger one, in particular, looked so like her mother. They were bright and engaging with an infectious enthusiasm for life.

Beth told them all about how brilliantly their mother was rowing. How she was one of the best female rowers in the club and how she'd learned to scull in no time at all. Kate squirmed and protested, but they seemed thrilled to hear someone talking about their mother's achievements in this way. It was obviously a new experience.

Beth described their dream of a veteran squad and explained they were on the verge of realising it. Kate caught her eye at that point, as if imploring her not to tell her daughters what had happened. She needn't have worried. Beth had already planned on giving a whitewashed version of events. Because Beth had planned this. Oh yes, she'd planned it all right. She was actually rather pleased with herself how cunning she was becoming in her old age.

She knew Kate was at the limit of what she could achieve

through willpower alone. What she needed was some female solidarity and encouragement. And Kate's daughters, so obviously like their mother, were clearly the women to provide it. Beth just prayed it would be enough.

The Sunday of the taster day finally dawned and the weather could not quite make up its mind whether to be fair or not. It was one of those typical August days when it's nice one minute, then grey clouds cover the sun the next. Not quite warm enough to be comfortable, it was perfect for rowing.

Beth felt more nervous than before a big race and it was a huge relief when Kate's car finally pulled in to the car park. Beth had made the most monumental effort to arrive before her and it was obvious from the look of relief on Kate's face it had been worthwhile. She knew how much courage and determination it was taking for Kate to return to the club. She just hoped to God the day worked out and gave Kate a reason to keep coming back to the river.

Kate would not be rowing with the senior squad any time soon, so if she were to keep rowing, they would have to create their own squad. Beth hadn't really thought about it before, but she had her own little niche at Albion. People were nice to her because they needed a cox. But if truth be told she knew it was a superficial sort of friendliness. She doubted many of them would have stood up to defend her if she'd been attacked the way Kate had been. Plus it was all a one-way street. She was an incredibly experienced coach, so it was not surprising people wanted her help. Kate was the only person in years who'd asked about her rowing and what Beth wanted to get out of the club. She was not going to burn any bridges, but as well as helping her friend, Beth could see she too stood to gain a lot from this project.

Kate had brought a large folding decorator's table from

home. She covered it with a checked tablecloth and laid out mugs, plates of filled rolls covered in cling film, and cake stands laden with extravagant cupcakes.

'I think you forgot the bunting,' said Beth.

'Are you taking the piss?'

'As if!' said Beth and they both laughed. Beth was pleased to see Kate able to take a joke. They'd just finished filling the kettles with water from the outside tap when Stanley and Molly arrived carrying cans of petrol for the launch. When Beth had first known her, Molly had been tiny, quick and slightly fragile but she'd obviously piled on the weight since she'd injured her knee. Beth ran a professional eye over her. She moved awkwardly, still with a slight limp. She guessed Molly had still not achieved full mobility in the new joint and had suffered significant muscle wastage. All of the extra weight she was carrying couldn't be helping either. She hadn't noticed how disabled she was when they had met at the skittles night as Molly had been perched on a stool for most of the evening

'Hello, Molly. How are you?'

'A bit stiff, as you can see. And a bit nervous. I haven't coxed for a couple of years since I first injured my knee. My main concern is getting in and out of the boat,' confided Molly quietly. 'I may need some help with that.' Molly was shaking slightly. Her voice was even more acerbic than usual. Beth saw Stanley out of the corner of her eye and realised he hadn't taken his eyes off his wife.

'Don't worry – we'll look after you. One advantage of being menopausal is it does make you sensitive to the needs of others.'

'About that – I was so sorry. The whole thing was disgraceful. Poor Kate – that isn't the Albion I know and love.' Molly was getting quite pink in the face as she said this. It was the most empathetic Beth had ever seen a member of the Butcher household in all the years she'd known them. Perhaps her own suffering had opened Molly's eyes to other people's troubles.

'Are you sure you're up for this?'

'I'm absolutely sure,' said Molly with grim determination. 'I've rather plateaued with my rehab, so needing to get in and out of a boat is just the kick up the pants I need to get me going to the gym.'

'Well, if you're sure. There'll be no rush getting you in, and once you are in, it'll be just like riding a bike.'

'Except ten times longer.'

'Exactly.'

Just then the first of the women started arriving and Kate went over with her clipboard to introduce herself and tick them off on the list. Everyone knew at least one other person there, and of course they all knew Beth, Stanley and Molly. For such a large group they were extremely prompt, and everyone was present and correct with a few minutes to spare.

'Who's that?' asked Kate, indicating a woman with long blonde hair who looked as if she was about to doze off.

'That's Abbie. She was quite the party girl, back in the day.'

'Looks like she still is. I'm guessing she had a late one last night. Well, so long as she doesn't throw up in the boat . . .'

Kate called them all over and they squished together on the grubby sofas or sat cross-legged on the floor. After a brief introduction, Kate asked Beth to give a safety briefing.

Although Beth didn't particularly enjoy speaking to a crowd, she thought it important as she reckoned the biggest risk of injury to the women would be from moving the boats. They had been so used to lifting them, once upon a time, it would be easy to underestimate how heavy they were. Those not doing regular weight training would be much less strong than they had been last time they were out on the river.

Beth had never seen or heard a coach at Albion taking these sorts of issues in to consideration: rowing was set up for young men, and anyone else could take part, so long as they could cope on those terms. There was an expression that Beth had heard many times:

'If you can't lift it, you can't row it.' Given that all of the boats were designed for large men, this was obviously nonsense. And totally unfair as the problem only affected women. She and Kate would have to work it out as they went. It would require some careful thought.

'Remember that back in the day you were rowing with crews you'd spent hundreds of hours with. You moved together as one, which made it easier and safer. It won't be like that today. We'll get it back, but it won't happen overnight. So we're all going to be CAREFUL! Got it? If necessary, you ask for help.'

'Got it!' they chorused. When Beth had finished, Kate consulted her clipboard and called out the two crews by name with their seat numbers.

'Don't worry if it's not where you used to sit, or would like to sit in future. We can move it around. This is just to get us out on the water. Beth's crew – you can start with a warm-up on the erg while my crew get our boat out. Once we're done we'll swap over. OK, everyone?'

'OK!' they all chorused, and with a surprising level of compliance, seven women followed Beth to the ergs. Beth was not used to anyone following her anywhere, unless they were patients. Molly was to be the cox of Beth's crew and she took them through the warm-up drill. It was impressive. All of the women clearly had solid technique and had forgotten very little.

Once they'd finished, the crew went out to the other boatshed where the eights were stored. Kate's crew already had their boat out on trestles and were intent on adjusting the distance between their seat and their stretchers, and also the height at which their shoes were set. All of the women leant a hand to get the second shell out, and Beth busied herself adjusting her own stretcher. Out of her peripheral vision she was vaguely aware of a powerfully built figure having a meltdown at the far end. She walked casually down the boat, checking rigging and hatch covers as she went. When she got to the bow she spoke to the mixed-race woman at Two:

'Everything OK, Lesley?'

Lesley was clearly not OK. She looked flushed and agitated. Her eyes were red and puffy. The state of her hair was always a useful barometer of Lesley's mental state: today her wild ringlets had blown and frizzed into a giant puffball.

'No, it's not. I don't know what I'm doing here. Mike was right. I'm too old, too fat and too useless. I can't think why I ever said I'd do this. It's just a terrible, terrible mistake.' With this, Lesley started sobbing, big heaving globs of misery. Beth put an arm around Lesley's shoulders and walked her away from the boat.

'Now look, my friend, I've known you a long time, and I can tell you why you're here. You're here because you're a bloody good rower and it's time you got back in a boat. You're not too old – for God's sake, you're younger than me. And you're not too fat. If you really can't get your arse between the gunwales then I'll let you go home. But I can tell you now that isn't going to happen. You're here because you used to be one of the best rowers in the club and you're going to be again. You're here because we want you. More to the point, right now we need you.

'Look over there: it might not be obvious but those women are feeling just as scared as you are. But they've put their hand up to do this. They want to do this, even though they're terrified. If you back out now we can't go out. You don't have to do this again, Lesley, if you don't want to. But you are going to do this now. Just once. If we get out there and it's all too awful, we can come straight back in. But you're going to get in that boat and give the rest of the crew a chance. OK?'

'OK,' sniffed Lesley, rubbing her forearm across her snotty nose. 'I've got this.'

Beth was far from convinced, but she would just have to cross her fingers and hope Lesley held it together. As she walked away Beth had a curious out-of-body sensation. Was that really her who'd spoken to Lesley like that? What had come over her? She normally left that sort of thing to other people. Maybe some of Kate's determination was rubbing off on her.

'OK, Cox. Let's go,' said Beth and she scurried towards her seat at Stroke. Molly was waiting there, trussed up in an overly tight buoyancy aide with an elasticated band stretched across her forehead holding her microphone in place. The tail end was too long and dangled down in front of Molly's nose. She stuck out her lower lip and blew hard to shift the blue fabric. It swung away and then back. For a moment Beth did wonder whether Molly should really be trusted with a £30,000 boat and eight lives. At least Stanley would be there in the safety boat. He wouldn't let anything happen to his precious shell. Or Molly come to that.

Suddenly, for a split second, Beth saw them as they must have looked to others: a crowd of middle-aged women, some overweight, some greying, attempting to do something ridiculously challenging for women half their age. She'd been quietly rather proud she and Kate had managed to make today happen. But now she was panicking. What on earth had made them think this was a good idea? Thank God the place was deserted and there were no Facebook users to see them.

Carrying the boat was easier than they'd anticipated. Everyone remembered what to do, even if there was a bit of dithering about which side to split to. An eight is reasonably forgiving because if one person does something daft there are still seven other people taking the weight. Getting everyone in the boat was more problematic. Beth suggested she wait on the pontoon and help Molly in last, but Molly was having none of it. Stanley was hovering around like an anxious mother hen and he said he would get her in.

There was a good deal of puffing and complaining as the crew manoeuvred themselves into position. Beth could see Lesley was still looking shaky. Fortunately, Abbie at Bow took no nonsense, so Lesley was forced to get on with it. Finally all of the rowers were in their seats and there was just the cox left on dry land, standing with one foot through Stroke's rigger. Stanley practically lifted Molly in his arms and lowered her into her seat. There was a certain amount of difficulty in manoeuvring her in and it was a tight fit between the sides of the boat, especially with her life jacket on.

'We need to get you one of those skinny buoyancy aides next time,' said Beth. 'Then you won't be so wedged in.'

'Perhaps you could install a hoist on the pontoon as well for next time,' muttered Molly.

'All set?' asked Stanley, and he took Stroke's blade and slowly pushed the eight away from the pontoon. As Molly manoeuvred the eight into the stream and over to the far side of the river, Stanley sprinted over to the tethered motorboat and leapt into the driver's seat. Beth thought to herself that if ever a film company were in the market for a seventy-year-old action hero, Stanley would be a shoo-in.

They set off in fours, giving everyone a chance to check their set-up and reacquaint themselves with the equipment. To begin with, the crew responded slowly to commands and at one point Seven failed to respond to Molly's request to back down a stroke.

'Can you hear me OK, Geeta? Do you need the cox box turned up?' she asked sarcastically. There was only Beth sitting between Molly and Seven, so a microphone was surplus to requirements.

'It's not my hearing, cox, it's my dementia. I can't remember my number. What did you say my name was?' This was met with low-grade tittering in the bows, which Molly chose to ignore.

If there were some preliminary difficulties in responding to commands, there was no issue with technique and not one person missed even part of a stroke. They were barely halfway to the lock before it was obvious caution was unnecessary. Stanley had caught up with them now and was cruising along in their shadow, observing silently. By the time they reached the top of the river he'd forgotten the circumstances of the outing and was simply analysing the crew and identifying what needed to be done.

Molly spun the boat and, once it was pointing downstream, the crew sat to attention, all eyes on Stanley.

'That was all very tidy, but this isn't bloody dressage. Cox – take them off – thirty strokes of half pressure, and then put in bursts of ten firm. Repeat that all the way to the top of the straight and wait for me there. I'll peel off at some point and have a look at the other boat.' If the crew were disappointed by the lack of praise, they didn't show it. They were back.

Molly ordered them to the backstops position and they moved as one like a well-regulated machine. The concentration was palpable.

'Backstops –
Half pressure –
Are you ready?
Go!'

With this command the boat pushed forward with conviction. There was no tentativeness. They meant business. This was their business. As they worked through the drills, Molly made calls to sharpen up their technique and each instruction was met with an obvious improvement. It took about twenty minutes to reach the section where they were to stop, and in the final few hundred metres a number of the crew were obviously shortening up as a way of coping with exhaustion. When Molly finally called out, ***'Easy oar,'*** there was a chorus of groans and sounds of collapsing.

'Oh my God, I thought I was fit!' said Seven.

'I'd forgotten how much it hurts,' said Six.

Everyone was chatting to the woman behind or in front, drinking from their water bottles and taking tops off. Just then the sun came out from behind a cloud and the river was flooded with sunshine. Apart from the excited chatter from the women, there was not a sound. A small breeze produced a gentle rustling of the rushes next to them.

'Kingfisher!' said Molly through her microphone, and they all turned to see the flash of brilliant turquoise land on a branch of the tree on the far bank.

'Wow, will you look at that,' said Three. 'It's magic.' The

women all gazed at the tiny bird as if trying to commit it to memory.

The sounds of an outboard motor were heard from around the bend, and the launch appeared and came along side.

'Right, ladies. The other crew will be here in a moment. If the straight is clear, you're going to paddle half pressure down to the 1,000m mark and then race each other side by side. We'll do a rolling start, so Cox, try to stay level with the other crew. I'll start you somewhere around the mark when you're level. OK?'

As Stanley finished talking, the other eight came into view. Beth's crew watched with keen interest. Their perfectly synchronised blades chopped into the water and levered the boat forward with intimidating power.

'Crumbs, they look good,' said Beth, to no one in particular.

Molly covered her microphone and whispered at Beth:

'Don't tell the others but you lot look just as good, and possibly even have slightly faster catches.' Beth was taken aback. Was it possible the middle-aged rabble she'd observed on the bank were rowing like this crew in front of her? If you didn't look too closely at their faces, you could mistake them for an elite university crew. They looked terrifying. Beth had coxed every crew at Albion and only a couple of the men's crews could come close in technique to the eight in front of her.

'You're kidding me,' said Beth.

'I think you know me well enough to know that kidding is not really my style,' said Molly. 'Just wait until we've got this together. Once we get it running properly, this boat is going to fly!'

Beth was euphoric. She felt ashamed she'd ever doubted

these women, just because they were past the first flush of youth. She turned around to speak to the crew.

'How are we doing, ladies? Everyone feeling all right?' There was a chorus of positive noises, and then Molly was moving them off. The other crew was already on the other side of the river, having overtaken them. Molly kept to the right-hand side, hugging the bank as closely as she could to maximise the distance between the two sets of oars. It only took one person missing a stroke for an eight to swing across the river and crash. In the excitement of a race there was always a distinct possibility of some sort of mishap.

'River's clear!' bellowed Stanley through a megaphone. ***'Coxes, hold those courses steady at half pressure!'*** Beth felt the crew sharpen up. Suddenly there was no weight on her blade as she put the spoon in the water: her crew were there at exactly the split second she was, lifting the boat for her. It felt effortless.

'Hold it there, crew. When Stanley says go, increase the pressure but don't rush the slide. Stroke will take the rating up, but follow her.' They took another half dozen strokes in studied concentration, and then Stanley yelled through his megaphone:

'Attention.

Go!'

From the first stroke the boat leapt forward with a sudden increase in power and adrenaline.

'Don't rush!

Follow stroke!

Hold the legs down!'

Molly's commands came in time to the rhythm of their strokes, and helped to calm everyone down. They settled into a steady rating. With every stroke, Beth could feel the crew coming together, ever more closely synchronised and precise. She could feel one or two people were still rushing the slide, and muttered to Molly.

'Don't rush Stroke!' called Molly, and immediately the rhythm settled down. Suddenly it came together. All eight women were moving as one and as they glided forward on the slide, they soared. Concentrating so hard on what she was doing, Beth had forgotten about the other crew until Molly called, ***'We're in front, so just hold it there and keep it relaxed.'***

Beth sneaked a look across to the right, which was always a mistake. From the stroke seat the angle made it look as if the other crew were winning, even when they were not. She saw a terrifying vision of oars and power and speed.

'Eyes in the boat!' shouted Molly, slightly too loudly given she had a microphone. Beth willed all her attention on the next stoke. The next catch. The next finish. By halfway down the straight Beth could clearly see they were ahead, but she also realised her crew were tiring rapidly.

'Finishes,' she hissed at Molly.

'Hold those finishes in,' called Molly over the cox box.

'Keep it long.' With this call solidity returned to the stroke and the boat speed lifted.

By the final 100m, every fibre of Beth's being was screaming for respite. Her lungs were burning, her muscles felt like jelly. But still she continued. She kept telling herself that if she felt that bad, what must it be like for the women who hadn't rowed in years? If they could do it, she could do it. She had to do it. For them.

'Last twenty strokes!
Empty the tanks!
Leave it all on the river!
This is what we do!'

As the race came down to the last few strokes, it was as

if the bubble surrounding her had burst and Beth became aware of the crashing of blades on water, the shouting from the two coxes and the cheering from a group of ramblers on the towpath. It was like an epic movie in glorious Technicolor remembered from her childhood. She was jubilant. She was intoxicated. And then it was over.

Molly brought them to a halt and they drifted. Silent. Spent. There was not a sound from the crew. Everyone was fighting for breath. Someone was coughing. Another person was retching. Beth was exhausted but almost beside herself with delight at the performance of both crews. She slowly came to, and saw the other crew drifting towards them.

'Did we win?' asked Beth.

'Oh yes, we won all right,' said Molly.

'Three cheers for Kate's crew! Hip hip hooray! Hip hip hooray! Hip hip hooray!' The women did their best to cheer and then collapsed in more coughing and groaning. Kate's crew responded. In her wildest dreams, Beth could not have imagined the day's outing turning out like this.

Once both eights had been washed and put away, everyone gathered round the tea table. Kate was busy passing round mugs of tea and checking in with each of the women in turn to make sure they were OK. She wanted to establish there were no injuries and that everyone had enjoyed themselves. It was fine. Not a single person had a problem, although nearly all of them insisted on showing Kate their blisters, and a couple actually started competing over whose were worse. Kate ended their argument by collapsing laughing between them. She was in her element.

The women were so thrilled with their afternoon and suitably grateful to Kate and Beth for making it happen. They didn't seem to have stopped chatting since they docked.

Without standing on ceremony the women dived into the sandwiches and cakes, talking excitedly. The volume rose rapidly as they all spoke louder in order to make themselves heard. Beth wandered over to where Lesley was standing talking animatedly to Molly, shoving a huge piece of salted caramel cupcake into her mouth.

'Well done, Lesley. How was that?' asked Beth. 'Sorry I bullied you into it back there. Did you enjoy it in the end?'

'Did I enjoy it?' spluttered Lesley, showering Beth with cake crumbs. 'I bloody loved it. And do you know what? I'm good at this. I'm bloody brilliant! When are we out next?'

Pair: *A shell with two rowers. The coxless pair is a demanding but satisfying boat to master.*

15

LESLEY

'Cooee! I'm home' Lesley exploded through the door leaving a trail of water bottle, sticking plasters and tissues leaking from her bag. Silence. 'I'm back.' Nothing. 'Humph,' said Lesley. The whole drive back she'd anticipated seeing Mike and telling him how brilliantly she'd done. He'd be so pleased. He hadn't thought she'd be able to manage it after all these years. No doubt he'd been worried she'd hurt herself. But she hadn't. Not apart from a few blisters, and they'd soon heal. She'd done it and she'd been bloody brilliant.

Just wait till I tell him. He'll be so pleased.

Lesley put the kettle on and as she waited for it to boil she noticed her belongings scattered on the floor. As she bent down to pick them up she felt a sharp twinge in her back.

'Better get in a nice hot shower before I stiffen up.' The kettle boiled and she opened the cupboard to find a mug, but then realised she didn't actually want anything. She was already full of tea and cake. She was in such a state of exhilaration and fatigue, she really didn't know what she wanted. Except to tell Mike about her afternoon and for him to be pleased.

As she headed upstairs for a shower, she poked her head in the lounge to see Mike in his normal Sunday afternoon position, sound asleep on the settee. Lesley smiled to herself, thinking how much better her news would sound when she was dressed and had sorted her hair out.

The shower was blissful, pummelling her stiffening back and shoulders. She could have stayed in there until the hot water ran out, but she eventually persuaded herself to make a move. She hoiked up the pile of stinky Lycra on the floor with her foot and turfed it in to the laundry basket. Perhaps it was lucky Mike had been asleep when she got back if she'd stunk that badly. She thought how funny it was you never noticed your own smell until you were clean again.

Lesley slathered herself with moisturiser then dressed and dried her hair with far more care than usual. She even put on some bronzer and mascara. She wasn't one of those women who spent forever fiddling about with skincare products and make-up. She was more of a two-minute routine sort of gal.

Mike was awake and sitting at the kitchen table flicking through the *Rowing Gazette* when she finally went back downstairs.

'Have you seen this article, talking about reorganising the points system for racing? Honestly, I've never read such a load of rubbish.' Mike eventually looked up from the magazine and did a double take.

'Are you going somewhere?'

Lesley smoothed down the sides of her tunic.

'I just got back. From rowing.'

'Ah yes. How was that? Did you manage to get out on the water?'

Lesley sat down opposite Mike and put her elbows on the table.

‘Oh Mike, it was brilliant. We were out the whole time. In two boats.’

‘Two boats, ay? How far did you get?’ asked Mike.

‘The whole way. To the top of the river then back down to the weir at the far end and back again. Everyone was fantastic. I thought we’d have forgotten how to do it, but we hadn’t. It all came back. And you know what? We had a race down the straight – and my crew won.’ Lesley’s joy spilt over and flooded the kitchen.

‘You had a race? You had a race!’ Mike’s face darkened and flecks of angry spittle flew from his mouth. As he stood up violently his chair crashed back on the floor. ‘How bloody stupid can you get. I knew this was a mistake. I just knew it. Not content with risking our two most valuable boats, they decide to have a fucking race. Well, I’m not having it. I’m not. Just you wait until I tell Stanley what they’ve been up to! Where’s my phone?’

Mike stormed out and the kitchen suddenly felt chilly.

‘It was Stanley’s idea,’ whispered Lesley to herself. Then she got up and found the biscuit tin, her eyes stinging with tears.

Connection: *Used to describe the link between the power of an athlete's legs to the force applied to the spoon of the blade. Should be made as soon as the catch is taken and held through the core muscles for the length of the work section of the stroke.*

16

BETH

Beth was the last to arrive at the Cross Baths, clutching a plastic bag with her swimming costume and flip-flops. 'I bet this place is a breeding ground for verrucas,' she muttered to herself. It was dark and the night was heavy with damp. Hurrying along the cold, slippery pavements, a fine haze of drizzle clung to her hair. It was a particularly unappealing night to get naked.

Lesley hadn't been the only one who'd wanted to keep rowing. Beth wondered if it was the heady intoxication of the home games. Or it might simply have been that sunny afternoon in August when they were reminded of something they'd all but forgotten: they loved rowing and they were good at it. Whatever it was, she and Kate were thrilled to find the whole group of women signed up to row Sunday afternoons, and quite a few asked to row Saturday afternoons as well. They had their squad.

More importantly, Kate was rowing again. She'd so enjoyed that first outing and meeting the other women - it was just what she needed. It was early days and they hardly knew each other, but it was obvious these women would have Kate's back if anything awful happened again. They weren't on their own any more.

The training was going well, although the vets were still working through the stiffness and blisters that Kate had endured a year earlier. The difference was they had each other to compare war wounds with and Kate and Beth to advise and watch out for them. Beth took the whole squad through the exercises and stretches she'd taught Kate in her kitchen, what seemed like a lifetime ago.

There was a huge amount of work each week organising crews, boats, coxes and sit-ins. Fortunately for the squad, Kate had a real gift and they simply had to turn up at the appointed time and sit in the seat specified in Kate's email, which arrived punctually every Friday lunchtime.

It seemed to be doing Kate good too. Beth still kept a close eye on her friend and was always on the lookout for signs that her mental health might be deteriorating. On the contrary, Kate seemed to be positively flourishing. Beth just hoped it continued and the squad's enthusiasm didn't fizzle out once the weather turned cold and wet. Kate said they needed to maintain the momentum, and the women were keen for the chance of a more extended conversation than outings allowed. They were all agreed: they needed a social evening. Which was why Abbie had told them all to be at the Cross Baths tonight with their swimming things.

There was a gaggle of women at the entrance, huddled in the pool of light cast by the overhead lantern. They all talked excitedly to one another. Some were flushed with excitement, like young girls on a school outing and one or two looked drawn and pale. Beth had last seen them this uncertain at the start of the taster day back in August. She imagined she was not the only one who felt uncomfortable about taking her clothes off in front of other people, despite all her years at boarding school.

The Cross Baths were in a bijou, single-storey building that might have been mistaken for an eighteenth century bungalow. It was squat and reminiscent of the top tier of a wedding cake, all hung around with swags and wreaths. Beth had walked past the building many times, but had never thought to wonder what lay inside.

She squeezed past the group blocking the entrance. Inside Abbie, who'd organised the outing, was remonstrating with the young woman in charge. Abbie looked washed out. *Burning the candle at both ends again?* She was showing the official the email confirming the booking, but the girl was having none of it. She'd been told a group of elite rowers were coming and she was not going to let them down by allowing this rabble in first.

Beth could see the thought of ripped male athletes cavorting in the thermal waters might have sounded attractive. She noted the girl's perfectly blow-dried hair and carefully applied make-up. It was little wonder she didn't want their superannuated girls' night out to gatecrash what promised to be a magical evening. Beth sympathised. Most people were more likely to take them for a book club outing than a group of athletes. Refusing to be fazed by the difficulties, Abbie produced her driving licence to prove she was the person who'd made the booking. When this made not a jot of difference, she realised the difficulty lay in the woman's refusal to accept they were actually rowers. Exasperated by the hold-up, Abbie resorted to persuading Kate and a couple of the more suitably dressed women to sit on the marble floor in a line behind her and pretend they were rowing. Realising what was going on Beth slipped past the crowd, sat cross-legged opposite Abbie, and barked the orders.

'Whole crew –

Backstops!

Light pressure!

Are you ready?

Go!'

The squad was reduced to silence while the four women in front of her went through the motions of rowing. Then, in time with their strokes, Lesley at Bow started mimicking the sound made by the blades as they bit into the water and then emerged:

'Chooo . . . . .

Haaa!

Chooo . . . . . .

Haaa!'

The rest of the squad picked up Lesley's riff to produce a soundtrack to the demonstration.

'Next stroke . . .

Firm pressure!' ordered Beth and the chorus increased the tempo as the rowers picked up the pace, following Abbie at Stroke. The crew were within striking distance of the finish line, when a man in his forties wearing the same logoed polo shirt as the girl pushed his way through the crowd.

'What on earth is going on?' he asked. With this interruption the crew collapsed giggling on the floor. Kate looked like she would never be able to stop laughing and Beth was afraid the young woman might burst into tears.

'My friends and I are trying to convince your colleague that we are rowers and that we have a reservation at your baths.' A scowling Molly gave Abbie a hand and pulled her up to her feet. Pulling her sweater down, Abbie led the manager over to the far side of the entrance hall and appeared to give him the full benefit of her opinion on his running of the facility. Beth was not someone who made a fuss, and she really admired people who were prepared to take a stand when required.

'Isn't she amazing?' Kate whispered to Beth as the pair of them watched, mesmerised.

'Blimey – she's definitely the right woman for the job.'

It only took a couple of minutes before the manager retreated, visibly chastened. He spoke briefly to the girl in the polo shirt who looked similarly shaken and then scuttled off into the night.

'This way, ladies! Apologies for the delay,' and Abbie shepherded the squad into the changing room. Curiously, they were open-air, as were the baths themselves, which meant a quick strip in the autumnal chill and a dash to the warm water. They ripped off their clothes, yanked up their swimsuits and ran on tiptoes to the water's edge. The steam rose enticingly, illuminated from within the bath and everyone waded straight in. After the nervous anticipation, the altercation in the foyer and the shock of undressing in the cold night air, the warmth enveloped them like a mother's hug.

The baths themselves were circular, and the women arranged themselves around the edge. They'd barely finished spacing themselves out and complimenting each other on their bathing suits, when the door opened and two youths in polo shirts walked in carrying trays of glass flutes and bottles of Prosecco. As they walked around, handing the chilled glasses to the group, the women stared at Abbie, open-mouthed.

'How did you do that?' asked Kate.

'It's like dealing with five year olds – I find a little

firmness goes a long way. I hope you're all planning on taking taxis because there's going to be as much as you can drink. They'll be bringing smoked salmon sandwiches as well shortly. Cheers!'

'Cheers!' chorused the women and they all raised their glasses in the swirling steam, chinking them together with their neighbours and drank deeply. The ice was well and truly broken, and everyone chatted away, nineteen to the dozen. Beth noticed Kate through the haze on the other size of the baths, quietly taking it in. She looked so happy. Beth caught her eye and mouthed at her:

'You OK?'

Kate smiled broadly in reply and nodding, mouthed back: 'You?'

Beth didn't reply to Kate but surprised even herself by calling out to the group, 'Ladies – can I make a toast? First of all, thank you to Abbie for convincing us this would be a good idea and making it happen.' With this everyone cheered and slapped the surface of the water with their free hand. 'Can I also say a massive thank you to Kate. If it was not for her, neither I nor any of you would be back rowing, our squad wouldn't have happened, and I know I for one would be the poorer. I give you – Abbie and Kate!' Once again the women raised their glasses, clinking them together and chorused,

'Abbie and Kate!'

Through the steam Beth could just make out Kate trying to disappear, which was impossible in the circumstances without sinking underwater. Beth smiled to herself.

They passed an extremely pleasant evening, taking it in turns to dash out of the water for more sandwiches and fresh bottles. They all moved around from time to time, so that by the end of the night they'd talked to nearly everyone.

Kate had barely drawn breath. All of the squad wanted to get to know her better.

As their time was drawing to a close, the women were quieter, content to wallow in the rich minerals and luxuriate in each other's company.

'Do you know,' said Lesley, attempting to disguise the smallest of ladylike burps, 'I was really worried about this evening. I didn't have time for a bikini wax. Or a pedicure. And the elastic in my cozzer's gone, so it's nearly as saggy as I am. I didn't want to come because I didn't want you to have to look at me, the state I'm in. But you know what – I've had a bloomin' brilliant time. You're all such gorgeous women. I wouldn't have missed this for anything.'

'I could've told you not to bother with the bikini wax,' said Abbie. 'I can't see a thing without my glasses and I don't suppose the rest of you can either.'

'You know what,' said Lesley, slurring her words. 'With or without my glasses on, I think we're all beautiful. Here's to us,' and she raised her glass for yet another toast.

Beth looked round the pool. Lesley was quite right. They were beautiful, and it wasn't just because she didn't have her contacts in. They were all shapes and sizes: Kate and Hilary were skinny with chiselled muscles; Abbie and Lesley tended more towards the voluptuous. Abbie reminded her of those vintage postcards of big-bosomed ladies with round smiley faces and enormous bottoms. She radiated kindness. As she looked around the billowing vapours, she saw hair scraped back or frizzy with humidity and smudged mascara. But all of them glowed with happiness and their fondness for the shared company. It was loveliness indeed.

'Do you know,' Lesley continued, 'when I told Mike what we were doing tonight he said he couldn't imagine anything more revolting than a group of middle-aged women without their clothes on.' With this she started sobbing quietly, having reached the maudlin stage of drunkenness. Abbie put her arm around her.

'Well, more fool him. I'd take us over a group of middle-aged men with no clothes, any day of the week. Can you imagine – all those beer bellies and saggy scrotums?'

'Eww!' squealed a couple of the others, and they all fell to laughing and splashing each other as if to wipe the image from their minds. Amidst the uproar, Kate waded over to Lesley and signalled for Beth to help her. The three of them staggered up the steps towards the changing rooms, Kate on one side gently holding Lesley by the arm, and Beth on the other. Lesley would need help getting dressed.

As they walked outside into the night, the cold hit them like a slap. By each taking one arm, they manhandled Lesley in the direction of the taxi rank by the station. They'd just missed the arrival of the London train, so when they reached there was one solitary cab waiting on the cobbled forecourt. They bundled Lesley into the back seat and told the driver where to take her. Kate made a note of the driver's number and knowing he could hear, instructed Lesley to text her when she arrived home.

'Not that I'm neurotic or anything,' said Kate as the car pulled away.

'No – just sensible,' said Beth.

They were left on their own in the dank gloom to wait for another taxi. Beth pursed her lips and blew out hard to produce a cloud of vapour. The street was deserted, although they could hear carousing students in the distance and the wail of a siren from the other side of town.

'Poor Lesley,' said Kate, breaking the silence. 'Living with Mike must get her down.'

'What I don't understand is, why she doesn't leave him.'

There was more silence, then Kate replied, 'Maybe she's thought about it. Maybe she thinks it isn't quite bad enough. Maybe she's afraid the alternative could be worse.'

Beth absorbed what she'd said – and for just a second she wasn't sure whether Kate was talking about Lesley or herself.

'But you know, it was dreadful of him to talk to her like that. Just dreadful. Apart from the fact it's plain rude, it's ridiculous as she's still a gorgeous woman. OK, she doesn't look the way she did twenty years ago – but then who does? Mike doesn't, for sure.'

'When I was younger . . .' Kate hesitated, but the wine had lowered her inhibitions. 'When I was younger, I was quite attractive. I used to catch men looking at me. A lot. They don't do that any more. No one looks at me. It's like I've become invisible.'

Beth had often thought how beautiful her friend was. It hadn't occurred to her that might make ageing even harder.

'I was wondering – how are things with you and Tim? How's he adjusting to rowing taking over your life?'

'Do you know, I'm not sure he's even noticed. He's usually out when I'm at the river and I don't really talk to him about it because – because we don't really talk.'

Beth was conscious her friend had made a significant confession. She hesitated. 'Does that bother you? The not talking, I mean?'

'Well, I suppose I'm used to it. He's so rarely there. But now the girls have left I'll admit – it is lonely. I think I'd go mad if I didn't have you and the others.'

'Do you think you could change it? I don't know – do a date night once a week or something? Sorry, Kate, I've no idea what I'm doing offering relationship advice. Forget I said anything.'

Kate swayed suddenly, having momentarily lost her balance. She held on to Beth's arm.

'But you're right, Beth. I should try and change it. Everything is different now the girls have left home. I'm so fricking good at fixing everyone else's problems but I don't seem to spend any time thinking about my own.'

The two friends stood in thoughtful silence. Although she'd made light of it, Beth had the impression Kate found it deeply troubling. She wondered how much Kate's marriage contributed to the state of her mental health and silently gave thanks that she herself was single and contented with her lot. Relationships seemed to cause so much misery. Having Kate as a friend had helped her see things more clearly and she'd never been happier than since she'd ended things with Mark. Her life was already full between work, rowing and friends. With their new masters squad, her cup overflowed.

Just then a black shape with its orange light illuminated loomed into view at the end of the street, signalling they would soon be home.

Part Three

October 2012

***Burst:** A small number of strokes (usually less than a minute) taken at full pressure in training.*

17

KATE

'Oi, Katie! Over here!' Half the crew were already at the club and huddled together when Kate arrived. Apart from them the place was more or less empty. It was cold and bleak. Kate hurried over to join them and greeted her crew warmly.

It was now late October and Somerset Union, the club at the end of their stretch of river was holding a head race. Training had been going well and Molly was pleased with their progress, so Kate had taken a deep breath and entered an eight. There had been minor setbacks, of course: Lesley had a heavy cold, a couple of them had child-care issues, Abbie had a few non-specific family problems. Such was the fabric of these women's lives. Achieving anything required a level of tenacity and flexibility that was exhausting in itself.

Fortunately they'd managed to form a squad large enough to cope with the vicissitudes of life. Increasingly there was a sense of solidarity amongst the women, so those who'd only signed up to row on Sundays moved heaven and earth to act as substitute on Saturdays when required. Beth regularly asked the Senior Women to help out, but they were always too busy.

In some ways the race that day was a non-event. Kate's eight was the only women's masters crew entering, so there was no one comparable to race against. As the oldest women rowing, they would expect to be the slowest adult crew on the river which had the potential to be demoralising. On the other hand, it was an opportunity to row under race conditions without having to travel to another river or transport their boat anywhere.

Their boat. Of course the shell they trained in was not actually 'their' boat. It was easy to start thinking of *Cressida* that way as she was always sitting on the shelf for them, quietly waiting when they arrived for their outings. They noticed the footgear had to be readjusted each time, and some of them had to remember to reset the height of their gate. Sometimes they would joke about the irritation of other people using 'their' boat.

The reality was that in a small community club the equipment had to be shared, and inevitably the best equipment and sessions tended to be assigned to those with the sharpest elbows. Beth and Kate had so far avoided wrangles over boat use by making the decision to row at times when no one else wanted to.

Entering this race had been the first real opportunity for a showdown as both Kate's crew and the Senior Women wanted to row in *Cressida*. However, as everyone wanted to be in a morning division, Kate had a quiet word with the entry-secretary and made sure they were in the last division of the afternoon, deftly side-stepping the potential for a punch-up.

They'd all arrived promptly and even Beth was only a few minutes late. As predicted, the races were behind schedule and it would be quite a wait before they boated. Kate was relieved they had the club to themselves. Most crews had already raced and were no doubt rehydrating in the Waterman.

Apart from not wanting to run into any of her tormentors, she really didn't want them watching her veteran crew. She could imagine the sniggering and snide remarks. She just wanted to be able to complete their row without worrying what anyone else was thinking. The other members would see her crew's time when it was published, but at least Kate wouldn't be present to hear their mockery.

It had rained heavily over the last few days, and there had been concerns the race might be cancelled. Beth, Kate and Molly went down to the dock to take a look at the river. It was not as high as one might have expected. The water barely covered the fixed pontoons. The sky was leaden and heavy, but mercifully there was no wind. Mysterious eddies swirled in the sombre stream, taunting and enigmatic. People drowned in this stretch of water every year. Alcohol was invariably involved but it was easy to underestimate the river's potential as a malignant force.

Eventually the solitary Albion crew from the previous division returned, which meant it would soon be time to boat. Molly and Kate had a word with the returning boat's cox to ask about conditions.

'It was fine going down but we ran into an awful lot of debris coming back. I've a feeling they've just opened the sluice gates to release the flood-water as the head was supposed to be finished by now. Keep a good eye out. Those big logs can really take a dent out of your boat.'

The crew finished their warm-up on the ergs. The boat was already out and adjusted, so they took her straight down to the river and paddled up to the start.

As Molly slowly guided the eight upstream, ahead lay some fifty boats of all sizes from singles to eights. Her task was to position their boat on the far bank in start order. This was tricky enough at the best of times, trying to steer an expensive piece of kit in a tight space. But the number of entries from schools compounded the problem. Not only were the crews inexperienced, but the coxes were normally the same year group and struggled to assert themselves over their classmates.

Hence the river was jammed with eights drifting with the powerful current, each bearing nine small boys bickering. Marshals bundled up in fluorescent buoyancy aids and bobbing up and down on safety boats, bellowed through megaphones at the hapless crews. As no one could make out what they were saying, all it did was add to the noise and confusion.

Molly stopped alongside a safety boat and asked where their number would slot in. The marshal indicated a stumpy willow tree about fifty metres further up, and Molly moved the crew on. They inched along at half slide and light pressure, creeping forward as openings in the mayhem appeared. The current was getting stronger. Kate felt anxious. It was such a relief to know all she had to do was row. It was up to Molly to look after the boat, and Kate had absolute confidence in her. It was a good feeling.

After a couple of skirmishes and near misses, Molly guided her crew into the space between the boats before and after them in the running order. They would have to maintain this position until they were called forward, in spite of the current which seemed particularly fast. It was likely to be quite a wait. Before they boated, Molly had made sure her crew were well wrapped up so they didn't get cold waiting at the start. Now her job was to help them to stay calm. Nerves were running high and waiting in a state of tension would not help their performance.

Kate, at Stroke, was facing downstream in the direction of the start and updated Molly on progress. Finally she whispered that the boat ahead was starting to turn. Molly snapped into action.

'Tops off, ladies. We've a race to get to.' While the women stripped down to their green vests, Molly reminded them of the game plan.

'Remember, this is just like a regular outing. This is our river and you've rowed this piece dozens of times before. You can do this. You have the fitness and the technique. We're not expecting to beat any course records. We just want a solid, proficient row. Make sure that when we go past the boathouse we give the rest of Albion something to think about. And don't hold anything back. We need to lay down some solid work in the first half. You've done the training. That and the adrenaline will see you through to the end. Number off from Bow when ready.'

The women numbered off promptly, and as she called out 'Stroke!', Kate had a momentary jolt of fear. Molly moved them away from the bank, spun and headed down towards the start. The priority was to settle the crew into a solid, efficient rhythm they could maintain for three kilometres. As soon as they started rowing Kate felt better. The boat had never sat so well or the timing been better. With the pressure of a race, every woman was focussed like never before. Their blades chopped in together and they sped along.

'I can see the start umpire up ahead.

Next stroke!

Half pressure!'

As they approached the invisible line across the river, Molly opened the throttle. When they crossed it a horn sounded and she called out:

'And we're racing!
Keep it steady!
Keep it long!'

Never had Kate felt the boat move at this speed. They were galloping. After a couple of hundred metres they passed the Albion dock. A solitary voice called out, 'Go, Albion!' but was lost on the wind. Metre after metre the women worked, focussing element by element on every aspect of their craft: catches, drive, finishes, recovery. Then back to the beginning, polishing and perfecting as they went, ensuring every stroke was as near perfect as they could make it.

Kate knew the real challenge would come once fatigue set in. At that point it was as much a mental challenge: could you maintain your efficient stroke when your whole body was screaming for mercy?

'Catches!
Drive!
Finishes!
Recovery!'

The cox's calls become a mantra to focus on every tiny component of each stroke.

They rounded the first bend shortly after the start and passed the wreckage of the junior eight that had been in front of them. It had become impaled on the bank after taking too tight a line. Marshals were running to their aid as boys abandoned ship and splashed their way to the bank.

'Eyes in the boat!' Kate snapped her gaze firmly to a point above Molly's head.

Having overtaken the schoolboys' eight, there were no other crews in sight. Without another boat as pacemaker it would be hard to tell if they were doing well or badly. Molly steered an impressive line through the series of bends. There was a significant home advantage in head races, knowing the optimum course and how to position yourself.

They shot through the road bridge. *Halfway.* This was when the tiredness would start to show. Kate could feel her blade becoming heavier as the crew's catches grew sloppy. Molly shouted ***'Catches!'*** and the weight vanished from Kate's oar. The boat leapt forward. Once they were on the straight the excitement would see them through. The important thing was not to lose speed in the middle section of the race.

'You're on the way home!
You've got this!
You've done it before!
You know you can do it!
Another seven minutes and it will all be over!
Keep it crisp!
Keep it long!
Hold those finishes in!'

Each call was in time with their stroke, and with each instruction the blade work became crisper. The boat speed on Kate's display jumped up. *Look up, Kate. Don't worry about the speed. Concentrate on your rowing.*

'Keep it there, ladies!
This is good work!'

They were on the final straight. As the crew recognised how close they were to the finish, Kate felt a surge in energy from them, like horses quickening to a gallop as they turn for home. With 1,000 metres to go they would all be hurting. Kate's legs felt limp and her chest hurt. Everything was begging for rest.

Catches, drive, finishes, recovery.

On she went, gritting her teeth and concentrating hard

on not letting anything slip. At this stage she could not take squaring for granted. Placing the spoon in the water just a few degrees away from true would result in a crab at this speed. Exhausted hands could not necessarily be relied upon to do this accurately. One momentary loss of concentration could see their race end in disaster.

Focus. Drive. Push . . .

Wash: *The wake from a motorised boat, disliked by rowers as the wash affects the boat stability and can cause water to flood over the gunwales.*

18

BETH

Beth and the crew burst through the door of the Waterman, cheeks flushed and eyes shining. They'd finished their race. They hadn't messed up and there'd been no disaster. It had been a good solid row with nothing to be ashamed about.

It was late afternoon but most of the crews who'd rowed earlier were still there, on their second or third pints. A couple of them waved to Beth. She wasn't sure Kate would agree to come as she hadn't entirely managed to put the online bullying behind her. Beth assured her that most people in the club either hadn't read the stuff on Facebook or had long since forgotten it, but even as she said it she knew that wasn't the point. Thankfully, Kate was persuaded to join them, not wanting to miss out on the team celebration. Hopefully she'd feel safe with her seven crew mates as wingmen.

She noticed none of their crew had invited their families along, Kate included. Beth realised head racing was not an especially spectator-friendly sport, and besides, she could imagine the women wanted to focus on what they were doing without other distractions. When you had no partner to invite, it was easy to imagine having someone come and watch must be a good thing. She was starting to learn from her crew that wasn't necessarily the case.

As this occasion came loosely under the umbrella of a 'social', Abbie took charge and made camp at the far end of the bar room. She announced she was buying Prosecco for everyone and wouldn't truck any argument. With everyone else deep in animated conversation, Beth suggested to Kate it would be politic to say hello to the other members. She whispered, 'We don't have to speak to everyone. And I'm right here with you.' Beth recognised it took considerable courage and determination on Kate's part to mingle with the rest of the club. Hopefully, after this first step, she would find it easier.

Everyone was in high spirits. Beth stopped to ask Jack's crew how they'd got on as she'd coxed them from time to time. The four men were in their forties. One was exceptionally tall and lanky, his cheeks pitted with acne scars. The others were not short but carried a staggering amount of ballast around their waists. They were friends of old and fiercely loyal. Jack was at the bar ordering drinks.

'Nice to see you ladies getting out,' said the skinny one. 'Did you manage to finish?'

Beth was floored by the question but fortunately Jack interrupted them with a new round of beers.

'Wotcha, Beth. Kate. Great to see you guys here. I can't believe you got a racing crew together after – what? – a couple of months? What an achievement. Boys – do you have any idea what these two women have achieved?'

They were all too busy arguing about which was their pint and who had ordered what, to treat the question as more than rhetorical. Kate asked how the race had gone for them and Jack was characteristically upbeat while acknowledging the unlikelihood they would be troubling the umpires for medals.

'Seriously, though, I'm totally in awe of what you're doing. Just make sure you keep it going,' and Jack beamed his warmest smile at them. The two of them moved on. Beth spied Stanley at the bar in earnest conversation with Mike, the Club Captain.

'If you're going to let so many junior small boats enter you're just asking for trouble . . .' Mike said as Beth joined them.

'Afternoon, gentlemen. How are you doing?' asked Beth.

'Not bad,' said Mike. 'I'm hoping for some good results from today.' He'd rowed in a veteran men's eight first thing in the morning and had been helping with the marshalling ever since.

'When do we hear?' asked Kate.

'I expect the times will be on the noticeboard at Somerset quite soon, if someone wants to drive down there. They'll put the times up online at some point as well.'

'What did you think, Stanley? Did you see us?' Beth couldn't help herself.

'Yes I did, just before the start. You were looking pretty tidy then. So long as you all had fun and got the boat back in one piece.'

Beth felt deflated and could see Kate making a face so she turned away and squeezed through the crowd to reach the Senior Women's table. Chloe was sitting at the far end and all heads were turned towards her. Kate said hello to the Women's Captain and Three who were closest to them and they were soon deep in conversation. The Women's Captain was obsessing about how her crew had done against the Somerset Senior Women.

Taking place on their own river, this race was a local

derby between the two neighbouring clubs. When they saw each other away at distant and more prestigious races, they cheered for each other and shared logistics and equipment. When racing at home, it was a grudge match and the Albion Senior Women were entirely focussed on beating the Somerset eight. The local university had entered a crew that included a number from the GB development squad and Beth knew they had no realistic hope of beating them, but a Somerset scalp would see honour satisfied.

They chatted about the race, the weather and how the Senior Women's training was going. No one asked Kate or Beth how their crew had fared, despite both of them standing there in race kit. Finally the captain remembered her manners and asked, 'And how did your ladies get on? Did you get my boat back in one piece?'

'Yes, *Cressida*'s still in one piece,' said Beth slightly wearily. 'We'd been told there was a lot of debris in the water but we managed to miss it.'

'They must have opened the sluice gates early,' said the captain. 'All that rain we had over the last few days, they were going to have to let it down some time. What a shame they couldn't wait until the end of the day. I'm sure someone will be going home with some nasty dents.'

'To be fair, it should have been over well before. The head was running so late by the last division,' said Beth.

'The Somerset Head always runs hours behind. They should know that,' snipped the captain. Crowing laughter interrupted them from the far end of the table. Chloe was enjoying holding court, laughing at someone's whispered comment and bestowing cloying smiles on her entourage. Beth decided to retreat and signalled to Kate to follow.

'Well done,' said Beth as they made their way back through the crowd.

'Well, no one can say we didn't make an effort,' Kate whispered back.

They rejoined their crew who were opening their third bottle. Abbie knew how to make a party go and her companions needed no encouragement. Beth looked at the joyful faces around the table and basked in their elation. To see these women, who barely knew each other a few months ago, bonded by this shared achievement, it was truly heart-warming. Yes, it was only the poxy Somerset Head. All they had done was row their own river while someone timed them. But it was more than that, and every one of them knew it. Every single one of them had conquered her own personal demons to be part of that race today. Simply finishing the race in style was a real achievement. Their time was immaterial.

Abbie came back from the bar carrying yet another bottle of Prosecco and a couple of plates of steaming chips.

'Tuck in ladies – you've earned it,' she called. The women dived in, then dunked great handfuls of fries in the bowls of ketchup before shoving them into their mouths, laughing at their appalling behaviour.

'Steady on,' said Sal. 'Leave some for Molly.'

'Don't worry about me,' said Molly. 'I haven't done any exercise,'

'Oh I think you'll find you burnt off quite a lot of calories in nervous energy back there,' said Beth.

'More chips coming,' said Abbie, as two more platefuls were deposited on the table.

'Oh my God, isn't this bliss?' said Kate. 'Being able to make a complete pig of yourself and feeling completely justified.'

'I suspect we all smell like a farmyard as well, but no one cares because we're all as bad as each other,' said Lesley.

They carried on slurping their drinks and gorging on fries.

'This is rich living,' said Abbie, and they all laughed for absolutely no good reason other than they were perfectly contented.

Just then Beth noticed the pub had fallen silent, but for a quiet but frantic buzzing of voices. She looked across the room and saw the Senior Women clustered about Chloe. A couple of them had their arms around her. She was crying. Bow proffered handfuls of red paper napkins in lieu of tissues. Beth noticed the men were all staring at the group and speaking among themselves in hushed tones. All attention was focussed on Chloe. Beth wondered what on earth had happened. Bad news of an aged relative perhaps? A blip in a romantic liaison? It was difficult to imagine something so terrible that it could transform the mood of the entire pub. By now the other women in Beth's crew had noticed the change in the atmosphere and had lowered their voices.

'What do you think it is?' whispered Kate.

'I don't know,' said Beth. 'I'll go and ask Jack.' He was standing at the bar, waiting for his round to be poured. He had his back to the bar and was looking over towards the Senior Women. Beth sidled in beside him and ordered a bottle. She didn't say anything initially, but waited until Jack turned back to the bar and smiled at her.

'Is Chloe OK?' asked Beth. 'Has she had some bad news?'

'You could say that. One of my crew just got the results up on his phone,' said Jack, his habitual wide grin firmly in place.

'Oh, don't say they got beaten by Somerset. I'm not surprised she's upset,' said Beth.

'Oh, it's much worse than that. They were beaten by your crew, Beth. Cheers!' and with this Jack raised his pint and took a giant slurp of Doom Bar.

As Beth made her way back to her crew, she struggled to contain the conflicting emotions competing to explode from her breast. As she put the bottle down on the table, all eyes were fixed on her.

'Well?' asked Molly. 'What on earth has happened?'

'You're not going to believe this,' said Beth quietly. 'They've just got the results up. Apparently we beat the Senior Women.'

'What?'

'You're kidding me!'

'That's ridiculous!' The chorus of voices sounded with shock and disbelief.

Molly said firmly, 'Let's not get ahead of ourselves. Can someone check it out?'

With a flourish Abbie produced her pink sparkly smartphone to look up the Somerset website. There was a hiatus as no one had their reading glasses to hand, but finally Kate had the list and read out the times.

University of Wells	12 minutes 45 seconds
Albion Women's Masters C	13 minutes 5 seconds
Somerset Senior Women	13 minutes 15 seconds
Albion Senior Women	13 minutes 25 seconds

No one quite believed it and they all had to take their turn with Abbie's glittery phone and Kate's specs. When they'd all confirmed it for themselves, there was a silence like a vacuum around the table.

'Holy shit,' said Lesley staring at the empty bowl of chips.

'Holy shit indeed,' said Abbie who was also staring down at nothing in particular. Then like a chemical reaction, the women simultaneously leapt to their feet, shouting and screaming and hugging each other. Kate and Beth remained seated, too stunned to move.

'Christ. The brown stuff is really going to hit the fan now,' said Kate gloomily. 'If they didn't like us before, they're really going to hate us now. You do know we only beat them because the stream got faster when they opened the sluice gates? All that floodwater that was being held back would have acted like a tidal current, carrying us along.'

'Yes, I'm sure the stream did get faster which will have made us a bit quicker,' replied Beth, 'But all the same, we beat them by quite a margin. I would love to know how we'd have compared racing at the same time. And I don't think it matters what Chloe and her mates think. They never did us any favours before, so how much worse can it be? Plus, we may have won ourselves a few supporters.'

Indeed, when they finally filed out of the Waterman, they were met with calls of 'well done' and 'well rowed'. Kate tugged at Beth's arm excitedly, clearly thrilled by the enthusiasm of the other members. Beth felt positively giddy as they headed out to the road to find their taxi. It was not just the wine that had gone to her head.

***Fin:** A piece of metal or plastic attached to the underside of the boat towards the stern. Provides directional stability by preventing sideways slippage.*

19

LESLEY

The next morning dawned bright and unseasonably warm. After the rain of the previous week it was a relief to wake to sunshine forcing its way round the faded edges of the chintz curtains. Lesley stretched luxuriously. She couldn't remember the last time she'd stayed in bed this late. Mike woke her so early at the weekends as he dressed to go to the rowing club, she normally got up shortly after and started her day. This morning the senior men's crew that Mike coached had given themselves the day off because of the race. Mike was not rowing himself until later, so he was crashing around downstairs.

Lesley rolled onto her side and winced. Everything hurt. She'd thought she'd been getting fitter, but yesterday's race had really taken it out of her. She flung on a shabby but comforting housecoat, pulled it around her pudgy stomach and shuffled downstairs. Mike had what looked like an outboard motor sitting on the kitchen table. On closer inspection Lesley could see it was indeed an outboard motor. He was bent over it muttering and gesticulating with a spanner.

'Morning,' said Lesley cheerfully. There was no reply. She filled the kettle, opened the fridge door and stared inside for inspiration. 'Can I make you some breakfast?' Still there came no reply. Lesley shut the fridge door and went over to where Mike was bent over the motor. He was still recognisably the man she'd fallen in love with thirty years ago, still lean as a whippet although his hair was quite white now. She put her arms around his waist, leant her cheek against his back and murmured in a husky voice, 'Can I tempt 'ee to a full English?'

'I just can't get this blessed thing to shift,' said Mike throwing the spanner down on the kitchen table and shaking off Lesley's embrace in the same forceful movement. He walked over to the place where his toolbox lay on the floor and rootled around among the jumble of spanners, screwdrivers and odds and ends.

'Tea?' asked Lesley, and when this met with no response she gave up, and went back to trying to decide what to make for herself. She switched on the radio only to find the morning service. She shuddered at the sound of the pious singing and switched it off. She made tea and scrambled eggs and sat at the table eating it, watching what Mike was doing. Finally he decided he was satisfied with his repair and threw his spanner back in the toolbox. It missed and skidded across the kitchen floor. He made himself a cup of instant coffee, spilling it on the counter as he stirred it, and sat at the table opposite Lesley. She eyed him cautiously as he sipped at his coffee, still too hot to drink comfortably.

'What did you think about yesterday?' asked Lesley.

'What do you mean? What about yesterday?' queried Mike sounding tetchy.

'What did you think about my crew?'

'What about them?'

'How did we row?'

'I haven't really thought about it. It was a busy day for me, you know.'

'Yes, I do know. But we're a club crew. You might have taken some interest in what we were doing. Do you realise, you never actually said "well done" or anything? Were you proud of me, rowing like that? Were you proud of all of us?' She was starting to feel slightly tearful. Mike leant over and took Lesley's hand.

'Of course, I'm proud of you,' he said in the sort of voice people normally reserve for small children. 'I'm always proud of my little Dinkums.' With this he got up, kissed Lesley on the top of her head and left the room. A few minutes later he reappeared with his foul weather jacket on, heaved the motor off the kitchen table and left the house, leaving a faint odour of engine oil behind.

Lesley sighed. That was Mike's baby voice, something they'd shared at tender moments since they first met. It used to make her feel loved and close. For some reason it didn't work any more. Why was that? Was it her fault? Had she changed? She sighed again and got up to put some coffee on to brew. She needed something to go with it. A doughnut. She'd earned it after all. She'd buy a newspaper at the same time and have a really spoiling morning. With this thought Lesley threw on a pair of jeans and a baggy sweater and headed out of the door.

At the supermarket she picked up a few things she needed for supper, her newspaper and a bag of doughnuts. It really was outrageous you could only buy a bag of ten when all you wanted was one. If she had any sense, Lesley thought, she'd have emptied nine of them into the bin outside the supermarket before she left the car park, but it seemed such a waste. If she were truly honest, she knew she was going to eat them all, and then would hide the bag under the other rubbish in the bin so Mike wouldn't see it. Lesley knew because that was what always happened. She also knew that even the whole loathsome mess of grease and sugar couldn't fill the emptiness she felt inside. She flung the offending package onto the passenger seat and headed home, trying to ignore the siren call of sugary temptation wafting up from the paper bag.

A few minutes later Lesley passed the turning to Kate's. Then without consciously thinking about it or knowing what she was doing, she turned the steering wheel, went round the roundabout again and drove to Kate's house. As she knocked on the door Lesley suddenly felt ridiculous. What was she doing there at that time on a Sunday morning? Kate would be busy. She was bound to have lots of things to do with her family. It wasn't as if she even knew her that well, certainly not well enough to pitch up unannounced. She'd just decided to scuttle off home when the door opened. Kate's broad smile on seeing her crewmate was reassurance enough. Lesley raised the brown paper bag level with her face and rattled it at Kate.

'Don't suppose I could beg a coffee off you?' said Lesley.

'Of course. What a lovely surprise,' said Kate, pulling her crewmate in through the door. 'I was feeling quite flat after yesterday with no one to talk to about it. You're just the person I need. Come on in.'

'I don't want to interrupt if you're busy with your family . . .' said Lesley.

'Actually, I'm quite alone. The girls are away and Tim's out cycling. You're saving me from a pile of ironing.' With this she marched Lesley down to the kitchen, put the coffee on to brew and arranged the doughnuts on a plate. Lesley eyed up the large and comfortable kitchen. A shelf above the Aga displayed a collection of green jugs, all slightly quirky and each a thing of beauty. Everywhere was clean and tidy, but it had the feeling of having been well used. It was scuffed and homely and all the more welcoming for that.

They talked through the race of the preceding day, reliving the experience. Lesley didn't mind when Kate repeated herself. Some things have to be said out loud, and sometimes they have to be said several times. After a while, they'd retold everything that needed to be remembered, and they sat quietly, lost in pleasant thoughts about the day before. They'd been so busy talking, neither of them had touched the doughnuts.

'Tell me – can I ask – what did Mike have to say? About our performance, I mean?'

'Erm . . . he didn't say anything,' said Lesley, slightly embarrassed.

'He must have said something.'

'Actually, no, not a word. I did try to ask him this morning but he just fobbed me off,' said Lesley, feeling her eyes prickling with tears.

'Does that mean he thinks we're rubbish and didn't want to hurt your feelings?'

'No, it doesn't mean that,' said Lesley emphatically. 'At least, he might think we're rubbish, but that isn't why he wouldn't talk about it. He never talks about my things. He's not once asked me how an outing went in all these months. It gets me so cross. He's obsessed about every other crew at the club. Do you know, today was the first Sunday since I can remember I haven't been woken up at half five by him getting up to coach another crew. He spends every spare minute he's not at work helping other people at the club, but he hasn't lifted a finger to help us.' By the end of this

Lesley was feeling quite overwrought, and she could feel her colour rising.

Kate put a calming hand on Lesley's and said, 'I know it's not the same, but if it's any comfort my husband hasn't asked me anything about it either.'

'Really?' asked Lesley, eyes widening with genuine surprise. 'But you have the perfect family, the perfect husband . . .'

'Oh really? Who told you that?'

'I don't know, I suppose I must have assumed . . . The perfect house, two lovely children. I guess I imagined you had the whole package. I mean – you've got an Aga, for pity's sake!'

'I hate to break it to you, but I think you've been watching too many chick flicks.'

'Well, at least you got married.'

'How long have you two been together?'

'Nearly twenty years,' said Lesley.

'Wow, that's a long time. Would it be nosey of me to ask why you never got married?'

'Oh, I don't know. I suppose there was never a time when we both felt simultaneously it was good enough to make that sort of commitment. When we met we were moving around a lot with our jobs so it wasn't even on the cards. Then, when we were more settled, we both had doubts. Mike has proposed a few times – usually when he was in the doghouse for one reason or another. So I was never likely to accept. Plus Mike never wanted kids so it wasn't like there was any pressure to make a decision.'

They both sat in silence for a moment, absorbing what she'd revealed. Finally Kate broke the silence, asking in a tentative voice, 'And how about you? Did you ever want children?'

Lesley hesitated, weighing up whether to fob Kate off with a flippant comment or to trust Kate with the truth.

'Yes. I did. I wanted them very much. I wanted everything you've got. But how could I have a child with a man who didn't want them, especially when it was all so . . . brittle?' She had to think hard to find the right word.

Her thoughts went back to that time when it had felt as if both her mind and body craved a pregnancy as if it were heroin. She'd struggled to think about anything else, and each month when the blood came she'd mourned another child that was not to be. Her unhappiness had placed a strain on the relationship and it had felt even more precarious than before. It was an impossible situation and the one thing she knew was not an option was to bring a baby into that toxic environment.

She could have left. She probably should have left. But she loved Mike, and it felt as if their relationship, however shabby, was better than nothing. So she hung in there and gradually the sharpness of her monthly sorrow lessened. And as the regularity of her periods began to falter she almost felt as if she were reconciled to the way things were.

'Somehow Mike and I made it through and we're still together. I'm still here, but there are no children and now it's too late.' The enormity of this reality hung in the air, heavy with pain and regret. Both women stared at the plate of doughnuts, examining the individual grains of sugar that clung to the greasy lumps. Kate looked as if the idea of her friend's unfulfilled longing was almost unbearable. Softly she asked, 'Did you ever think of leaving him?'

Lesley hesitated. Unused to baring her soul, she was already finding the conversation difficult. She hardly knew Kate, after all.

As if sensing her uncertainty, Kate said, 'I've never

actually told anyone this . . .' She stopped, and Lesley noticed she was screwing up her hands into tight balls. Lesley looked at her quizzically. Kate took a deep breath as if she was mustering all of her inner resources. 'I've never admitted this to anyone, but I regularly ask myself whether I should leave Tim.'

Lesley's eyebrows shot up to her hairline and her own misery was temporarily forgotten.

'You're kidding me! Oh Kate, I'm so sorry. There's me and my big mouth. Assuming you were living the dream. I had no idea it was so bad. You always look so . . . I don't know, like you've got your shit together.'

'Well, how can I explain? It isn't so bad. We don't argue. It's not like Tim hits me or has other women. It's just – I'm not happy and it's so long since I have been I don't even realise it most of the time. I'm just used to it.' She paused here and looked up at Lesley's astonished face. 'Do you know what, I don't think I know a single woman who's in a long relationship who doesn't sometimes wonder if she'd be better off out of it.'

'So what stops you leaving?' asked Lesley.

Kate was now staring at the plate and had started pushing a couple of grains of sugar around in a loop.

'You'll laugh – I make a mental checklist of pros and cons.'

'You do love your lists, Kate!'

'The thing I've always got stuck on is the kids. They're the best thing I've ever done and I gave up so much to give them the upbringing I wanted them to have. Moving to Bath, giving up a promising career for a part-time job. Why would I blow all that by leaving their father? It would be like all the sacrifice had been for nothing.'

'But your youngest has recently left home, hasn't she?'

'Well yes, exactly.' Kate finally looked up and met Lesley's gaze. 'So speaking personally, I'm all out of excuses. Either I find a way to be happy as we are or I need to do something about it.'

Lesley was looking deep into Kate's eyes as if seeing her for the first time. Kate's face was a study in warmth and empathy.

'So how's it for you, Lesley? Do you ever make a list?'

'Oh, regularly.' Lesley laughed. But as she reflected on what Kate was asking, she could feel herself getting angry. She knew her face would be soon be flushed and mottled. 'I think about it all the time. Never quite good enough to get married. Never quite bad enough to leave. So here I am, twenty years later and stuck.'

With this she felt a tear trickle down her plump cheek. Kate fetched a box of tissues and Lesley blew her nose noisily and mopped up her face. They sat in silence, her friend holding her hand, lost in sad thoughts of missed opportunities and unborn children.

After a few minutes Kate brightened and said, 'Do you fancy a walk? It's the first nice day we've had in ages.'

Lesley agreed readily as she could feel herself stiffening up, and the two of them set out. It was indeed a glorious day for October and the sunshine had to be savoured when it appeared. The fresh air lifted their spirits and they were soon joking and laughing. If truth be told, it was not just being outdoors: the exchange of confessions had been cathartic. Lesley felt lighter for unburdening herself. She didn't have many close female friends, and she was not in the habit of revealing too much about herself.

They headed up a track that led to woods, winding its way through the trees to a series of lakes concealed in a bowl scooped out of the landscape. Its meanderings were punctuated by first, a mock-gothic ruin and then a confection of a Georgian orangerie, all glass and pale limestone.

As they dived into the spinney above the lake, they were enveloped in a world of russet and coppery brown. Lesley loved the beech trees at this time of year. It was a joy to see the first fluorescent green leaves emerging in spring, but their real glory lay in the explosion of autumnal colour. Just as the world was anticipating the bleakness of the winter to come, they staged this glorious display as if in defiance.

Back at the house they let themselves into the kitchen through the back door, re-energised by the fresh air. Kate shrugged off her shoes and went to clear the table.

'We never ate the doughnuts.'

'Do you know what – I don't think I fancy them now,' said Lesley, and she emptied the plate decisively into the bin.

Pressure: *The amount of effort applied by the athlete to the power phase of the stroke.*

20

KATE

'We need to set our next goal.' Kate had come over to Beth's house for a quiet Wednesday night supper. It was early December and they were making the most of the last few weeks of peace before the Christmas frenzy began. She was sitting in Beth's kitchen nursing a glass of wine while Beth stirred something on the stove.

'Ta da!' said Beth, putting a plate in front of her. Beth had knocked up a very passable pea risotto, although Kate had to stop herself from trying to identify how she might have improved it. As she forked it into her mouth she had the sensation of being watched and glanced up to see, high on top of a cupboard, a stuffed pine marten in a glass case peering down at her. Beth's kitchen was eclectic. The shelves of an over-sized dresser were crammed with ornate porcelain and a white bust of a coy young woman perched incongruously on a countertop. It could not have been more different to Kate's and she adored it.

'Without a tangible goal there's a danger everyone will start losing interest when it all gets too difficult and will drift away.'

Taking part in the Somerset Head a few weeks earlier had

clearly had an impact on the squad and Kate sensed a change in the women's attitude to their training. There seemed to be greater commitment and they needed a sit-in far less often. Indeed, a number of the squad were pulling double outings by sitting in for the Senior Women's crew. More of them were becoming regulars at erg training and circuits, and three of them now had a regular Thursday afternoon slot when they trained together on their own. There was a sense of determination that was encouraging. But despite everything, Kate was only too well aware it would not last forever. They needed to maintain the momentum.

'Well, how about doing Vesta next March?'

They'd talked about the veterans' head race ever since Jack had mentioned it at the skittles night. It was a daunting prospect. It was the same race course as WEHORR, the Head of the River and all the other big races that took place on the Tideway. It was long but it was more the conditions that made it so testing. The Thames was nothing like their own familiar river. It was wide, deep and fast. The tidal stream was a force to be reckoned with, and the currents and whirlpools could be lethal. It would be a huge challenge and complicated to organise.

'How on earth will we get *Cressida* to London?' said Kate, already considering the problem.

'Actually, our first task will be to persuade the committee to even let us take her,' said Beth darkly. Kate was confused. Why should there be a problem? Beth reluctantly owned up to the difficulties she'd encountered in securing the use of the boats for the taster day. Kate was bewildered.

'No, there must have been some misunderstanding. It makes no sense. Why would they behave like that?'

'Well, interestingly, the lovely Jack happened to overhear

what was going on. His take on it was the problem was because we're women.'

'Not that we're too old?'

'Well . . . that too, he said.'

'Crikey,' said Kate, and they both sat in silence for a few minutes, turning the thing over and over. Finally she asked, 'Do you think he's right?'

Beth didn't know, but the experience had made her cautious about assuming anything where the club was concerned.

'One thing I can tell you - the first question the committee will ask is, who's coxing us, as that's the person who'll be responsible for getting the boat back in one piece.'

'Sounds like we'd better have a chat with Molly.'

It was crucial to convince Molly it was a good idea. If she wasn't prepared to do it then all bets would be off as they'd struggle to persuade anyone else to cox them. And it was far from a given she'd agree. Racing on the Tideway was as daunting for a cox as it was for a crew. The stream on the Thames was so fast, a cox could win or lose a race depending on the course she took. It was essential to stay in the jet of fast water but following its course was fiendishly difficult as it was pushed from bank to bank as the river meandered in massive loops.

Apart from steering, the cox was responsible for their safety and the conditions on the Tideway could be treacherous. Coxing Vesta would be a challenge, and Kate knew they'd already pushed Molly hard to simply take up coxing again. She was an outstanding cox, but she'd lost confidence in recent years and Kate knew, from personal experience, how hard that made things. She'd seen how each time Molly had confronted her fears and overcome them she'd visibly grown in self-belief. But Molly could easily decide this was too hard and she didn't want to test herself in this way. To be fair, there were those who thought a woman of Molly's age should stick to Tai Chi rather than extreme racing on the Tideway. It would not be unreasonable if Molly chose to agree with them.

The good news was that Molly had coxed and rowed the Tideway on many occasions in the past. The less good news was it was quite a long way in the past.

Kate and Beth broached the subject with her over tea the following Sunday after their outing. As ambushes go, it was pretty subtle, although Kate's freshly baked lemon drizzle cake was possibly a clue they were after something.

'So, Molly. Beth and I, that is, we were wondering . . . what do you know about racing on the Tideway?'

Without any need for prompting, Molly started reeling off the occasions she'd raced or coxed it: the year, the race, who was in the boat and so on. Anxious to get Molly on side, Kate hung on her every word. But by the time Molly had got to the Head of the River, 2002, and was racking her brains to remember who had been at Stroke, Kate was starting to lose the will to live. Beth interrupted:

'The thing is Molly, you're obviously terrifically experienced. How do you fancy doing it again? With us?'

Beth had taken a deep breath before she asked this last question and Kate sat on tenterhooks, waiting for the response. They both looked at Molly expectantly. It was ominously quiet. Molly didn't look particularly surprised by the question. Presumably the idea of Vesta had already occurred to her. She looked deep in thought, as if she were turning over the question in her mind.

'We know it's a big ask. You wouldn't have to give us an answer straight away, but we would love you to do it,' gushed Kate.

'There's a lot to think about,' said Molly, picking her words carefully. She paused. 'One thing I will say is, I've no doubt your crew can do it and put in a respectable performance.' There was another pause. 'Have you worked out how you're going to get the boat there?'

'We haven't even asked if we can use a boat yet,' said Beth. 'We thought we should secure a cox first.'

'Oh, that won't be a problem. I'll sort it out with Stanley. I'll ask him as well if any other crews are going and the club is planning to send the trailer,' said Molly.

'So does that mean you'll do it?' asked Beth excitedly.

'I suspect I'm going to live to regret it, but yes I'll do it,' said Molly, and the two younger women flung their arms around her and jigged up and down. Kate felt as if she'd won something already, and in a sense she had. There would no doubt be many more obstacles to overcome before they found themselves on the start line at Vesta, but already they seemed to have solved the biggest problems.

The following Sunday, the conditions were particularly blustery. As Kate, Beth and Molly checked out the river before the outing, it was running dark and high. The wind was whipping up the surface of the water into white horses and sinister vortices peppered the water in front of them. It was not good.

'Are you OK for us to go out in this?' asked Kate.

'Any other crew and I wouldn't be,' said Molly. 'But it'll be good practice for the Tideway. Plus Stanley is coming to have a look at you, so if the worst comes to the worst, he'll be able to fish us out.'

Beth caught Kate's eye and raised an eyebrow. Kate swallowed hard. Stanley was clearly there to decide whether to allow them to use a club boat for Vesta. Without his blessing they wouldn't have a chance with the committee. This outing was going to be make or break for their Vesta dream.

At the briefing before they boated, Molly talked the crew through the conditions and the necessity to be alert at all times, ready to respond to instructions.

'Now remember, when we're rowing downstream we'll be going like the clappers between the wind and the stream. Make sure you keep your hands light and nimble and keep them moving. If anyone gets caught up at the speed we'll be going you'll be ejected from the boat. If necessary, shorten up slightly but keep the rating up with Stroke. I want to see nice light, fast catches. On the way back it's going to feel heavy, going against the stream and into a head wind. Make sure you hold those finishes in and keep the power on. Above all – everyone listen out for instructions in case I need to manoeuvre quickly.'

Molly knew exactly how testing this was going to be and yet had clearly resolved to do it anyway. Now she looked carefully, Kate could see the skin pulled tight across Molly's pinched cheeks. She could tell from the laboured way Molly was swallowing that her mouth was dry. Molly was frightened. What was Kate thinking of scaring an old-aged pensioner? Putting her in a position where she felt this intimidated? It was too late to back out now, plus it wasn't what Molly wanted. Kate knew the best thing she could do was make sure the crew were on the ball.

Without having seen the river for themselves the crew had heard enough to realise the situation was serious, yet no one questioned the decision to go out. Like old warhorses, they clicked back into fight mode, focussed and in the moment. As they left the confines of the boathouse the wind caught the side of the shell and tried to rip it from their hands. The crew knew they were in for a battle, but no one flinched, no one wavered. Molly believed they could do this and they had absolute trust in her.

As they set off upstream into the wind, it felt like rowing through treacle. At least no one else would be mad enough to go out on a day like this so they wouldn't have to worry about a collision.

They rowed for a few minutes at half slide, and then stretched out to full slide. Molly didn't want to risk a more thorough warm-up as she had less control over the boat with shorter slide work. Spinning was the most dangerous manoeuvre. The river was only slightly wider than the eight and once the boat was sideways to the wind and stream they would be blown all over the place. They needed to complete the turn in as few strokes as possible. Everyone had seen or heard of an eight that had been impaled in conditions like these and ended up being broken in half by the current.

The crew didn't let Molly down. They all understood the situation was critical. They'd never spun a boat as swiftly. Molly gave the crew a moment, even though they were already being carried down the river at an alarming speed.

'Take your layers off. Have some water. We won't stop again until we get back to the boathouse. You have one minute, ladies.'

The women were silent as they quickly pulled off their fleece tops and stowed them away in the hatches, shivering in the wind.

'Attention!

Backstops!

Light pressure!

Go!'

The crew took off with precise, deft catches, gradually

increasing the pressure and rating with Stroke until they were mastering the stream. They flew though the archway of the bridge, with inches to spare between oar and brickwork.

'Harden up, Bowside!' came the call, and the boat eased away from the side. By the time they passed the club, Stanley was putting out in the motor launch.

The crew were rating nearly thirty strokes a minute and ripping through the water. They were flying. Water was sprayed around with every blade that clipped a large wave and Kate was soon soaked. It was nuts! It was exhilarating! What were they doing?

In no time at all they'd reached the far end of their stretch of river. Molly was not going to stop. They would spin and carry on. And it would have to be really quick: at this end the river would drag them over the weir if they took too long and became caught in the current. This was not a drill.

Despite their fatigue from the sprint down, the women executed a perfect turn and were rapidly back in position, ready to make the return leg. This would take twice as long, and then some.

'You have one minute to grab some water,' barked Molly, as they floated rapidly past the moored narrowboats, back towards the weir. ***'Number off when ready.'***

Seeing the all too apparent jeopardy, the women shouted their numbers in rapid succession. They were off. It was a relief to be rowing and in control of the boat again, although their forward progress was painfully slow. The contrast between the two halves of this outing could not have been more marked. While the first half had been madly exhilarating, this section was just a slog. The pace had slowed but Kate did her best to keep up a decent rating. It was all about maintaining long strokes and using the power of their large leg muscles. It was hard. It was heavy. By the time they reached the home straight everyone had had enough. But they kept going, and as the wind dropped momentarily, Molly changed gear and pushed the crew into a final sprint. As they put out their hands to grab the dock the crew erupted into howls of relief. They were done in.

'Everyone quiet! This isn't over until the boat is back on the shelf. We won't wash her outside. This once we can run a cloth over her inside the boathouse.' This last instruction really made everyone pay attention. The conditions must be serious.

They lifted the boat out of the water and swung her to heads and were drenched in the icy water that had accumulated in the bottom. This produced a chorus of squeals, quite at odds with the gritty performance the women had just delivered. Kate had thought she couldn't get any wetter but it turned out she'd been mistaken. Even her socks were now squelching with every step.

Once the boat was back on the shelf, everyone put on extra layers over their damp Lycra ready for their team talk.

'Tea's ready,' called Kate. Next to the old sofas she'd set up a large picnic table crammed with mugs of steaming tea and plates of cake. 'There's ginger cake and carrot cake. Lesley – can you give a couple of mugs to Stanley and Molly? Everyone – grab a mug and a piece of cake then find a seat as soon as you can.'

As everyone swarmed around the spread, Sal called out, 'Oi! Katie! What happened to the checked tablecloth and napkins? Standards are dropping!' Everyone joined in the banter and the tension of the outing evaporated along with the spirals of steam from their mugs of tea.

Molly cleared her throat. 'Congratulations, ladies – that was an incredible row. The conditions today were as testing as it is possible to row in. Had it been any worse we'd have been swamped rather than just soaked. You acquitted yourselves admirably and you should all feel extremely proud.' The women erupted into excited chatter, feeling the need to comment to their neighbours. Molly raised her voice slightly and carried on:

'Kate and Beth have asked me to talk to you about an idea they have – a dream, if you will. They'd like us to enter the Vesta Veterans Head of the River Race next March. I'm going to ask Stanley to talk you all through the race, but you should know that I would be delighted to cox you in it. After that outing today you've proved you're more than up to the challenge. Stanley?' With that Molly squeezed herself into a tiny space at the end of one of the sofas. There was a murmuring amongst the women.

Kate and Beth exchanged glances. Kate was irritated Molly had deferred to Stanley. She was their coach and knew more than enough to be guiding them through this challenge. She wished Molly would believe in her own abilities, rather than assuming she was only listened to as an adjunct to Stanley. Still – Kate recognised there was a significant advantage in a senior member of the committee buying into the project.

Stanley stepped forward and clicked on the projector to light up the first slide. It was a diagram of the River Thames from Mortlake to Putney that looked like a massive U-bend in a piece of industrial plumbing. In his broad Yorkshire accent, he talked them through each section of the course, the bridges, the eyots, which bank had the stream at the different sections, which stretches normally had a head wind, pilings and buoys and so on. As he did so he clicked through photograph after photograph.

The details blurred into one for Kate. She didn't know

the river so it meant nothing to her. If anything, Stanley was making it sound more difficult than she'd imagined. After the punishment of the last hour she was starting to slide into a warm, sugar-enriched fug that was making it difficult to concentrate. She suddenly realised Stanley had ended his talk and there was silence. Beth fortunately was still alert and she jumped in to fill the void.

'Thank you, Stanley. I know everyone appreciates you taking the time to share your expertise with us. Hilary – could you get Stanley another cup of tea? Another piece of cake, Stanley?'

Molly was also now back on her feet and Kate was just praying she would come up with something a bit more rousing.

'Ladies – the main thing you need to know is this: the race is 6.8 kilometres long. That's what we just rowed today. In fact, as we'll be rowing with the current the whole way it will feel more like rowing five kilometres. I can also tell you the conditions will not be worse than today, because if they are, the race will be cancelled. What I'm trying to say is, this race is completely within your grasp and I'm happy to cox you in it. In fact, I'll go so far as to say I'd be proud to cox you. So who's up for it?' There was a momentary pause, during which Molly, Beth and Kate all held their breath. Abbie was the first to say,

'Hell yeah! Count me in.' A chorus of assents and nodding rose to a crescendo, swiftly followed by an enthusiastic clamour for more tea and cake.

'Help yourselves, ladies. I don't want to have to take any home,' said Kate.

'I must just try a small piece of the carrot cake,' said Molly primly, 'just to see what it's like.'

'Too right,' said Abbie. 'You have to try everything once.'

Recovery: *The part of the stroke phase between the finish and the catch when the blade is out of the water.*

21

December 2012

Kate heard the front door smack against the hall wall and the sound of voices. They were home. Despite trying to pretend otherwise, she'd been counting the days until her two girls came home for the Christmas holidays. Without bothering to take off her pinny, she hurried up to the front door.

'Mumsie!' they chorused and flung their arms around her. Kate breathed in the smell of them and hugged them as tightly as she could. She could have stayed like that forever, knotted into a tight parcel of hair and arms and affection.

'What time's supper?'

Kate disentangled herself to greet Tim who'd collected them from the station, having spent all day out on a bike ride.

'Hello, darling,' and she gave him a chaste kiss on the cheek. 'Thanks for getting them. It'll be about half an hour. Does that suit?'

'Sure, Mumsie!' and the sisters started dragging their bags upstairs, giggling and whispering as they went.

Kate smiled after them. 'Isn't it lovely to have them back?' she confided to Tim.

'Makes you realise how quiet it was without them. And tidy.' Tim started picking up the various rucksacks, carrier bags and black bin liners in which they'd transported their worldly possessions, now littered around the hall. 'I'll help them with their bags. Then maybe we could all have a drink together, before supper?'

'Sounds good to me,' and Kate headed back to the kitchen, humming a jaunty Christmas carol as she went. The Chicken Basque was already in the oven and she only needed to throw a salad together and tidy the kitchen.

Kate had come to the conclusion the girl's homecoming was the best part of Christmas. The day itself, the twenty-fifth, always contrived to be less joyful than it was supposed to be. And definitely more trying. They either spent too much of it on the motorway visiting extended family, or the whole time was spent in the kitchen preparing and clearing away meals for the endless waves of people visiting. And the relatives seemed to get trickier with every passing year. Tiptoeing around the various unspoken tensions and grievances while wearing a forced smile became more exhausting with every passing year. Of course the girls were a huge help now. But still.

She was convinced the Americans had the right idea with Thanksgiving, a holiday when the only thing you're expected to do is spend time together with those you love. And eat great food as well, of course, as no celebration was complete for Kate without a wonderful meal. Without the presents and pressure for everything to be picture perfect you could focus on what really mattered: enjoying spending time with your family.

She'd thought about it quite a bit at odd times, and had come to the realisation it was the girls' homecoming that really mattered to her. Having said that, the welcome home supper the previous year had been a disaster, at least for Kate. After a wonderful meal that she'd lovingly prepared the girls had announced they were meeting friends in town and Tim had said he needed an early night.

She could still remember dropping off the effervescent girls and how the dark night had screamed with silence. She'd felt so bereft. She knew at the time it was silly. It was only the first night of the holidays – she'd have plenty of time to spend with the girls. They didn't need to stay home on their first night, especially as it was a Saturday. 'They didn't even say the meal was nice,' she'd told herself, knowing even as she thought it she was being ridiculous. Of course they'd all enjoyed it. They'd loved it. Yet despite knowing this it had all felt – well – just a bit rubbish.

So with her newfound resolve she decided this year she was not going to just let it happen, like she usually did, and then be frustrated and disappointed afterwards. She was going to manage it, so she got out of it what she needed, and her needs were met as well as everyone else's.

'How's it going?' Tim opened the fridge and started moving things around. 'I thought we might open a bottle of fizz. Celebrate the girls being home. Are you done?' He found the bottle he was after and then the champagne flutes high up on the top shelf of a cupboard.

'Perfect timing,' said Kate.

The meal was a triumph. After their long train journey the girls were ravenous. Kate also told herself a little smugly they probably hadn't tasted a meal as good as their mother's cooking for a while.

They were on really good form, so obviously delighted to be home and with each other. They told jokes and related their various escapades and the four of them laughed almost continuously. At one point Kate found something so funny she was helpless with mirth, bent over with tears rolling down her cheeks.

'Oh God, your mother's going to wet her pants now,' said Tim. It was said with a voice of such affection, as if seeing his wife in paroxysms of hysteria was the best Christmas present anyone could have given him. Having the girls there always seemed to make things easier between the two of them, as if they were essential components in the machinery of their marriage.

Tim even started telling the girls about Kate's rowing, about how she was hoping to take a crew to race on the Thames in London.

'Is that safe, Mum?' asked Poppy. 'I mean, you know . . .'

'I think you'll find your mother's perfectly able to look after herself,' said Tim, which pleased Kate immensely. She quickly changed the subject. She could tell her daughters regarded her rowing as a little hobby, and she had no wish to try to explain it or justify herself. These days she knew she didn't need anyone else's approval.

'I've missed this. Being together,' said Kate.

'Well, don't worry, Mumsie, we're here for weeks. You'll be completely fed up of us by the time we leave,' said Ella.

'How long do you think until you start complaining about the mess and us having emptied the fridge?' asked Poppy.

'Well, give me twenty-four hours and I'll be irritated by that,' said Tim.

'Pudding anyone?' asked Kate, holding up a large white plate bearing a tart crammed with toffee-coloured apples.

'Oh my God, my favourite!' squealed Poppy as Kate served up thick slices of the dessert and passed round a bowl of crème fraîche. They all had seconds.

'This is so good,' swooned Ella, completely transported.

'You two off to town after supper?' asked Tim, shovelling in a last mouthful of cream and pastry.

'Gosh no – we're all going to play Trivial Pursuit. It's all arranged.'

'Oh, is it?' said Tim, and he looked at his wife with an expression that might have been surprise, but was possibly also admiration. Kate just smiled.

Swivel: *The U-shaped plastic rotating piece mounted on the pin in which the oar sits while rowing.*

22

KATE

Kate had been absolutely right about the galvanising effect of signing up for Vesta. Not that she'd have dreamt of saying 'I told you so.' The squad seemed to be more committed than ever, despite January being the time of year when every ounce of willpower was required to keep training. Christmas came and went, and somehow the women managed to negotiate their various family and social obligations and continue with their training sessions. Even Kate had been surprised how easily her rowing had been accepted by her family, home for the holidays.

'If I'd known how easy it was just to walk out of the door I'd have done it years ago,' she'd said.

'What do you mean? Why couldn't you walk out of the door?' asked Beth and Kate realised, not for the first time, there were bits of her life she took for granted but which Beth didn't fully understand as she'd never had children.

'Well, you know how I was pretty much a single mother most of the week, with Tim away?'

'Well, yeah.'

'From the moment Poppy was born, I couldn't leave the house unless I'd arranged and paid for a babysitter. We had no family here and as we'd only recently moved here I didn't have friends I could call on. It came as quite a shock and took some getting used to. It was the end of spontaneity. I can't tell you how I longed to escape on nice summer evenings. I was trapped in the house by my sleeping baby and I felt like a prisoner on remand who'd been tagged.'

'Wow – is that what it's like? I've never really thought about it. Presumably it was different once they were older? Once they didn't need a babysitter?'

'Yes, it was different. Sure, they didn't need a babysitter, but I still had to organise what they were going to eat, check up on their homework, make sure they were all right. Maybe I should have worried less and just gone.'

'I don't think worrying less is in your nature, Kate,' laughed Beth. Kate smiled and shrugged her shoulders at her friend. She had a point.

By good fortune, the squad's newfound purpose was blessed with a period of dry weather that was remarkably mild for December. It felt as if nothing could stop them. Then January came in like a punch to the kidneys. The temperature tumbled and, more significantly the rain started to fall and looked like it would never stop. It was positively biblical, making up for the months of drought the previous year. The first two weeks of January, the women were soaked every outing and the jokes were beginning to wear a bit thin. Molly made sure they warmed up properly before they went outside, and then kept them moving until they were back in the boathouse where everyone peeled off their wet layers and replaced them with an assortment of baggy jumpers and tracksuit bottoms. No one lingered to chat afterwards.

There were no complaints, though. They could all see the water level climbing with every outing and they knew if the rain didn't stop it would soon be too high to go out. One of the steps down to the dock was marked with a slap of red paint. Once the flood reached that mark, no one would be allowed on the river until it receded. Kate had discovered a website run by the Environment Agency which showed the water level at a pumping station just downriver from the club. She refreshed it obsessively during the day and tracked the inexorable rise. If this kept up, the river would be too high for rowing within a couple of days.

It was really worrying. Competing at Vesta was at the very limit of the crew's ability, and that was assuming they trained flat out until the race. There was so much that could still go wrong and taking part meant so much to all of them. They were all investing heavily in their dream. Her dream. She didn't think she'd be able to bear it if they failed. Then inevitably, a couple of days later, the committee announced the river was closed until the flooding subsided.

Both Molly and Beth phoned almost as soon as the announcement was posted and they agreed the crew would meet as normal on Saturday to train on the ergs. They all splashed through the mud in their wellies, shrouded in waterproofs with a steely determination. Everyone showed up.

Molly gave a pep talk which went on slightly too long. The points she had to make, though, were well made: at this stage the best way to improve their performance would be through building strength and stamina. Their technique was already sufficiently good that any improvement they could make in two months would be negligible but there was no doubt that all of them had scope to improve on their power and fitness, even though they'd already improved massively since the previous summer. That seemed an awfully long time ago, now Kate thought about it. So yes – they could all get a great deal stronger and fitter in two months.

Five kilometres. It was a considerable distance. It should take them about half an hour, and that was a long time to sustain that level of effort. Molly had come up with a new erg training plan for them in which every session was either based on 5,000 metres rowing or thirty minutes work. The more the women could get their head around the distance they would be rowing, the more achievable it would seem.

Kate was worried some of the squad would baulk at erg training. Effective though it might be, it was much less enjoyable than being on the water, even in early January. But there were sage nods of the head from around the group as Molly was speaking, and everyone seemed to agree it needed to be done.

'Blimey, Kate,' hissed Abbie, 'you'd think this was a cult, we're all so compliant.'

Each time the women completed a session in their land-training programme, it became a little easier and slightly less intimidating. Kate even realised with a jolt one morning that she was actually looking forward to that evening's training session. That was a first for her.

Then, just as it felt as if the land training was becoming established and making progress, there was one setback after another. First Sal had to go and stay with her elderly mother who'd had a fall and then insisted on sacking the carers provided by Social Services. Lesley had to cancel as she'd gone down with a virus, and a couple of others were struggling on with coughs and sniffles. Kate found herself wondering whether squad morale might be wobbling, but then good old Abbie came to the rescue with team T-shirts in Albion green with 'Vesta 2013' written on the back in large letters. As she handed them out, Beth grinned at Kate.

'Finally, we get T-shirts.'

From then on the women wore their green tops to every session, and with it came a reinforced sense of solidarity. They all seemed proud to be wearing them. Hilary wanted to take a squad photo so they could post it on the club's Facebook page but Lesley objected vehemently.

'Mike's already told me he thinks we look like a geriatric hen party. I don't think I want to post a picture of us so people can make even worse comments.'

Abbie gasped. 'That's so mean! How could he say something like that? Even if he was joking?' The idea was quickly dropped.

The following Sunday was Abbie's birthday. She hadn't said anything about it, but Sal had somehow worked it out and she took it upon herself to organise mugs of tea after their erg session and produced a birthday cake. It was covered in a puddle of cobalt icing, with a brown sugar-paste boat complete with eight sugar-paste rowers – all wearing green tops. The cox even had a paper megaphone. They called Abbie over and presented it to her, candles lit, and sang 'Happy Birthday'. Abbie burst into tears. The singing petered out and the friends crowded round her, competing for space to hug her.

'Oh my God, what is it? Is the cake that bad?' asked the anxious Sal.

Abbie was sobbing too much to answer, so Kate and Beth led her away to a quiet bench on the other side of the boathouse. Sal diplomatically bustled about offering tea and slices of cake to the crowd, giving the others space. Beth and Kate sat with their arms around Abbie, just holding her until she'd cried herself out. Kate produced a packet of tissues and Abbie blew her nose noisily.

'Better?' asked Kate.

'Yeah – sorry about that. I don't know what came over me. I feel so awful after Sal went to all that effort. But that was the trouble. That was easily the nicest thing that's happened all day. In fact, that was the only nice thing I can remember in weeks. It's been just one shitty day after another, and I don't know how much more of this I can take.' With this she broke down in big gulping sobs.

Kate didn't really know what to say. Despite all of the time they'd spent together in a group, she didn't know Abbie that well and had no idea what could be causing her so much grief. Beth was clearly in the same position but had the wit to remain quiet and allow Abbie to talk while she held her hand. Kate kept her arm around Abbie and stroked her shoulder, hoping that would provide a crumb of comfort.

'It's my husband. I know I haven't told you about him. He's . . . He's got a thing called Pick's Disease.' Here Abbie paused to blow her nose and shake her head as if to toss out her despair. 'It's a hideous form of brain rot. I've managed to keep him at home with a rota of carers so I'm very lucky, really. But he's getting worse. Much worse.'

'Oh my Lord,' said Kate. 'I had no idea.'

'It's not like Alzheimer's – Pick's starts in the frontal lobe, so the first thing that goes is the ability to communicate. He probably only has about twenty words left now which is such a terrible irony for a man who used to speak three languages.' Kate squeezed her hand.

'They also get personality changes and become disinhibited. If I'm honest, it's absolutely appalling. We were on a reasonably even keel for a while. But he got this bug that's been going around and he's deteriorated so much over the last month. I have respite carers that come in, but the latest has just handed in her notice because she can't cope. That was this morning. Nice birthday present.'

'Christ, Abbie! Why didn't you tell us?' asked Beth.

'Do you know – I really enjoyed coming somewhere I was just Abbie, rather than Martin's carer. If I had told you, that's all we'd have talked about. Rowing with you guys, I really feel I've managed to reclaim just a bit of myself again.'

'You're incredible, do you know that?' said Kate giving Abbie a squeeze.

'I know what you need,' said Beth. 'A piece of your birthday cake!' and giving Abbie yet another hug got up to fetch it.

'What do you want me to tell the others?' asked Kate. 'They're all very fond of you and they'll be concerned.'

'You can tell them,' said Abbie sniffing. 'Just so long as we can keep talking about green T-shirts and Prosecco and that doesn't have to change.'

'That's a promise,' said Kate. 'You know – it makes me realise I don't know anything about you. What you do for work, do you have kids, do you have a dog?'

'This is starting to sound like a blind date,' said Abbie sniffing. 'If it helps, I like Piña Coladas. Getting caught in the rain, not so much.' Kate laughed, and just then Beth arrived with mugs of tea, closely followed by Sal bearing slabs of cake with puddles of lurid blue icing.

'Sorry about the cake,' said Sal. 'It does taste better than it looks.'

'Oh, come here,' said Abbie, and she grabbed Sal round the neck and gave her a massive hug. As the two women embraced, Beth caught Kate's eye and they exchanged smiles of relief, affection and solidarity.

Lateral pitch: *The outward angle of inclination of the pin to the vertical.*

23

LESLEY

Lesley needed a dress. A black dress to be precise. Audrey, a long-standing and much loved neighbour had died, and the funeral was at the end of the week. Lesley was not one to spend much time in front of a mirror, but she had an inkling that she should probably check out her outfit ahead of time. She'd tried on her most promising pair of black work trousers with a jacket and stood squarely in front of the full-length mirror on the landing. Light poured in from the double-height sash windows, illuminating her ensemble. She was shocked how tired and washed-out it all looked. Had it always been that baggy? Or was that just her that was drooping? Either way, Audrey deserved better. It was a matter of respect.

So she'd decided to finish work early today as time in lieu, and hit the shops. She just wanted a simple, black dress. How hard could that be? She pushed though the heavy swing doors leading off the dank high street which was suitably quiet for a grim February evening and made her way across the vast expanse of grubby marble floor tiles past rail after rail of clothing. The floor alternated between pools of startling white from an overhead searchlight, and puddles of dingy shadow. Lesley felt the ceiling pressing down upon her. She walked through the shoe department and the faint aroma of plastic made her heave. She had to get out of there. Lesley didn't like shops.

As she was about to give up, she saw a sign: dresses. Girding what remained of her inner resources, she went straight for the numerous plain black shifts. She picked up a size sixteen and an eighteen, just to be on the safe side, in a number of styles and marched over to the fitting room before her determination failed her.

The scruffy marble floor gave way to a faux bleached-wood laminate, hinting at beach houses and driftwood. The cubicle was spacious and it had a proper door, which was something. She hated those changing rooms screened with a curtain that didn't quite cover the opening. Even better, there was a bench, and Lesley plonked herself down on it. Shops like these sapped her energy.

The dresses were on flimsy hangers with a coloured cube of plastic on the hook indicating the size. Lesley liked this system as it meant she didn't have to bother ferking around in her bag for her specs while shopping. It was not unusual for a dress to end up on a hanger with the wrong-coloured cube, but somehow the whole glasses thing made this seem unimportant.

Lesley reached for the most promising-looking garment and tried it on. She turned and looked in the mirror. It was enormous. She checked the rail. The size eighteen was still hanging up. She must have picked up the wrong size – there was no way this was a sixteen. On the plus side, she liked the fabric, which looked a great deal smarter than the subfusc offerings in her own wardrobes. The neckline suited her as well. She opened the door and peered out to look for an assistant.

Another customer was standing in the corridor between the cubicles, checking out her reflection in the mirror on the end wall. She was wearing a calf-length dress in a harsh lilac. *Always a difficult colour to wear*, thought Lesley. The shiny synthetic fabric wrinkled between the woman's shoulder blades, clinging to the rolls of back fat. The customer was smoothing down the material at the front, turning this way and that, staring deep into her own eyes with a flirtatious smile.

Lesley wanted to shout, 'Don't do it!' But she knew how much she would hate it if someone attempted to intervene when she was on the verge of a hideous purchase.

A shop assistant with overly bleached hair stiff with lacquer clacked down the laminate floor towards them. A slash of red emphasised her fake smile.

'Now, ladies. How are we getting on? Ooh, that colour is fab!' She spoke with a heavy East European accent, standing directly behind the lilac lady, one hand on each shoulder. The shopper simpered and retreated to her cubicle.

The server had red-framed spectacles perched on the top of her head that matched her acrylic talons. Lesley had difficulty in making out what she was saying due to her accent, but it was clearly intended to be encouraging. She asked if she could check the size as she was after a sixteen but must have picked up the wrong one. She turned round so the woman could check the tag attached to the back of her neck.

Lesley started explaining about the not wearing reading glasses thing, but realised the woman was carrying on a parallel conversation in another language. Cringing with self-loathing, she assumed the assistant must be fat-shaming her, despite her oleaginous tone. With no idea what the saleswoman was really saying, Lesley was startled when she turned abruptly and click-clacked back to the shop floor.

For a moment Lesley contemplated throwing her own clothes back on and making a dive for the exit. The whole business of undressing in a brightly lit changing room and offering herself up to be judged was excruciating. She wanted to escape, to be outside in her usual shapeless disguise, able to breathe and disappear into the background. Then she thought of Audrey and convinced herself to see the miserable business through.

Before her resolve failed again, the assistant returned with a different size of the same dress. Lesley retreated to the changing room, peeled off the dress she was wearing and tried it on. It felt tight as she zipped it up. No – actually it wasn't tight. It was close to her body. It skimmed it. As a rule, Lesley liked her clothes to waft in the general vicinity of her outline. Whisper it softly, but Lesley had also of late come to appreciate an elasticated waistband. She figured it had something to do with the menopause, the change in hormones making the weight gather round your waist rather than on your bottom or thighs. Perhaps that was why she found it slightly shameful and had not even mentioned it to her best friends.

She looked at her reflection. She was dumbfounded. Was this one of those trick mirrors you get at the fair? The person opposite her looked slim. Trim. Verging on lithe.

'It's good?' The assistant was knocking on the door. Lesley opened the door cautiously and stepped outside.

'Aah – it's good! You like it?' Lesley found herself imitating the lilac lady, and admiring herself coquettishly in the mirror. She noticed her cheeks were slightly flushed.

'You need a good fit – you no size sixteen. What you think of blue?' and the server held up the double of the dress Lesley was wearing but in a bright cerulean blue.

She's good, thought Lesley, admiring the woman's sales skills. *'She's really good.'* Lesley bought the dress in the black and also the blue. Of course she did. When she hung them up in her wardrobe at home she was shocked to discover they were a size twelve.

Audrey's funeral was the next day. Lesley was still wearing her new black dress when she arrived home in the evening. She'd gone back to the office to work on the quarterly report after putting in a brief appearance at the pub where wine and sausage rolls were being served to the mourners. So when she arrived home, later than usual, Mike was already there, sitting at the kitchen table fiddling with a cox box, a screwdriver and some electrical tape.

'Why do so many coxes have to remove the charger by pulling on the wire? That's three of them not charging now because the wires have been pulled out.'

'Good evening to you too,' said Lesley cheerfully, hanging up her coat. She headed to the fridge and poured herself a glass of wine. She stood there for a moment, gazing vaguely in the direction of the top of Mike's head, still thinking about a tricky section in her report. Mike looked up. He stared at her for a moment. His gaze drifted down to her ankles and back up again. Coughing slightly he turned his attention back to the electrical equipment in front of him.

'You're late,' he said.

'It was Audrey's funeral. I had to go back to the office and finish something after. Have you started supper?' asked Lesley, without any real expectation he would have done.

'How was it? Big turnout?' asked Mike, still peering at the task in his hands.

'It was lovely. The church was packed. Everyone liked Audrey,' said Lesley slightly wistfully, and turned to the fridge and started pulling out various items. 'Now, what are we having tonight?' she muttered to herself, as she consulted the list pinned to the fridge door. 'Tarragon chicken with spinach and brown rice.'

The last few months they'd been having pre-packed ingredients delivered every week. They came with the recipes, and none of them took longer than half an hour. Lesley was a perfectly competent cook, but the bit she struggled with was working out what to eat each night and planning the shopping. There was no doubt they'd been eating a great deal better since they started this system. Mike complained about the expense, but Lesley reckoned they were actually saving money as they no longer bought food they didn't eat and ended up throwing away. Fortunately, he approved of the recipes once cooked and occasionally prepared them himself, when the mood took him. It was a pity the mood didn't take him more often, especially on evenings when she'd warned him she'd be home later than usual. But the food was soon prepared, and Lesley collected cutlery to lay the table.

'Supper's nearly ready. Would you mind moving all that so I can lay the table?'

Grudgingly, Mike picked up the various bits of equipment scattered over the table, muttering to himself like a truculent teenager. Lesley gave the table a quick wipe, then laid it. She added wine glasses and napkins, and adjusted the lighting.

'Supper's ready,' she called a few minutes later, and she carried two plates of steaming food to the table, poured the wine and sat down. She sipped at her wine, admiring the plate in front of her, and waited for Mike to join her. And waited. What was he doing? Lesley hated seeing food that had been lovingly prepared going cold. Why did he always seem to go AWOL just as it was about to be put on the table?

She called again. No answer. There was no longer steam rising from the food. She felt the side of the plate. It was cooling rapidly. It was such a shame to let it spoil. She waited some more. Did he do this on purpose? Dammit, she wanted to enjoy her chicken while it was still hot.

She then did something she'd never done before. She picked up her knife and fork without waiting for Mike and started eating. She savoured every morsel: moist chicken with the beautiful light taste of tarragon; slightly nutty rice with a hint of a bite to it; just wilted baby spinach that tasted of health and vitality and provided the perfect foil to the chicken. She topped up her glass and relished the contrast of the chilled oaky wine with the meal. She revelled in every mouthful. She didn't rush, but there were only a couple of forkfuls on her plate when Mike finally appeared.

'You started?' he said.

'It was going cold. How was your day?' she asked smiling.

'Same as usual,' said Mike. 'I spent quite a lot of time on the phone trying to organise to get the trailer repaired before the Bristol head. I don't know why people can't mention these things when they realise there's a problem, or better still, sort it out themselves.'

'Talking of trailers,' said Lesley. 'You know my crew is planning to do Vesta? No one else from Albion is going up to London that weekend and we're trying to find someone to drive the trailer. I was wondering – how would you feel about driving it up? We could make a weekend of it. Maybe stay with Steve and Rosie?'

'Yeees, I did hear something about Vesta. To be honest, I was surprised Stanley thought it a good idea to let you take one of the club's best boats up to the Tideway. But far be it for me to question his judgement on these matters,' said Mike.

'So what do you think – about driving the trailer? I know you're driving it to Bristol in a couple of weeks,' said Lesley.

'Only because none of the other approved drivers are going. I'm not doing it out of choice. I really can't spare a weekend from coaching my crews at that time of year. It's a critical time, you know, just coming up to the start of the regatta season.'

Lesley didn't say anything. She just stared at Mike, as if she'd never seen him before. Then slowly and deliberately she placed her wine glass on the table, blotted her lips with her napkin and rose imperiously from the table.

'I'm going to have a bath then an early night,' she informed him icily. 'You are going to clear up, including taking every bit of bloody rowing kit out of my kitchen. Then you will sleep in the spare room.' She paused, considering what she'd just said. 'In fact, you can sleep there every night until you start treating me with the respect and consideration I deserve.' Lesley positively spat out these final words, turned on her heel and strode magnificently out of the room.

Attention!: *To start a race, the umpire calls out the names of the crews competing, says 'attention', and after a definite pause, calls 'go'.*

24

KATE

Kate was sitting in bed propped up on a pile of pillows, studying the sudoku on the back of the newspaper. Her reading glasses had skidded down her nose on the slick of moisturiser still glistening on her face. She sucked her biro as she contemplated where to start. The 'fiendish' puzzle always took some getting in to.

Tim was lying on the floor. He was wearing a pair of green checked pyjama trousers with a tie waist and was otherwise naked. He had one leg out straight, and the other, with the knee bent, flung across his body. His arms were laid out flat on the floor as if he were being crucified.

Despite being obsessed about fitness, he'd always poo-pooed the advice to stretch before and after exercise. However, a number of minor injuries had persuaded him to go through this ritual every night before getting into bed. Despite having done this for several years now, Kate could not honestly say that she'd noticed any change. Tim was not a man noted for his flexibility.

She looked down at her husband, grimacing and gurning with the effort of holding his position. His head had not been shaved for a number of days, and the dark stubble clearly defined the expanding bald patch, which had originally driven him to adopt this look.

'What time do you think you'll be back from your ride tomorrow?' asked Kate.

'I'm not sure. Two o'clock, maybe. Why?'

'I thought we might go out together. For a walk. Or visit somewhere – you know – a National Trust place. Or whatever.'

'A walk? Hmmm. Nice idea, but I'll have work to do, and I'll probably want a nap as we're going out in the evening with the Milners.'

'I just thought it would be nice to do something together . . . spend some time together.' Kate had really enjoyed spending time as a family when the girls were home for the holidays. Since they'd left she and Tim seemed to have reverted to their separate lives.

'We'll be together in the evening – we're going out.'

'Yes – I know – with the Milners. But you'll spend all evening with Bob discussing your bikes and the rugby. I just thought we might spend some time on our own. You always seem to be behind that laptop when we're alone.' Kate was conscious this sounded a touch whingy.

'If I am, it's because I've a lot to do.' She'd pressed a raw nerve. He was sounding defensive. 'You've no idea the pressure of a job like mine.' Tim started untangling his limbs and getting to his feet. He stood at the foot of the bed, his hands on his hips, glaring directly at Kate. He looked fierce.

Ordinarily Kate would have backed off but she was feeling indignant. All she'd asked was that he spent a couple of hours with her doing something enjoyable. Was that really too much to ask given they were apart all week? She felt rejected by his lack of interest and angry that work and cycling took priority over her. Took priority over their marriage. Worst of all, asking for a crumb of attention and being refused made her feel pathetic and she didn't want to be that person.

'Funnily enough, I do have an idea about the pressure. You may remember I used to have a proper job, before I gave it up to have your children. And just for the record, I would give my right arm to have it back.' Kate's voice was getting louder and had a definite edge. She didn't often raise her voice to Tim, not least because it never proved an effective strategy. Tim didn't move but his stare became more intense and his face was darkening. Kate could imagine a cartoonist might depict him with steam coming out of his ears.

'Would you stop playing the martyr? If you want a proper job – why don't you go out and find one? What's stopping you?'

'What's stopping me? How about the fact that I'm nearly fifty, I've been in the same mummy-graveyard at my firm for twenty years and no one does the sort of work I want to do in Bath.' Now she did sound pathetic. And sorry for herself.

'Well, find a job you want somewhere else then.' Tim turned away and marched to the bathroom. He took a long time to do his teeth. A very long time. By the time he came back into the bedroom Kate was curled up with her back to his side of the bed, pretending to be asleep.

Apart from her work situation, the other issue preying on Kate's mind was transporting their eight to London for Vesta. She'd never had any involvement in the transporting of boats back at Cambridge, so there was a lot to learn. Given their size and fragility, the only way to transport an eight was with a purpose-built trailer. These were designed to carry a number of boats at the same time as usually a club would send several crews to a regatta or head race. The trailer had racking welded on top, and three or four boats or sections of shells could be secured each side. The oars, riggers and seats were stacked in the base.

Once loaded, the trailer was a challenge to tow, being both long and heavy. Kate was told you didn't need a special driving licence but you had to be approved by the committee as a trailer driver. Given the responsibility and the stress of the driving, it was hardly surprising the number of people prepared to drive the trailer was limited.

With only five weeks to go until the race, Kate was starting to panic. She'd emailed Mike, the Club Captain, about the issue but she hadn't heard from him, so she collared him at the club the following weekend. He told her they were the only Albion crew going to London that weekend and no one on the club's list of approved drivers was available to help. He walked off pretty sharpish after delivering this piece of news and Kate was taken aback by his abruptness. Jack came over to her.

'Problem?' he asked cheerily. She told him what had happened, although she had the impression he already knew.

'Your best bet's to ring round the local clubs. One of them is bound to be sending a trailer that weekend. Even if they don't have a crew rowing in Vesta, it's the Head of the River Race the day before.' He promised to dig up some phone numbers.

When she called, the person from Frome Rowing Club was friendly but a bit vague. The bloke she called at Somerset Union Rowing Club, however, came up trumps. Yes, the club was definitely sending at least one crew to Vesta and he knew who was dealing with logistics. Kate immediately sent off a pleading email to someone called Jonny.

She was half expecting this Jonny might not be desperately helpful, as that had been her experience so far in rowing. It occurred to her to wonder how the Albion Committee might have responded to a similar request from a middle-aged woman from another club.

As it turned out, sometimes when you are becoming the most despondent, the universe sends someone along to restore your faith in mankind. Such a man was Jonny. Kate had barely pressed send on her email before the phone was ringing and Jonny introduced himself.

'I can't tell you how relieved I am you've called. I'm supposedly responsible for logistics and I've absolutely no idea what I'm doing. I've never rowed at Vesta – or organised a crew before.' Kate, realised she was verging on the slightly hysterical as she let this all gush out.

'Well, aren't they lucky you agreed to take it on,' said a deep voice that sounded like it had been soaked in honey. 'It's no problem. We can sort this out. I promise you I'll get you there.' As he said that, Kate exhaled deeply, and the anxiety she'd been hugging to her chest for months drifted away.

'I coach a veteran women's crew at our club and they're doing Vesta, so I agreed to drive the trailer. I'll actually be going up on the Friday night because our men are doing HORR, which is on the Saturday, so their boat will be on the trailer as well. We'll come back Sunday afternoon after your race.'

'Are you rowing on the Saturday?' asked Kate, conscious she knew nothing about Jonny. Did he even row or was he just a coach, like Stanley?

'I wish! No, I'm far too old. I row with a masters' D crew, but we haven't managed to get our act together for Vesta. Do you realise how well you've done just to get this far?'

asked Jonny, in a way that sounded genuinely impressed. 'People who've never tried to get a crew together have no idea how hard it is.'

'Herding cats comes to mind,' laughed Kate.

'Oh no – cats are way easier than my old curmudgeons. The key thing you need to know is that we're boat loading on the Thursday evening. I'll bring the trailer round to Albion for about six o'clock if you can be ready to load,' said Jonny.

'That's perfect,' said Kate, writing herself a note in the diary. 'So how come you got talked into coaching the women at your club? Is your wife in the crew?' Even as she said this, Kate realised she was crossing a line.

'No,' he laughed. 'Maybe if my ex-wife had rowed we'd still be together. I've recently been through a fairly messy divorce and had time on my hands, so I guess I was a bit of a sitting duck when the women were looking for a coach. To be honest, I'm happy to do it. It beats sitting around feeling sorry for myself.'

'Well, I'm sure they're lucky to have you. And my crew is extremely lucky you'll be helping us out like this. You must make sure to tell us what our share of the costs will be.'

'Don't worry about that for now. There'll be plenty of time to sort that out nearer the time. I forgot to ask what category you're rowing in,' said Jonny, almost managing to sound disinterested.

'We're C class – aged forty-five to fifty,' said Kate, who'd already done the calculation that Jonny must be in his early fifties when he mentioned his crew.

'Snap. Same as my women. We should have a race some time.'

'Well, hopefully we'll be having one on the Tideway.'

'Indeed. No doubt we'll speak again soon. Just call me if

you've any questions. But please feel assured we'll get your boat there.'

If Jonny had been in the room, Kate was in no doubt she'd have kissed him. The logistics had been preying on her mind since they'd first contemplated the race and no one at Albion apart from Jack had offered any help or advice. To have someone so competent agree to look after them was more than she could have hoped for. She must tell Beth right away, and while she was at it she might just drop in the conversation that Jonny was single . . .

The weeks flew by and training really stepped up yet another gear. Every woman in the squad now had her sights firmly set on the Tideway and thirty minutes of racing. They were back on the water now on Saturdays and Sundays, but they also met twice a week to erg. They were on a mission. They seemed to be past the worst of the winter viruses and Abbie was on more of an even keel. So as long as no one was injured or fell ill, they should have their crew on the start line.

Someone suggested they all gave up alcohol until the race, which Kate assumed was a joke. But when most of the squad agreed and said what a good idea it was, Kate realised she was going to have to do it as well. What sort of a monster had she created?

Abbie had taken it upon herself to check up on everyone's racing strip. A few of them had borrowed all-in-ones for the Somerset Head, and as she was planning to invest in a new vest for herself she offered to do a group order. Kate made sure Lesley ordered one, as the top she'd been wearing at the last race had seen better days. It had been washed so many times it was closer to grey than green, plus it was so baggy it must have interfered with her tap down.

Abbie also used her initiative and purchased a shiny new rigger jigger for every crew member. This was the essential spanner required to undo or tighten the numerous nuts and bolts that held the boat together and attached the riggers.

Jonny had thoughtfully forwarded to Kate the list of kit and instructions he'd supplied to his own crew. Kate went through it with Molly, slightly surprised at the need for 'Vaseline, white spirits and gaffer tape'. It sounded as if Jonny thought they were going to a swingers' party rather than a rowing race, but Molly had studied the list carefully, nodding away, and pronounced herself impressed with its thoroughness. She said she'd organise it in time for boat loading.

By the time the week of the race came round, the women were at a fever pitch of excitement and nerves. Kate had spent so long nursing the squad to this point, she hadn't had much time to consider her own rowing. Now responsibility for the boat rested with Jonny, and the crew with Molly, Kate had time to consider her own role as Stroke – and had a massive wobble.

'Suppose I blow out halfway through? Suppose I can't do it?' she wailed at Beth on the phone.

'You're going to be fine, Kate. We've done this so many times now. Of course you can do it. It's just nerves.'

Beth was absolutely right, of course, and Kate did know it, deep down. She just needed to hear someone else say it. In fairness, she'd been providing the same reassurance to everyone else in the crew. It wasn't surprising she might need some bolstering herself.

She'd started dreaming about the race, and invariably woke up just as she caught a massive crab. At least in her nightmares they were racing, rather than driving around the South Circular trying to find the river, or worse still, trying to find their boat. With Jonny taking care of transport, even Kate's fevered brain couldn't devise a way for that to go wrong.

The Thursday before Vesta finally dawned and their carefully made plans swung into action. Feeling slightly jittery, Kate arrived at the boathouse early and went down to the river to wait. The icy depths were dark and quiet. The levels had dropped considerably since the recent floods so the dock was now clear of water. It was a fine day although quite bracing: a good day for rowing. She watched the swirling eddies gliding past, mesmerised by the never-ending stream. It was extraordinary how just being near the water had the capacity to soothe. She'd heard talk of a storm coming in, but no doubt it was another of those overcautious warnings that would come to nothing.

She was called back from her reveries by a holler from Lesley. A few of them had already arrived and they were going to strip the riggers off one side while the boat was still on the rack. They wouldn't be able to move it out until everyone was there, but they could make a start. Molly was talking them through what to do. The key thing was to put the washers and nuts back on the bolts as soon as each rigger was taken off and to tighten them properly. The boat would be shaken around for several hours on the journey, so anything that could work itself loose was likely to. Molly had a supply of extra nuts and washers in her comprehensive racing kit, as recommended by Jonny, but no one wanted a washer flying off the top of the trailer at sixty mph as it could easily cause an accident.

With time to spare the whole crew had arrived and Molly had them lift the boat outside onto trestles. There was no chatting. Everyone was uncharacteristically quiet and focussed. Kate could sense their anxiety. Barely had the boat been set down on the slings than the remaining four riggers were whisked off, the rudder, wires and impeller taped down and the two sections unbolted. Once the boat had been separated in two, Molly cleaned off the blunt ends with a cloth and white spirits. They were good to go. The blades had been laid out, and the riggers were placed in two neat piles.

Headlights appeared at the end of the track and a large SUV with a trailer attached pulled through the gateway. It drove slowly over to where the women were waiting and pulled up close to the equipment. A tall, athletic-looking man with close-cropped black hair jumped out and approached the group. Kate walked over to him, hand outstretched.

'Jonny! I'm Kate.'

'Nice to meet you,' said Jonny, shaking her hand.

'Thank you so much for helping us like this.'

'Really, you don't have to mention it. I'm only too pleased I could help.'

'Jonny – this is Beth,' said Kate, practically shoving Beth forward. 'And Molly our cox.'

Asserting her position, Molly said, 'We're all set, I think. Where would you like us to put it?'

'As you're first, I think we'll put you on top, one section each side. Do you think you can manage that?' asked Jonny, slightly unsure. Kate could see he was eyeing up the crew, and for a moment she saw them through his eyes. If Jonny had seen one of them on a train with a large bag he would have probably offered to lift it onto the luggage rack.

'No problems,' said Kate, possibly more confidently than she felt.

After a quick conflab, Molly called the squad to attention and ordered them into action. First the blades and riggers were stowed in the body of the trailer. Then Molly called for four volunteers to climb onto the trailer and up the scaffolding.

'Shotgun!' shouted Lesley, and there was an unseemly scramble as five of the women raced to the trailer. It was like school kids fighting over who was next on the climbing frame. Hilary graciously conceded and the other women clambered up. On Molly's command the four of them still on the ground lifted one half of the shell to offer it up to the racking and the women waiting to receive it who were clinging to the racking. Kate was on tiptoes, stretching herself out, but the end of the boat was still tantalisingly out of reach of the outstretched hands. It was too high. They were simply not tall enough to reach the top rack.

'Hang on a minute,' said Kate, 'Can you hold this without me a sec? I've got an idea.' She ducked into the boathouse and found a couple of short stepladders. They were just high enough to allow the women to lift the boat sections up to their crewmates perched on the racking.

Both sections were in place. The next job was to secure them to the metal structure using brightly coloured lengths of strapping. Kate stood back and watched as four women of a certain age hung like monkeys from the scaffolding and expertly secured the hull. They chattered to each other and checked out each other's work, testing the tension on each tie.

Having finished her own checks, Lesley lingered a moment and surveyed the scene from her eyrie on top of the trailer in the fading light, one leg curled round an upright to secure her. Seeing Kate she waved at her.

'Look – no hands!' she yelled. Then she threw back her head and ululated in a passable impersonation of Tarzan, beating her chest. A couple of the women applauded, but

Abbie and Sal rolled their eyes in a good-natured fashion and carried on testing the straps were securely fastened. Once they'd all agreed they were satisfied, they climbed down and hopped off the trailer as if this was something they did every week.

'Do you want to check it?' Kate asked Jonny with a certain amount of trepidation. It was vital the boat was properly secured. It would be unthinkable to have to tell the committee that *Cressida* had fallen off the trailer in the middle of the M4. Jonny jumped up onto the trailer and made his way around, testing each of the ties and making sure there was no play in the shell.

'I think that should hold. Good job,' he pronounced, and Kate positively puffed up with pride. *Perhaps we're not just a bunch of middle-aged women.*

With the task complete, everyone started chatting excitedly. Molly shouted above the din, 'OK, guys, that was really efficient . . .' Everyone fell quiet. 'Thank you all for your cooperation. Your job now is to rest, stay off the booze, rest, eat properly and rest. You're all officially tapering. We'll meet here on Sunday morning at 7.00 a.m. Sharp. Any questions?'

There were no queries, but clearly everyone had a number of issues they felt they needed to get off their chest. Kate grabbed Beth's arm and dragged her over to speak to Jonny who was making his final checks before driving off.

'How many more boats have you got to load tonight?' asked Kate. 'The light will be gone soon.'

'Just two eights, but we have floodlights at Somerset so we'll be able to manage. It's helpful you guys were so efficient. My men's crew usually fanny around for ages, with everyone arguing about the best way of doing it.'

'Oh, we're quite happy being told what to do and Molly knows what she's about,' said Beth.

'I can see that. You're in safe hands with her.'

There was a pause, then Beth added, 'It's jolly nice of you to do this. I can't tell you what it means to us to have someone help us get to Vesta. It's been quite a journey.'

'It's my pleasure,' said Jonny, and Kate noticed him looking straight into Beth's eyes, and Beth holding his gaze for a fraction longer than one might have expected.

As the trailer bearing *Cressida* disappeared down the track, Abbie called out, 'Just three more sleeps till Vesta!' and a rousing cheer erupted from the whole squad.

Hold it up!: *Instruction to bring the boat to a stop quickly in an emergency stop.*

25

KATE

That night Kate slept better than she had in ages. There was nothing more to organise. Everything was in place and all she had to do now was row five kilometres on Sunday. At the time she couldn't work out why she was so chuffed about the slickness of the boat loading. This morning it was obvious: her rag-tag bunch of older women had been transformed into a professional crew and it was Kate who'd made it happen. If she could pull that off, then of course she could stroke them on the Tideway.

They'd done the preparation. They were ready. After all the tribulations, she was finally going to realise her dream. After all these years, on Sunday, she'd be rowing again in a race that mattered. And aside from her sense of satisfaction, she realised she was looking forward to the rowing itself, to testing herself against this mythical stretch of river. She was excited about racing.

She positively leapt out of bed and hummed to herself as she went about her morning chores. She was working from home today as she had a complex deposition to draft and she installed herself in the office with a large mug of coffee ready to attack her to-do list. With each item checked off, she felt a warm glow of satisfaction. She hadn't felt like this in a long time. She was completely engrossed in her work when the phone rang. It was Jonny.

'Hiya. Everything OK? Did you manage to get all the other boats loaded last night?'

'Well, we did,' he said, all seriousness. 'But have you seen the British Rowing website?'

'No – what have I missed?' asked Kate, frantically tapping away at her laptop. The website sprang up. Across the home page was a banner:

'HORR cancelled due to severe weather warning at 10.15 a.m., Friday 22 March 2013.'

'W-what?' stuttered Kate, struggling to process what she was reading. 'What does it mean?'

'There's a storm coming in tomorrow and they're forecasting high winds for the Thames. They've cancelled HORR because it simply won't be safe. Too many boats will get swamped, not to mention how dangerous it is for everyone to tow boats in high winds.'

'Oh my God! But what about our race on Sunday?' asked Kate, as the reality of the situation started sinking in.

'There's no news yet. It's possible the storm will blow through and it'll be calm enough on Sunday. If the race does go ahead, I can drive up early Sunday morning, once the wind drops. Let's not panic just yet, but I thought I should give you a heads-up.'

'Yes – thank you,' spluttered Kate. 'I don't know what to say. It never occurred to me the race could be cancelled. It's nuts – the sun is shining here and there's hardly a breath of wind.'

After she hung up, Kate sat for quite a while staring out of the windows at the daffodils. How dare they look so cheerful at a moment like this? She didn't want to acknowledge it, but it was evident a freshening breeze was ruffling their bumptious heads. Kate clicked through to the Vesta website. No news. She went to the Met Office's page to check on the forecast. The warnings were there, but it was still uncertain which course the storm would take and how long it would last. The weathermen were hedging their bets.

With a heavy sigh, Kate tried to reapply herself to the task in hand. She could barely type two sentences before she was overcome by the need to pull up the Vesta website and hit 'refresh'. It was hopeless. She debated contacting the others, but decided against it: there was no point in worrying them unnecessarily until there was news.

As the day wore on, Kate gradually became absorbed in her work and managed not to think about the race for a whole ten minutes at a time. She'd almost forgotten about it completely by mid-afternoon. She clicked absent-mindedly on the Vesta web page, more as a tic she'd repeated a hundred times that day than in the real expectation of news. There it was: the announcement.

'Vesta Veterans International Head of the River Race 2013 – CANCELLED

Due to severe weather warnings from the Met Office and forecast high winds, the race organisers have reluctantly taken the decision to CANCEL the race on Sunday. We will notify your race entry secretaries if any part of your entry fee can be refunded.'

Kate slumped back in her chair. It was impossible to take in. They'd overcome so many obstacles. It had never occurred to her this could happen. She was so shocked there was no emotion. There was only incomprehension.

Eventually Kate rallied herself and wrote a brief email to

the crew telling them what had happened. Having pressed Send, she staggered upstairs and crawled into bed. She felt cold and utterly exhausted. She lay on her side, hugging a pillow to herself, knees pulled up. She was devastated. How could she have been such an idiot as to invest so much in one stupid race? It was so humiliating. No doubt Facebook would be awash with the Senior Women's schadenfreude, full of comments mocking their failure. Her failure. Just the latest in a long line.

The phone started ringing and Kate flung out an arm, switched it to mute and reburied her head beneath the duvet. As the silence crept over her, Kate felt the need to cry rising from her chest. She did not resist. She gave in to a cathartic howl, and sobbed into her pillow. She cried out all of her frustrations and disappointments, the petty humiliations and casual rudeness. She grieved for the irrelevance and invisibility that were now her lot. She cried until she could cry no more. Then she slept, her cheek resting on the sodden linen, a deep dreamless sleep of one who was past caring . . .

She had no idea how long she'd been asleep when she was roused by banging at the front door. She looked at the bedside clock: it was gone five. She'd been asleep for nearly two hours. She ran to the bathroom, splashed some water over her face, ran a comb over her hair and raced downstairs. It was probably a delivery, so it really didn't matter how she looked. But it wasn't. It was Beth and Molly holding the largest bunch of white roses she'd ever seen.

'Oh my God, guys! What is this?' gasped Kate.

'Well, we couldn't get an answer on your landline or your mobile, so we thought it would be simplest to come round and discuss it in person,' said Beth. 'The flowers are from the squad. We were planning to give them to you on Sunday after the race, but right now seemed the appropriate moment. Are you OK?' asked Beth, concern drawn large on her face.

'I am now,' said Kate. 'Don't stand there. Come on in and have a cup of tea. I've a mountain of flapjacks someone needs to eat. I made them for us to eat in the minibus after the race.'

'I wouldn't go giving those away just yet,' said Molly, 'we've still got a race on Sunday.'

'Whaaat?' asked Kate, confused, wondering if the whole Vesta debacle had just been some terrible dream.

'It's all arranged. As we have to collect the boat on Sunday anyway, we're going to race the Somerset crew. Jonny said his club will do the timekeeping and umpiring, and Albion are organising to close the river and provide marshals and safety boats,' said Molly, the image of efficiency.

'Whaaat?' croaked Kate again, conscious she sounded like a clueless teenager.

'Let's make tea and we'll explain,' said Beth and, in a reversal of roles, led Kate down to the kitchen.

Over tea the two friends explained that as they couldn't get hold of Kate they'd decided to organise the race themselves.

'It seemed the obvious thing to do,' said Molly. 'We'll have to be down at Somerset anyway to collect the boat and both crews are free. Beth sorted out the arrangements with Jonny and I cleared it with the committee. Stanley will drive one safety boat and Mike has said he'll drive the other.'

'What – Mike is helping us? How did that happen?' asked Kate still struggling to get up to speed. Molly and Beth exchanged a look.

'Well, I might have suggested to Stanley that he give Mike a call, and Lesley just might have said that he'd be sleeping in his car if he didn't help,' said Molly who succeeded in looking simultaneously both slightly sheepish and terribly pleased with herself.

'Jesus – and what did you have to threaten Stanley with?' asked Kate genuinely astounded.

'I think some secrets are best kept within a marriage,' said Molly pursing her lips.

'Oh my God, what have I turned you all into?' wailed Kate, laughing and shaking her head.

'Do you know what, Kate? I don't think you've got a clue what you've started,' said Beth.

Cover: *The distance between one set of puddles and the next.*

26

LESLEY

On Sunday morning Mike's alarm sounded at 5.30 a.m. as usual. What was not usual was that before he left he brought Lesley a mug of tea and laid it on her bedside table. He planted a kiss on her tousled head and whispered, 'Good Luck, Dinkums.'

Lesley was awake but made no response. The gesture was so unexpected and sleep soon engulfed her again. When her own alarm sounded a couple of hours later she was shocked into a state of instant alertness. She had a race to get to.

Lesley threw on her new race strip, carefully laid out on a chair the night before. She couldn't help but admire herself in the mirror on the landing, turning this way, then that. She was still surprised at how much better she looked in clothes that fitted. She was ready in double-quick time and headed out of the door earlier than planned. In her haste, she failed to clear away the mug of cold tea next to the bed.

She was meeting Abbie at the Albion car park to grab a lift round to Somerset. They would need some of the cars left at their own club as they'd be rowing back there after the race. Abbie was also ahead of schedule.

'How are you feeling?' Abbie asked as Lesley climbed in the passenger seat.

'I don't know . . . disappointed, obviously. But if I'm honest, a bit of me is relieved as well. But I'm glad we're doing this today. We had to do something after all the let-down. How about you?' asked Lesley, studying Abbie's profile as she drove.

'Pretty similar, I guess. I just hope Kate's all right. She's put so much into making Vesta happen. She must be absolutely gutted.'

'All the more reason we have to give it everything this morning,' said Lesley as they drew into the muddy field that served as Somerset's car park. The trailer still loaded with the Albion eight was parked at the far end.

'Is that Beth's car?' asked Lesley, pointing to a small navy hatchback.

'I think it is. Did we get the time wrong? I thought we were early.' They both exchanged quizzical looks.

As they picked their way through the puddles to the boathouse, Lesley felt the mud squelching beneath her wellies. They found Beth deep in animated conversation with Jonny.

'Hiya,' called Abbie. 'How's everyone this morning?'

'Great,' replied Beth and Jonny in unison. They stole a furtive glance at each other then gave the two newcomers their full attention. Lesley couldn't remember when she'd seen her old friend like this before. She was positively girlish.

'You've obviously seen where the boat is,' said Jonny. 'I suggest we set up trestles here and bring everything round. We can make a start on the oars and riggers before the others arrive.'

'That's a plan,' said Abbie. 'The others shouldn't be too long, not if Beth's here already.'

'Cheeky!' said Beth, still beaming impishly.

The four of them went back and forth to the field carrying

the various pieces of equipment. By the time the rest of the crew arrived, the riggers were laid out in their correct order on the ground and the blades were neatly stacked against a rack by the river.

Kate arrived looking a little pale and the crew all flocked round her to give her a hug. Lesley gave her a tight squeeze and whispered,

'We love you, Kate. We think you're brilliant.'

Once they were quorate, Molly took command and gave the orders for the women to untie the sections of shell from the trailer and carry them round to the boathouse and the waiting trestles. Once again there was an unseemly scramble to be one of the four climbing the frame to undo the boat ties. Lesley simply couldn't help herself and threw herself at the scaffolding. This time Abbie was the one who lost out.

'You snooze, you lose,' shouted Lesley from the top of the trailer. As soon as she'd said it she regretted it. Fortunately Abbie took it in good part:

'Don't worry, I'll take you next time,' she growled.

'Let's save the aggro for Somerset, shall we?' said Molly. 'I want focus from everyone, from now until we put *Cressida* back on her shelf at Albion. Clear?'

'Clear, Boss,' they all replied, and they set to their task with determination. High above the ground, the breeze tugged at Lesley's loose curls. She loved the ridiculous freedom of clambering on the trailer. Her right leg was wrapped around one of the uprights and she worked with both hands to free the boat ties. She felt like a trapeze artist swinging in the breeze. She had an overwhelming urge to put both hands in the air and shout, 'Ta-da!' However, she'd noticed a few of the crew rolling their eyes on Thursday evening so she resisted the temptation.

They'd nearly finished rigging *Cressida* when the Somerset crew arrived and carried their own boat out. Molly took her team to a quiet corner for a briefing.

'OK, ladies. This isn't Vesta, but this is still a race, and a race that matters to Albion.' As she said this Lesley caught Kate's eye. This was a frank admission coming from Molly. Lesley's involvement with the crew had always been complicated by her partner being a club official, and she'd sometimes wondered if the same might be true for Molly.

'A race against Somerset is always a grudge match, and the whole club wants us to win. We'll have a number of committee members out on the river in safety boats, so I want them to be impressed. I have no idea how good the Somerset crew is or whether we should expect to beat them. All I know is that we're going to have the best and the fastest row we're capable of.'

No one said anything. All eyes were fixed on Molly.

'We'll be running it like a head race as that will be safer than racing side by side. We'll paddle up to the top of the river and turn there. Somerset won the toss so are going first and we'll be chasing them. As we come back with the stream, the race will start as we pass the pumping station, just like when we did the Head in the autumn. The finish is the final marker just before the Somerset boathouse.

'Your job is to row as cleanly and efficiently as you can. Don't hold back. If you pace yourself, then we'll have lost the race by halfway. You're all fit and strong and this is half the distance we should have been doing today. When we get to the finish, I want the tanks to be empty. You all know this river like the back of your hand, so you can do that. Be brave! Let's row this to win it! Let's do it for Albion!'

With this lasting rousing exhortation the women gave a cheer, and the group broke up into a chattering mob, hugging each other and patting each other on the back. The Somerset women were huddled around their boat for their own briefing with Jonny. Lesley noticed Beth was watching them.

'Whole crew – hands on!' The order from Molly snapped them back to the task in hand. Boating from an unfamiliar dock on the other side of the river presented a challenge. Even the prevailing wind was pushing them away from the dock rather than blowing them in, as they were used to.

They listened intently to Molly's instructions and they were soon pushing off as smoothly as if they were leaving Albion. Molly moved them into their standard warm-up, and the crew worked their way up through the slide. The sky was overcast and there was a frisky breeze. There was no sign of the hazardous conditions that had been forecast for the Tideway, although there was time for the wind to pick up. It was one of those days it could go either way. The Avon was running fast, but there was no indication of dangerous eddies or currents. From a cursory glance you would say the river conditions were good. But who could really tell by looking at the surface? It was only by testing its true character would be revealed.

They made their way to the top of the river. As they passed Albion, out of the corner of her eye, Lesley could see two figures making ready the club's launches. *At least Mike has shown up. That's one less thing to worry about.*

They rowed past and she could see Molly peering back at the club's dock, no doubt relieved that Stanley had not let her down. At the pumping station, two Somerset members cocooned in down jackets were perched on camping chairs with a laptop set up on a small picnic table. The starting marshals. At the lock gates they turned and waited for Somerset to join them. With a few minutes respite the women sucked on their water bottles and made their last-minute adjustments.

Finally Somerset Union were there. Both crews stared at each other, more wondering than menacing. Are you bigger than us? Are you fitter than us? Whose technique is better? No one spoke except the two coxes who agreed the protocol. Somerset would go off first then Molly would set off after about half a minute. The aim was for both boats to stay within sight, but with enough of a gap that overtaking would be unnecessary. No one had any idea how close the race was likely to be, although the Somerset cox seemed pretty confident.

Molly told the crew to number off. Once the numbering reached her at Stroke, Kate yelled out, 'Good luck, Somerset Union!'

'Good luck, Albion!' came the reply.

With that, the Somerset cox called her crew to back-stops, and they were off. Lesley studied them intently as they rowed away. After a pause Molly set her own crew off in pursuit. She'd instructed them to row at light pressure, but each precise stroke suggested a racehorse performing caprioles as it waited for the tape to go up at the start of a race. Lesley felt the adrenaline in front and behind. The boat was as light as air and going like a rocket.

As they approached the pumping station, Molly instructed them to take it up to race pace, following Stroke. They didn't need telling twice and the boat leapt forward with the change of gear. This was fast. The rating felt higher than usual. Could they sustain this? Lesley dismissed the thought, confident Molly and Kate knew what they were doing. In any case, she could keep it up. That was all she needed to worry about.

After 500 metres or so, Lesley felt the rhythm click down

a gear to something more sustainable. Their catches were sharp and fast, and the power in each stroke was evident. It was wonderful. A few more strokes and they'd be rowing past Albion's dock. Lesley found herself resetting her core control and lengthening her neck. As they went past the pontoons, a cheer rose up:

'Come on, Albion!'

'Go, Albion, go!'

'Keep it going, Albion!'

At the sound the boat lifted and soared.

Don't look! Don't look! she told herself. The pontoon with its small crowd of green-clad spectators came into Lesley's field of vision. *Concentrate!*

'Rudder going on!' called Molly. The balance wavered as they negotiated a sharp bend, but the crew corrected for the steering and drove hard though the curve, maintaining speed.

'Focus on catches!' called Molly, and once again the crispness returned to their stroke and was rewarded with an increase in speed. Coming up to halfway, they were starting to tire. Lesley knew this was the section of the course where races were won or lost.

As their opponents were ahead and she was facing backwards, Lesley couldn't tell for herself whether they were winning or losing. Like the rest of the crew, she had to rely on feedback from their cox. Molly had said they were gaining, but then she would, wouldn't she? Lesley had completely discounted it.

It was completely different for Somerset: the rowers could all see Albion and judge for themselves who was going the fastest. Conversely, the cox only knew what Stroke was able to convey in spluttered sound bites during the recovery between strokes. If they were faster, Somerset would be enjoying the ride, able to relax and row more efficiently. If they were struggling to match Albion it would be a complete nightmare. They would lose efficiency as they tensed and lost concentration. Lesley was glad the coin toss had resulted in them pursuing. Rowing in a bubble like this was hard, but nothing like as difficult as having to go first and watching their opponents gain on them, stroke by stroke.

As they negotiated the series of bends, Molly wouldn't be able to see the crew in front. It was crucial to maintain effort and keep the speed up. Sometimes that middle section could feel like rowing through fog, weighed down by resistance from the rudder and with no sense of distance or time. No matter how many times she rowed this river, Lesley would never be able to distinguish one bend from another. All Lesley knew was that it was 1,000 metres until they reached the bridge just before the straight. One hundred strokes. She dug deep. They were all digging deep.

'Keep it going!
This is where we win this race!
You can do this!
You've done the training!
Give me speed!
Give me power!
Show me what strong women you are!'

With each call, the boat accelerated forward. As they shot round the last bend and under the glowering metal bridge, the women were ready for the kill. At any moment Molly would be able to see the opposition.

'You've done it!
We're only two lengths behind!
We're winning!
It's just the straight left!

1,000 metres to the finish!
Anyone can row 1,000 metres!
I want you to catch them!
I want you to take them!
Let's do it!
Let's finish this race!'

They were all exhausted. They'd given it everything in the middle section. The fatigue made it hard to detect the movement of muscles so at this point what mattered was focus and technique – and an overwhelming desire to win. The crew sharpened up, their catches crisp with attention.

'Keep it long!' called Molly as one or two started to shorten up. With that command Lesley could feel finishes being held further in. The power was still there. They just had to maintain it to the end of the river. Stroke by stroke. Catch by catch. Finish by finish. It only took a momentary lapse and anyone could catch a crab bringing the boat grinding to a halt. No one wanted to be that rower, least of all Lesley, who was ever conscious of Mike's presence.

750 metres left. Tired as she was, Lesley knew the rest of the crew felt the same. Hopefully, the opposition felt worse.

'They're putting in a burst!
We're not going to lose them!
We're going to give it ten!
In five,
in four,
in three,
in two,
in one,
go!'

With this there was a change of rhythm as the exhausted crew attempted to squeeze even more power from their legs. The rating picked up and Lesley used everything she had left to stick with the pace Kate was setting. Good old Kate.

It will be hurting them more. Lesley repeated this to herself like a mantra.

'We're holding them!' bellowed Molly, excitedly.

'Keep it going!

'We're going to hold them there and then have a final push in the last 250 metres.

Keep it long!

Keep it relaxed!'

By now Lesley was counting down the strokes in the last 250 metres. Ten more. Then another ten.

'We're going to catch them!

Wind with Stroke!

In three,

in two,

in one,

go!'

The rating shot up, and the women set to the task with a renewed sense of purpose. Shattered as they were, they knew how many strokes were left. They knew they had to hang on. Lesley felt a rush of exhilaration from the increased rating and lift of speed.

'Only one length behind!

We can do this!

We're going for the line!'

Again the boat surged forward with a final burst of acceleration. Out of the corner of her eye, Lesley at Six realised she could just see a blur that must be Somerset's stern.

Shit – we're really doing it! At each stroke she concentrated on making it her strongest ever, as if it were her last.

'Last ten strokes to the line!

Make them count!

Leave it all on the river!

Empty the tanks!

Ten!

Nine!'

As Molly's count reached seven, Lesley could see them accelerating past Somerset. She was nearly level with her opposite number. The two sets of blades were dangerously close, and the splashing and shouting from both boats felt like the chaos of battle. *Shit, shit, shit!*

'Three!

Two!

One!

And three more strokes!' With this the Albion boat lurched forward and overtook Somerset, just as they crossed the line and the umpire's bell sounded.

'Light pressure!

Keep it together!

I know you're exhausted but we can't stop here,' said Molly frantically, and the crew limped to a small bay at the side of the river.

'Easy oar!' roared Molly. With this, everyone collapsed in their seat, gasping for breath. The sound of retching floated up from the stern.

'We won!' screamed Lesley, 'We fucking won!' and with this the middle-aged planning officer for the local authority broke down in floods of unstoppable tears. She hadn't allowed herself to even imagine this moment, so used had she become to disappointment. When had she last succeeded in something she'd worked for and deserved? She'd thought being passed over and ignored was now her lot. She didn't know when she'd last savoured the sweet nectar of victory.

'Three cheers for Somerset! Hip hip!' yelled Kate, as their opponents' boat drifted into view.

'Hooray!' replied the crew.

'Hip hip!'

'Hooray!'

'Hip hip!' shouted Kate one last time, her voice cracking with emotion.

'Hooray!' sang out the crew.

Rowing gate: *The metal bar tightened by a screw that closes over the swivel to secure the oar.*

27

KATE

'I could have brought some of my salted caramel cupcakes if I'd known,' said Kate, slightly resentfully. The table in the Somerset clubhouse had been laid out ready with an urn and plates of tempting cakes.

'Kate!' hissed Abbie. 'Having just whooped their asses at rowing, I don't think this is the moment for competitive cake baking.' Kate gave her a weak smile back. She was right of course. Sometimes Kate just couldn't help herself.

They were warmly welcomed by a couple of cheerful women with large metal teapots, and they were soon cramming slabs of coffee cake or millionaire's shortbread in their mouths and gulping down the milky coffee. By now the Somerset crew had arrived along with Jonny, the umpires, and the Albion marshals. The atmosphere was festive. Refreshingly, even the Somerset rowers were in good spirits, fired up by taking part in such a spectacular race. Kate made a point of finding the Somerset Stroke and going over to her.

'You know, on Friday I was inconsolable when I heard the news. But honestly, this has been the best day I've had in a long time. Racing you guys – it's been wonderful.'

'Wasn't it great? Even though we lost. It does seem kind of crazy we have to miss out on a national Head to make us race our neighbours down the road. We should do this again. Although I warn you – you won't find us quite such a soft touch over 1,000 metres,' said the Stroke.

'You know, I've no idea what we'd be like over a shorter distance. I don't think any of us have done a racing start in thirty years,' said Kate.

'Are you trying to make me feel worse?'

'Oh, don't worry – we've done a lot of training and a lot of ergs,' said Kate quickly. 'A lot!'

'I'm joking! You don't get to row like you guys did today without a shedload of training. We know that. Someone said you only came back to rowing a year ago. Is that true?'

'It was about eighteen months ago for me, but most of them only started back last August,' explained Kate.

'Woah – that's seriously impressive. And I thought we had the best coach on the Avon.'

'Well, you certainly have the nicest. He totally saved my life offering to trailer our boat,' said Kate.

'Yes, that's typical of Jonny. He's definitely one of the good ones,' said the Stroke. 'You might pass that on to your number Seven,' she added confidentially with a knowing look. Kate smiled and promised she would.

Just then, one of the Somerset officials climbed onto a chair and called for silence. He was a rotund balding gentleman wearing a moth-eaten Oxford blue blazer. A stained Vincent's Club tie dangled over the bulging mound straining at his shirt buttons. It was with a jolt Kate realised he must be a similar age to most of the toned, sleek women in the room dressed in tight Lycra. He was Somerset's president.

He made a brief speech thanking everyone involved, then he called on one of the urn ladies to present the prizes. Sheepishly, the Albion crew went up to be presented with Somerset china mugs, and then posed on request for photographs.

As the noise died down, Kate realised someone from Albion needed to say something. She looked over to Mike and Stanley. They were deep in conversation in a corner and it didn't look as if either of them were going to do anything. Then just as if she were twenty-five again, without thinking about it, without worrying what anyone would say, she climbed on the chair herself and raised her voice to command quiet.

'Ladies and gentlemen. My name is Kate and I'm the Stroke of the Albion Vesta Eight. I'd like to thank Somerset Union Rowing Club for inviting us to race today.' She went on to explain for the benefit of anyone who didn't know that both crews should have been on the Thames, and how much the race had meant to them all. At this point the assembled crews started applauding furiously.

Raising her hand to quieten the din, Kate went on to thank everyone, including the people who'd provided the refreshments saying, 'I'd like to add a personal note of thanks to whoever made that fabulous coffee cake.' This too provoked another bout of cheering and whistles.

'Finally, I'd like to thank Molly our cox and coach, without whom we would not be here today, and all of the committee at Albion for their unstinting support of our project to put together a women's masters squad at Albion. Please raise your mugs and drink a toast to Somerset and Albion Rowing Clubs.'

With this, everyone raised their mugs aloft and bellowed, 'Somerset and Albion!' They then broke into unbridled clapping and stomping of feet. As Kate clambered down, Beth was at her side.

'Well done, Kate. That was perfect. You never said you were good at public speaking.'

'That's kind of you. I wouldn't say I am but I did have to give a lot of speeches at one time in my career. I guess some things you don't forget.'

'Do you know – contrary to popular opinion – I don't think there are many things you forget. By the way – you laid it on a bit thick about the support we've had from our committee,' said Beth quietly, looking around to see who was standing in earshot.

'There's no point in trying to score points – and anyway, I'm feeling magnanimous right at this moment.'

'If you say so,'

'Right – I must have a word with Jonny before he disappears – you coming?' said Kate, and they made their way over to where he was chatting to Lesley and Sal.

Lesley was reliving the last 250 metres of the race with Jonny chipping in his observations from the bank. She was on amazing form. When she finally paused for breath, Kate took the opportunity to thank Jonny again for all his efforts, not least in organising that morning's race.

'Honestly, the biggest stress of this whole enterprise was trying to find someone to drive a trailer up to London. I spent months trying to solve it and was really starting to lose sleep over it. When you agreed to help it was a lifesaver,' gushed Kate. As she said this, she noticed Sal frowning.

'Honestly, it was my pleasure,' said Jonny. 'As it turns out, you've done me a favour racing my crew. They were in danger of becoming a bit complacent after their big win last year. Losing to you lot so decisively today is going to make them all sit up and think about their training. This is exactly what they needed at this stage of the season.'

'What was their big win last year?' asked Lesley.

'Gold at the Nationals,' replied Jonny and Lesley choked on her coffee, spraying fine brown droplets down her new vest.

'They won at the Nationals? Oh my God, I'm so glad I didn't know that before the race!' spluttered Lesley.

'Didn't I mention it?' asked Jonny airily, with a twinkle in his eye. 'You guys are seriously good. We're going to have to work extremely hard to beat you next time. By the way – what is your next race?'

'We haven't got that far,' said Kate. 'Any suggestions?'

'You could go in for the usual local regattas, but if you want to row as a masters' crew it can be tricky finding competition. You should definitely be thinking of the Nationals up in Nottingham in May, and Henley Masters in July,' said Jonny. 'You'll have plenty of competition there, and both regattas are extremely well run. Believe it or not, they run exactly to time.'

'Sounds like my sort of regatta,' replied Kate. 'We'll have to give it some thought.'

The group fell silent, munching on their cake and considering the glittering prizes that might lie in their future. Except Sal, who was hopping from one foot to the other. Finally she broke the silence.

'Kate, I had no idea you were so stressed about the transport thing. Otherwise I might have mentioned it sooner. Back when the issue first came up, I asked a committee member if I could tow the trailer. You see, I got my HGV licence when I was in the army—'

'What – you were in the army?' Beth asked, incredulous. Which regiment?'

'The Royal Hussars. I did five years. I left after I met Erica and started my nursing training. Anyway, I got my HGV—'

'You can drive a lorry?' interrupted Lesley, astounded.

'Well, yes. And a tank which is rather harder.' Sal looked quite pleased with herself about the tank bit. 'So although it's lapsed now, towing the trailer would be a piece of cake compared to the things I used to drive—'

'So what happened?' asked Kate, realising she too was interrupting. 'What did they say?'

'I'm afraid they rather fobbed me off. If I'd known how much difficulty it was creating I might have pressed harder. You see, you don't need a qualification to tow the trailer, you just need to be confident in doing it safely.'

All of the women stared at Sal. There was silence. Finally Kate voiced one of the many questions they were all wondering:

'Why wouldn't they let you tow the club trailer?' She spoke quietly, her mouth dry.

'Oh, I think he said my experience was too out of date and I'd need to be retrained by the club. Apparently, no one was available for that. So I kind of gave up,' said Sal. 'I wish I'd known how much trouble it was causing.'

'Seems a bit odd,' volunteered Jonny. 'If you were a Somerset member I'd put you in charge of training trailer drivers. You would easily be the most qualified person around here.'

Kate noticed the expression on Lesley's face. She looked as if she were about to explode. Beth must have noticed it too because she suddenly said, 'Jonny, could I trouble you to get me another coffee? I think we need a quick team talk. I'll catch up with you in a few minutes.' Jonny took the hint and quickly took himself off. By the time he'd left them Lesley's face was one livid flush with pale splodges on her cheeks. She stared at Sal and spoke softly but with careful emphasis.

‘Who was it Sal? Which committee member did you ask?’

Sal sighed and looked down at her feet, shaking her head. Then raising her gaze, she looked straight at Lesley and replied, ‘I’m sorry, Lesley, but it was Mike.’

Ratio: *The ratio of the time taken for the power phase to that of the recovery phase of the stroke. Ideally time taken for the recovery will be about three times that of the power phase. 1:3.*

28

BETH

The Waterman was crowded, but the manager was able to find them a table as a booking had failed to show. Beth and Lesley slunk into the corner, grateful to be away from the crowd. It had been gruesome rowing back to Albion after Mike's treachery had been uncovered.

Lesley put her elbows on the table and held her head in her hands. Beth wondered whether this was the point when the tears would start, but Lesley seemed beyond crying. Beth spoke softly.

'Lesley, if you don't want to go home, I have a guest room with the bed all made up. Just say the word and it's yours for as long as you need it.'

Lesley finally peeled her hands away from her head and looked up.

'Oh, thanks, Beth. You're such a good friend. I'll bear it in mind. But I need to talk to Mike about this today. I know I won't get any sleep until I have.' She paused. 'Do you know, I'm so used to the shitty things he does, it's almost like I don't even notice them any more. Right from the start, when you first called me about coming back to rowing, Mike has not given me so much as one word of encouragement. Not one. Would it have killed him to coach us occasionally? I know Molly would have appreciated the input. He'll go out all hours of the day and night coaching every single person in the club – except me and my crew.'

Beth gave a wry smile and nodded, trying to convey her support.

'Do you know, I asked him if he would drive the trailer to London and we could make a weekend of it. He didn't even consider it. He had no interest in how we were going to get there. I think he assumed we wouldn't be able to find a trailer driver so we'd have to scrap the idea. He obviously didn't realise how resourceful Kate is. Why would he do that? Why would he try to wreck this for me?' At this Lesley ran out of steam, and Beth took her hand and held it.

'I don't know what to say, Lesley. You're going to have to hear his side of the story, but it doesn't look good. And you're right – Mike hasn't really done much to help us, but then, to be fair, nor have the rest of the committee.'

'No – that's true.'

'I got the impression they were hoping it would all fizzle out and we'd lose interest. And it probably would have done without Kate and Molly. Have you noticed, Molly's one of the best coaches in the club and yet they treat her as if she's a novice cox - Stanley included. She has no sense of her own ability and it's hardly surprising when she's constantly put down and undermined. God, I could spit!'

Fortunately, before Beth could follow through on this threat, their roast pork arrived, piping hot with driblets of fat and the comforting sweetness of apples. Food always helped Lesley's mood. The women tucked in with the enjoyment reserved for those who've earned their appetite with hard, physical labour.

The pub bustled with activity: family groups with nothing to say to each other, undergraduates eager to make full use of their student loans, lovers more interested in making physical contact than availing themselves of refreshment.

Her meal half-finished Beth hesitated, wanting to speak but afraid of saying the wrong thing.

'You know – playing devil's advocate – it is possible Mike wasn't trying to be obstructive and he genuinely thought Sal couldn't or shouldn't tow the club's trailer. It is a massive responsibility after all, towing the club's most expensive boat up the M4.'

'Well, if he thought that it's even worse. What possible objection could he have, other than her being a woman pushing fifty? And if that's the case, what does that say about the way he thinks about me?' Lesley was starting to get herself quite worked up again.

'You're right,' sighed Beth, sawing at a particularly tempting piece of crackling as she spoke. 'It's all of a piece, isn't it? They don't think we should be rowing, towing trailers or anything else for that matter.' She hesitated, weighing up whether to continue. 'You may not know this as it was just before you joined, but around the time of the Olympics, there were a load of really poisonous comments about Kate posted on the club's Facebook page. Things like – "we don't want menopausal women in our club".'

'No! You're kidding me! Poor Kate. What on earth was that about? What could she possibly have done to deserve that?' asked Lesley, starting to shriek again.

'Well, it all started when Kate was interviewed by the BBC after Kirsty and Karen won their gold medals. They interviewed lots of us, but hers was the one they showed. At the time I thought it was just envy – I'm pretty sure it was started by that Chloe in the Senior Women's eight.

Everyone thinks she's so sweet, but I've been coxing her for a couple of years and trust me, she's pure poison. She's incredibly manipulative and everyone just seems to fall for it, especially the middle-aged men.'

'Now you come to mention it I've heard Mike saying how nice she is more than once. But then he always was a sucker for a pretty face.'

'It's shocking the lies she tells. Yet everyone just laps it up. I couldn't believe no one called her out about the Facebook thing – assuming it was her. In fact, quite a number of other members piled in with nasty remarks of their own. It was bewildering the way these people didn't seem to realise they were talking about an individual with feelings who was going to read their comments.'

'That's just awful.'

'Now, looking back, I wonder whether it wasn't just Chloe, but something deeper. Whether our presence somehow reminds the other members that none of them are young, elite athletes. It's as if our being at the club cheapens what they do. You know – if a bunch of old women can do this sport then maybe they aren't the gods they thought they were.' Beth ground to a halt, and placed the now cold piece of crackling in her mouth and chewed thoughtfully. She normally tried to avoid speaking ill of other people and was surprised how cathartic it could be.

'Poor Kate!' wailed Lesley, who was now more herself. She stared down at the plate of food in front of her as if unsure why it was there. Finally she laid down her knife and fork: 'Who was that American woman who said, "There's a special place in hell for women who don't help other women"?'

'I don't know but my friend Lorna has it written on a T-shirt.'

'It's just too awful for words. I mean, what sort of a cow does that? How did Kate take it?'

'She was devastated. Completely devastated. It was so totally unprovoked. There's no question she'd have given up rowing there and then but for the fact that very same day we heard from fourteen amazing women – yourself included – who were all dead keen to get involved in this project she'd started.'

'I can't believe it. I just can't believe it. Kate has done such an amazing job – not to mention bringing fourteen new members into the club paying full subscriptions.'

'That's true, I hadn't thought of it like that.'

'By the way – wasn't she great today at Albion, that speech she made? You look at her and you think she's just another middle-aged woman. Then she does something like that and you realise – wow! – you're really somebody.'

Both women cupped their wine glasses and drank, pondering all that had been said.

'Changing the subject, you seemed to be getting on really well with the lovely Jonny,' cackled Lesley, brightening.

'He is lovely, isn't he?' said Beth, unable to conceal her pleasure. 'He asked if I wanted to go to a lecture about nutrition tomorrow evening, up at the university.'

'Wow. A date. That's exciting.'

'It's not a date, Lesley,' Beth said firmly. Yet despite her protestations the simple mention of Jonny's name produced a fluttering in her lower abdomen that made her squirm.

Standing start: *A racing start done from stationary.*

29

KATE

Why are these trousers tight across my thighs? This suit's always fitted perfectly. And it's gaping round the waist. With this Kate stuck her thumb in her waistband to gauge the size of the gap. It was one of her favourite suits, bought in the days when her salary stretched to Italian designers. A fashion expert would have recognised the cut of the jacket was subtly dated, but it didn't trouble Kate as it spent most of the day draped on the back of her chair. She hadn't worn it since the previous summer as it was relatively lightweight. *Who has trousers that fit on the hips but are too small for their thighs?* It was a mystery.

Kate was in the office, despite it being a Monday morning. She didn't officially work the first two days of the week, but she'd been so distracted on Friday she felt the need to put in a couple of hours to get on top of things.

There was a steady flow of staff walking past her glass office wall. But this morning she barely noticed the comings and goings and didn't once dwell on the deficiencies of her office arrangements. She was on fire as she pored over her stack of medical reports, witness statements, HR records and the multitude of other documents required to build a case. By lunchtime she'd brought all three of her most pressing files up to date and felt happy to call it a day.

As she saved the document she was working on, she stretched out her back and listened to the ligaments and vertebrae click as they rubbed over each other. Life was good. She felt whole. Complete. She reflected on the events of the weekend with immense satisfaction. She'd never thought of herself as someone who needed to win, but goodness, it had felt fantastic. She couldn't have predicted their quest would take the turn it did, but it felt fine none the less. They'd rowed their race – not a Race that Mattered, as Beth would say. But it would do for now. They'd shown themselves what they could do – and a few other people into the bargain.

Kate thought back to standing on the chair in the Somerset clubhouse and for once she didn't cringe at the memory. She was pleased. She'd done what needed to be done and she'd done it well.

With Vesta over, she finally had the mental space to consider other matters. Only now it was at an end could she appreciate how every waking moment had been dominated by Vesta: the crew, their training, the logistics, appeasing the committee.

Firstly, they needed to work out where the vet squad was going from here. Kate knew there would be a lull in motivation and it was essential they made the transition to the next challenge before it all fell apart. She drew up a list of calls to make when she got home, starting with Beth and Molly.

Next on her list was her job. Tim had been right that night a few months back, when they nearly had an argument: she shouldn't simply accept this was all there was. After that conversation she'd scoured the ads in the legal journals, updated her online profile and had long conversations with a couple of headhunters. This simply confirmed what she knew already: she was only qualified to do the work she was already doing, and she was unlikely to find a job that was significantly better paid, and definitely not one that was as convenient. *Would it be terribly unprofessional to tell the headhunter you just wanted a window?*

Kate now found herself wondering whether she'd simply gone through the motions of looking for a job just to prove a point to Tim. For in truth that was all she'd done.

Come on, Kate. You can do better than that. If you'd just gone through the motions at Albion you wouldn't have built your own veteran squad. If you can do that, surely you can create your own job?

She considered the problem. She had two major assets in her favour: firstly, she was in the privileged position of not needing to earn more money, so she could gain experience by volunteering on her two free days. Secondly, as Beth had pointed out, she could easily work in London as Tim already had a flat there.

It would also mean they could spend more time together – and a different quality of time. It would be like going back to the days before they got married when Tim had moved into her small but perfectly formed one-bedroomed flat. There'd never been enough storage space, but somehow that hadn't mattered, as if the dimensions of the rooms had forced them closer together.

It was extraordinary how suddenly her brain felt energised: it was like a smouldering fire that receives a gust of oxygen to its glowing embers and bursts into flame. She reopened her laptop and tapped at the keys, bringing up page after page, until she found what she was after: a charity working with asylum seekers. *They're bound to need another lawyer.* Before she could lose heart or start doubting herself,

Kate composed an email asking about volunteering opportunities, attached her CV and pressed Send.

Having completed her to-do list for the day, she packed up her things and headed out of the office. As she walked along the wide corridor to the main stairs, Rick, the tosser who'd stolen her almond croissant, emerged from a side office and fell into step beside her.

'How's it going?'

'I'm fine, Rick. How are you?' Ahead were a pair of heavy swing doors, and through the glass Kate could see an elderly woman with a mop of white curls hunched over a walking frame. Kate recognised her as one of the firm's oldest clients. She'd managed to push open the door on one side and was busy transferring her frame to the other hand. In that moment Rick stepped forward and was about to barge in front of Kate and past the client. Kate grabbed him by the arm and held him firmly in place as she held the door with her other hand.

'Hello, Mrs Stringer. What an absolute pleasure to see you.'

'Good afternoon, young lady,' and Mrs Stringer tottered through the opening and off down the corridor. As they watched her depart, Kate let go of her grip on Rick's arm.

'Please remember your manners, Rick. Around clients. And colleagues,' and she walked on through the door leaving Rick for once the one without a response. As she strode down the stairs she breathed out a deep sigh of satisfaction. And allowed herself just the merest hint of a smile.

Fixed Seat: *When the athlete rows arms and/or body only without moving their seat.*

30

BETH

Bugger, bugger, bugger. Every time Beth found a likely looking space it turned out to be reserved for permit holders or disabled parking. Beth had meant to be on time. She really had. But as someone who'd always taken a relaxed approach to timekeeping, she'd fallen into the habit of deceiving herself how late she really was. So today, when for some reason being on time seemed to matter, she didn't have a realistic idea of how much time she needed to allow. She'd even worried she'd be ridiculously early.

Unfortunately she hadn't factored in the time it would take driving round and round the university campus looking for a visitor parking space. Then she had to negotiate the ticket machine. Finding she didn't have enough money in her purse, she returned to her car and scrabbled about in the glove compartment. She found several used tissues, a comb and a previously sucked humbug, but eventually she had sufficient shrapnel for her purposes. Trying to feed them into the machine she dropped two coins and then one of them jammed. *Bugger, bugger, bugger.* Finally she secured her ticket.

Next was the not inconsiderable challenge of finding

where the lecture was being held. Being not so much a red-brick university as a reinforced concrete one, it was made up of an endless sprawl of apparently identical buildings. By the time she had found the correct amphitheatre the lecture had already started.

The entrance emerged right next to the lecturer, an arrangement that could have been designed expressly to deter latecomers. As she opened the door, the speaker paused and all eyes turned to Beth.

'Do make yourself at home.' The sarcasm was clearly well-practised. Fortunately Beth caught sight of Jonny sitting in a row near the back, high up in the raked seating, semaphoring madly with both arms. Good old Jonny. Beth completed her walk of shame, cheeks glowing and slid into the orange seat next to him.

'OK? Glad you made it. So pleased to see you.'

Beth gave him a wry smile and continued her efforts to shrink into the back of the plastic seat and disappear from view. The lecturer, a Dr Harper, was a PhD rather than a medical doctor, and was peppering her talk with as many scientific and technical terms as she could. She wasn't a natural speaker, and in her attempt to sound more impressive had lost all sense of what she was trying to convey. Beth could understand each word, but strung together the meaning eluded her. The audience was largely composed of members of the Sports Science Faculty, and they all seemed to be paying close attention.

Then Dr Harper let slip the word 'protein' – followed by the word 'molecule', to be fair – and one of the swimmers shot up his hand to ask a question about protein supplements and a heated debate ensued. Beth knew the official line was that athletes should obtain their protein from a balanced diet. The reality was they all relied heavily on commercially produced supplements, even though these were frowned upon or even banned by some sports. The reasoning seemed to be a Luddite, 'you never know what else is in them'. Unfortunately this logic failed to recognise that the same could be said of the instant noodles and fast food the average student willingly subsisted on, so was unlikely to be much of a deterrent.

While the uproar continued, Beth stole a glance at Jonny. He looked at her and smiled encouragingly.

'Not too bored?' he whispered.

'Not at all – it's . . . interesting,' she whispered back, just as the good doctor called for quiet and resumed her thread. She'd moved on to amino acids. Beth couldn't imagine this was going to be of any direct use to the swimmers, badminton players and gymnasts in the audience, but they all sat listening intently, one or two of them nodding sagely and taking notes.

Beth looked down at her lap, her hands clasped together. Then she glanced sideways at Jonny. He was gripping his seat on both sides as if he were concerned he might be ejected at any moment and it would be important to maintain contact with the chair. His sleeves were pushed up above his elbows – it was hot in the lecture theatre, particularly high up in the back rows. Beth studied his muscular forearms, lightly covered in soft black hair. As she looked at the tendons rippling beneath the skin, she felt a jolt like an electric shock somewhere deep in her pelvis. She looked up to find him gazing at her. The air between them crackled.

'. . . I cannot stress enough the impact of long-chain saturated fatty acids on the blood lipid profile . . .' Beth smiled and turned away to give Dr Harper her full attention.

After the lecture they stood in the gloom next to the

harshly lit entrance. A sudden blast from a northerly wind made Beth shiver. They stood facing each other, hands in their pockets, jiggling around on the spot to keep warm. Neither seemed to know how to behave around the other.

Beth was in no rush to go home. She wanted to stay and get to know Jonny. She didn't want to call an end to the evening. It was just friends. Obviously. But still she felt something powerful drawing her towards him that scrambled her thoughts and made speech near impossible.

Perhaps Jonny had an early start in the morning? He was bound to be busy. He didn't say anything, and some internal conflict made him twitch and fidget. The students streamed past them, talking animatedly and calling out to friends as they went. A few of them headed towards the neon sign for a café further along the building.

'Do you fancy a coffee?' asked Jonny finally, indicating the café by inclining his head towards it.

'Yes!' said Beth, way too quickly.

The place was brightly lit, and housed a number of students working at laptops.

'What would you like – coffee?'

'Actually, I'll have a herbal tea – mint if they have it.' She installed herself in the far corner in a group of low-slung easy chairs and watched as Jonny bought the drinks at the counter. He smiled as he walked over to her and Beth found herself beaming back at him.

'Well – you really know how to spoil a girl.'

'I'm sorry – could this be any more grim?' said Jonny, and they both laughed, relieved to break the tension.

'So – what did you make of the lecture?' asked Beth, raising her brows to peer up at Jonny as she sipped at her scalding tea.

'Honestly? Not a lot, I'm afraid. I'd been hoping for

something a bit more . . . well, applied. You know? Some specific dos and don'ts I could share with my crews. How about you? You're medical, I hear.'

'Well, not medical as such. I'm a physio.'

'That could definitely come in handy. I always seem to have one injury or another. In fact, my rotator cuff is throbbing quietly as we speak. So what did you think about the lecture?'

'Honestly?' Beth looked around as if Dr Harper might be eavesdropping. In hushed tones she whispered, enunciating carefully, 'I thought it was a load of utter bollocks.'

'Oh my God, I knew it was a mistake asking you,' said Jonny, burying his face in his hands. 'I'm such an idiot.'

'Don't be silly,' laughed Beth, pulling his hand away from his face. 'I'm so glad you did. And you weren't to know what it was going to be like. Anyway, if we hadn't come, I wouldn't have got my mint tea.' Beth suddenly realised she was still holding his hand, and she dropped it hastily.

'Yeah, in a caff that makes a motorway service station look upmarket.'

'Well – you have a point. Anyway – enough of that. Tell me about yourself.'

With that, Jonny gave her a potted version of his life story, spun to make humorous the various everyday tragedies that had brought him to this point. As Beth listened, she decided he was a decent and kind man who'd been dealt a slightly shoddy hand by life. He was simply lovely.

There was no doubting his physical appeal. He wore his powerful masculinity as casually as some men wear cologne. He was funny, too, in a self-deprecating way that made Beth warm to him all the more. He couldn't have been more different from Mark and she knew Kate would really like him. For a moment she pondered which of her single friends he'd be right for, given he wasn't suitable for her. Obviously.

'Hello, Beth. Fancy seeing you here. What brings you to my manor?' In front of them stood a swarthy young man wearing tracksuit bottoms and an oversized hoodie with the word 'Physio' written in enormous letters front and back. Without invitation he sat down at one of the vacant chairs.

'Oh, hi, Liam. We just went to a lecture. Liam – this is my friend Jonny. Jonny – Liam did part of his training in our department at the hospital.'

'I think I recognise you from the gym here,' said Jonny.

'Probably. I spend a lot of my time there, know what I mean?' And he laughed a huge belly laugh. Beth was wondering what to say, not wanting to encourage Liam to linger, but equally not wanting to appear rude. Just then the lights flashed a couple of times.

'Chucking out time,' said Liam. 'I was lucky to grab my protein shake before they shut. Nice to see you, Beth.'

Outside they stood awkwardly once again in the pool of light in front of the café. Liam's arrival had broken whatever spell they'd started to weave and they were both unsure what to do or say next.

'Well, goodnight then. I guess I'll see you on the river,' said Jonny and they exchanged a clumsy and mistimed peck on the cheek.

'See you on the river,' called Beth as she hurried away.

Release: *At the end of the drive portion of the stroke when the blade is removed from the water.*

31
KATE

The village hall was ablaze with light when Kate arrived. Abbie was inside directing operations. She'd called Kate the evening after the race to suggest a curry night to celebrate, but Kate's immediate reaction had been Tuesday was too soon.

'Why don't we do it next weekend?'

'I'm afraid it has to be Tuesday,' Abbie replied firmly. 'That's my only overnight respite care this month. And don't worry – I'll organise it. Just leave it to me.'

Kate enquired gently whether Abbie would really be able to manage it in two days.

'Katie, once upon a time I ran a company with 2,000 employees. I think I can organise a curry night in the village hall with forty-eight hours' notice.'

Embarrassed to find she'd done to Abbie the very thing she hated people doing to her, Kate meekly asked what she could do to help. Despite Abbie's protestations, she insisted on providing pudding.

'You know I feel uncomfortable if I'm not in control of the stickies,' she joked.

'Yes, I do know, Katie. And you really ought to see someone about that,' said Abbie.

The evening was not just an opportunity to celebrate their victory, it was a chance for the whole veteran squad to regroup and talk about what they would do next. After long discussions with Beth and Molly they'd agreed it made sense to break down into fours. The clocks were going forward the following week, which meant people could start rowing after work as well as at weekends. To be competitive, crews needed to train at least four times a week over the summer. Realistically, not all of the women in the squad could commit to that. So, much as they'd enjoyed rowing together in an eight, it made sense to divide into smaller crews based on how many times a week each woman was able to train.

To avoid arguments, Kate insisted Molly should make the decision on crews, but the new arrangements would need to be sold to everyone, and Kate had taken the time to speak to each member of the squad beforehand to check they were happy with the plan, in principle. A few of them didn't want to commit to anything, but were happy to act as sit-ins for the crews when required. A couple of them had started saying who they did or didn't want to row with, but Kate had cut them off. Crew selection would be based on availability and suitability, not friendships.

She recalled squabbles she'd sorted out between her two girls over the years. She'd told them they didn't have to be friends but they did have to be sisters, and had insisted on kindness and loyalty irrespective of the provocation. This seemed to be a good rule for the veteran squad too. Despite Kate's assurances, Molly was anxious there would be objections to her crew assignments. It seemed to be a common occurrence at Albion.

The squad arrived en masse as they were sharing lifts and got stuck straight in to the bottles of wine Abbie had chilling in a large cooler full of ice. Then a couple of waiters turned up from Manzil's, the best Indian restaurant in Bath. They manhandled in half a dozen massive catering trays covered in silver foil. Abbie had already set up plates and cutlery on the trestle table, and once everything was uncovered, she yelled, 'Grub's up!'

Being amongst friends, none of them felt the need to hold back. They loaded up their plates as if they hadn't eaten in days: vivid orange tikka masala, fragrant yellow rice studded with cardamom, pungent onion bhajis and pillowy nan bread. They sat either side of one long table. Kate was impressed. It all looked so welcoming and everyone was clearly loving it. *Well done, Abbie. I'm sorry I doubted you.*

The noise level rose exponentially as the rowers conducted animated conversations about the food, the race, and rowing in general. The glasses were filled and refilled. After a month's abstinence the Vesta crew quickly become tipsy. Not wishing to be left behind, the rest of the squad downed their drinks enthusiastically. No doubt they all felt the need to justify the expense of a taxi home.

Once they'd finished eating, Kate got to her feet and thanked everyone for their contribution to the Vesta project and the victory over Somerset. She spoke from the heart and managed to convey something of how much the endeavour and their support had meant to her. Her words were met by a chorus of cheering, whistling and stomping of feet. She thanked Abbie for organising the evening and this was met with more applause, although without the whistling this time, as it turned out that had been coming from Abbie, who sheepishly removed her two fingers from her mouth.

Finally Molly called for quiet, and said a few words about

the crews going forward. It was a repetition of what Kate had discussed with all of them on the phone, so several of them carried on chatting in the background. Molly directed a scowl in their direction. When she announced she was about to call out the lists of crew, there was an ominous hush. She read through the names of the four crews, and Kate was delighted to find she was with Beth, Lesley and Abbie. They all hugged each other with squeals of delight.

Abbie muttered, 'Looks like I'm with the Three Musketeers. I guess that makes me D'Artagnan.'

It hadn't been a coincidence that Molly had assigned Abbie and Kate to the same crew. It was the only request Kate had made but she knew it was important Abbie was in a crew that went out regularly. Abbie still didn't tell them much but they heard snippets and caught glimpses of the grind of caring for a loved one disintegrating in such a cruel fashion. Occasionally she mentioned when they had to call out a police helicopter as her husband had gone missing. Again. Or the time her husband decided to relieve himself against a wall in the local shopping centre. She tried to relate these events for comic effect, but there was not much to laugh about.

Kate found it difficult to hear of her friend's struggles, feeling impotent. She knew they were helping Abbie by having her in the crew. 'First take care of the carer.' Kate couldn't remember where she'd heard that, but she recognised the truth of it. That was what they were doing and would continue to do, even after Abbie lost her husband, as she inevitably would. It still felt inadequate.

She'd once been driving though a busy intersection on a day when the rain was coming down like a tropical deluge. The traffic had slowed down because of the conditions, but as they approached the crossroads the whole snarling mess ground to a halt. Kate's windscreen wipers were on double speed but she still struggled to see through the stream of water over the glass. She could just make out a man standing in the road, waving his arms. He was tall and well-dressed but something about his movements was off-kilter. People are frightened of bats in part because of their unpredictable and skittish movements. It was the same with this man. There was nothing intrinsically threatening about his behaviour. It was just . . . odd.

Then Kate realised the cause of his anguish: a dog running manically amongst the traffic. It was a liver and white spaniel, and Kate was just thinking it looked vaguely familiar when she saw Abbie running between the cars, attempting to catch the errant dog while shouting at the poor, bewildered man. Her hair was plastered to her scalp, and her clothes were sodden. She was wearing fuchsia high heels, of all things.

Cars further back were tooting their horns, but the drivers closest to the drama remained silent. No one moved. No one offered a hand. Including Kate. She'd been rooted to the spot, dithering with uncertainty. What should she do? Did she have a waterproof in the car? An umbrella? Anything to act as a leash for the dog? Just as she decided to get out and simply do what she could, the situation resolved itself. Abbie caught hold of the dog by the scruff of the neck and, taking her husband's arm, dragged him to the pavement. The traffic started moving again, and Kate found herself driving slowly past on the other side of the road.

It had taken days to shake her deep sense of shame that she'd done nothing to help her friend. Finally Kate assuaged her conscience by vowing to do what she could: she'd ensure Abbie's time at the river was as rewarding as possible. If she couldn't relieve her burden, she could at least provide her friend with some respite.

Kate had never told Abbie she'd seen her that day in the rain. She'd never told anyone – but she hoped by being in a crew with Abbie, she could make it up to her.

Now Abbie climbed on a chair and announced, 'Oi, you horrible lot. Before you get pudding we're having a boat race!' This was greeted with a raucous cheer, although it was not clear whether the crowd were excited about the game or the pudding.

Kate wondered whether Poppy or Ella did boat races at university. Drinking games were always popular with students. She'd never forget her daughters making her elderly mother join in a family game of Beer Pong the previous Easter.

Sal and Hilary went round topping everyone up and Abbie checked everyone had a full glass. Molly started raising an objection, but Abbie shushed her quiet and said she could be the umpire. As the rest of the squad were enthusiastically attempting to form teams, Molly gave in and shouted at them until they were just about in two lines.

'Albion A.

Albion B.

Attention.

Go!'

Sangeeta and Abbie both started downing their wine. Bizarrely, Geeta seemed to pour the liquid straight down her throat without swallowing, while Abbie was taking more ladylike sips. Geeta was the first to invert her dripping glass on her head, signalling Ling to start drinking. Sal took over from Abbie and demonstrated she might have learnt more than HGV driving in the army by pouring it straight into her mouth, although in fairness, half of it did go down her top. It was bedlam with everyone shouting and shrieking, stamping their feet and wine going everywhere. A crash and the tinkle of broken glass were rewarded by a roar from everyone.

Finally, Lesley and Hilary were the last to go and started almost simultaneously. Both of them poured the wine in the general direction of their mouths and some of it even ended up being swallowed. It was a dead heat. The cheers were deafening. The boat race triumph required a toast of celebration and Abbie and Geeta went round filling everyone up.

With her glass replenished, Lesley clambered on a chair and stood swaying gently, holding her wine aloft.

'I'd like to propose a toast: to the best bloomin' group of women in the whole world.' With this, she attempted to drink. Concentrating on carrying her glass to her mouth, which she'd temporarily misplaced, Lesley forgot to control her balance and gradually started toppling over sideways. Fortunately Ling noticed what was happening and shouted, 'Catch her!' and Lesley fell neatly into the arms of four of her crewmates.

As they set her back on her feet, Lesley didn't miss a beat and carried on shouting, 'The best bloomin' women in the world! I need another drink. Why's my glass empty?'

All around her was laughter and delight as Kate reflected on the group. They scrubbed up well, this squad of hers, glamorous in sequins and beading. Two of the women were wearing the exact same brightly patterned wrap dress, which caused much hilarity and Lesley was a knockout in an elegant blue dress. The women she knew barefaced and dishevelled on the river were transformed into sleek creatures of the night, with styled hair and dangly earrings.

Kate was so pleased they were up for some fun. She

hadn't behaved like this in years. It wasn't that she hadn't wanted to. She hadn't changed. But as they aged, she and her friends felt judged if they drank too much or were loud. It was so liberating to kick back with a group of women her own age. No one was judging anyone tonight.

'OK, guys!' shouted Abbie over the cacophony of sound. 'Kate's about to bring out her famous Lemon Polenta Cake.' Everyone erupted into thunderous cheers and whoops. Abbie raised her hands for quiet.

'Anyone who wants a piece though has to do a turn with the karaoke machine,' and here she waved an arm in the direction of the machine she'd installed in the corner.

'Crikey, Abbie – you really know how to organise a party,' called Beth in amazement. They were interrupted by the sound of scuffling from the end of the hall as Lesley and Hilary attempted to elbow each other out of the way to be first in line. Beth rushed over and persuaded the two women they could sing together. They then started bickering over what to sing. While they were arguing, with Beth desperately trying to act as intermediary, Kate intervened.

'Ladies – would you mind if I went first? I think it's time for our song. You can both help me.' She whispered the chosen title in Abbie's ear as she bent over the controls and scrolled through the song titles. The insistent rhythmic tattoo of a drum beat out and Kate started singing,

I used to always be alone
Said I didn't need anyone
I could do it all myself
Then my crew adopted me . . .

'Shit – you can sing!' shouted Lesley.

'Go, girl!' yelled Abbie.

And now I don't go anywhere
Without my boyz surrounding me . . .

'Way to go Kate!'

So if you see our gang coming,
Just remember . . .

As the verse gave way to the chorus the women linked arms around each other's shoulders, spraying sauvignon blanc everywhere as they did so. They threw back their heads and gave it everything they had:

We are young
Let's live our lives,
Strong and free . . .

Stride out!: *Instruction to reduce the rating after a racing start.*

32
BETH

Vesta Eight Trounces National Champions

> *The cancellation of this year's Vesta Head Race in London was not going to deter two of our plucky local crews from testing each other's mettle. Somerset Union and Albion Rowing Clubs organised a mini Veterans' Head of their own to allow the two women's masters' C crews to battle it out. The smart money was on the Somerset crew who triumphed at the National Championships last summer, but plucky underdogs Albion refused to be beaten, and not only caught up with Somerset who started first, but overhauled them at the line.*

Above this paragraph was a photograph of the Albion crew, sucking in their stomachs and self-consciously brandishing their trophy coffee mugs. Beth and the other three stood in a tight knot of Lycra, heads touching, as they held the paper up for scrutiny.

'I wish I'd brushed my hair,' wailed Lesley.

'I wish I'd had a facelift,' said Abbie.

'I wish they hadn't taken a photo at all,' said Kate. 'Who on earth gave it to the paper?' The women fell silent as they minutely examined the picture and reread the text. Beth guessed Kate was anxious about the Albion trolls. Someone was bound to have posted the article to the club Facebook page.

'By the way, I forgot to ask: how was your date on Monday?' Lesley asked.

'It wasn't a date,' muttered Beth, her face buried in her rucksack as she rummaged around for her diary.

'What's this? A date?' asked Abbie.

'It wasn't a date,' repeated Beth. That came out more forcefully than was strictly necessary. And possibly sounded a little tetchy as well. She didn't know what she thought about the whole Jonny thing, except it felt tumultuous. She simply wasn't ready to discuss it with anyone, or to put labels on it.

After Molly's announcement of the new crews, the four women had quickly arranged to go out late on Friday afternoon, and secured Molly to cox them. Lesley was able to flex out early as she had so much time owing, and Beth and Kate were able to rejig their schedules. Abbie had the most difficulty as she had to make sure there was a reliable carer available to take care of her husband. Kate was still reluctant to row at the same time as the members who'd trolled her on Facebook and she justified her preference saying it was easier to secure the boat they wanted at quieter times. They would be rowing in *Desdemona*, the better of the two fours allocated to the women's squad.

The four women had arrived before Molly to discuss dates and schedules. They were all happy with the idea of four water sessions a week and soon roughed out a potential timetable. Once they'd agreed their training schedule, the next matter to be settled was the races they were planning to enter.

'The thing is,' volunteered Abbie, 'just speaking

personally, it's obviously difficult for me to get away at weekends. Plus, if I'm honest, I'm not sure quite how much I actually like racing. I'm pleased to have done it, and I wouldn't train as hard or be as committed if I didn't have a race in sight. But it's the training I really enjoy. Does that make sense?'

'Perfectly,' said Beth. 'I used to love going away with the club for the weekend to some ghastly local regatta, camping in a muddy field, living on burgers and boogying to Ted's disco in the clubhouse until it shut down at 10.00 p.m.'

'Ahh – those were the days,' agreed Lesley wistfully.

'I think I'm just too old for it – I've come to realise I don't like camping and I don't like cheap burgers. When I've coxed in races the last few years, I've tended to drive up, do my thing and then drive back. Of course it's different when you're part of a crew. But I think I'm with you, Abbie – I'd be quite happy with just one or two races to aim for.'

Following on from Jonny's suggestion, they all checked their diaries for the dates of the Nationals and Henley Masters. Lesley had a conference over the weekend of the Nationals, but all them could make Henley Masters.

When Molly arrived they shared their plan with her. She frowned and sucked in air through her teeth. Beth studied the deep, parallel grooves between Molly's eyebrows, with a horizontal gash just below them, the result of a lifetime of disapproving.

'I can understand your thinking, but really you ought to do some of the local regattas as well. You could do with more race experience before you get to Henley. There's also the matter of getting a few local pots under your belt. That win on Sunday really helped with your standing in the club. I'm afraid going out in the first round at Henley won't impress anyone—'

'Whereas beating some scratch novice crew who've had two outings will impress them?' interrupted Lesley. Beth could see she was irritated.

'I'm not sure it makes much difference what they think of us,' said Abbie. 'They're never going to row with us, so why should we care what they think?'

'You have a point,' said Kate. 'Shall we see how we go? If there's a local regatta we fancy, we can always enter nearer the time. I don't think we have to decide now. One really good thing – if we stick to rowing in *Desdemona*, she splits in two so we can transport her ourselves. If someone has a roof rack, that is. So we can be pretty much self-sufficient. No more worrying about trailers.'

'So long as you get permission to use *Desdemona* for the races you want to do,' added Molly sounding prissy.

'Of course,' said Kate. 'I'll drop the captain a line about Henley Masters right away, just to put a marker down.'

Good old Kate, thought Beth. *She's always good at smoothing over potentially divisive issues.*

The river was deserted as they pushed away from the bank. It was a fine day if overcast, although there was still a chill to the light wind. The stream was at a normal level for spring, and ambled benignly past. The willows along the water's margin were just starting to show tips of vibrant green. With a few more weeks of fine weather, the river-banks would be transformed by an explosion of growth. A heron perched awkwardly on a bare branch hanging low above the rippled surface. The Avon was still clothed in the greys and brown of winter, but the buds struggling to contain the new growth within hinted at the glories that lay ahead.

They completed their warm-up, then Molly set the crew to the first of the exercises she'd mapped out. Rowing in a four was a challenge after being in an eight: every tiny movement out of sync with the other three was magnified and made the boat fall over to one side. Beth couldn't remember the last time she'd rowed in a four: it was tough. At their first attempt at rowing all together, rather than in pairs, the boat lurched around quite alarmingly. A couple of times when the boat crashed over to one side, Lesley gave an unhelpful yelp. Beth was irritated by this, and then cross with herself for being so intolerant.

But they persevered and, as they worked through the drills, bit by bit the balance gradually settled down and they started to feel they were rowing as a crew. Once they were sprinting sections of 250 metres, the added speed smoothed out the boat's trajectory and the wobbles were forgotten. Molly worked them hard, making them perform eight sprints with only a few minutes of light pressure to recover in between. To make matters worse, she was using an electronic gadget that calculated their boat speed. If their velocity started dropping, she bawled at them to pick it up. By the end of their set pieces they were exhausted.

'I thought I was fit after all that winter training,' howled Lesley. The rest of the crew were too busy catching their breath to say anything, but Beth had been thinking the same thing.

'It's a different sort of fitness,' said Molly. 'Don't worry - you're doing well. A couple of weeks from now you'll have got used to the sprinting and all of that winter training will come into its own.'

'If I live that long,' Beth caught Lesley muttering under her breath. They had come to rest at the far end of the river, not far from Somerset Union's boathouse. Beth caught herself looking back towards it and wondering whether Jonny might be going out.

After a decent rest and having drained their water bottles, Molly edged them out into the river to begin practising their start. Unlike winter head races which involved a rolling start, summer sprints began from stationary which made it extremely difficult to create the momentum to accelerate up to race pace. It required perfect coordination and balance as well as strength. Learning to execute a decent start would be immensely challenging, but without one they wouldn't stand a chance in a race. It was going to take time.

Molly began the task with just one stroke. The women were sitting at three-quarters slide, their backs as strong and upright as they could make them and the spoons of their oars buried in the water.

'Come forward!

Attention!

Go!'

They pushed hard with their legs, drew the handle into their bodies, flung their hands down and away and paused with their arms outstretched. *Desdemona* fell over violently to the left and Beth felt a sharp stab in her back.

'Hold her up!'

The crew dug their blades in the water to bring the boat to a standstill. Molly repositioned the nose of the boat, then repeated the exercise. Then again. And again. They proceeded one stroke at a time until they were on the home straight before Albion. Finally Molly let them relax and they paddled in to the dock. Beth's back felt really sore. Being rocked to the side so violently was not good for anyone. There was a limit to how long they'd be able to keep this up if they didn't sort the balance out.

'My brain's hurting,' said Abbie, as they climbed out of the boat.

'My back's killing me,' said Beth.

'But do you know what? I didn't think about the carers' rota once while we were out,' Abbie added.

'That was a serious mental workout,' agreed Kate.

Despite trying to remain upbeat for the others, Beth felt despondent. She was worried she'd done some serious damage to her back. Even if it was only a minor strain, she didn't know how much more of this she could take. Rowing in an eight had been one thing. Their lack of recent experience had been flattered by being in a heavy boat that muffled the impact of any one person's movements. In a four there was nowhere to hide and the balance would remain horrendous until they melded together as a crew. She didn't know if she could keep going physically until that happened. The last thing she wanted was to end up with some awful back problem and to be off work for months, stuck at home on her own. It didn't bear thinking about.

It was all very well talking about Henley. Right at that moment Beth was far from confident they'd be able to get it together as a four in time – or that she'd survive the experience. It was only four months away. Getting four athletes to row as a crew didn't happen overnight, it could take years to be fully synchronised. How on earth were they supposed to achieve that in four months? More to the point, would she be able to cope with the strain on her back until they did?

She decided not to let Kate know how she was feeling. Her friend had been through more than enough drama in pursuit of her dream. Beth would have been quite happy just to go out a couple of times a week, the way Jack's crew did. In her heart of hearts though, she knew Kate was right: if they settled for rowing without a goal, it wouldn't take long before it fizzled out. They all had so many other calls on their time and if it wasn't sufficiently important it would soon be squeezed out. That was the story of her life, if she were honest. It was so easy to settle for a quiet life. But nothing worthwhile lasted for long unless you invested in it. No, Beth would keep her doubts to herself for now.

Their next outing was barely twenty-four hours after the first and Beth's back was still recovering. Her colleague had given her a thorough examination and reassured her it was nothing serious and would settle. But it was sore.

'I'd normally advise you to rest it and just keep it mobilised, but I'm guessing you need to keep rowing.' They'd agreed Beth should continue with her training but take sensible precautions. She felt better for the reassurance but her back felt miserable as the painkillers wore off.

It was dull and a sharp breeze was making itself felt. Beth made sure she was well wrapped up with plenty of layers, and dosed herself up before she left the house. For good measure she slipped a hot water bottle under her fleece to warm her back on the drive over. When she arrived at the boathouse there was no one there, and all she could hear was the sound of the wind tugging at the corrugated iron roof and some faint scratching from near the sofas.

She put herself gingerly through a series of stretches to ease the stiffness, and then climbed on the erg to go through the warm-up. She was halfway through her drill when the others arrived.

'Blimey – what's this? Did we get the time wrong?' asked Abbie cheerfully.

'Ha-bloody-ha,' said Beth through gritted teeth, focussing intently on every aspect of the movements she was putting her back through. By now she was feeling pleasantly warm and sweaty and her back felt much easier. She couldn't feel any pain at the moment, but she'd taken a strong painkiller before she'd left. One of the perks of her job was knowing the good drugs.

Their work this time consisted of two pieces of 1,000 metres. They completed the task assigned but Molly was unimpressed by the speeds they were achieving. They'd been pacing themselves too much and rowing it like the first kilometre of a head race.

'You need to learn to empty the tanks completely over 1,000 metres, which means giving every stroke the maximum effort, right from the start.'

Despite Molly's lack of approval, Beth was relieved her back seemed to be holding up. The balance was far from perfect, but by keeping up the pace they'd avoided the really damaging lurches. They paused in their normal place near the weir and Beth found herself looking round for signs of Jonny's presence.

Stop it! she scolded herself. *Eyes in the boat!*

When the time came to practise starts, Beth was anxious. She debated saying something about her back, then changed her mind. They continued working on the first stroke. The third time the boat tipped over she felt a sharp twinge in her lower back and bit her lip. By the fifth time they performed it and the boat tipped over, everyone was becoming frustrated. Beth could feel the tension around her and felt she had to say something. She hesitated, not wanting Molly to feel undermined.

'Molly – would you mind if we had a quick paddle, just to release some tension? I can't help thinking we're all trying too hard.'

Despite her misgivings, Molly readily agreed and they rowed a couple of hundred metres further on at a relaxed half pressure. They repositioned themselves.

'Come forward.
Attention!
Go!'

This time the blades came out of the water as one, their hands went away and *Desdemona* continued to glide forward as if she were poised on a knife-edge. Once Molly gave the order to easy, they all erupted in cheers. They'd cracked the first stroke.

'Fantastic – just another twenty strokes and we'll have ourselves a racing start,' groaned Abbie.

But Beth was elated by that one stroke. It was so perfect. They could do it! They were going to make this work and she didn't care how much her back complained. It was ridiculous how one perfect stroke out of an outing lasting an hour and a half could make your whole day better. By the time they'd reached the end of their outing they could just about control a two-stroke start.

'Wow – this is going to be a slow process,' said Kate.

'We'll get there. There's plenty of time to sort it out before Henley,' said Molly.

'Alternatively, we could see if there are any extremely short races?' suggested Abbie.

Beth left the boathouse at the same time as Kate, her rucksack slung over one shoulder. She'd taken some more of the strong painkillers when they got back to the boathouse, but they hadn't yet kicked in so she walked gingerly.

'You OK? You look a bit stiff?'

'I'm fine. My back's a bit sore. It doesn't like all the tipping over when we practise starts.'

'I know what you mean. I'm feeling a bit battered as well. Hey –a little bird told me you had a date with the lovely Jonny?'

'It wasn't a date. We just went to a lecture on sports nutrition up at the university.'

'But you do like him, don't you?'

'I don't really know. I mean, I barely know him.'

'But you do think he's cute? And he rows.'

'Well . . . yes.'

'So take a chance – make it happen. Ask him out on a date. If he's not as nice as he seems you haven't lost anything.'

'What? Me? Ask him out? I haven't even got his number.'

Kate was holding her phone as she'd just sent a text to Ella so she jabbed at a few buttons with her finger and Beth's phone beeped somewhere in her rucksack.

'You've got it now. Go on, Beth. No more excuses. Make it happen. Before one of those Amazons at Somerset snaps him up.' With that Kate kissed Beth lightly on the cheek, climbed into her car and drove off.

Kate's intervention gave Beth pause for thought and she considered what had been said as she cautiously lowered herself into the driving seat. She sat with both hands on the steering wheel, staring at the fluff on top of the dashboard.

Kate was right, of course. The interesting question was why Beth needed to have it pointed out. She was pretty certain she could and would have asked Jonny out off her own bat if she'd definitely been interested in him, if he'd ticked all the boxes.

All the boxes. Now she was getting to the nub of the problem. She hadn't even been aware she'd been doing it, but at some point in their brief acquaintance, Beth realised she'd run her slide-rule over Jonny and calculated that He Would Not Do. Without thinking, when she first met Jonny, she'd asked herself the question she posed about every available man she'd ever met: would Mummy have approved?

With a Damascene flash of insight, Beth realised she'd spent her life ignoring or discounting the men who'd failed this simple test. Worse still, she was still worrying about what her mother would have thought, even though she'd been dead for two years. Why had it never occurred to her before? The worst part was, she'd never cared about that stuff herself. It was nonsense, the things her mother thought were important. What mattered to Beth were the attributes she looked for in her friends: kindness, integrity, loyalty, honesty – possibly bravery as well – all the qualities she so valued in her crew. Why would she judge a man any differently?

'Oh my God, he's lovely!' Beth slapped herself on the forehead. How on earth had she been so dense? 'Now – where's my phone?'

Stern: *The end of the boat that travels through the water last.*

33
BETH

The pub felt warm and inviting as Beth pushed through the door, leaving a miserable day outside. The barroom smelt of roast potatoes and wet dog. A few of the lunchtime punters were still toying with their sticky toffee puddings while a couple of students in white shirts plodded through the business of clearing the other tables.

She was there to watch the Oxford and Cambridge Boat Race with the Albion members who met up for it each year. No one really cared about the race, but it was an excuse to spend the afternoon drinking, so the usual diehards could be relied upon to be there. Beth had joined in occasionally over the years, when she had nothing better to do. She would probably have given it a miss this year, but it seemed to strike exactly the right note for an invitation to Jonny: if he wasn't interested, it was just rowing after all. It wasn't a date. However, Jonny had already replied to her text by the time she'd driven home. Presumably he'd been out of the dating game for so long he'd no idea how uncool this was. In a panic she called Kate and insisted the others should come too. For moral support.

'How old are you – fourteen?'

'Oh, come on, you're the one that made me do this. Be a

sport. There won't be many other members there and we're heroes at the moment, don't forget. We're the crew that slaughtered Somerset last week.'

A dozen or so Albion members clustered around the bar. Kate and the rest of their crew had made camp at a table in prime position to watch the TV. An impressive number of amber-coloured pint glasses were lined up in the middle of the sticky table in front of them.

'I hope you drink cider. I got in spares so we won't have to go to the bar halfway through,' said Abbie. Beth was pleased Abbie had managed to get away to join them.

'How's the back, buddy?' asked Kate. Beth made light of her injury, but it encouraged everyone else to have a moan about their aches and pains. Even Molly was feeling the effects of the balance problem. In truth, Beth's back was no better but, there again, it was no worse. She was able to keep moving thanks to her stash of pills, but now they were beginning to irritate her stomach. If it wasn't one thing it was another.

This time it was Jonny's turn to be late and the two university crews were already positioning themselves on the start line as he made his way through the pub to join them at their table. He kissed Beth on both cheeks, and gave a small, self-conscious wave to the other four. Molly was confused why a Somerset member was gatecrashing the Waterman until Kate whispered in her ear.

'Ah ha!' said Molly as the penny dropped, and she was so distracted she knocked her cider all over the table.

All eyes were fixed on the television screen fixed high on the wall and Jonny lifted his pint up to his mouth without breaking his gaze. Beth took the opportunity to scrutinise him, as if she'd never seen him before. He had a neat, elegantly shaped head that made his buzz cut look like a fashion statement. His face was regular and well-proportioned, although with the lean, spare look of someone who trains hard. In his tight-fitting black Lycra jacket and jeans he blended in seamlessly with the Albion crowd.

Beth became conscious of Kate watching her looking at Jonny. As she transferred her gaze to her friend, Kate winked at her and took a deep draught of her cider. Beth would normally have felt self-conscious, being caught like that. But she didn't. Far from it. She felt elated and light. Above all, she felt a liberating sense of belonging, of being her true self together with the people she wanted to be with.

On the television, the Tideway looked cold and inhospitable. According to the commentators there was a brisk south-westerly, with the odd flurry of snow. It was odd to think that a week ago their crew should have been waiting to race at the same place on the same river.

A famous Olympian who'd rowed for Oxford once upon a time was the umpire. He was stationed on a large motor launch behind the crews. The year before some attention-seeker had swum in the path of the boats and brought the race to a halt. This year they were taking no chances and the route was lined with police in motor boats

With both crews more or less aligned, the umpire read over the names of the crews through a loudhailer:

'Cambridge!

Oxford!

Attention!

Go!'

They were off. As the crews went through the brisk opening strokes of their starts, the Waterman erupted to half-hearted cries of, 'Go Cambridge!' and 'Come on, Oxford!' Apart from Kate, Beth was not aware of anyone else who had a personal connection with either university. She guessed the members of Albion chose their allegiances the way small boys picked their football team: some preferring the favourite as they had to be on the winning side, some supporting the underdog in that great British tradition, some just going with the shade of blue they preferred.

As the eights reached the Harrods Depository, just before Hammersmith Bridge, Oxford made their push. Large crowds lined the banks on the north side of the Thames and the noise there was deafening. In the Waterman there was one feeble cry of 'Come on Oxford!' followed by an embarrassed silence.

Both crews took it up a gear. Cambridge pressed hard for advantage and the crews momentarily clashed blades. Later that evening, when Beth thought back about the race, she concluded that was possibly the most exciting moment of the entire race. From the aerial view, it was clear the relative positions were unchanged. Apart from the shape of the river, this shot looked identical to every view over the last ten minutes. For the rowers, each stroke was a life and death struggle. For the television audience it all looked a bit ho-hum.

By now the two crews had reached the Surrey bend and the commentators seized upon this fact, like men lost in a desert falling upon a half-empty bottle of warm water. With great enthusiasm they explained the relative advantage of each bend and which crew would benefit and by how much.

Unfortunately, by the end of the Surrey bend Oxford had clear water so were able to move in front of the Cambridge crew and steer the same course, making the long explanation about the bends redundant. With Oxford in front there was nothing to expect from the last five minutes except a stately procession towards the finish, just before Chiswick Bridge.

The atmosphere in the Waterman might have been described as attentive rather than exuberant. There had been the occasional self-conscious call of, 'Come on Cambridge/Oxford!', but mostly the watching crowd had generated a quiet hum as they analysed deficiencies in technique for the benefit of their neighbours. As they discussed the finer points of finishes and tapping down, Jack came over and stretched out his hand towards Jonny.

'Have we tempted you over to the dark side, Jonny? Glad to see you here. What are you drinking?' With this, the crew and Jonny were absorbed into the crowd of Albion supporters. Even Kate seemed to be enjoying herself, surrounded by Jack's crew joshing her about the triumph over Somerset.

For a moment Beth stood quietly and watched the scene. She felt a warm contentment, not solely due to the two pints of cider. This was her family, her rowing family. She belonged here. And so did Jonny. What did it matter if her late mother wouldn't have approved of him? Her rowing family did, and that was all that mattered.

'Mini golf? Is that a date? Is it even a thing?'

Beth had never played mini golf. She'd walked past it often enough, although in her mind the course in Victoria Park was always full of cocky French adolescents on exchange trips. Not grown adults. And especially not adults with designs on each other. Jonny's invitation sent her spiralling off into yet more uncertainty. Having finally decided she really liked him, she was now worried he wasn't interested in her. At least, not like that.

'You're worried he's friend-zoned you?' Kate had acquired

the phrase from her daughters and Beth was impressed they had a word for it now. It was obviously a common problem.

'Trust me, Beth. Jonny really likes you,' Kate had said, but Beth was far from convinced.

'I mean – mini golf?' She wrestled with the problem all day at work, dissecting it in excruciating detail. Maybe, she pondered, Jonny was doing what she'd done with the Boat Race, sort of fudged the issue, so that if Beth wasn't interested in him then it was – well – just golf. It was doing Beth's head in, trying to second-guess Jonny's intentions.

'What I need is a clear, unambiguous signal. I'm too old for this nonsense,' she said to the elderly lady whose knee she was attempting to manipulate. She was one of Beth's regulars. The woman's A-line skirt had ridden up showing thick American Tan tights wrinkled around her thighs. Beth pulled it back down and patted the hem in place. The patient glowered at her.

'Young lady,' said the woman sharply. Beth held her breath, waiting for the reprimand. 'What you need is to give him a good seeing to. Once you've sorted my knee out, of course,' and she gave a sharp kick of the leg Beth was holding, finally succeeding in straightening it out.

When Beth arrived at the course after work, she was relieved to see the other people playing were all adults, including groups of students and work outings. In fact, the whole thing was better than she'd imagined. The course was cleverly landscaped around the natural slope, and the holes were screened from each other by mature shrubs. Someone must have put a good deal of thought into the planting, as the overall effect was extremely pleasing, charming even, with the mature trees in the park as a backdrop. The holes themselves were carpeted with artificial grass, which Beth decided wasn't as bad as it sounded once she'd got used to it. Dusk was falling fast, and as she waited for Jonny, tiny white lights twinkled into life in every hedge and bush. In point of fact, the whole thing wasn't as bad as it sounded. Lit up you might almost describe it as romantic.

'Hey! Beth!' Jonny called to her from the path that ran down the hill to the entrance. He was jogging with a huge rucksack on his back as if he were out on manoeuvres with the paras. Beth's heart lurched as she saw him.

He bounded up to her and gave her a peck on the cheek. Beth went in for the second cheek but Jonny was already pulling away.

'I hope this is all right. One of my C crew suggested it.'

'Jonny, this is wonderful. I can't believe I've lived in Bath all these years and never seen it at night before.'

Jonny jiggled his head about as if trying to process the joy her answer generated. *He really is lovely.*

There was a short wait for the first tee and they stood awkwardly, making small talk about their day. In front were a party of accountants from a firm in Queen Square. They were wearing T-shirts emblazoned with their corporate logo over their normal clothes. Several were still wearing ties. One, in a red baseball cap, dominated the conversation with a riveting explanation of how his handicap had evolved over the previous six months, and which of the courses around Bath he'd played.

Beth was mesmerised by the performance. Jonny leant in to her ear to whisper:

'Have you seen he's wearing a golf glove?' which reduced Beth to fits of giggles.

Then it was their turn. On the first tee Beth completely underestimated the speed of the plastic grass, and her ball shot out the end and disappeared through the shrubbery on to the fifteenth.

'Here – I've got a spare,' said Jonny, and Beth had another go. This time she was more judicious with the power behind her shot, but sadly this too ricocheted out of sight.

'Oh dear,' said Beth. 'I'm not sure mini golf is my game.' But Jonny produced yet another ball from his pocket and encouraged her to persist. Each time she fired her ball off into the darkness, Jonny quietly produced another ball and set it on the ground in front of her. Finally she got the hang of it, and as her ball sank into the hole she turned triumphantly to Jonny who was possibly even more pleased than she was. By the fifth she was managing to hole the ball in sufficiently few strokes they could have kept score, if they'd been minded to.

Jonny was no better and if they had been keeping score, Beth would probably have had the edge. But neither of them could read the slight rises and bumps in the greens and they were constantly thwarted by their ball veering away from the hole at the last moment. It was infuriating. Beth realised it would have been even more irritating if she'd been with someone who could play. Or even worse, someone who resented her for doing better than him. Not many men would have been as relaxed as Jonny at being quite so rubbish. She wondered how the accountant with the golf glove was faring on the plastic grass.

By the time they finished on the eighteenth Beth felt exhausted. The odd moment of competence had lulled her into a false sense of security then was swiftly crushed as she returned to form and balls squirted in all directions. But she'd enjoyed being with Jonny. With every small act of thoughtfulness and kindness she'd become even more convinced he was the nicest man she'd ever met.

'A drink?' asked Beth weakly, trying to think of the nearest half-decent pub, but Jonny said he'd brought supplies with him, and patted his bergen. Beth suggested they walk into the park, which was now lit by the glow from the city below, and they made their way over to a Victorian bandstand. Further up the slope the Royal Crescent was ostentatiously illuminated. It was a magical setting.

From his rucksack Jonny produced a tartan rug and a small cloth, followed by a magnificent picnic: French bread and pâtés, tubs of coleslaw and rice salad, jewel-like tomatoes still on the vine, olives, marinated artichokes and grilled peppers. Beth gasped and held her hands to her mouth. She couldn't believe Jonny had organised all this. For her. By now he was half-submerged in his pack trying to reach the very bottom, and he emerged brandishing a bottle of wine. Beth was enchanted. He'd even brought two proper wine glasses, carefully wrapped in socks to stop them breaking.

'They are clean,' said Jonny quickly. 'I was in a bit of a rush.'

It was wonderful. It really was a date and Beth could not have been happier. Jonny poured the wine and then raised his glass, looking directly at Beth. Disconcerted, she had to glance away, but after a moment studying the coleslaw, she looked up again and boldly returned his gaze.

'I think we should drink a toast to your Vesta crew,' said Jonny. 'Because without them I wouldn't have met you.'

'Well, in that case we'll have to drink to your Vesta crew as well,' said Beth.

'Here's to all the Vesta women,' said Jonny brandishing his glass and they clinked their glasses together.

'Here's to Vesta women everywhere,' said Beth.

The wine wasn't terrible and after their exertions it wasn't long before Jonny was refilling their glasses. Beth heaped her plate with food and tucked in enthusiastically. Her morning clinic had over-run so she'd barely managed a bite at lunchtime. In between spreading pâté on her bread and popping olives or cherry tomatoes in her mouth, she still managed to keep up a near-constant stream of chatter about work and her crew's balance problems.

Jonny wasn't really eating, but he didn't take his eyes off her as she talked. Finally he lunged forward to kiss her, taking her by surprise. His movements were clunky, like he'd been thinking about it for a while, but Beth didn't mind. She found it endearing that he was as hopeless as she was. She was simply relieved he'd finally made a move. It wasn't the best kiss she'd ever had – she was too startled to participate fully and Jonny seemed solely intent on making contact, with no clue what to do once he got there. She was just glad they'd got it out of the way.

'Um – Beth. There's something I should tell you,' he said as they came up for breath, Jonny still perched over her. Beth panicked. *Oh God. His ex-wife wants him back. He's moving in with his mother.*

'I'm afraid I've put my hand in the Pâté de Campagne.' It took Beth a moment to recognise this wasn't an announcement that need dash her hopes. In fact, she thought it was the funniest thing she'd ever heard, and the pair of them howled with laughter.

Wind: *The final sprint for the line in a race.*

34
KATE

'What – you batch cook? How did I not know that?'

It was Monday night and Kate was at Tim's tiny London flat having spent the day volunteering at the refugee charity. It was her first day and everything was new. Including, it would seem, her husband's domestic routine. Monday night supper was apparently always spaghetti with a portion of Bolognese sauce from the freezer. Tim leant over and kissed Kate on the mouth.

'Stick around, kid, and I might have some more surprises for you.'

She'd been absolutely right about the refugee charity being able to use another lawyer who came free of charge. Like most such organisations the scale of need they were trying to address overwhelmed them, and Kate was thrown in the deep end. There was an impossibly long list of people needing help. With no way to triage whose plight was the most desperate, they simply took the next name on the list. They were all scared and completely without resources, anxious to secure leave to remain from the Home Office so they could begin the monumental task of building a life out of nothing: finding a job and somewhere to live in a country that felt increasingly hostile.

But who was genuinely in fear of their life and had escaped persecution rather than simply wanting a better life where they could eat every day? Who was genuinely at risk of being trafficked? Could any of these people be described as less than vulnerable? It was impossible to know. So Kate's role was to take each of them at face value and expedite their claim as effectively as she could. It was up to the Home Office to make the tough decisions and to say who they didn't believe and send them back.

'You know the thing that troubles me?' Kate told Tim, as he sucked up strands of pasta, leaving a slick of brown sauce at the corner of his mouth. 'It's just how many of them are young men. Who's looking after their mothers and sisters if it was so terrible back home?' She realised it would be easy to become cynical, yet the misery driving these desperate people to leave their homes and families to seek sanctuary in a foreign land was only too real.

The problems were incredibly complex, with the issues constantly changing with every shift in geopolitics, like sandbars in a storm. There was no simple right and wrong. It was a world of relative values, not absolutes. It was completely fascinating.

The legal aspects of the job were intriguing as well. It was completely new to Kate, so simply mastering the procedures and rules currently in operation would be challenging. And apparently nothing stayed the same from one week to the next. With every new crisis or appointment to the Home Office, it all changed. The number of asylum seekers was growing and between the threats of war and global warming no one was predicting it would slow down any time soon.

No one had worked out how to deal with the situation in a way that was humane without encouraging others to take the same treacherous journey. In a sector that was exploding with barely any resources servicing it, Kate could see there might be a chance to become an expert the government would need to listen to. The opportunity it presented to her personally was intoxicating.

But that first Monday evening Kate was just as excited about starting a new chapter with her husband. She'd only be staying with him on Monday nights as she'd get the train home after work the next day, but it was something. He'd seemed genuinely interested in what she was saying over dinner, and that hadn't happened in a long time. She probably hadn't sounded this enthusiastic about anything in ages. Well, apart from rowing, but that didn't seem to interest Tim in quite the same way.

After supper she fetched a large glossy carrier bag that she'd deposited by the front door when she arrived home, and waved it at Tim.

'What's that? Do you need different clothes for your new job?'

'No,' said Kate, opening it up. 'It's a present for you,' and she held up a brand new game of Scrabble. Kate had the strange feeling of being a guest in her husband's home. It was hardly surprising that after all these years he'd developed his own routine – including batch cooking. Perhaps one day Scrabble with her could become part of it.

Part Four

June 2013

Settle!: *A command telling the crew to bring down the stroke rate while still maintaining the pressure. This usually occurs in the middle of the race.*

35
KATE

Kate was early for her outing. The air was delicious and she felt the tug of a growing connection with the river. It was mid-June and after a disappointing spring, summer had finally arrived with a flourish. Checked earlier by the cool temperatures, the natural world was now exploding with the recent burst of heat and light. The willow trees along the river's edge were heavy with fluffy new growth and between their sweeping boughs trailing tendrils in the water, the bank was frothy with cow parsley, the umbrellas of florets clinging on late due to the unseasonal weather. The last few days of heat had seen them go over, shrivelling brown and shedding their seed. They perfumed the air with a faint hint of aniseed, nearly masking the usual river smell of rotting vegetation.

As she watched the ripples playing on the surface of the water, a group of mallards swam past, three fluffy ducklings scurrying to keep up with their mother. The women had watched the family's progress over the weeks, seeing the youngsters' desperate race to grow before the numerous predators caught up with them. A band of ten originally, they disappeared one by one, falling victim to pike and mink, buzzards and kestrels, magpies, crows, weasels and foxes: a whole host of photogenic carnivores. Kate was pleased to see three of them had made it this far.

Her four had made good progress on the training schedule set out by Molly over the weeks. With four crews wanting coxing and coaching, Molly was greatly in demand. She'd agreed to cox Kate's crew twice a week, but also provided detailed plans for the other outings. Almost the hardest task now was finding people to cox these sessions, not least because they were at off-peak times as far as the rest of the club was concerned. Considering how many people Beth had coxed over recent years, Kate found it disappointing how vanishingly few were the offers to help. Instead, they focussed on the women in the other three masters' crews and made sure they took it in turns to reciprocate.

They suggested Abbie needn't worry about coxing as it was so hard for her to arrange cover for her husband, but she'd been adamant she would do her share and had turned out to be a natural. The crews she took out raved about her and always asked for her first. Kate had to admit to feeling a bit peeved by this, but gave herself a stern talking-to and they soon had a regular cox-swap established.

Gradually, it all began to improve and even Kate could see the progress. Beth had struggled with her back when they first started training in the four, but she seemed fine now. The four had really come together as a crew: they now had a solid platform to push against and their fitness on sprints had picked up. The strength they'd acquired over the winter was now coming into its own and being measured in boat speed.

The ducks disappeared into a bed of reeds to the side

of the dock and Kate's thoughts drifted back to the crew's progress. They'd plugged away at their relaxation and fast hands, and the ratings were coming up nicely. They were also now at a point where they were confident in their start. It was neat. It was clean. And it was fast. Still Molly kept them practising, outing after outing.

'Remember – it's no good just being able to do a perfect start here on a quiet river in training. When we're at Henley the wind will be blowing us sideways, motor launches will be milling about, I could be getting Bow to take a stroke just as the umpire shouts "Go!", and all you'll be able to think about is who's watching. You need to be able to do this in your sleep. As one. With power.'

'She's spot on,' said Beth later. 'So many races are won or lost on the start. And it can be so difficult to concentrate with all the commotion.'

'Remember the pandemonium at the Somerset Head start?'

'Exactly. That's where having a jolly good cox makes all the difference. You need someone who'll take charge and dominate the situation. So the crew know they can ignore everything else and just focus on what they have to do.'

'Did you notice – Molly talked as if she'd be coxing us at Henley?' said Kate.

'Gosh – you're right – she did, didn't she?'

Beth and Kate had discussed a number of times who else they could ask to cox the race. They by no means took it for granted that Molly would be prepared to do it. Side-by-side racing was challenging for a cox and required either huge amounts of confidence or lashings of courage. No one wanted to be the cox whose crew crashed at Henley. Molly's self-belief had clearly grown since they'd started on this adventure, but was it enough to cope with the pressure of racing at Henley? She was nearly seventy, after all. It was a big ask.

They attempted to replicate some of the pressure by practising starts against other crews. Beth was now seeing Jonny regularly and he suggested training at the same time as the crew he coached so they could all get some start practice. They were closely matched: sometimes Albion won, sometimes Somerset. It always came down to who had the cleanest start.

It occurred to Kate that as the four of them forged an ever-closer bond of friendship, their rowing was also becoming more and more synchronised until every movement they made was effortlessly in tune with each other. Their starts were now reliable every time. But were they fast enough? It was impossible to know how good they needed to be. It was reassuring to know they'd held their own against Somerset who'd been tested on a national stage. But was their four as good as the Vesta eight? How fast were they? How fast did they need to be?

A sudden gust of wind made Kate shiver as a small, dense cloud briefly covered the sun. Henley was only four weeks away. Would they be ready? Were they up to it? They'd trained so hard and invested so much. Would it be enough?

Everything was organised. The draw had been published a few days ago and they had a bye through to the semi-final on the Friday afternoon. On the remote off-chance they won, the final was the following day. Win or lose, they agreed to stay the night and make a trip of it given that Abbie needed to organise two days' respite care, whatever happened. And as Abbie had pointed out, there were lovely shops in Henley. Good old Abbie.

'Wotcha, Kate!' Beth's cheerful cry from the top of the slope brought Kate back from her reveries. She pulled herself up from her wooden seat, grimacing at the complaints from her body.

Come on, Kate. We've got work to do.

Extraction: *The removal of the blade from the water by application of downward pressure to the blade handle.*

36

KATE

'Hang on, Abbie. Slow down a minute. I can't tell what you're saying.' It was Sunday afternoon, and Kate was heading out of the door for one of their last training sessions before Henley. The regatta was less than a week away and they'd be resting for the final two days. Until then their outings would be relatively light, aimed at keeping them sharp but still allowing their bodies to recover.

'I can't come,' wailed Abbie down the phone. She was completely incoherent.

'Abbie, you need to try to calm yourself. I'll call the others, but then I'm coming over. OK? We'll sort this out. I promise.' Kate was not at all sure what she was promising and what needed sorting out, but clearly Abbie was in crisis. She was about to start phoning when she realised the simplest thing was to call in at the club on the way to Abbie's and speak to the rest of the crew together.

'There's no need to panic,' was the first thing Molly said. 'You ladies are so well prepared, missing one outing isn't going to make any difference at this stage. We can do a light erg instead as we're all here.'

Kate had a worrying feeling it wasn't going to be that simple.

'I'm sorry – that's a great idea but I said I'd go over to Abbie's. To see if I can help,' said Kate.

'I'll go with you,' said Beth quickly.

'Me too,' said Lesley. Molly harrumphed at this and looked most put out.

'We can all come back and do an erg together later,' said Kate, trying to placate her. 'I'm sorry you've had a wasted journey. And I'll text you this evening – to confirm about Tuesday's outing.'

They all watched their elderly cox stomp away, Kate conscious the atmosphere had soured. She was the only one who'd heard Abbie's distress, but all of them knew Abbie well enough to know it must be serious if she'd cancelled at the last minute.

They piled into Lesley's car and drove out to the village on the other side of Bath where Abbie lived. None of them had been to her house before and it took a few false attempts to find it. It was on a slope looking down towards the water meadows below.

'What a great spot,' said Lesley. 'Do you see how her house was built just above the flood plain? Those Georgians knew a thing or two about construction.' The others barely answered. No one was in the mood to appreciate scenery or discuss the finer principles of urban planning.

Abbie answered the door, her face etched with worry. No one said a word, but all three women dressed in matching green vests trooped in and flung their arms around her. This of course reduced Abbie to tears.

'Oh, now look what you've done!' she sobbed. After a good long hug and the shedding of more tears they repaired to the kitchen.

'Where's Martin?' asked Beth. 'Is he OK?'

'He's asleep right at the moment, poor thing.' While Kate made the tea, Abbie told them her sorry tale. A couple of hours earlier the carer on duty received a call from back home in Poland: her mother had been rushed into hospital after a suspected stroke.

'She had to go straight away. I checked and luckily there's a flight from Bristol airport in a couple of hours so with a bit of luck she should make it. You know, it seems so terrible, her being here looking after Martin and there's her mother so far away all on her own.' Abbie was obviously fond of the woman. She'd been with her for several years and Abbie found her thoroughly competent. 'And she's so kind. To Martin, obviously, but to me as well.'

Kate was struck how much Abbie knew about the carer's life. She must have had many hours to talk to her over the years.

'So where does that leave you now, with carers? For the next week?' asked Kate, ever practical.

'In a fix,' said Abbie grimly. 'I was already a person down so I spoke to the agency last week. They weren't too optimistic about getting someone in before the end of the month. I was relying on Sylwia to make up the extra shifts. Now she's gone . . . I'll have to wait to speak to them tomorrow, see what they say.'

The others were silent. Kate could sense they were all contemplating the ramification. If Abbie couldn't row then Henley was over for all of them. You couldn't just drop a reserve into a four. They all remembered only too well the painstaking process of learning to synchronise their starts. Anyone new would wreck the balance and speed, no matter how brilliant a rower they were.

'I could look after Martin so you could get out to row,'

said Lesley enthusiastically, but then she realised the snag. 'Ah, but then you wouldn't have a Bow.' The others made sympathetic faces, rather than the 'doh!' noises this suggestion would normally have elicited.

'I tell you what,' said Beth, 'how about I look after him now and you go for an erg with the others? It would do you good to get out.' Despite the kindness of the offer, Abbie just wasn't feeling up to it.

'I know,' said Kate. 'How about I nip to the supermarket then make supper here for the four of us? Well, five, with Martin.'

Beth and Lesley thought this a wonderful idea and Abbie finally gave way.

'Everyone happy with steak? Keep it simple?'

When Kate had been at Cambridge the college used to lay on steaks for the First Eight the week before the Bumps races. Maybe that's why she suddenly fancied one. It was funny how, with only a few days to go before their big race, she had such a strong memory of her time at Cambridge.

Lesley drove her to the supermarket and pushed the trolley as they wandered round the aisles. Kate found some baking potatoes and then threw in a couple of bags of salad, saying, 'I was just thinking back to my time at uni. How simple it all was then. My biggest problem was having to grovel to my tutor when training got in the way of my weekly essay.'

'The only problem I can remember was trying to avoid a hangover on race days.'

'Well, that too. Obviously. My twenty-year-old self wouldn't have had the faintest idea what we all have to overcome now to take part in a race. Not the foggiest.'

They were now in front of the shelves of meat and Kate

was squinting at the various packages, trying to figure out which cut they were without putting on her glasses.

'Do you know – I called Mike to say he'd have to get his own supper and I told him what was going on with Abbie. Guess what he said?'

Kate looked up from the slab of beef in her hand to see her friend's anguished face. She wanted to suggest he might have said something supportive, but she already knew that wouldn't have happened.

'He said, "Well if you're not going to Henley you can visit my mum at the weekend and check how she's coping. I'm too busy to do it myself."'

Kate shook her head and grimaced at her friend. 'I'm sorry. Lesley. That's really rubbish.'

They pushed the trolley round the next two aisles, hunting for the dairy section.

'Do you think we're going to solve this, Kate? I mean, do you think we'll get to Henley?'

'Do you know what, Lesley? If I'm honest, right at this moment, I've absolutely no idea.'

It wasn't the jolliest meal Kate had ever shared. She could tell they were all struggling to come to terms with the situation, not least the uncertainty. But having a meal together helped. She doubted Tim or the girls would have understood what she was going through but she, Beth, Lesley and Abbie all felt the same, and by sharing a meal they could lick their collective wounds.

Bleak as everything looked, Kate was not feeling as terrible as she had over previous setbacks. This time she felt they were in it together. It wasn't only her who'd be missing out on realising her dream. For once it didn't feel like her personal failure. It just felt like – well – life.

As she watched Abbie cutting up Martin's steak, she was

forced to admit that sometimes life was just a bit shit. In fact, that was the main reason they were all trying so hard to remain upbeat. They didn't want Abbie to feel any worse than she already did. No doubt her distress was a mixture of frustration and disappointment, combined with the ongoing grief of losing her husband one day at a time.

It hadn't even occurred to Kate to consider what Henley must represent for Abbie. She knew how much it meant to her and, frankly, she had nothing to complain about compared to Abbie's lot.

Martin was unable to speak, and it was not clear how much he understood of what Abbie said to him. A couple of times he tried to respond and produced a string of unnerving sounds. Abbie persuaded him to take his seat at the table with them and he could just about cope with eating unaided, once his food was cut up. Ketchup dribbled down his chin. Abbie took a napkin and wiped it away, talking softly to her husband and gazing tenderly into his eyes as she did so. He rewarded her with a look of utter devotion and Kate felt privileged to share this meal with them. Their palpable affection was humbling.

It must be completely devastating. To watch someone deteriorate day by day. It's too cruel. Then, on top of the grief, Abbie had to deal with the practicalities, making sure Martin was properly cared for while keeping life going. She wondered how often Abbie had to cope with setbacks like this. No doubt it was too frequent to bother counting.

Kate looked across at Beth. Her friend's face betrayed the maelstrom of emotions she was feeling. They were all hurting. Instinctively she reached out to take Beth's hand and, as one, all four crew members joined hands, encircling poor Martin as he ate.

*

The next morning Abbie phoned Kate. It wasn't looking good. The care agency said they'd phone round, but at the moment they didn't have anyone available before the end of the month.

'Is it worth trying another agency? I could have a word with Sal. You know she's a nurse? She might have some ideas.'

'Well, anything's worth a try, I suppose. On the bright side, I've got cover for Tuesday so we can still go out then.'

'That's great. Let's try to stay positive.' Kate didn't feel positive. There'd been so many setbacks along the way, but this one felt insurmountable. As much as anything, Kate was struggling because it was out of her hands. She'd happily have looked after Martin single-handed for the whole week if it would help. She knew all of them would have. But none of them could be in two places at once.

No, she simply wouldn't allow herself to be upset. It wouldn't be fair on Abbie. Anyway, it wasn't as if Henley was the only race. They could do one of the local regattas later in the season. There would always be another race. They just had to keep going and stick together.

Having resolved not to get worked up, Kate still managed to become quite emotional talking to Sal. She was hoping she might have some contacts in the caring sector. It was a bit of a long shot, but then they were officially desperate. She explained the problem and how Abbie needed round-the-clock care for forty-eight hours so she could go to Henley. So they could all go to Henley.

'She's got someone covering our outing tomorrow evening, but then after that she's on her own.'

Sal was suitably sympathetic and made all the right noises about Abbie's plight. 'I can't promise anything, Kate, but I'll ask around.'

★

By Tuesday evening, the agency still had no solution.

'They're trying hard,' Abbie assured Kate. 'I've been with them for so long, I know they're doing their best. But they can't just magic people up out of thin air, even for me.'

No one said it, but Kate had the impression they'd all pretty much given up on Henley. Even Kate had started thinking about what she might do on Saturday. The girls were home, so maybe she could persuade them to go out somewhere for the day? She was desperate to look on the bright side, for Abbie's sake.

Despite trying to remain positive, Kate sensed a definite air of melancholy clinging to their crew as they took *Desdemona* out. It was as if they were all on Death Row. No one talked about what was happening, but it hung over everything. Molly seemed quite oblivious. Under the circumstances it was probably just as well, and she took them through their session in her normal no-nonsense fashion. Once they were out there was no time to brood and, in Kate's opinion, they all did a marvellous job of pretending it was just another outing.

It'll do us all good to get out. Abbie most of all. It was ironic, but now the pressure was off, the boat simply flew. Their rowing had never been as relaxed and fluid. Molly kept it short, as specified on the training programme, and they headed back in to the dock.

As they pulled alongside, out of the corner of her eye Kate saw a crowd of people standing on the steps. Their blades came to rest on the dock and she turned round to see Sal pulling in Two's blade. The rest of the veteran squad were there too.

'Funny – I didn't know they were going out now,' said Kate as Molly clambered out. *But why are they all in mufti?*

'Hi, guys. You look like a reception committee. Where are you all off to?' asked Beth.

'We're here to see you. Well, Abbie really,' said Sal. She seemed to hesitate and Hilary nudged her with her elbow. Sal had a large piece of paper in her hand. The others clustered round, fidgeting. They were all looking straight at Abbie.

'The thing is, Kate told us about your – your situation. I called round everyone I can think of.'

'I tried too,' interrupted Geeta. 'A couple of my friends are nurses.'

'The thing is,' continued Sal, clearly annoyed at the interruption, 'despite everything, we couldn't find a professional carer who could help. So we've all discussed it. As a squad. And we're going to do it.' This was met by total incomprehension. The 'pee-pee' of a buzzard far overhead disturbed the silence.

'I don't understand. What do you mean, "you'll" do it?' asked Lesley, confused.

'Exactly that,' said Sal. 'We've drawn up a rota. There'll be two people with Martin at all times and I'll be on call throughout.' She handed Abbie the piece of paper.

'But you guys don't know what to do, how everything works,' protested Abbie.

'Abbie, look at us. We're not just your friends, we're nurses, mothers, daughters and sisters. Between us we've got hundreds of years' experience of caring for people, young and old: feeding them, bathing them, wiping their bottoms, cooking and cleaning and keeping them safe. And not just safe. Keeping them happy and feeling loved. I promise you, Abbie, this is going to be fine. Martin will be in good hands. We want you guys to go to Henley. We need you to do it for all of us.'

Abbie looked down at the paper in her hand, dumbfounded. She tried to speak but nothing came out. Her lip trembled and she looked as if she might cry.

Unable to contain herself Lesley blurted out: 'Are you serious? You mean we can go? We get to race?'

At this the women standing behind Sal broke ranks and poured down the steps to engulf the crew, shrieking and hugging and repeating reassurances. It was mayhem. Kate was so overwhelmed it took her a moment to absorb the news and its implications.

'Oh my God,' Beth whispered to her. 'We're going to make it, Kate. We're going to race at Henley. We've been rescued. Thank Heavens for menopausal women.'

'Thank God for the Sisterhood,' she replied.

Regatta: *A competition with events for different boat types usually involving heats, semi-finals and finals for each event. Boats compete side by side from a standing start.*

37
KATE

They were actually here at Henley-on-Thames, on one of the most iconic stretches of river in the world, and the four of them were paddling up to the start. After the months of training and dreaming, after all the drama of the previous week, they were finally here. Sal had done an amazing job of convincing Abbie she had nothing to worry about. She'd checked in a couple of times as they drove up, and then she finally decided to trust them and concentrate on the task in hand.

They rowed past the stand and through the booms with their Sunday-best technique, backs straight and heads high. For a moment Kate imagined they were a team of dressage ponies with arched necks and swishing tails.

It was so different to their quiet backwater on the Avon. The Thames was wide at Henley and one half was sectioned off with heavy wooden booms to create a racecourse. The other side was frantic with river traffic. There were motorised pleasure craft of all sizes with skiffs and canoes weaving in amongst them.

Through this chaos, Molly steered downstream past the

course, the start and Temple Island until they reached the point where the river opened out and normal navigation rules applied. The women rowed as if they were wearing blinkers, blocking out everything except the stroke they were executing at that moment.

If Molly was feeling the pressure, she was doing a first-rate job of hiding it. She deftly picked her way around the various obstacles while giving her crew the impression they had the river to themselves. The adrenaline-induced focus made the crew's bladework crisper than ever. When Molly gave the order for a five-stroke start, they went off like a rocket.

Not dressage ponies, thought Kate, *we're racehorses ready for the off.*

Their warm-up complete, they spun, crossed to the other side of the river and paddled back upstream to the holding area below the start.

'Just a word of warning: there was a nasty crosswind coming up to the start. We're sheltered from it now, but once we row past the end of the island we might well be hit by a strong gust. I want you to be ready for it.'

'Got it, Skip,' called Abbie from the bow.

Kate rolled her shoulders and did a few waist rotations. She was incredibly nervous, yet weirdly, at the same time, felt as if she had superpowers with heightened awareness, speeded-up reactions and pent-up strength.

There was no denying this regatta was incredibly civilised, even apart from the scenery. Races started at exactly the time scheduled and there was calm and order. Each pair of competing crews was followed down the course by an ancient and highly polished teak slipper launch carrying the umpire and a few favoured spectators. The officials wore white trousers and navy blazers set off by a jaunty panama hat or a vintage rowing cap.

The first of the two races ahead of them started and both crews shuffled forward one place. This brought *Desdemona* alongside Temple Island, a gem of an outcrop in the middle of the Thames, which consisted of a manicured garden and an ornamental folly. As the women tapped the water to avoid drifting downstream, they watched a couple of men on stepladders threading strings of light bulbs through the trees. They were all lost in their own thoughts when the marshal called them forward.

'OK, ladies, this is it. Get your game faces on!'

Molly took them on, past the stake boat anchored in the middle of the stream and they backed up expertly on to the start. A lad lying flat on the pontoon caught hold of their stern and clung on, arm outstretched. Kate gave a silent prayer of thanks they'd practised the manoeuvre so many times. This was not the moment to be faffing around.

Kate's crew were on the Berkshire side, closest to the bank. Ardingly, their competitors, were on the Buckinghamshire side, which at the moment was next to the island, but further down the course would be closest to the boom and the middle of the river.

'Take a tap, Bow! Back it down, Three!' Molly kept making micro-adjustments to the position of their bow. She kept her right hand raised until she was satisfied they were perfectly positioned. Twice she lowered her arm only for Ardingly to continue their manoeuvring and the wind to blow *Desdemona* off course. Finally they were both straight and the two coxes lowered their hands simultaneously.

'Coxes – you are aligned.
Albion.
Ardingly.
Attention.
Go!'

The umpire hurled the tip of a large flagpole down towards the water, the white silk fluttering behind – and they were off.

You can do this, Kate. You can do this. Explode off the start. No back. Fast hands. Half slide. No back. Fast hands. Half slide. Don't use your back. Drive with the legs. Push. Push!

With each stroke they pulled away from the start and gained speed. Kate was dimly aware of noise and splashing around her, but she was insulated in her own little bubble. *Bring in the back. Full slide. Lengthen out. Give it everything, Kate. Give it everything. Push. Stroke eleven. Stroke twelve. Stroke thirteen. Stride coming. Keep the rating up.*

'Next stroke!
Stride out!'

At Molly's signal the change the crew changed down two gears in one synchronised movement: they pushed even harder through their feet, threw their hands away, rocked over fully, and held their legs down until the last possible moment. As Kate kicked into the new rhythm she caught a glimpse of the other crew out of her peripheral vision.

We must be ahead! They had to maintain this lead and stretch it out. *Harder, Kate. Harder.* Gradually, stroke by stroke, she could feel them stretching out the distance between their two sterns.

'Keep it going!
You're in front.
You can do this!
Maintain the pressure!
Keep it relaxed!'

Kate could sense the other crew slipping back a few inches with each stroke. Then Ardingly were holding them. Kate forgot about the 800 metres remaining and channelled all of her strength into that stroke. And the next one. And the next one. *They're coming back at us! Shit! Drive harder!*

'Keep it focussed!

Keep it long!

Quick catches!'

Kate hung on to Molly's words, directing all of her concentration to the single instruction barked in time to each stroke. Suddenly there was a commotion of splashing and shouting, and the Umpire's launch started falling back. As they continued down the river Kate could see the Ardingly boat was stationary, close to the boom. What had happened? Would they be called back to the start?

'Keep it going, ladies. Concentrate! It looks like our opposition have crashed, but they'll no doubt start rowing again, and we haven't won until we've crossed the line. Remember – everyone is watching. I want this to be showcase rowing.'

It took a moment for this information to register, but they soon readjusted and set about executing the most dynamic but relaxed rowing they were capable of. Keeping an eye firmly on Ardingly, Kate dropped the rating a couple of pips, and stretched out on the recovery. The boat speed did not drop. This was the ideal way to row: they had adrenaline powering their drive, but the knowledge they were in control allowed a textbook recovery between strokes.

As they processed past the main enclosure, Kate could see Ardingly in the distance, limping home. She was only dimly aware of the cheering and shouting from the bank.

'You're looking great.

We're coming up to the line!

Twenty more strokes!'

Kate felt herself straighten her back ever so slightly and reinforce the engagement of her core muscles. *Anyone can do twenty strokes.*

'Five!

Four!

Three!

Two!

Light pressure!'

They had won their heat.

'Congratulations, ladies. I think we can call that a convincing win,' said Molly.

'Oh shit – does that mean I can't have a drink tonight?' wailed Abbie, and they all collapsed in a mixture of laughter and coughing.

'How's it going? How's Martin?' Abbie's sparkly mobile phone was pressed to her cheek. 'How did we do? Oh – we won . . .' Abbie yanked the phone away from her ear and grimaced. They could all hear the squeals and screams. As it subsided Abbie picked it up again and said, 'I think everyone got that. Yes, we'll do our best.'

The five women studied the menu. They'd debated going for a curry, but in the end they compromised on an old-school Italian in the high street. Molly said pasta was a good option before a race.

'Are you sure we need to carb-load for a sprint?' asked Abbie. 'Isn't that supposed to be when you're racing a bit longer than five minutes?'

'I don't know about you, but that race today was the longest five minutes of my life,' said Beth.

As the others tried to decide between tagliatelle and lasagne, Kate leant over to whisper in Lesley's ear, 'Do you mind me asking – how are things going with Mike?'

At this Lesley threw both hands up in the air, as if the surroundings were encouraging her to gesticulate like a Neapolitan.

'Oh – I don't know, Kate. I feel as though I've finally

learnt how to stand up for myself in our relationship, and the more I do that, the nicer Mike tries to be to me.'

'But that's good, isn't it?' asked Kate.

'Well, I suppose it should be. Except the harder he tries, the more he gets on my nerves. It feels like he's just sucking up to me, and the moment I forgive him he'll be back to his old ways. Maybe it's too little too late. Or maybe I only love him when he's being a bastard. Either way, I don't think I can carry on like this much longer . . .'

The atmosphere in the crew was far from triumphant. They were all pleased with the result, but it was fundamentally unsatisfactory to have won in such circumstances. As Molly had predicted, Ardingly had been caught by a strong gust as they cleared Temple Island, causing Bow to miss a stroke. That was enough to shift the nose of the boat, and before the cox could steer away from the boom, they'd hit it. On the bright side, no one was hurt and there was no serious damage to the boat. It still wasn't how you wanted to win and so the women were in reflective mood. It was almost their first chance to relax after all the anxiety of the previous week. It sounded as if Martin's care package was running like clockwork, so all they had to do was row their best and enjoy the experience.

Their final was the next morning and they were up against an Australian crew who were the national champions in their age group. No one voiced it, but Kate sensed an unspoken assumption that they didn't stand a chance, although Molly seemed extremely chipper. No doubt she was relieved it hadn't been her crew that had crashed. Kate couldn't imagine what it must have felt like to be pulling hard on the rudder strings and yet be unable to prevent the boat storming into the barrier.

Kate couldn't work out how she felt. Was it pure relief

they hadn't lost? Or a sense of achievement that they'd simply taken part? They'd been fixated on this race for months now and so much of their lives had been directed towards those five minutes of reckoning. In her usual self-deprecating style it had never occurred to her they might actually win at Henley. She just didn't want them to embarrass themselves or let Molly down. So this was a good result, if not a fantastic one. There would be no shame in losing in the final, especially to the Australian champions.

The waiter arrived with plates of steaming garlic bread, glistening with butter and speckled with parsley. Lesley topped up everyone's glasses with sparkling water and Abbie said, 'You know, whatever happens tomorrow, and despite Ardingly torpedoing themselves today, I feel like a winner. Rowing down the course today in front of all those people – I thought I was going to burst with pride.'

'Me too,' said Beth.

'It felt so amazing to be part of this incredible crew. I know I don't talk about it much, but this week you've probably got some idea of what being involved in this has meant to me.'

They all chewed their crusts and licked the garlic butter dribbling on their fingers thoughtfully. The candles stuck in raffia-covered chianti bottles spluttered as new customers arrived, creating a draft. Anywhere else and the décor might have been thought ironic, but Kate was pretty sure the place had been like this since the dawn of time.

'I can't imagine what it must be like for you,' said Lesley. 'Day in, day out.'

'You know, when I've had a rotten night, just being on the river makes everything better: the sound of the water, seeing a kingfisher flying past. Even without the rowing or seeing you guys, the river alone does me good.'

'I know it does me good,' said Kate. 'So much good.'

'And me,' chipped in Molly. 'Plus needing to hop in and out of boats has got me back to the gym and working out again.' Kate wondered whether the others remembered the sorry physical specimen Molly had presented when she first came out with them. Seeing this spry, slightly abrasive elf in front of them, it was hard to imagine she was the same person.

'You know, I think we've all been changed by this project of Kate's,' said Beth thoughtfully as she reached over for another breadstick.

'Well, it helped you find your Handsome Prince, that's for sure,' said Abbie.

'Mmm – I don't think it's so much that I found my prince,' said Beth nibbling at her breadstick, 'it's more like I've found myself. I've known so many lovely people like Jonny over the years and I was just too stupid to realise I was allowed to date them.'

'You shouldn't be too hard on yourself – lots of people never work out what's good for them,' said Abbie.

'Well, maybe, but something about being part of this crew has really made me pull my socks up.' She reached for another bottle of water and refilled everyone's glasses.

'Me too,' said Kate, 'I've been pulling my own socks up recently.'

'You, Kate? I can't imagine you've ever allowed your socks to slip,' said Molly.

'Oh, trust me, they slipped all right. When we first moved to Bath I was reliably informed it was "the graveyard of ambition", and I think I just accepted that. I sort of gave up. But since we've been rowing together, everything feels different. It suddenly all feels possible again.' Her friends nodded in agreement. 'So no more just accepting things. I want to start making things happen again.'

'Well, I have to say it's incredible what you've managed to do at Albion,' said Molly with uncharacteristic generosity. 'Even apart from this crew you've created a whole new veteran squad. And trust me, I know how tricky Albion can be and what an extraordinary achievement that is.'

'That's kind of you to say, Molly. But now I need to attempt the same trick with my law firm.'

'What – recruit a squad of middle-aged female lawyers?' asked Lesley.

'No,' said Kate laughing, 'although maybe that's not such a terrible idea. I want to build a human rights practice at the firm. Oh my God! I can't believe I just said that out loud. How pretentious does that sound?'

'I don't think it sounds any more pretentious than a year ago saying you wanted to race at Vesta,' said Beth quietly.

What Kate didn't tell them was that the week before, the senior partner had dropped by her windowless office, his white shirt as fluorescent as his teeth. He'd been chatting to a partner at one of the Magic Circle firms who just happened to be a trustee of the charity where Kate was volunteering.

'Great stuff, Kate,' said the partner. 'Really important. We have to think about our ethical image these days. As a firm, I mean. Corporate Social Responsibility, and all that. Can I get our PR girl to talk to you about using it in some of our social media?'

This was totally unexpected. Not that long ago Kate would have been thrown and simply grateful for the crumbs of attention. But with her newfound sense of purpose and resolve, she was ready. Fizzing with adrenaline and confident she could solve anything life threw at her, she'd replied, 'Yes, of course, Derek. I'd be delighted.' She'd stood up and walked round to the front of her desk and leaned back against it. 'You're absolutely right, Derek. Demonstrating we take our Corporate Social Responsibility seriously is so important these days. Which is why I know you'll be interested that I've come across a client who lives in Bath – a victim of modern-day slavery. I think the firm should take her on, pro-bono. A case like that will attract a lot of media interest and I'd be happy to spearhead this new specialism. It would be fantastic for our image.'

Kate didn't know how Derek was going to react, but she was shocked at her own sass. There was a pause while Derek worked out how to respond. The old Kate would have apologised in case she'd overstepped the mark, but new Kate didn't. She'd simply folded her arms and waited for Derek to reply.

'That's a fantastic idea, Kate. I like your style. I'll have to put it to the partners of course, but I think it's inspired. I might even be able to persuade one of my corporate clients to sponsor it, and then it won't even cost us anything. I'll be in touch . . .'

Kate recalled the encounter with satisfaction. Whatever the outcome of the partners' meeting, she would always be proud of the way she'd stood up for herself and asked for what she wanted when the opportunity arose.

Just then two waiters arrived with vast open bowls of spaghetti and tagliatelle. Molly was making do with a small salad. A youth with a lascivious grin came round brandishing a massive peppermill. A second waiter followed apologetically, offering spoonfuls of Parmesan the consistency of dust.

Lesley sucked in a wayward strand of spaghetti with a squelching sound then dabbed at her mouth daintily with her napkin and nodded.

'What Kate said, about feeling things are possible, that's

happened to me too.' She paused, staring dreamily into the distance, possibly in the direction of the waiter with the pepper grinder. 'In fact I've got some news . . .'

The other four women froze, mouths open, forks mid-air. No one made a sound. Kate swallowed hard. What was she going to say?

'I've been promoted at work! Tee-hee!' And Lesley sat back in her chair roaring.

'Gosh, that's marvellous,' said Beth. 'When did that happen? I thought you missed out on a promotion only a couple of months ago?'

'I did. They decided to parachute some dickhead with half my experience and qualifications in above me. So I had a word with a colleague of Kate's, and a couple of weeks ago I went to see HR. I told them if they insisted on going through with this appointment then I would be suing them for "sexual and racial discrimination and constructive dismissal".'

'Golly, you did that?' asked Beth, clearly impressed.

'What did they say?' asked Kate.

'It's taken a couple of weeks but I just heard from them. They've changed their minds and given me the job. Tee-hee!'

'Blimey, Lesley,' said Abbie, 'you're a dark horse. Who'd have thought you'd pull off a stunt like that? I'm so proud of you! Another toast everyone: to Lesley – our dark horse!' They all clinked their glasses again.

'Anything else I can get you, ladies?' asked the waiter, waggling his pepper grinder suggestively.

'No thanks – we've got absolutely everything we need,' said Kate.

Repêchage: *The 'second chance' race given to those crews which fail to qualify for the finals from an opening heat.*

38
KATE

Kate was hunched at front stops, core muscles clenched, back straight, head held high, looking up over Molly's head. They were attached to the stake boat, ready for the start. Kate felt as if she were in a film being shown in slow motion with the volume muted. She checked her blade: the spoon was squared and just buried in the water. There was a familiar black bile in the pit of her stomach. She stretched out her fingers and wiggled them while maintaining her hand positions on the blade. *Relax. You can do this. Keep breathing. Big breaths. Relax. You've got this.*

It all came down to this: who was faster, Albion or Wallaroo? It didn't matter who was stronger, who had the best technique, who wanted it the most. Ultimately, the only question was who could move their boat the quickest and cross the finish line first.

How often these days were Kate and her friends judged purely on what they could achieve, rather than someone else's assumptions? How often were they in a position where sagging jowls and greying temples were irrelevant to the outcome? Where being a woman and an older one at that, was not unconsciously taken into the calculation and held against them?

Deep breath in. Slowly exhale. Deep breath in. Slowly exhale. They were ready. The umpire announced their race.

'Wallaroo!

Albion!

Attention!

Go!'

1000 metres. Kate drove down as hard as she could, exploding off the footplate. *You can do this! Come on, Kate!*

'Lengthen out!

Lengthen out!'

Stroke twelve. Ready for the stride. 900 metres. Come on, Kate!

Somewhere in the distance, or possibly far below her, Kate could hear the sound of amplified commands and water splashing. She was flying. She was strong.

'Next stroke –

Stride out!'

The crew changed gear as neatly as a show-pony switching from a trot to a canter.

The umpire's launch bore down on them. On it were Mike, Stanley and Jonny. They'd turned up unannounced as they were sprinting shuttle runs to warm up before they boated. Kate was conscious of their scrutiny from such close range.

'You're doing well! You're holding them!' called Molly.

750 metres. 250 metres down. You can do this, Kate. If Wallaroo hadn't taken them on the start, they were in with a chance. *500 metres.*

'Halfway!

We're still holding them!

Dig deep!

This is where it counts!'

Kate had no sense of whether one boat was marginally in front of the other. It was too close to call. From the stroke's seat she knew she only had a distorted perspective in her peripheral vision. One thing was for sure – this race was far from lost.

'Keep the focus!
Fast hands!
Keep it relaxed!
Quick catches!'

250 metres. It was really hurting now. Every muscle in Kate's body was begging for respite. She could barely feel her core muscles. Her legs seemed to be made of jelly, yet the boat was still flying. She had to keep going. She had to. She couldn't let her crew down. If they could keep going, so would she.

'They're as tired as you are!
But we want this more!'

She's right – I do. I do want this. Drive. Drive. Fast hands.

'Last twenty strokes!
Wind it up with Stroke!
Go!'

They're not going to take us now. Not after all this.

'Final effort!
Empty the tanks!'

Kate pushed down through her feet as hard as she could, as if her very existence depended on it. Then from the bows a primeval roar rose up:

'PUSH!'

It was a raw sound, as old as time, the battle cry that has echoed through the ages – one woman calling to another in her labour, supporting her, giving her strength when she doubted she could go on. Since the dawn of time women have carried each other's burdens, held each other up, shared each other's pain.

The crew responded with a final surge. They were across the line. They collapsed over their blades, attempting feebly to go through the motions of rowing while trying to fill their lungs with oxygen, their mouths turned upwards, like dying goldfish.

'Did we win?' panted Kate to Molly.

'Did we win?' called Abbie from Bow between gasps.

'I don't know. I honestly don't know.'

'Cox, do you know who won?' the Wallaroo stroke called across to them.

'Sorry – we don't. We'll have to wait for the official verdict. But well done, you guys. That was an amazing race. I hope it was worth coming all this way for!'

'You betcha!' called the Australian, and she gave the command for three cheers. The Albion crew reciprocated, and both boats paddled back to the pontoon.

Back on dry land, they'd just finished stowing *Desdemona* back on her rack when Stanley and Jonny found them. Stanley put an arm round Molly. After hesitating for a moment, he put the other one round for good measure and gave her a self-conscious squeeze. Jonny suffered no such hesitation but swept Beth up in an ardent embrace.

The other women watched with expressions that suggested satisfaction with a light sprinkling of envy. Kate felt for Abbie. At least Tim could have come if he'd wanted to. She hadn't been sure whether she'd been disappointed when he'd said he was busy today. She'd said she didn't mind, and at the time she hadn't. But watching Beth with Jonny she realised she did. She minded terribly. She wished Tim were here, giving her a hug and telling her how proud he was of her. Next time there was a race she'd tell Tim she wanted him to be there. At least she could be clear about how she felt. It would be up to him what he did about it.

Abbie must be missing Martin too. How bitter must it be to know she would never again have him by her side, to cheer her on, to tell her 'well done'? Kate quietly moved over to her and put an arm round her waist. She gave her a tight hug and whispered in her ear, 'He'd be so proud of you.' Abbie's eyes glittered with tears as she returned the hug.

Mike came over to speak to Lesley. 'Apparently the umpires are asking for the photograph. It was too close to call. I really couldn't tell from back in the launch. That was a tight finish.'

Neither woman said anything, but Kate could feel Lesley groping for her hand and taking it in hers. She felt Lesley's callouses rubbing against the patches of dead skin on her own palm.

'You know, Dinkums,' said Mike, lowering his voice and Kate could feel Lesley's stubby nails digging into her hand, 'when we were in the launch – before the race – I got a good look at Temple Island and I was thinking . . . it would make a great venue for a wedding. How about it?'

Oh my God, did he just propose?

Lesley said nothing and the question hung in the air like a bad smell. Beth finally let go of Jonny's face and skipped over to them, breaking the tense silence.

'Well – any news?'

'Just one item,' said Lesley, clearing her throat. 'I've made a decision. Is that spare room of yours still free, Beth? I'd like to move in with you. For good.'

Lesley's announcement exploded like a hand grenade. Kate realised she was holding her breath. As she waited for someone to say something, anything, she heard cries of 'Mumsie!' and saw her two daughters in floaty summer dresses running across the grass towards her. They flung their arms around her, laughing and crying and hugging, all at the same time.

'Why are you crying?' asked Kate, who had tears running down her own face. 'It wasn't that bad, you know.'

'Oh, Mumsie, you were incredible! We had no idea . . .' sobbed Poppy. 'We couldn't believe that was you racing down the straight. You're so strong, so good at this! Why didn't anyone tell us?' And she hugged her mother some more.

'What an amazing woman you are!' said Ella tearfully. 'Did I really need two years away at university to work that one out?'

Kate was lost for words and the three women held each other, heads close together, savouring the familiar and reassuring physical presence. Ella was still blubbing, and screwed her head in closer to her mother's neck. Poppy moved her arms to get a tighter grip. Ensnared in their arms, her head buried in skin and hair, Kate patted her daughters and whispered words of love.

They were interrupted by Jonny, corralling the crew into a tight group for a photograph. Side by side, with Molly kneeling in front, the women put their arms around each other, a wall of green singlets, muscular arms and bold smiles. With the stately river behind them and bucolic fields beyond, they presented a timeless image of heroic victory. As the supporters snapped away with their phones, Kate knew exactly what to say to her daughter.

'We're all amazing, Ella. Don't ever forget that. But women are stronger together. We all need a crew.'

Let her run!: *Instruction to allow the boat to glide for a distance leaving no paddle wake in the water.*

39
KATE

Kate sat on the broad step, leaning back against the wooden upright. Small eddies licked against the sides of the pontoon. The late afternoon sun bathed the dock in warmth. Kate turned her face up towards it, eyes closed, and breathed out a long peaceful acknowledgement of contentment. The uncomplicated pleasure to be had from sitting in sunshine seemed all the sweeter in a busy world. Kate stretched out her legs, pointing her toes and letting her flip-flops dangle. She admired her neatly painted toenails and smooth, honey-coloured calves, shiny in the sunshine. She twisted her legs from side to side to check they were completely satisfactory from all angles.

They were a vast improvement on the start of the summer. The sudden arrival of warm weather had caught out the whole crew. They'd stripped off furtively at the last minute before boating, having had no time for the necessary maintenance. It was bad enough that Kate's legs were nearly hairy enough to plait, but her skin looked blue. Beth's legs had a purplish tinge and Abbie's varicose veins were particularly alarming. Lesley's calves, however, were smooth and soft and the colour of chewy toffees.

Twirling her toes in the sunlight now, Kate revelled in their splendour and considered how much else had improved. Of the four of them, probably Lesley had seen the greatest change compared to the anxious and unhappy woman she'd met the previous summer. Physically, she was transformed. But it was more than that. She was confident. Assertive. More at peace with life. She'd recently moved into a flat down the road from Beth's house and seemed to be going from strength to strength. It humbled Kate to realise how Lesley must have been crushed by her toxic relationship. Thank God she'd found the strength to escape.

And what of her own relationship? It had been crushing her too, in a way. She still wouldn't describe it as perfect. She didn't think she was ever likely to describe it as that. She'd tinkered with it at the edges and made some minor improvements. Spending time in London with Tim had definitely helped. But it was still a work in progress. What had changed was her attitude towards it. Now she was more fulfilled by her work and her rowing, her relationship simply didn't matter as much. Her crew provided so much emotional support that it hurt less when Tim failed to do the same. It wasn't a fairy-tale ending, but this was real life, and Kate was realistic enough to know it was a good result.

Kate sucked in great lungfuls of air that tasted of new beginnings, and luxuriated in the moment. The opportunity for a period of quiet reflection next to the water was now almost as important to Kate as all the other aspects of her rowing. She had increasingly found herself arriving early for her outing, without realising why. The truth was, she knew now, that over time the river had almost become one of her dearest friends, as important to her as any of her crew.

Looking back she could see how precarious her mental health had been. But she'd treated her rowing as if it were medicine, and the cure had worked. She felt stronger and more resilient than she had for years. The sessions on the river had given a new rhythm to her life. Training was sacrosanct in her diary, and everything else had to fit around it. She'd been pleasantly surprised, indeed slightly astonished, how readily her family accepted her new commitment.

It set Kate wondering how much of what she did was really expected by her family, and how much was the result of her own ideas about what a wife and mother was supposed to do. No matter how much she liked to think of herself as a feminist, she knew some of the cultural stereotyping that surrounded her growing up had taken hold. Juggling her rowing with her family had forced her to reassess her reasons for some of the things she did. Like her compulsion to bake cakes. Abbie had been right – it was a symptom of a deeper problem, this need to demonstrate she was a 'proper' mother. The trouble was, even if the world had stopped judging women in these terms, how was she to stop judging herself by the rules she'd grown up with?

The wind picked up and ruffled the leaves on the willows and a swan glided past, eying her suspiciously. The ripples on the surface of the river glinted cheerfully as they barrelled downstream.

Ella would be heading back to Durham next week. By train. It was her final year and she'd hopefully find a job at the end of it. Then she really would be gone for good, like her older sister who was fully engaged in her new life in London. There'd be no more long university vacations, just fleeting weekend visits.

And Kate was fine with that. Just fine. Her life had already moved on to the next chapter.

Glossary

Attention!: To start a race, the umpire calls out the names of the crews competing, says 'attention', and after a definite pause, calls 'go'.

Backstops: The 'ready' position. The rower sits with a straight back, leaning backwards slightly. Legs are flat and straight. The blade is held flat on the water with the handle against the body. This is the position the rower adopts immediately before commencing rowing.

Blade: Rowing term for oar.

Bow: The front end of the boat. Also, the rower closest to the front or bow. In coxless boats, often the person who keeps an eye on the water behind them to avoid accidents.

Bow Four: The four rowers closest to the bow.

Bow pair: The two rowers closest to the bow.

Bow side: The rowers whose blades are on bow side (the starboard side of the boat). In a conventionally rigged boat, bow side are the odd numbered seats: e.g. 1 and 3.

Burst: A small number of strokes (usually less than a minute) taken at full pressure in training.

Bye: When one team proceeds to the next round of a competition without competing.

Capsize: When a boat turns over in the water due to

poor technique or a collision. Not uncommon in sculling boats.

Catch: The moment at which the spoon of the blade is immersed in the water and propulsive force applied. Immersion and force application should be indistinguishable actions.

Catch a crab: When the oar becomes caught in the water at the moment of extraction and the blade handle strikes the athlete. Often causes unintentional release of the blade and significant slowing of boat speed. A severe crab can even eject a rower.

Clams: Plastic device that clips onto the blade between the button and the rowlock, effectively shortening the outboard section of the blade and lightening the gearing.

Collar: A wide plastic sleeve placed around the oar. The button stops the oar slipping through the rowlock.

Come forward!: Instruction used by the cox or athlete to bring the crew to the front stops position ready to row.

Connection: Used to describe the link between the power of an athlete's legs to the force applied to the spoon of the blade. Should be made as soon as the catch is taken and held through the core muscles for the length of the work section of the stroke.

Cover: The distance between one set of puddles and the next set of puddles.

Cox: Short for coxswain. The person who steers the boat using wires attached to the rudder and gives commands. Eights always have a cox. Fours can be coxed or coxless.

Cox box: An electronic device that plugs into wiring in the boat. It has a headset with a microphone attached, and amplifies the cox's voice. The sound is relayed to the rowers through speakers built into the boat.

Drive phase: After the blade is placed in the water the rower applies pressure to the oar, levering the boat forward. This is called the drive phase of the stroke.

Easy!: Also – 'easy oar' or 'easy there'. The command to stop rowing.

Eight: A boat designed for eight rowers plus a cox to steer. Each rower has one oar, so there are four oars on each side.

Ergometer: An indoor rowing machine, commonly found in gyms and essential for land training. Known as an 'erg'.

Extraction: The removal of the blade from the water by application of downward pressure to the blade handle.

Fin: A piece of metal or plastic attached to the underside of the boat towards the stern. Provides directional stability by preventing sideways slippage.

Finish: The end of the drive phase of the stroke when the blade is extracted from the water by tapping down. In coaching it is often thought helpful to consider it as the start of the recovery phase, rather than the end of the drive phase.

Firm: Firm pressure. Rowing with maximum force in the drive phase. (See also Light and Half pressure.)

Fixed Seat: When the athlete rows arms and/or body only without moving their seat.

Front stops:	The position at which the rower sits forward with arms straight and out, legs fully compressed, ready to take the catch.
Gate:	Bar across the top of the rowlock, secured with a nut, which prevents the blade coming out of the rowlock.
Gunwales:	The top rail of the shell (also called the saxboard).
Half pressure:	Rowing with a level of force in the drive phase between Light and Firm.
Hands away:	The position after the Finish where the arms are out straight but the rower has not yet rocked over.
Hands on!:	The command for a crew to stand by their boat ready to move it.
Head race:	Time-trial that takes place in the winter months when conditions are normally too challenging for side-by-side racing.
Henley Masters:	A masters' regatta run at Henley, usually in mid-July.
Hold it up!:	Instruction to bring the boat to a stop quickly in an emergency stop.
HORR:	Head of the River Race. A time trial for men that takes place on the Tideway in London, usually at the end of March each year.
Lateral Pitch:	The outward angle of inclination of the pin to the vertical.
Let her run!:	Instruction to allow the boat to glide for a distance leaving no paddle wake in the water.
Light:	Light pressure. Rowing with minimal force in the drive phase.
Nationals:	The National Masters Championships. A side-by-side race over 1,000m for veteran crews.

Held on a multi-lane lake, usually in mid-June.

Number off: Quick way of ensuring the whole crew is ready to start. Each rower from Bow in turn says his number as soon as he is ready.

Overlap: The amount by which the scull handles overlap when the athlete holds them horizontally at right angles to the boat.

Pressure: The amount of effort applied by the athlete to the power phase of the stroke.

Puddles: Disturbances made by an oar blade pulled through the water. The farther the puddles are pushed past the stern of the boat before each catch, the more 'run' the boat is getting.

Rating: Number of strokes rowed per minute. Measured with a rate meter attached to the boat. Normally used by the cox and/or stroke.

Ratio: The ratio of the time taken for the power phase to that of the recovery phase of the stroke. Ideally time taken for the recovery will be about three times that of the power phase. 1:3

Recovery: The part of the stroke phase between the finish and the catch when the blade is out of the water.

Regatta: A competition with events for different boat types usually involving heats, semi-finals and finals for each event. Boats compete side by side from a standing start.

Release: At the end of the drive portion of the stroke when the blade is removed from the water.

Repêchage: The 'second chance' race given to those crews which fail to qualify for the finals from an opening heat.

Rigger: Short for outrigger. The riggers project from

the side of a racing shell. A pivot for the blade, called a rowlock, is attached to the far end of the rigger, away from the boat. The rigger allows the racing shell to be narrow thereby minimising drag, while at the same time positioning the oarlock at a point that maximizes the leverage effect of the blade.

Rock over: From backstops, after the arms are fully extended, with the legs still flat, the rower hinges at the hips to rock from an 11 o'clock position to the 1 o'clock position.

Rolling sixes: When only six rowers in an eight row at a time. The two who are not rowing help to maintain the balance of the boat by resting their blades on the water. The cox will alternate the rowers sitting out.

Saxboard: The sides of the boat above the water line made to strengthen the boat where the riggers attach.

Sculling: Rowing with two smaller blades, one in each hand.

Settle!: A command telling the crew to bring down the stroke rate while still maintaining the pressure. This usually occurs in the middle of the race.

Shell: Short for racing shell. A lightweight narrow boat designed for speed.

Sit-in: A substitute rower.

Slide: Parallel metal runners upon which the rower's seat rolls on small wheels.

Slow firm: Rowing with a low rating (fewer strokes per minute) but maximum effort in each stroke.

Split: Measure of speed on an ergometer or a rate meter. The 'split' indicates the time it would take to row 500m if every stroke were the same level of power as the one just performed.

Spoon: The painted part at the end of the oar that enters the water.

Squaring: To turn the oar so that the spoon is at 90 degrees to the water. This action should be done early during the recovery to ensure good preparation for the catch.

Standing Start: A racing start done from stationary.

Steer: Rower in the bowseat responsible for steering a coxless boat.

Stern: The rear of the boat. 'Stern pair' refers to the two rowers closest to the stern. 'Stern Four' refers to the four rowers closest to the stern.

Stride out!: Instruction to reduce the rating after a racing start.

Stroke side: The rowers whose blades are on stroke side (the port side of the boat). In a conventionally rigged boat, stroke side are the even numbered seats: e.g. 2 and 4.

Swivel: The U-shaped plastic rotating piece mounted on the pin in which the oar sits while rowing.

Take a look!: Steer in a sculling boat looks over their shoulder to check their position. Also used to warn approaching boats of an impending obstruction.

Tap: 'Take a tap' or 'take a tickle': instructions for the rower to take a small stroke to adjust the direction the boat is facing.

Tap down: To lower the hands at the end of the stroke to remove the spoon from the water.

Tapering: The practice of reducing exercise in the days before a competition.

Vesta: The Vesta Veterans International Eights Head of the River Race. Held on the Tideway in London, usually at the end of March.

Wash: The wake from a motorised boat, disliked by rowers, as the wash affects the boat stability and can cause water to flood over the gunwales.

Washing out: When the blade is extracted before the end of the stroke which results in a loss of power and drive. Washing out may be caused by finishing too low, or by a loss of suspension.

WEHORR: Women's Head of the River Race. A time trial for women that takes place on the Tideway in London, usually in the middle of March.

Wind: The final sprint for the line in a race.

Acknowledgements

My heartfelt thanks go to the following for their support and encouragement: my crew Sue Lees, Jocelyn Nichols and Rosie Culling; my agent Sophie Lambert; and everyone at Conville and Walsh my editors Harriet Bourton and Charlotte Mursell and everyone at Orion; everyone at Curtis Brown Creative and my writing group Gill Ryland, Julia Walter, Caroline Raphael, Clemency Marlowe, Camilla Emerson, Kate Ereira, Jack Meggitt-Phillips, Saya Yada, Neil Stringer, Zina Rohan, Becky Howard, Alice Goulding and Kate Warner; Jane Riekemann; Bath College and especially Gabrielle Malcolm and Becky Newnham; and not least my husband Grey and children Imogen, Miranda and Hugo.

Credits

Jane Turner and Orion Fiction would like to thank everyone at Orion who worked on the publication of *The Way From Here* in the UK.

Editorial
Harriet Bourton
Charlotte Mursell
Lucy Brem
Sanah Ahmed

Copy editor
Kati Nicholl

Proofreader
Francine Brody

Audio
Paul Stark
Jake Alderson

Contracts
Anne Goddard
Humayra Ahmed
Ellie Bowker

Design
Rachael Lancaster
Joanna Ridley
Nick May

Editorial Management
Charlie Panayiotou
Jane Hughes
Bartley Shaw

Finance
Jasdip Nandra
Afeera Ahmed
Elizabeth Beaumont
Sue Bake

Production
Ruth Sharvell

Marketing
Tanjiah Islam
Yadira Da Trindade

Publicity
Ellen Turner

Operations
Jo Jacobs
Sharon Willis

Sales
Jen Wilson
Esther Waters
Victoria Laws
Rachael Hum
Ellie Kyrke-Smith
Frances Doyle
Georgina Cutler